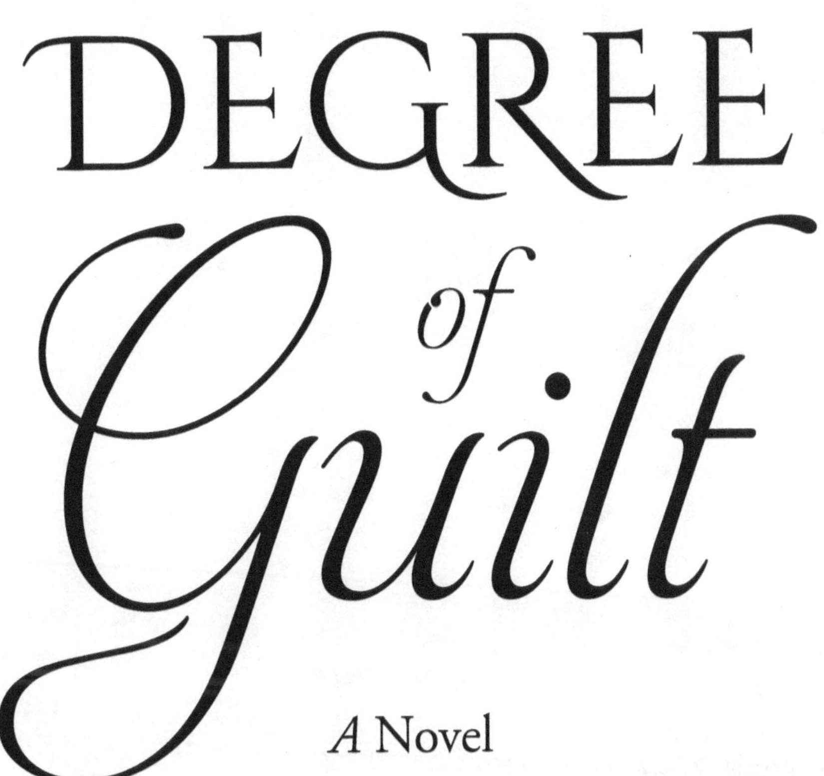

DEGREE of Guilt

A Novel

Barbara Harken

ISBN
978-1-957895-15-4 (Paperback)
978-1-957895-14-7 (eBook)

Table of Contents

*The degree of guilt depends on the degree of
atonement, what you do to correct the wrong.*

— *Chapter 1* —

Maggie Witkowski's thinking was pretty basic. Any day nobody pissed her off was a good day. That's why those birds were driving her nuts. While the mist of a Wisconsin June morning swirled around her calves, she pressed her feet against the gravel, stretched her long legs – they hadn't called her Maypole Maggie for nothing when she was a kid -- and listened to the fresh outbreak of twittering from the trees surrounding the cabin.

"They oughta' outlaw chirping before ten o'clock."

The gravel felt like old friends, but those birds --they might as well have been her high school students on the first day back from vacation.

She grabbed her ankles. *No good talking to birds. Focus on the goal, woman. She would run.* For the first time in too many years, she had returned to Hornsboro Wisconsin and Wall Lake, the summer home that had defined her youth. Before she was old enough to throw snits as a teenager, before she had grown into a woman who dealt with the same kind of snits from streams of teenagers in her classroom these past four years, she was a child who came to Wisconsin every summer to stay for eight glorious weeks with her grandparents. Three months ago, after months of living in hell from a debilitating stroke, her grandmother, Jean Witkowski, had died and left Maggie the family place. The papers had been signed and mailed back to Jean's lawyer with feelings bittersweet. She was an heiress. She was a grandchild orphan.

The roots of her past clung to her. She would offer up a ritual of physical exercise, her sweat as a blessing and goodbye, followed by several days of moving in, the cleaning and rounding up of all the childhood heirlooms that had been stored while renters had vacationed here.

She grimaced. Lord, she hated running. A little yoga, maybe a tape or two – she had brought enough of those to whip herself back into fitness. But running. Running meant no turning off the tape or breaking for a Snickers. Running meant bugs, icky things that swarmed around her like first graders on sugar.

While she wiped her hands on her shorts, she gave herself a short slap for her carping, felt the roll of her shoulders, the circling of her neck. *This is for you, Grandma Jean. You, too Grandpa Lou.* Drawing in a breath, she took in the sharp sweet smells, tasted the freshness and promise, so different from the sting of diesel in her neighborhood in Chicago. Just as she filled her lungs, a new rash of bird noise broke out.

She picked up an acorn and hurled it at the nearest tree--let those twittering fools think about that-- and after one more deep breath, lifted her torso higher, set her hands on her thighs. As the wetness of the morning lapped around her ankles, and the sun struggled to break through the timber, she dug in her heels, grunted, and took off--ten paces, then twenty. On went the count as she jogged up the lane toward the road.

Midway up the lane, the past tugged at her. She turned around and looked back. There was something about this very spot, the slight turn toward the cabin, the beginning of the leveling as the lane stretched toward what for the child Maggie had become a promise – the perfect marriage of fun and safety, the tranquility, the unconditioned love of a summer with her grandparents. The best of her childhood was all around her, this primal world of green ferns, gnarled brush, the dappling of sunlight through the forest growth. Her past.

Folding her arms while she ran in place, she paid homage to the two most loving people in her childhood, the grandparents who had her heart long before they won the hearts of the citizens of the community, that tight-knit group of mostly Norwegians who at first had listened to the name *Witkowski* and raised their eyebrows.

"Love you to the moon and back!" Her voice tumbled forward, gathering momentum, until the words -- her childhood morning greeting to her grandfather--spilled through the trees to the left and the cabin to the right. The thought touched her like a comforter keeping out the cold Wisconsin night.

Maggie turned back to face the road and took off with a quick hiking pace as the grade of the lane turned steeper, each crack of a stick under foot, each crunch of gravel a sound of ownership. At the top of the lane, she turned east, feet to blacktop on County Road HH. Swept by a light breeze, the early June morning wrapped itself in the smell of sun and wildflowers. While Maggie ran along the shoulder, she let the past run with her, warming her as much as the sun in its muscle memory.

Then the next half-mile hit. June still wrapped itself in the smell of sun and wildflowers, but Maggie was not so fortunate. Sweat and celebration started their battle, and she remembered just why she hated to jog. By the curve that turned south, sweat won. Another half-mile and Maggie sat on the side of the road, thighs wrapped in red spandex, gasping like a fish in the last throes of life. She had reached the turn-around point, the old Willson barn, long deserted and left to fall apart on its own time schedule.

She and her cousin used to sneak out and smoke cigarettes behind it when she was twelve. That is, until Grandpa found out found out. That deep voice. Those huge hams of arms crossed against a barrel chest. Cigarettes were history. She smiled at the memory.

The barn meant she could turn around. Arms folded over her head, she looked at the building across from her once more and chuckled. Then she took a whiff. Lord. She smelled like old pee, and she was only half done. Her mind issued a command.

"Off your duff and on your feet, woman. Go." Maggie obeyed and took off.

Familiar markers along the road mocked her. *Curve ahead.* Great. Not only did she have to run, she had to be able to navigate. *Look out for deer.* That's all she needed, a run-in with Bambi. Who needed large game? With her luck, she'd trip over a lost badger looking for water. Her throat rasped to a road that didn't care, "Don't bring up water. This was your idea."

Then sweet Jesus, there it was, the battered mailbox her grandfather had long ago painted orange. It looked tie-dyed now, mostly rust and gray with a couple of patches of orange that had earned survivor status. Never had one woman been so happy to see something so blatantly ugly. She llumbered up to that piece of junk and leaned against it.

Her black hair was a mass of spirals twisted by sweat and humidity, her eyebrows two black swaths over ice blue eyes that threatened to roll inward. Even the cleft in her square jaw begged *Mercy.* Armpits awash with the truth of her state, she unwrapped herself from the mailbox, leaned over and grabbed at her tee shirt, now spotted with pockets of sweat. Maggie Witkowski – runner with a mission -- had come full circle back to grumbling, punctuating her angst with *What is with sweat, anyway? People act like it's the Holy Grail.* She allowed herself a good belly scratch, then exhaled a last huge puff of air and hobbled down the lane toward the house, the aspen, oak, and birch of Northwestern Wisconsin lining the path as she drew closer.

Nothing wrong with taking a moment. The place was simply too beautiful to pass up a look, and just maybe her body would forgive her if she stopped for a few seconds of thankfulness. Oblivious to the gravel and sticks beneath her, she eased down and scanned the scene, knees up, arms folded over them. Silence graced the scene she surveyed. There was the tree where she had buried her grandfather's silver dollar collection when she was nine – held it for ransom so that he would take her to town for homemade chocolate-covered peanuts at Winnie's. He threatened to kidnap her comic book collection if she didn't start digging pronto, that and wash her hands, he had said with a wink. Ten minutes later, fingernails only moderately grubby from raking through the ground cover, they were on their way.

She'd plant perennials around that tree base, bleeding hearts, she decided, that is, once she recovered. Maggie had her breath back, but her legs and butt tightened up. Memories – sweet as they were -- could not compete with muscles. She heaved herself up and cursed her strained hamstrings.

Get to the porch, woman. Get there and it'll all be over. For another second, she slipped into memory as her mind's eye saw the prize. The glider waiting for her. Lou Witkowski had built it by himself, working the wood in the boat house, hung the glider with pride. "No sense having a place to relax without a glider. A porch and a glider, that's heaven."

She'd melt into the softness of its cushions and begin her recovery. She loved that glider. As a child, she'd lie in it for hours, feeling the presence of forest and lake all around her. A mental blow slapped her. This morning, she had stretched out before her run on the porch – the bare porch. The glider was gone.

Why hadn't she noticed? She dismissed the problem even as her mind filled with the absence. It was probably stored with the other things. In that moment, gone was the hardness of the road under her feet, the wetness of the sweat on her face and under her arms. She felt the joy coil in her arms, the anticipation of restoring the place to its rightful glory.

She looked at her watch. A full hour had passed since she'd started this insanity. All she had to do was survive a slow jog down the lane toward the dock where she could dangle her feet, or – what the hell – jump full bore into the lake. Bad idea. Too much work. The lake was past the cabin. She tossed aside any hope of cool and staggered the last fifty feet, climbed the wood stairs and lay on the front porch, sweat and all.

I need a beer. She didn't know whether she'd drink it or wear it, but a Miller Lite seemed like the perfect reward for what she'd just endured. One was right inside the front door, nestled in a cooler she had iced down before she left.

Somewhere out on the lake, a fisherman was putting toward bass heaven, the motor on his boat a purr. A light wind, just the barest wafting reached her on the porch and glided across the back of her neck All right, she'd live. Even without a beer. Lord, she needed a nap. She could lie here all morning – maybe forever. She'd die here, face flat on the wooden steps. Chipmunks and squirrels would use her petrified body as a bridge to the house.

Last night, fresh from Chicago, she had seemed so organized, boxes of supplies stacked on the trestle table immediately inside, clothes hung in the back room, juice, beer, and yogurt on ice. Any teacher worth her chalk well knew the rite of moving from school year to summer, the tasks that shut down the adrenaline and promised the unknotting of stress.

Last night her hamstrings hadn't cried for mercy.

You can gripe later. Wash your face and get to work. Her conscience was totally without sympathy. It was also right. She'd better put her body – aching or not – into this project full force, hands, back, whatever it took to restore this place to its former bliss.

Minutes later, she was standing at the kitchen sink, alternating between drinking water straight from the tap and throwing it on her face when a noise outside brought up her attention, a crunching punctuated with the squeal of breaks that said *old car.* Who'd be out here at the crack of 8:00 except another jogger or a North Woods critter, a big one that could make that much clatter? Maggie took one last drink and turned off the tap. Then wiping her hands on her running shorts, she left the kitchen, stepping up the single step to the great room, opened the screen door and stepped outside.

A Chevy truck -- half blue, half rust – had rumbled down the lane and parked right next to the front porch. *Handy Guy* was inscribed on its door, right above a bumper sticker that bragged, *I'm from Wisconsin. Bite my cheese.* The realtor had promised a handy man once she moved in. Judging by the condition of the vehicle, Maggie just wasn't sure what constituted *handy*. The car door creaked open and out stepped a distantly familiar figure, a lumbering man, his large upper body hoisted onto short, bowed legs.

"Yo'. Miss Maggie. Knew you'd need me from the get-go." Marvin Federinc looked at Maggie and smiled. That is, he looked at her as much as he could. His left eye focused on her face while his other eye seemed to peer at whatever lay forty-five degrees to the right. The local handyman used to scare the bejesus out of her when she was little and up here visiting Grandma Jean and Grandpa Lou for the summer. Grandpa had called him "Ferdie, the wall-eyed wonder," and told her to never mind him, he was harmless, but every time he showed up flanked by his tool set and that eye, she'd gone running for the boathouse.

What had seemed terrifying at the age of six was now simply mildly distracting. Maggie had no idea how Marv knew she needed him this morning, but then most of this part of Wisconsin had its own psychic hotline when it came to someone's business. No need to call for help. The locals read signs or talked to fish, whatever it took to know the community's business – often before the subject of said business knew it herself.

Knock it off, Witkowski. The guy's here to help. Cut him some slack. She shut down the residual stress of a tough school year. No point in making her a crank punishing the innocent. Sarcasm was a defense mechanism best served to the deserving.

Good thing Maggie listened to herself. Marvin Federinc was not a man to waste time. Two hours after his arrival he tackled the last of the jobs – cleaning out the fireplace. Maggie sat on the edge of a wicker chair and watched him -- or at least his bowed legs -- as he stood inside the cabin's stone fireplace and banged away. In between grunts and foreign clanks

Maggie wanted to ignore, Marv kept up a conversation." I figured this old girl would need me. Critters and soot. They love a home."

Maggie shuddered. Soot she could handle. Critters? No way.

"Yep, I knew soon's as I drove up we'd be cleaning her out today. No need to haul in all your loot and get everything all sooty. The mumbled *her* was the ceiling high

gray rock fireplace now cursed with built up gunk in its chimney, the only source of heat in the summer home of her childhood. The place had been closed for the last three years. For all Maggie knew, the chimney was something's condo.

"Glad you're opening the place after all this time. Worried about it the whole time it was rented out. At least when it was closed, I could check up on it once in a while.

"Don't get me wrong. Renters is okay. Can't blame your grandma Jean for what she done back then. But them guys was from Minneapolis," He raised his voice to a soprano lilt that bounced off the chimney's stone walls. "You know. *Decorators*." His voice lowered into a snort. They was more interested in matching their towels than making sure this thing was cleaned out and working."

Maggie didn't know whether to laugh or climb up and slap him — probably on the shins since his upper half was still hidden as he worked away. Instead, she turned around in her chair to face the outside and looked out the window toward the lake, indulging in memory as she thought of her grandmother. All the tension from the jogging left her, so immersed was she in thought. One year after Lou Witkowski had died, Maggie's grandmother had pulled up stakes and rented the home to yuppies who wanted a "cabin" but couldn't commit enough to buy. That had lasted four summers. Now that Grandma Jean had died, it was Maggie's. In truth, it had been Maggie's for years. She might curse a morning run, but in her heart, she was home.

The swish of the birch and the crunch of the oak leaves beneath her feet. The sweet smells of dirt and lake water. She had carried them like talisman.

Maggie shifted in her chair again, turning back to the present and watched Marv, narrowing her eyes. She didn't know which was worse, the guy's soot-soaked John Deere hat, or his abuse of grammar. Since she was an English teacher, one who made her living keeping maimed language at arm's length, she had to go with the grammar. But that hat . . .

Finally, the last shower of creosote. Finished. "There you go, Ms. Witkowski. Flue's open and she's slick as morning bass. Good thing, too. Nights get pretty cold up here, even in June." The man bobbed his head. "Course, you know that, beings how you lived up here when you was little, and all.

"Say what, that'll be all fer today. Unless you want me to clear out that garbage dump next to the bunkhouse. What is it with some people thinking they can just throw their trash anywheres? Gotta be outsiders. I can get . . ." The handyman stopped mid-sentence and cleared his throat. He grabbed his sooty hat off his head and beat it against his hip. "Ms. Maggie, you okay?"

"What?" Maggie's head jerked. She crossed her arms and faced him squarely. "Sorry, Mr. Federinc, I'm always letting my mind wander when I should be paying attention." She shook her head and smiled. "My students tell me I have attention deficit. Just like them."

"My nephew, Bart, has that. He can't sit still long enough to take a shit. "His face reddened. "Whoops. I been talking too much to the guys down at the café. Better watch my language before it runs away with my tongue and gets me in trouble."

Maggie smiled and laughed. "Don't worry. That doesn't compare to what I've had to wash off of desks at my school." She bent over to pick up some of the tools scattered in front of the fireplace.

"Don't you go now and do my work for me." He tipped his hat. "And the name's Marv. I've known you and your family too long to be Mr. anything." While he gathered his equipment, he told her, "I won't drop off a bill until we're sure everything's done. This place has been closed up for a long time, and who knows how many times I'll be back." He nodded his head and started for the door, then turned to face his client. "You come into town now and see us. We all remember you and your brothers, and how you all could guzzle down Green Mountain Floats. Bet you're a fancy coffee drinker now, beings from Chicago, but Winnie could fix up a green fizzer for old time's sake."

He had taken two steps down the porch stairs before he came back and opened the screen door. "And don't you worry about folks talkin', little girl. Everyone loved your grandma and said it was a shame she left after your grandpa up and . . . well, after he died and all. It's good to see one of your family's back here in spite of all the troubles." He slammed the screen door shut and walked off to his truck.

Maggie watched him leave with her eyes wide. *Troubles?* When did anyone refer to death as "troubles"? Trouble is getting caught speeding or swiping cookies from a bake sale. Grandpa Lou's death wasn't trouble. Grandpa Lou's death had been a cement truck dumping concrete over a child's delight in heroes. Residual pain sifted through her as she sat there. She'd been a child filled with a sadness she couldn't even name. The thought rumbled through her as she sat there.

She swallowed hard and refocused, pushing down her remembering, letting it dissolve from her awareness, Marvin's comment about troubles with it. The present restored itself. There was simply too much to do to worry about the ramblings of a handy man with only one good eye. The cabin so needed cleaning. Years of neglect probably meant at least three days of scrubbing, not to mention unpacking the boxes inside her Explorer.

Thank God the realtor had electricity and water running. Maggie scanned the room, taking in the long living and dining area that stretched the entire length of the cabin. There was something about the rite of cleaning, the way chaos and grime turned to clean lines and clean smells. Last night, she'd stripped the white sheets that covered the furniture and swiped at the first layer of dust so that she could sleep without sneezing. The sheets lay piled in the back room waiting for a good washing. The big rag rug that centered the furniture, faded from decades of dancing feet, lay there like an orphan. She'd haul the behemoth out to the metal clothesline that still hung between two big trees. And those windows! The good Lord had not made enough vinegar and newspaper to get those clean. Newspapers, rags, and spray cleaner set onto the trestle table ready for action. Grandma Jean's ghost might be watching. She'd better get this right. She smiled at the thought.

Get your rear going, Witkowski. You can't scrub down a floor until the rug is out. And the rug won't jump onto the line all by itself. Armed with an old rug beater stuck in the back waistband of her shorts, she walked over to the fireplace area, lugged the old sled that acted as the closest thing to a coffee table her grandmother would have allowed, and, one foot planted solidly, hauled it off of the rug. Then, after she dragged the rug across the long room and out the front door, she hipped the door shut, dropped the rug, and bent over to catch her breath. Her back and legs sent her a clear message. *Are you out of your mind?* Aching hands answered back, *Yes, but there's work to do, so shut up and deal. Move it.*

Pulling the rug down the porch stairs wasn't so bad, but oh that gravel and wood chip path. Drag the rug and stop. Drag some more. Kill her hands cleaning off debris. Such a dance. Finally, climbing the boulders that had once separated the perennials from the wood chips that served as a lawn, she managed to heave the rag behemoth over the clothesline. She eased down onto one of the boulders, her body twinging, her mind begging, her hands flexing open and shut to dull the ache. Surely, the rug was the worst of the tasks. Nothing else could weigh that much.

While she waited for her heart rate to slow, she looked around. The boat house and dock to the left of the cabin were in good shape – surprisingly so – and the kid's place off to the right, surrounded by scrub bushes, might be salvageable. Maggie could see what was left of the curtains Grandma Jean had made to dress up the shed they'd laughingly called the bunkhouse. Her grandmother had insisted that the shed was not just that – a shed – no, it was a summer home for her grandchildren, and by golly, it would look like one. She could feel the warmth of the quilts that waited for snuggling, the handmade rug that kept their feet warm on those cool Wisconsin nights.

She grabbed the beater she had laid beside her and rose. Slowly. With several creaks, in fact, and one long grimace. Then she tightened her grip on the tool she held in both hands.

A noise startled her, some creature off in the leaves, she thought. Too loud for a squirrel. Probably a raccoon scrounging for garbage. She dropped the rug beater and picked up a handful of small rocks nestled between the boulders, threw them, one-by- one, at the sound. The motion of the throw, steady and aimed, calmed her, let her slip again, back to a time when she was seven or eight and playing guardian of the forest. *Margaret Mary Witkowski, don't you hit those squirrels.* Grandma would yell at her and then laugh. *Never mind, child, keep up your aim. All those rascals ever do is steal the seed from the bird feeder. Come on in when you're done and have a cookie. Then we'll play some Motley Crue and boogie.*

When the rocks were gone, Maggie stood up and returned to the rug, stopping only when the three-year layer of dust grabbed onto her lungs and pulled. Even then, she whacked one last time before she bent over and hacked, then drew in large gulps of air. She stood up, gripping the rug beater and talking while she attacked the rug. Whack. "Here's for you, Punky Riley. You pulled your sweatshirt hood over your head in disdain one too many times. Now one for you, Tristi Williams. See if your whining helps now. You thought I was brash in class? Watch this. Whack. And Ryan Kellerman? Look what happens when you pass gas and blame it on school lunch."

When every deserving student had been figuratively flayed, still, Maggie wielded that rug beater with demonic fury, this time power coursing up from a place that had nothing to do with school and its Punky Rileys. This was yet another roil that lay in waiting like rats behind a wall hoping for the slightest hole to sneak through.

She closed that part of herself down, fast. The rat might be skulking in her mind, even trying to climb hand over hand up to awareness, but he didn't deserve to see daylight. An old boyfriend turned scum was neither. Even acknowledging his name would tarnish her sense of now. She pressed him back down where he belonged. Just because, she doubled up her grip and smacked away until nary a dust mote dare show its face.

She collapsed onto the boulder, her face flushed, her breath once again heaving as she surveyed the rug. There in the upper corner was the section that she and her grandmother had patched after Maggie had spilled nail polish on the rug. A couple of inches of hot pink and lime green from one of Maggie's tee-shirts in a sea of denim and barn red, all of it faded and melded together like the best parts of families. Jean had hugged Maggie after the patching. *You're in there for eternity now Mags. Can't have much more redemption than that.* Only Jean Witkowski could turn discipline into a matter of pride.

Maggie bent over laid her forehead onto her arms, cradled her head. Her sense of childhood wound around her, slipping into crevices of her mind and then leaving, nothing but empty space where memory had played. Grandpa Lou. Grandma Jean. Fate had snatched them away. Grandpa Lou had fallen so very long ago when she was eighteen – freak accident they called it. Last year, Grandma Jean had slipped away.

"Was it so bad, Grandma? Too many memories and too much isolation to be here without him? Was that why you walked away after Grandpa died?" Only the Wisconsin landscape heard her. The words fell and evaporated. Marvin's words returned and echoed inside her. The "troubles".

What had Marvin meant by troubles?

Her last grandparent had died. Died alone. Without her by her side. Maggie let the knot of pain in her chest expand. She deserved pain. She was the one who had ignored reaching out. Forgot to call. Forget to check in with Mom. Grandma Jean had slipped away in Blue Mound, Minnesota while Maggie graded papers and lusted after a Chicago boyfriend not worth one warm breath from Jean Witkowski.

She pressed the palms of her hands against her eyes until sparks of light swirled, an offering to whatever forest gods might be around to hear of her foolishness.

Students were off to wage war on summer. The boyfriend was long gone, good riddance. But her grandma. That left a gap that Maggie could not yet define.

She stayed there seated on that rock, eyes sore and shoulders taut as she sought control. Maggie never cried. Never. Not smartass six-foot Maypole Maggie Witkowski.

The tension in her upper body – that was as far as she would allow herself to feel. When she was done, she stood up and rolled her shoulders, then went inside and lay on the couch, grit and all, and slept the fitful sleep of the hurting.

Outside, something stirred up, the bed of leaves left by autumns gone by. They circled in a dance around the boulders that had been Maggie's resting place. No breeze there on a late June morning. Everywhere else was still.

Inside the cabin, Maggie, too, stirred, pulled on a quilt throw against a sudden cold. She dreamed of the lane to the cabin, heard a crash on the shoulders at the top of the lane, a skidding, a scream, then moans. Unspent tears formed inside her for a victim she had never met, did not know had even existed, a sadness that crawled into her without invitation and waited.

Chapter 2

By the time she awoke, the sun was half way past on its way to sunset, cabin warmed, dreams faded. She sat up, back in control. As if a reminder, her stomach growled while she stood and stretched. Lord, she was hungry. Time for a trip to town.

She was too grungy for the café. Bif's would have to do. The once single gas station she remembered from another time, the one near the last turn of the road before turning off for the cabin, had evolved into a mutant strip mall – gas, bait, the best in camouflage casual wear, walleye fashioned cozies, not to mention pizza and soft serve ice cream. She could live without the fish, but pepperoni and vanilla swirl. Perfect. Tomorrow she'd talk to the lawyer who had settled the estate to find out where the good stuff of her memories – furniture, lamps, goodies like the wicker moose head that hung over the fireplace – had been stored. Right now, though, time for food, that and the bare necessities. Her mother always warned her about being low on toilet paper. Her dad worried about too little booze. Better check the liquor shelves when she got there.

She allowed herself two minutes in the bathroom, enough time to pull back the black kinks she referred to as hair, wipe her face, and brush her teeth. A little lipstick. No need to bother with more makeup. Dark eyes and dark eyelashes could survive a trip to town without any refinement.

Bif's was packed. Tourists stopping for gas and a snack. Old-timers drinking coffee, sitting at the row of scratched tables along the front window and trying to one-up each other on the latest gossip. Over the years, the décor had remained true in the hub of the store. Washed out signs for blue grass festivals, fishing contests, used bass boats had been plastered on windows when Maggie was younger. Some of the signs were probably the originals from days gone by. One lone garish newcomer advertised the casino thirty miles to the west. "Hottest slots in Wisconsin" it touted. Right. Best way to lose your pay check, it should have said.

She slid through the aisles. Holy cow! Cheesecake in the coolers. Go Bif's. Juice for the morning. Chips for tonight.

Time for the deli. Pizza. Chicken. Yum. She headed over, appetite applauding.

"May I help you, Ma'am?" The man behind the deli counter was dressed in a flannel shirt that almost reached across his upper body. He looked like an inverted triangle, huge head and chest narrowing down to normal legs. The jeans hung low, not out of fashion, but more as a response to the laws of physics. He had a hedgehog dark beard laced with gray and bushy eyebrows that met the brim of a baseball cap that said *Brainerd Moose Lodge* in bright green letters.

Ralph Whatshisname. Dinnows – rhymes with minnows, that was it. Maggie gave him her best good old girl smile. "Are you Ralph Dinnows? I swear I'd know your voice anywhere." Maggie slapped the counter. "How are you, Ralph?"

The deli server screwed his eyebrows together. He looked like someone had placed a cat's tail above his eyes. "I'm Ralph all right. But you got me on this one." His face relaxed as he checked her out. "Must say I can't believe I'd forget a girl like you."

A voice interrupted. "Raphie, don't you remember Maggie Witkowski? She used to stay with Jean and Lou Witkowski every summer until, what was it, ten, twelve years ago?" Maggie's first thought was *how could anyone call that behemoth Ralphie?* Her second, *Is this guy hitting on me? In Bif's?* She flicked away the questions and turned around.

A tall man with black hair too dark to be natural faced her. He wore a kelly green sport coat and yellow pants perfectly creased. He held his arms crossed and he leaned back as if taking in the local scenery. His wide smile advertised the best in dental care – no doubt the most expensive as well. Then she remembered. Cal Dinsdale, town realtor and mayor of Hornsboro, Wisconsin. When he held out his hand to her, she reached out and shook it.

No one would have the audacity not to shake the hand of the honorable mayor of Hornsboro.

"Imagine seeing little Maggie Witkowski all grown up. Who would think the years could've passed so fast?" He lowered his voice. "A shame about your grandma's passing. She was such a fine woman. A real Christian."

Here was a man looking like a Rotary Club advertisement gone leprechaun, a man who smacked his lips and sucked his teeth when he about to make a sale or tell a lie. Him sharing about her grandma? Dyed hair slicked back and smile empty, Cal Dinsdale not only assumed too much, he trod on the genuine goodness of a well-loved woman.

"Yes, she was." Maggie's gritted her teeth in her mouth, felt her jaw lock in anger. Cal Dinsdale overcharged people financially desperate to sell their homes. He feigned friendship with people he called sorry sinners behind their backs. Besides, as a girl, the pervert had pinched her behind with a smattering of too much glee.

Don't ever put yourself in the same category as my grandmother, you sorry-assed hypocrite.

The vexation passed and she relaxed. He wasn't worth the energy spent on conjuring up a good mad.

"Nice to see you again, Cal." Her smile was cream, a smile well-practiced on years of placating administrators. "I can call you Cal, now that I'm all grown up?"

His hand held hers firmly. "Of course. And look at what a fine woman you've become. I understand that you're a teacher in Chicago. Have you . . . "

"You two can have a reunion once I've paid for my tuna croissant. Some of us have to worry about our blood sugar."

Someone behind Maggie was not happy. Someone with a voice laced with soft Southern cadence. Maggie turned. A woman of indeterminate age stood at the counter, the fingers of her right hand tapping impatiently. Maggie's first impression was silver. The woman was silver. Silver hair. Shoulder length and curly. Gray eyes lined with silver shadow and liner. Hammered silver circles around her throat. A long white linen dress with a silver scarf tied below the necklace. Maggie bet the woman had on silver slippers. She couldn't help herself. She looked down. Sure enough. Silver slippers with tassels, no less. Hornsboro's own senior citizen fairy godmother.

When Maggie's gaze returned to the woman's face, the stranger put her hands on her hips and let out a laugh. "Every now and then, I like the one color look. But don't worry, my name isn't Glinda. It's Swoozie."

Swoozie. Not Glinda. Oh that makes much more sense. Maggie smiled and said, "Hello. Glad to know something in town still sparkles." She stood between the two citizens and leaned back into the counter while they continued sparring. What else could she do?

Cal's voice competed for attention now. "Swoozie Johannemeir's our resident hippy." His voice did not sound amused. "She caters to the city clientele hooked on New Age and shabby chic."

"And Cal, here, is, our resident town crier looking for witches and strange mushrooms."

Ah. A woman with a tongue as biting as Maggie's. She'd have to get to know this one. The smacking sound to her left brought Maggie's attention to the business at hand. Cal must be ready for a lie. He surely wasn't about to sell anything. The smacking stopped. Cal shook his head. "Swoozie, Swoozie, you're such a doosey."

God help us. Cal reciting poetry. Maggie forced herself to keep a straight face while Cal shook his head and tightened his lips. He turned his head away from Swoozie toward Maggie. "Remember when life in our town was simple and everyone knew her place?" The questions hung in the air for a second. "Too bad life can't be quite as simple now." Cal patted Maggie on the shoulder. "Remember me to your grandma when you next visit her grave. I'm sure she's up in heaven reveling in her just reward." He turned away from the two women and headed for the door, nodding and darting his hands at the locals who had gathered there. While Maggie watched the parade, Swoozie leaned in and whispered to her. "I don't know what's bigger about Cal Dinsdale, his ego or his mouth."

Maggie didn't remember all that much about the honorable mayor's ego, but she knew this much. If Cal Dinsdale knew Maggie Witkowski was back, soon everyone would know. She kept that thought while she paid *Ralphie* for her purchases. That and disquiet of the tightness of his face and voice when he said, "Welcome back," as if he were offering a to the edge of town – all the way back to Chicago. What had happened to pick-up guy?

Evidently there's a rural kind of PMS up here that is gender nonspecific. Maggie gave him her best people skill smile, picked up her groceries and said, "See you around" over her shoulder as she headed for the door. She missed how his eyes narrowed at her back as she walked away.

That night, by dusk, she had made serious progress. The must of years had been replaced with the scent of freshness and, to Maggie's surprise, the scent of Old Spice. She took in the scent, a gift she was sure from her mind, remembrance of Lou's favorite aftershave. Sheets had been folded and put away, groceries unpacked, and supper placed on the table next to a pitcher filled with fresh wildflowers – just like Grandma Jean liked. In Chicago, supper was never a time for the bliss of quiet. Television news, traffic noises, even an occasional thump of basketballs from a pickup game in the park across the street. They all were ordinary dinner guests. Here she was alone. Really alone.

You're going to love it here. You've got a pile of trashy novels to read, a tan to work on, and a lake waiting for paddling around on. Eat your supper, Witkowski. All six feet of you needs nourishment.

A sudden gust of wind swept through the nearest window. It swished through the wildflowers, threatening to dislodge them from the pitcher, and sent a chill across Maggie's face. Pulling her head back, Maggie closed her eyes and let the wind play with her. Its kiss cooled her, smoothed the strain of the morning's work as she took in the coolness, smiling at the sensation – the softness, the whisper of what she fancied was the kiss of a lover.

While Maggie slept, from the television in another living room of another Hornsboro resident, Fox news announced the latest economic woes. The segment was "Recovery is around the corner. Sit, wait, and pray for capitalism."

A book slid across a table, its journey directed not at the latest in media chicanery, but rather a source much closer to home. A bowl of peppermint candies careened to the floor, the crash against the wood a clank of petulance in the quiet summer night.

All right. She's back. Silly Amazon, strutting into town -- my town -- with those long skinny legs and smart-assed smile. Now is no time to stir up the past, Especially not mine.

Nosy thing. She'll be digging around the place like a pilgrim on crack. She'd already stirred up the customers at Bif's. Who knows what she'd be sniffing out next. Witkowskis. Bitches and bastards all of them. Thorns in the hand.

By the time a chair had scrapped against the wooden floor, the speaker's annoyance dulled, more a muttering laced with possibilities than frustration.

Old Lou was a joke, always yammering about how he couldn't get a good kolache in a town run by lefse-soaked Norwegians, like that was so funny. I showed him where he could put his pastry.

All that nosing around got him nothing but dead. So big Lou, you found out the truth. Where did it get you?

It got you dead, that's what. Bashed in the head like a piece of road kill. Nobody had even suspected. Lou always tromped around the woods. Jean always nagged at him to be careful. He could fall and hurt himself. Head wound? Nasty thing. Just look at those rocks.

Imagine that.

No one had suspected a thing. No clues left after old Lou had died. Made sure of that. The old woman was too stupid to lock her door on Sunday when she went to church. She prayed. I played.

Stupid. The whole lot of them.

So. What to do about Ms. Witkowski.

Nothing? She has no power. She's no more than smoke on a still night. *I could leave her alone.*

A laugh broke through the thought. A voice spoke to an empty room. *What would be the fun in that?*

"Naughty, naughty. You should feel shame, picking on a poor girl who lost her grandpa."

— *Chapter 3* —

True to her city roots, Maggie drove from the lawyer's office, cell phone in hand.

"I should have known as soon as I saw the glider was gone. Mom, how could you do it? Why didn't you ask me first?"

After only a block, one of the two that made up downtown Hornsboro, she pulled into a parking spot in front of the bank. Her hands were shaking too much to drive, at least the one in her lap. Her right hand clutched the phone.

"What do you mean, it's all junk? It's their lives! "I can't hug Grandma and Grandpa, but I can touch their things. Or at least I thought I could. I couldn't wait to reclaim them from storage." She said *storage* as if it should have been *ransom*. Her voice choked on the words. "Of course, it's just stuff. You don't get it. It's *my* stuff.

"I *know* the will didn't specify anything more than the house, but you sold everything that made it special. How could you! Six weeks I had to wait until I could get up here after this Bentley guy sent me the paperwork." She had gone for the name of the storage area and found, instead, a slap in the face.

"Yes, I'll calm down." Eventually. "I'll talk to you later." The click of the phone cut through more than a phone link. Her mother had carted off many of Grandma Jean's things to the local antique mall, what would be called a *vintage shoppe* in Maggie's neighborhood in Chicago. One minute, the cabin had nestled with all the earthly goods that had made it home, and the next, Mommy Dearest had carted them off, money signs blinding her to what she had done. What was the point of reliving the blissful parts of childhood if the story props were gone?

Even though her mother was no longer in range, Maggie carried on a one-sided conversation with a woman who was not there. Anyone watching would have thought her crazy. "I had to find out from the lawyer – the lawyer who could care less about the people I loved that my legacy had been hauled out in the back of a truck and deposited without a never-you-mind," Her jaw clenched and she gripped the steering wheel. "Will Bentley's not even part of the family." The local lawyer who had settled the estate couldn't have begun to register the degree of her anger. Her mother may not have wanted the things, but for Maggie they were necessary treasures. She was here to set things right. She would get back everything. If she had to pay extra, so be it.

*And how do you pla*n *to do that after paying that tax bill? Your bank account is one step away from moth-ridden as it is.*

She dismissed the obvious. How much profit could there be on "stuff" as her mother had called it? Still carrying resentment at her mother and conviction that the storeowner would be happy to work out a deal, she got out of the car, slammed the door, and stomped the four doors down to where her inheritance waited to be saved.

Exhale, Margaret. She only called herself Margaret when she was in turmoil. Still, the advice was sound. She stood back on the sidewalk shaded by a green and white striped awning. *Swoozie's World,* the sign said. *Treasure Trove and Emporium.*

Beneath the gilded letters and hand-painted delphiniums on the front window was a Help Wanted sign.

After meeting, the store owner yesterday, the gilding had not surprised her. But the sign. Why would Swoozie need help in a town this small? Maybe tourist trade had picked up since she had been a kid.

Somewhere off to the right, a car backfired. Maggie gave a sidelong glance, inwardly thanking the distraction as a sign of agreement, an omen. Her inheritance, the connection to her grandparents was in this store, sold by a turncoat. She'd get back every piece down to the Chippewa Falls salt and pepper shakers.

She pushed open the door. An antique brass bell above the door announced her. The building smelled of lavender and history. Like any one of a thousand small-town stores, the inside ran on forever, a long narrow space that split into tiny rooms promising surprises. But in a town that worshipped fish, road kill, and antlers, the surprises were hardly so native. *Swoozie's World* promised a different ambience for its customers, possibly a different universe. The scene swirled around her. Mission set aside for the moment of reaction, she could hardly take it all in.

Yes, there were the requisite antique duck decoys and wicker furniture. But local artists – painters, potters, sculptors, and weavers gave the place a gallery look, one tied together in a decorating scheme part French boutique, part 60's celebration of the psychedelic. The wood trim of the glass display case at the end of the room was painted Chinese red. Above it, glass bead curtains parted against a black wall. Handbags and scarves shared the space with antique photos of Wisconsin days long gone. The ceiling had to be eighteen feet high, a sky of blues spread with trompe' l'oeil clouds across its swath. Three cream-colored chandeliers hung from the ceiling, each with curved metal swirls and pointed bulbs. More crystal beads hung from them, these ropes of glass and silver. Armoires, metal baker's rakes, and wooden cabinets carved small spaces for display on each side of the big room. Some were the natural aged oak and maple of antiques. Others were painted the same cream of the chandeliers or enamel black. They all held a potpourri of merchandise ranging from silver gilded birds to a copy of *The Lutheran Ladies Handbook of 101 Recipes for Jell-O.*

"Kind of hard to take in with one look, isn't it?'

Maggie looked toward the source of the question . Swoozie was standing in the left doorway of one of the back rooms. "You haven't seen the half of it. After my husband died, I started collecting this stuff and couldn't stop." The owner walked toward Maggie gesturing at a trio of display shelves of extraordinary pottery. "Once I was up and running, all the local talent – and there is plenty – came in to offer their treasures on consignment."

The same southern inflection from yesterday, the one that could melt butter, but Maggie thought – only if this belle wanted it that way. Yesterday, Swoozie had been Paula Dean on steroids.

The owner stopped and fanned herself, dusting cloth in hand. Today she had changed from the silver Glinda Maggie had met at Bif's. She wore an orange caftan that reached to her ankles. Cats-eyes reading glasses hung at her chest suspended from a gold chain. Her silver hair was pulled away from her face, held back by a leopard print headband. Thick gold loops hung from her earlobes.

"So, what can I do for you, darlin'?"

All that's missing is a mint Julep and a parasol.

"Will Bentley suggested I come here. He told me that you sold on consignment, and you might have some of my grandmother's things." Reclamation was in full force. "Jean Witkowski. My mother's Eileen."

Swoozie tucked the rag in the pocket of her caftan, reached out and took Maggie's hands between hers. "I remember your momma coming in with all sorts of prizes. I could not believe at the time that she wanted to sell all of them." The shop owner's head shook, a nonverbal tsk that family could part with heritage. "Of course, I was so excited, I let her talk me into paying her upfront." She smiled. "I'm just a pushover for what I admire. Can't say no."

Maggie took back her hand and folded her arms. "Neither can I, but then Mom and I don't always share the same view on many things."

Swoozie smiled. "I know just what you mean, but then, darlin', after all a momma's a momma no matter what."

Before Maggie could finish clenching her teeth, the door opened and three customers swooped in. The first one held it open for the other two. "I'm telling you, Marion, you'll just love this place. Cindy, I bet you'll find a crock for a steal." She turned her body toward Swoozie as her two friends walked in. "I told you I'd bring the girls up from Minneapolis. They have to meet you and your delightful store."

Swoozie was all charm. "So glad to meet y'all. Why don't you look around." She waved her dusting rag as if it were a scepter. "I've been working, so I'm positively misting. You just take your time and I'll clean up a bit." She turned to Maggie and then back to the customers. "I'm sure my assistant here would love to give you advice. She's here fresh from Chicago and full of the latest news in trends."

Assistant? Since when . . . Oh yeah, the Help Wanted sign.

Never one to miss an opportunity, Maggie turned to the women and smiled." I'm so lucky to work here. For guiding fellow treasure hunters, Swoozie gives me 20% off anything I buy whether or not the customer does. And I never have to work on Monday." She did her best shopping addict voice. "I gotta tell you, this place is so delicious, you'll fall in love with just about everything." She turned back to her new employer and leaned forward, her voice a conspiratorial whisper. "Swoozie is so generous. It's all that steeping in Southern hospitality."

If she were hired without even applying, she might as well work the deal. Her pockets had been well-picked by her mother's impunity. Not only were the cupboards bare, her wallet was pretty desperate right now.

Shooing Swoozie along, she purred, "Don't you worry a bit, now. I'll take care of these lovely ladies while you're in the back. Take it easy. You've already worked so hard today." Then she turned back and held her hand out toward the right. "Why don't we start with the throws. They're hand loomed from local artists." They could be hand loomed from local truck drivers for all she knew. She needed more than what she earned as a teacher to buy back what was already hers.

As Maggie steered the customers toward the quilt corner, the owner called out a blessing. "You're in good hands with Miss Maggie." Then she swished toward the back of the store. Done deal.

Fiber weavings carefully oohed over and touched by reverent hands, Maggie had no clue where to go next. "I'm so new at this job, I have to confess I hardly know where to begin, so I'll let you browse. Let me know if I can help." The women took off in separate directions, all three caught up in exploration, an occasional "Oh, you've just got to see this," punctuating the air.

Lips pursed in amusement, Maggie listened to their explorations. *Barely out of school, and I'm employed. Good thing, given the check book balance.* She snorted, a small breath of humor, and walked toward the front desk to stow her purse. *At least I don't have to grade papers.* She heard Marion exclaim, "I just want to buy everything!"

Whoops. Better get back to the customers before they ended Maggie's own treasure hunt with their purchases. She headed toward the small room to the left and joined her customers. Marion was holding up a cane chair.

"That chair *is* darling, but it's back leg has been broken." Maggie ought to know. She had broken it when she was eight. If you have kids or a big husband, you might be in trouble." Maggie watched Cindy pick up the ewer from the bathroom. "That one has a crack in the lip. It might not stand up to heavy use or running children." No one seemed to wonder how a newly hired sales person could know so much about the merchandise much less discourage the customers who might want them.

The bell above the door rang again. Luckily, the three musketeers had wandered away from the Witkowski table. Maggie turned to face her first official customer. This time a man walked in. A familiar one. The lawyer who had handled her case. The one who had sent her on this mission in the first place. She'd just talked to him. Good thing. *Cute guy. Tall. Bet he was a football player once. Tight end.* A girl had to love a guy she could look up to, especially when she hit six-feet barefoot. It wasn't his fault her mother was a turncoat.

She walked over to him, reached out her hand, and took his, her voice a clone of Swoozie's. "Will Bentley, I do declare, a gentleman like you chasing after a little old gal like me." She laughed and let go of his hand. "I think you're responsible for my first job in Hornsboro, Wisconsin. If you hadn't steered me here, I'd be unemployed on my porch reading trashy novels." She folded her hands and opened her mouth in mock discovery. "Oh wait. That's what I had planned to do up here. Oh well, I guess I'm just a lucky girl."

The lawyer looked perplexed. "Didn't you just get to Hornsboro night before last?"

"Yep. I'm a woman of quick wit and quicker determination."

Will chuckled. "Lucky for me. And to think, until today you were only a name signed on the dotted line."

"Well, aren't you lucky I'm in the flesh, minus, a woman, of course, a few valuables." She cocked her lips and used her thumb to point to the back room. "The job's a necessary evil. I'll have to lull the tourists into firing up their credit cards so that I can buy back my own things."

Will shrugged. "That's harsh."

"I call 'em like I see them. Stick around. You may need my saleswomanship. Think of it as a tax on what you're making off the estate."

"How about after your shift, we celebrate your new status with a couple of beers at Winnie's." His brown eyes smiled behind his glasses. "I'll buy this time since I'm involved in the obvious plot to rob you of an inheritance. Of course, now that all this extra income is pouring in, I'll have to charge you for recruitment services."

Maggie's furrowed her brow. Will placed his hand on her shoulder and laughed.

"Don't worry. I'm kidding. I saw your car outside the bank and figured you were here checking out the only thing in town remotely resembling a tourist boutique." He took his hand off her shoulder and peered around her. "Where is Swoozie, anyway? I need to harness more of her invaluable decorating acumen." His eyebrows raised in punctuation. Will might be intelligent, even urbane. But decorating acumen?

"What? You need a couple of Walleye lamps? Maybe a life size loon as a centerpiece with some dried yarrow and silk spiderwort? I'm sure we have some around here somewhere."

"Hey, my place is outside the box – or the town at least. I may live out in rural Hornsboro, but I'm no hick. I've decorated my fireplace mantle with a collection of wooden bowling pins. Very vintage."

Bowling pins. The lift her eyes and Maggie's expression turned inward.

Will turned his head in question. "Something wrong with bowling pins? They're actually pretty cool. Swoozie got them from an estate sale. Some guy had a bowling alley in Blue Mound. Cream color with red stripes. Very masculine."

"I know. They were my grandfather's." Her lips made a straight line. "I was hoping to come here and buy them back. Not everyone in my family has a sense of personal history."

Will pushed his hand through his hair. "Good going, Bentley. Wasn't I the one who told you where to hunt for your grandparents' stuff?" He put his hands in front of him in a gesture of peace. "I'm still good for the beer." He lowered his voice. "But, Miss Maggie Witkowski, the bowling pins are mine. Nonnegotiable. They make me feel like a manly man." Then he laughed, turned around and started for the door.

Don't count your pins before they fall, mister lawyer man. I'll ply you with the liquor you buy yourself and have my way with you – in merchandise terms. Of course. No way was she ready for a man in her life, especially a man for only a short summer. The charm of the alternative disarmed her, and she swatted it away. Stick to the plan, she told herself. Swoozie has plenty of manly-man goodies here that would look just fine on his mantle.

And she could make a commission on them.

Swoozie's world, I'm here and ready. The wicker moose head that had hung above the fireplace was all but hers. Sure enough, Maggie worked her charm on the clientele that wandered in after the lunch shift. Hand glazed plates with trout motif. Glass ornaments blown by an artist up at Wall Lake. Wood boxes, a couple of wicker baskets.

By two o'clock, Swoozie had her arm around her new best friend. "Honey, you're a natural. It's like being handed a fresh glass of sweet tea every time a hot flash strikes."

Maggie took in the compliment and took advantage of a lull in business. "What's the deal on Will Bentley?"

"Deal?" Swoozie's face was a model of neutrality, but her voice had an extra helping of Southern praline-laced sweetness. "Whatever do you mean?"

"No biggie. Just wondering why a young lawyer would choose Hornsboro for his practice."

"Well, as I heard it, after Karl Nelson retired, the practice was for sale. Will bought it and hung up his sign."

"Karl I get. His folks are from the area. But a young guy like Will?"

"I asked him that one day, as a matter of fact. He told me that he was driving through out on Highway 206 and stumbled on some of the prettiest sights he'd ever seen. "A lawyer can find clients anywhere, travel to see them, use the internet like a highway if necessary' he'd said. 'But the beauty of this area, that's harder to find.' Raising an eyebrow, gleam in her eye, she asked, "Why ever, missy, are so interested?"

"Just getting a lay of the land -- and its folks."

Swoozie laughed and walked toward the back of the store. "Tell that to your face, Maggie. It's got Cheshire cat curiosity written all over it."

Winnie's hadn't changed in twenty years. Long bar with laminate top, now more than slightly chipped. A revolving dessert holder, three—tiered and covered with a plastic see-through cover. and worn down to the yellow base. Metal stools with cracked upholstery. Behind the counter toward the back, the fry kitchen, complete with the aroma of fresh grease, sizzling sounds spurting the promise of walleye and fries. Booths along the wall, a few tables in the back, all adorned with a Schlitz beer bottle containing two plastic flowers. Maggie had come in here with Grandpa Lou every Saturday for fried fish sandwiches and a green river float. Winnie would tease her about her steady beau. "Isn't he a little old for you? Maggie would reply, "Nope. He's my grandpa and the best beau I'll ever catch." Then the three of them would laugh and get down to the business of good food and better gossip.

Will and Maggie slipped back to the tables, the unacknowledged drinking section. Sitting there, Maggie smiled. "After the chaos of the city, it's nice to be in a place where nothing's changed."

A woman of indeterminate age came over to wait on them. Her hair, dyed black, was pulled into a bun. Her face, lined by life and hard work, did not match the hair. She had on a grease- stained apron and an air of welcome. The owner, herself. "Will, glad to see you. Who have you . . ." She stopped and looked at Maggie, lips tightening and welcome retracted.

"Winnie, it's me. Maggie Witkowski."

In a tone best described as hrrumph, the woman answered. "I know who you are."

The reaction stunned her. Maggie sat there, speechless. What had happened to Winnie?

There, in the back of the restaurant Maggie had known as a child, the owner's eyes glared at her, sharply condemning. "You're lucky, young lady, that you're with Will. I'll serve you, but I don't have to like it."

Will cleared his throat. "Winnie, we'll have two Miller Lites. Bottles."

"Got it." Winnie turned on her heels and stalked away. "Fred, these two need some beer. Take care of 'em." Her tone said, *Run the bastards out of town.*

Will stood up and pulled Maggie's chair out. "Let's get out of here." His voice was a harsh whisper.

"No problem." While he escorted the stunned Maggie toward the door, Will called out, "Cancel the order, Fred. Gotta go."

Maggie was a tumble of confusion, hurt, and anger. She turned to Will. "I used to call that woman Aunt Winnie."

"Don't worry. Sometimes Winnie gets something up her craw and needs a victim. It must be your day."

The hurt stung at the back of her eyes. Her voice was choked as she turned and walked away. *Mood* did not begin to explain that reception. "Thanks for the offer of a beer, Will, but I'm out of here. Some other time." Head down to hide the redness of her face and the glistening of her eyes, she hurried to her car, grabbed open the door, and climbed in.

Two hours later, during the best of the early evening, that time that lulled the busy townsfolk into a time out, Maggie sat on the cabin floor near the fireplace, arms around her legs, chin on her knees, caught up in her senses. The feel of whirling on the café's barstools, once an exercise in fun. The tickling froth of an ice cream treat. They were memories that melted, like an image in a photograph turned upon itself when set on fire. Her stomach burned a caustic reminder of today, proof of rejection.

While she poured through a collage of memories, she only grew more confused. Grandpa Lou was as gentle a spirit as his sister, Aunt Agnes, the nun. Agnes had callused knees from all that praying. Lou had callused hands from working and doing for other out of love.

Then she thought back to what Winnie had said at the café. The sign coming to town said, "Hornsboro, Wisconsin, home of the Hornsboro Hornets and friendliest people in the North." Hornsboro, Wisconsin.

Its residents were nuttier than the loons out on the lake.

She'd do more than find Grandma Jean's antiques. She'd find out why she had missed the town and landed on Mars. She stood up, wiped off nonexistent dust: hands firmly planted on her hips, she looked up at the wicker moose head above the fireplace, her first reclamation buy. "Ollie old buddy, we have more than a bit of mystery here." She tapped her foot and raised her forehead in salute. "Good thing nothing stops a Witkowski."

Outside, a dark form crouched against the side of the cabin. *Nothing stops a Witkowski? We'll see about that.* The form skulked away in the darkness, made for home and the joy of anticipation. Life had been moving along so smoothly as one step after another had fallen into place. Kind of boring, actually. What was the point of winning without a quiver of competition now and then?

Oh where to begin. The form slipped away, sure that the night, like so many things, belonged to him.

The early morning rain had left the ground soggy, soggy with a pair of size twelve footsteps imprinted by the night's visitor. By the next morning, they would be gone. Only the energy of a dark desire would remain.

Chapter 4

Two days on the job and the honeymoon with Swoozie was over. All because Maggie was forced to play merchandise hide-go-seek with the storeowner. From the get-go, Swoozie had promised her that the Witkowski items would stay tucked away as long as Maggie worked for her, but this morning, two of Grandma's ceramic Sacajawea coffee mugs had somehow wandered onto the shelves out front. One was being sold as Maggie walked into the store. The other set sat waiting for a buyer in front of a birch canoe loaded with lavender.

When Maggie asked about them, Swoozie had said, innocence personified, "You mean you wanted these too?" Of course she did. That's why they were in the side room in her cache. Swoozie dripped butter like usual. "There were so many in that collection, darlin' that I didn't ever think you'd want them all." The pool of butter had sluiced onward with, "And you know, a widow like me has to make sure that she has food on the table." With hardly a pause Swoozie smiled, "I knew you'd understand. I do, after all, run a business, and you have so many other things back there."

Fearful of an inopportune smart-aleck response – if not an all out hair-grabbing bitch fight, Maggie turned her head to the right to avoid responding to Swoozie's bomb, seemingly surveying that part of the store. "Well, Madam Employer, I guess I'd better get to work before the Witkowski heirlooms feed you too much."

Swoozie hadn't missed a beat. "I knew you'd understand, sweet thing. Now let's get to work. I have to run to the bank. You just stay here and guard all our treasures."

'Our treasures', my ass. Steel Magnolia had come to Hornsboro. Maggie had her work cut out for her. As soon as Swoozie closed the front door, Maggie reconnoitered between the rows, checking each shelf like a miser looking for a lost coin. Two more sets of salt-and-pepper shakers and one kerosene lamp later, she deposited her finds in the back and reset her lips into a smile. Grimaces and customers did not mix. The sooner she charmed a few sales, the sooner she could reclaim the bits of her home. Next up on the list, a tin lamp and reading chair. She'd take them home today. She closed her eyes grieving the rest that would have to wait.

That night, Maggie breathed deeply of the early summer air that filled the cabin. The day had been long, full of hard work and resentment. Winnie had been out watering her flower boxes when Maggie got to work. A friendly wave from Maggie earned a snort and a turned back. The locals who came into Swoozie's were less obvious – more just checking out the city girl come to Hornsboro.

Thankfully, coming home meant quiet, no more sound than the buzz of mosquitoes and a few loon calls. She rested on the porch, leaning against the screen door, taking in the promise of the cabin's comfort.

She almost didn't answer the phone when it rang. After all the betrayal this morning, she resented its intrusion. Better to sit and rest, replace her aching with the beauty of the night. But what, she thought, if it were her best friend Amber calling from Wyoming? She forced herself inside, turned right into the kitchen to answer the phone. Before she could even get out a hello, a gruff voice gave a distinct message. "You think you're so hoity-toity, little miss. After what that grandpa of yours did, you should be ashamed to show your face in this town." The call ended with a distinct click.

Maggie stood there, phone in hand. Its flat surface contacted her hand. It should have been warm from the caller's viciousness. She wanted to drop it like a letter laced with anthrax.

Who was *that*? How dare they spout accusations and then hang up. Outside the cabin, the early evening silence gave no answer. Even if it was a thing of beauty, nighttime in Wisconsin was not talking. Wisconsin took care of her own, not city girls who had left for too many years. Maggie's mind raced. *First Winnie. Now some nut case on the phone. What the hell?*

Two days ago, she had thought herself on Mars. Now she wasn't even sure of the solar system.

Maggie's questions turned to a dull anger, one surely to grow as she thought about the call. Her back straightened, shoulders pulled back as she grasped the phone. *Hoity-toity? Her? And ashamed of her grandpa? How could be ashamed of a man who lived to love? People! Think about it. Grandpa was one of the good guys. One of the best.* After slowly returning the phone to its cradle, shoulders sagging and head down, she walked into the great room. She felt his presence before she looked up and saw him. And stopped. Suddenly. A man was sitting in the chair, facing her, a big guy. Sexy brown eyes, chisled face, strong jaw. Dark and hunky in a George Clooney kind of way. One leg was crossed, his hands folded and resting on his knee. *Duh woman. Hunk did not necessarily mean safe.* She did watch *Criminal Minds* after all. She stepped back two paces, her favorite expletive tearing out of her, all in one breath. "JesusMaryandJosephandallsaintswhocanhearme."

Maggie's voice blurted so much louder than she had meant as a current of suspicion ran through her. Then again, strange men should not show up in her living room. Especially in the middle of nowhere. Especially on a night like this. Friendly neighboring was one thing, but strange phone calls and total strangers reeked of James Patterson.

She managed, "Who are you?" She meant, *please don't kill me.*

No answer. Just a visitor, one looking perfectly sociable, but an outsider nonetheless.

Could she back into the kitchen for a knife? She glanced around. *Where had Grandpa kept his shot gun?*

Jamming her hands into the front pockets of her jeans, she narrowed her eyes and watched him, just far enough away to grab the lamp from the side table and whack him if need be. Good lord. She'd brought it home today. Who ever would have thought she'd need it for protection. She braced her legs, set her midsection strong and breathed deeply . Then she conjured up her best teacher tone.

"Excuse me, sir, but I think I just asked you for your name. And a damn good reason why you think you can walk into my home and pluck yourself down." She slowed her voice. "This is a demand, not an invitation."

The man shook his head and tsked her. "My goodness, young lady, didn't your mother teach you not to swear? Then he smiled and nodded his head politely. "Name's Larry."

Larry as in neighbor guy?

She studied him. The sleeves of his shirt were rolled up, and he wore jeans with the cuffs rolled up. Red socks. The guy had on red socks. And penny loafers. Who wears red socks and penny loafers? And his hair. He looked like an ad for Brylcream. Surely North Woods crazies, even serial killers, did not dress this way.

Some comfort – the dressing standards of Wisconsin bad guys did not include penny loafers. The sheer absurdity of the thought gave her enough courage to continue speaking even though her chest felt baled with wire. She kept her awareness on the lamp.

"As a matter of fact, my mother tried to teach me a lot of things. Like not sneaking into people's houses. Start talking. What are you're doing sitting in my house in my chair?"

The intruder smiled, but didn't utter a word. He watched Maggie's face with apparent interest, his lips pulled in and straight, his eyes observing her, daring. Then he smiled, just a whiff of a smile, more just a release of his lips. His voice sounded noncommittal.

"Don't' worry. If I wanted to hurt you, I would have done something by now."

"Then what are you doing here?" *And where is that gun?*

"I live here." He said it with a shrug.

What? "You live here?"

"Indeed. Have for a while, in fact."

Was he some squatter sneaking in while she took that bizarre call? Hornsboro didn't have the same set of rules that most places did. Want to meet a neighbor? Just walk in. You don't even need to bring cookies. Maybe he was a friend of Marv's. She kept one hand on her hip and hit her chest with the other. "My name is Maggie. Maggie Witkowski. I own this place." Her words were clipped. The *own* came out particularly strong.

Larry seemed nonplussed. "I didn't say I owned the place. I said I live here." His *own* and *lived* were equally forceful.

That was it. Enough. All the frustration, all the disbelief and betrayal of the week coalesced into a single ball of outrage. There had to be a limit to craziness even in this godforsaken place. Lamp, knife, shot gun forgotten, Maggie stomped over to him, reached to jab him in the chest, and almost lost her balance. Her finger did not meet muscle and bone. Nope. It went through as if the guy were pure air. She snatched the finger away and looked at it as if the finger could explain what had just happened. She kept staring at it, absolutely stupified.

Then the air around the intruder shimmered, and he faded into a gray fog and disappeared.

Maggie screamed. Full. A bloodletting and perfectly justifiable scream. Bad enough a guy showed up in a living room. But then, vanishing? She closed her eyes like a child trying to make the night go away, shook her head before she opened them back again. Sure enough, no one was there. She looked around for sudden trick mirrors, cameras. Anything to explain away this insanity, all the while forcing down the panic that threatened to come sluicing out of her throat.

Before she had time to enjoy the empty space, *Larry* whispered behind her, "Boo." It was a mocking sort of *boo* but that was hardly the point. Maggie screamed again. And jumped. And lost her ability to keep her knees straight, they shook so much.

Time for another "Jesus, Mary, and Joseph, and all the saints" pouring out of her, this one a slow whisper, as much a curse as a prayer.

Sounding like a brawny male version of her high school Mother Superior, Larry's voice filled the space behind her. "I thought we had established that cursing was not nice for young ladies."

Maggie slowly turned around and saw . . . nothing. She could hear laughter, an echoing laughter, low and full of glee.

She collapsed onto the floor, folded her head into her lap, covered her head with her arms, and rocked.

If she just didn't open her eyes again, everything would be all right.

The ghost's words sounded conciliatory, also nearer. "I'm so sorry. I've been stuck out here for decades with no one to talk to. Where are my manners?"

A warmth settled over her, relaxed her in spite of her panic. A warmth that had not been initiated within her. She felt her skin crawl even as she sagged into the forced relaxation. Maggie raised her head slightly and forced her eyes to open. All she could see were the red socks and loafers, that and the cuff of his jeans. She slammed her eyes shut. This Larry thing might be back in living color but that didn't mean she had to look.

What the hell. She looked.

He was right in front of her, extending his hand. Smiling. "I seem to have that effect on people. Let's start over. Hello. I'm Larry, and, just in case you haven't noticed, I'm a ghost." Maggie hung on to her hands for all she was worth.

"C'mon, let me help you up." Maggie felt a swish, warm and airy. She was standing. She hadn't even started to unfold her legs, much less stand, but here she was. Up on her feet and face-to-face-with a ghost.

She should have whirled in spastic shock. That's what normal people would do. Instead, she faced the trespasser, hands on her hips, jaw forward. "Larry? What kind of name is that for a ghost?" Full fledged madness was certainly setting in.

The ghost shrugged his shoulders. "That's what my mother named me." His voice held a tinge of resentment. "We don't get to change our names just because we're dead."

Maggie had never been one engage in hysteria. Assertive behavior? Yes. Even a bit of ball breaking on occasion, but only when the situation warranted. Hysteria seemed like the most probable reaction at the moment, for beings faced with the paranormal.

Breathe in deeply, she told herself, let it fill all the space not stuck in shock, breathe out – slowly – get all those toxins out. She might have laughed at the scene, crazy woman one-with-the-universe deep breathing to deal with a dead guy, that is, if she had been hanging out watching, instead of living this. But if skinny old guys with loincloths and turbans could clear their minds to walk on coals, she could deal with this Larry thing.

She made peace with her panic, turned from her spectral visitor, walked to the trestle table in the dining area, pulled out a ladder-backed chair, and sat down. Her posture was perfect. Her face totally stilled. Her hands rested in her lap as if she were ready for tea. Of course, the tea was being served on the Titanic, and she was going to go down. With a ghost named Larry.

Eying him, Maggie turned her head ever so slightly. He was still there. Lips pursed. Tight. Like he had the right to be pissed? She jumped from her chair and turned to face him full front. Arms crossed, her right foot tapping in agitation, she nodded. "In spite of the fact that I've no doubt lost my sanity, I'll accept for now that you are who – or what you claim to be." Arms, akimbo, she tapped her foot.

"How did you get in here?"

"I was sent."

"Sent? By whom?"

"The Judges."

She pictured John Roberts with wings sprung from a flowing black robe, *The Universe in Black and White* aglow in his hands.

"Never mind. You wouldn't understand."

Maggie's eyes narrowed. "How did you know what . . ."

"I can read minds. Comes with the territory." Larry leaned forward. "Don't worry though. You have to be emotionally engaged at a high level for that ability to kick in."

His form intensified, took on a deeper color. "Let's get down to business.Maggie nodded her head, more of a bobble than a nod.

"You're my mission."

"Excuse me, for just a minute." Moving feet that felt like cement, Maggie stood up and headed past Larry Whateverhewas to the bathroom – where she promptly locked the door and leaned against the claw-foot tub, breathing in a blessing. Safe. She was safe.

Wasn't she?

The mirror across from her fogged up. For no reason. Larry's face formed within the fog, a swirling, blue-tinged apparition right out of the worst of Grimm. Except for his face. That was pure man wanting control.

"Knock off the hysterics, Miss Witkowski. We have work to do. I have an offer that will afford us mutual satisfaction. Get out of that bathroom and sit down and listen like an adult."

$$— \; \mathcal{C}hapter \; 5 \; —$$

S ign of a bad day – chip a nail putting on shelf paper, stub a toe cleaning the shower. And oh yes, hang out with a ghost, one who tells you you're his mission.

Maggie closed her eyes like she had as a child when confronted with unpleasantry, that time of innocence before she learned to face reality. She had grown up believing the laws of physics, good old pragmatic veracity, a grounding that lent permission to mock choices less down-to-earth. And where had it taken her? She was a mission. A mission for a ghost. Surreal hardly began to describe this.

She allowed her eyes to slowly open. By now, the sheer force of the moment should have killed the ridiculous grit of her initial response. The fear thermometer of any normal human being should have been shrieking at full alert. The guy was, after all, a ghost.

Be afraid. Be very afraid.

Her body should have been shaking. Her knees should have been mush. At the very least, for crying out loud, a shriek should be crawling its way toward her mouth at this very moment. Let's hear it for normal response.

No way.

Her mother's perennial warning, *Margaret Mary Witkowski, you are far too impetuous,* reared its head, but she swatted it away.

The guy, spectral or not, had altered the walls of reality. Sure, she was terrified. But curiosity could make a hangman's noose look like a swing. Besides, she was pissed. He had challenged her, climbed down her throat in all his wispy glory and demanded she "be an adult." The last hotshot who had thought he could give her orders had eaten his words under the baleful punishment of Maggie Witkowski's tongue. She simply did not abide control freaks. Even ghosts.

She crossed her arms and looked at her newfound acquaintance. Larry. The guy. ghost -- whatever -- had said his name was Larry.

"Larry -- you say you live here, 'live' being open to questions, of course."

"That's correct. Had a bad motorcycle accident right on there on the highway. My last girlfriend said it would be the death of me. "He chuckled. "Guess she was right."

She walked away from him to the sofa and sat down. Furniture was set in a conversation arrangement facing the fireplace, flanked by the hooked rug Maggie had beaten into cleanliness, two chairs at ninety degree angles placed strategically for conversation, entirely facing away from her new found acquaintance. Good thinking, Grandma Jean. You were always one for conversation. You'd love this one. I'm about to have a conversation with a guy who claims to be a ghost with a mission. Sure, right now I can't see him, but that's only because he hasn't whisked his ephemeral ghostness over here.

Maggie taught body language in her speech unit. She knew an invitation to be manipulated when she sat across from one. No way would she lean back to avoid him. By everything she deemed holy, no one, spectral or real would make her flinch. She was a Witkowski, and Witkowski women were a tough breed. They never flinched.

Then again, not too many Witkowski women had faced dead guys with red socks.

Her shoulders slumped and her head fell down to her lap, arms over her head. Her words were muffled. "Only because I'm overly tired and no doubt insane, I'll listen." She raised her head and straightened into perfect Catholic schoolgirl posture. Larry popped over, seated himself to the left of her in one of the chairs. Of course. Where else would he be since she was about to have a heart-to-heart with a dead guy? She turned to face him, nudged her body forward, one leg up, hands folded around her knee and studied him. His face was the epitome of composure. Had his mouth been more firm, his chin more strongly held, he would have been knighted by some Arthur looking for a Lancelot. She let herself feel a moment of appreciation. Hot guy.

Dead guy. Maggie slapped herself internally, then steadied herself and listened, chin in hand, fingers over her mouth. *I will not scream. I will not scream. Damn straight you won't.*

"First of all, again, my sincere apologies for scaring you. I seem to have that effect on people." He leaned forward. The two could have been best friends engaged in conspiratorial gossip.

Her hand came down and rested in her lap. She studied him, watching his eyes. Eyes were the window to the soul.

Did he have one? A soul?

"Judges. You mentioned them."

"Yeah. They're the . . ." Larry paused. "I guess I could call them beings for want of a better word. Their job is to weigh a life and decide on the proper . . . consequence."

"And those *Judges* came to a unanimous conclusion? No squabbling? Sent you down here on a mission. Me."

Larry nodded.

"Mary Margaret Witkowski. There's been a terrible injustice done to your family. It is not only my sworn duty, it is my eternal future that rests on righting the wrong."

She tilted her upper body forward. "The only injustice I see right now is some schmuck telling me I'm his . . ." Then she drew back, arms folded against her chest.

Larry leaned back and folded his arms. "You can spat all you want with me. But I'm just the messenger. If the Judges say there was an injustice, trust me an injustice there was. The Judges are never wrong." He had raised his head on the last sentence as if sending the message heavenward.

Injustice. No, she told herself. Couldn't be. A prickling played in her head. She shifted and brought her knees to her chest, leaned against them for balance. .Hornsboro this first week , a Hornsboro fresh out of Twilight Zone argued something was off. She drew one hand into a fist, rubbing her index finger against her thumb.

She would listen.

That is until the men with the white coats came to carry her away.

"Okay, Mr. Larry. I *might* buy your story -- please note my use of *might*—if you can give me some proof of . . ."

"Look in the pantry."

"What?"

"The pantry in the kitchen. That little space at the very top. Go check it out."

Suspicion and curiosity played on Maggie's face. Larry used a shuffling motion with his hands; Maggie responded, in kind, with a finger gesture, but, nonetheless, pushed herself off the sofa, gave Larry a long look, lips pursed, and went to the kitchen. "How did he know about the top of the pantry?" she muttered as she padded along.

The pantry door still creaked. Maggie closed her lips tightly as she hauled out the plastic stool and stepped up. A memory shot up. *Watch out for searching my hiding place. You never know where the ghosts live.* Grandpa had teased her relentlessly whenever she eyed the upper area of the pantry. It had been such a symbol of wonder.

Where ghosts live. Funny, Grandpa.

Maggie's hand swept across space. An old plastic lid. A penny. Plenty of dirt. So far not much in the nature of proof. At the far end of right corner, her hand stopped. Some kind of book. She slid it out. A red journal. The kind a teenager might buy to use as a diary, this one dusted and cobwebbed. Even as Maggie swept away the years, she held it like a precious find. When she stepped down, journal in hand, she didn't bother to take a chair; she sat on the floor and opened it gently. The pages had not aged at all.

"Dearest Maggie," the journal began. Her name. Her grandmother's writing. She recognized the neat linear penmanship. *"So much to tell you, to share with the little girl of my heart. Even as I write, I picture you, someday, reading my thoughts, part of your legacy. This home is as much yours as it is ours. You should know the joy we've had living here. Lou says, 'Tell her now,' but I want you to see the scope of our lives here. 'I'll tell her where the journal is when it's time,' I assure him. You just help me keep it hidden in Grandpa's favorite hidey-hole.' Now, my dear, you know why Lou told you ghosts lived in the pantry. Now that you're all grown up, you certainly don't have to worry about ghosts anymore. . . "*

Oh Grandma, if you only knew.

As Maggie watched and weighed in on the message, Larry's spiel about injustice beset on the Witkowski family was set on hold as she pictured her grandmother writing; a sense of warmth spread through her. While she rested her back against the kitchen wall, she settled into the memory for a few seconds before she turned toward the doorway.

"You knew about this. All along." He voice was merely a croak.

Larry nodded. Two small shakes of his head. His eyes said, *keep reading.*

"She writes she'd tell me about this. She never did." Maggie shook herself. Here, seated on the floor next to something otherworldly, armed with a mysterious journal, all Maggie could feel was disappointment. Her grandmother hadn't told her.

"Maybe she did. Or maybe she tried." Larry's voice slipped through her.

She pictured her grandmother in the hospital, after her stroke. Maggie had rushed to Minnesota after school. Jean lay in the bed, a pale wraith. She couldn't move her arms, her legs. She couldn't speak. When Maggie took her hand, Jean's eyes had been alert. They flashed at her, darted, eyes set deep in tired sockets but so active. Maggie had thought it fear, those old soul eyes trying so hard to talk. Had Jean been trying to communicate? Hand clasped firmly at the corners of the journal, she continued to read.

How excited she and Lou had been to come to this lovely place, she wrote, how they couldn't wait to turn years of investment into a dream retreat. Finding the right pine for the floor, the perfect light fixtures, even that silly wicker moose head that hung over the fireplace.

Entries took Maggie back to days of exploring, leaping off the dock, sword fights with her brothers before they chose Little League over Wisconsin.

Jean wrote of making new friends. "*Yes, Hornsboro does have its circles and clans, but so many have taken us in. This is a place of such community.*"

Taken them in. That was true. But now? The looks, the tsks from a few of the locals when Maggie waved or those who came in to buy but didn't quite look at her when they spoke. To some of that *community*, she was as welcome as the flu. And Winnie. What had turned her caring into vinegar?

Maggie read on. Lou and Jean had especially befriended a lonely woman only a few years older than they. Ida Ann. The poor thing. The whole town had seemed to love her "like they might love a decrepit old place that once housed local royalty but now had faded and started to peel." Lou took her to Bingo on Thursday nights; Ida loved the time she spent time at the cabin with both of them. She could be herself and share her secrets with her friends the Witkowskis.

Near the end of the journal, the entries became briefer. Ida Ann had died. They had lost a good friend. They also took on a darker tone. Gossip over Ida's death. "Batshit crazy," Jean had called several members of the community "who shall not be named. If they only knew what Ida Ann had been forced to endure. . . "Maggie was as shocked by the expletive as she was intrigued by the commentary.

The last entry was dated nine years ago, two weeks before her grandfather had died. Had Jean been too consumed with grieving to finish? Maggie felt a cloudlike shroud that covered her, a sense of must and sorrow. She sat on the floor, journal on her lap. She was hollow. She and Grandpa were devoted to each other. That's why she left here. She tried to stay. But she couldn't stand to stay in the place they had made their own without him."

"And you're claiming," she said to the presence behind her, "what I've found has something to do with this mission, this wrong done to my family?"

"Absolutely."

"And if I accept this *mission*, I'll correct whatever's been inflicted on my grandparents."

Maggie bent over in her seat and rested her head in her hands, elbows on knees, hoping for some sign or sense of illumination. Nothing came, that is except the promise that rose through her from her core. She rubbed her forehead with her fingertips, kneading against the strain of the evening. Discounting her unworldly mentor, she was alone, the only one who could take on this challenge. She laughed as a playful taunt came to her from childhood.

Tag. You're it.

— Chapter 6 —

Larry was back seated across from Maggie, arms crossed, face neutral. Maggie spoke first. "Okay. I accept. The least I can do for my grandparents is resolve this *injustice*, whatever it is."

"I'm delighted you agree."

"No so fast, mister. There's the deal breaker."

Larry's eyes narrowed.

"Nothing big, Mr. Dead Guy. Just final. You can't be scaring me. No more nudges from the supernatural, nothing to make me tingle. Let me repeat. A deal breaker."

Larry's face broke out into pseudo-shock. "Why Miss Witkowski, if I wanted you to tingle, I would most definitely not need to use anything remotely supernatural." He winked at her. "And you most certainly would not call it a nudge."

"Reign in the male superiority. The fifties are as dead as you are. We are a team. On a mission."

"I wouldn't have it any other way," said his words. His inflections? Not so much.

Great. She dealt with teenage boys and their bluster all year. Just when she'd escaped, she got an overgrown adolescent from the other side. *Steer ahead, Witkowski, and don't let him see you sweat.* She put on her Parents' Night face.

"That's a good girl," Larry said. Now we can get back to business."

Good *girl*? Maggie started to speak.

"Never mind. I'll be the one talking for now. You just listen."

Calm, she told herself. *Play his game. He can read you and he knows something.*

"Yes, I do as a matter of fact." There was that smile again. So he could read her mind. At least he knew where she stood.

"No, I can't always read your mind. Only when you're highly agitated. Which," he commented, "has been most of the last half hour."

"No, you can't kill me. I'm already dead." That had been said with a chuckle. His voice turned serious.

"Let's get to business, namely, my mission – which just happens to be you."

This should be good. She imagined him as Peter Graves slipping an envelope to the Mission Impossible team. When he was finished, would he go up in a puff of smoke and vanish like a tape of instructions?

"Here's what I know." His voice was clipped.

Hers was more of a yell. "What'd you mean, 'what you know'? I thought you knew everything."

"We'll get into that later. We know that you've inherited this place, I assume complete with all furnishings."

Not a good thing to bring up. Maggie looked at several conspicuously empty spots that had been raided before her arrival. "Oh really? Looks like I need a conversation with my mother." Before Larry could question her, she said, "Never mind. Go on."

"We know that your grandfather died suddenly. In an accident, the townsfolk said."

"Yes." The word was a whisper. She picked up the pillow and hugged on it again. "He was out walking. He loved to stomp through the woods." She paused. "He fell." Another pause. "Maybe he had a dizzy spell. No one knows. Who cares how? He fell. He hit his head.

"Ralph Winnows found him and ran to get the police." By now, she was rocking.

"That must have been so hard for you. Your grandpa. Your pal." Larry's voice carried the *sorry for your loss* typical of those who had tried to console her without a clue as to how.

Maggie stopped moving, bit down on her lower li p. Her eyes were focused on a spot of time long gone. The day still moved in slow motion. "I felt so damn helpless. Dad hovered over Grandma. She sat through the whole viewing and funeral back in Blue Mound hardly moving, never shedding a tear. Mom gathered up all the food that kept appearing at the door and organized taking care of the visitors."

Eyes closed, she brought up a memory as much felt as pictured. "What I really felt was guilt. The well-loved granddaughter, the one who had left the family for college in the city and never looked back. No fattened calf for this prodigal misfit. My folks told me what time to be ready and what to wear. Otherwise I wasn't even there." The last words were spoken slowly, softly.

Larry paused. "People get all caught up in their own business at times like those."

"Sometimes they let the blame fall where it may." She paused. "Or where it belongs." Maggie sat up straight, let the pillow rest on her lap. "Whatever. The weird thing, as far as my family was concerned, was Grandma. Why wasn't she crying? I mean, Witkowski women are tough – they never cry – everyone knows that, but this was Grandpa. He deserved reams of tears. The ones who normally wouldn't shed a tear fretted about it like choir ladies all ruffled about sinful chords. Maggie's throat had tightened. She couldn't make any more words come out. She sat there drawing in deep breaths, patting the journal.

Finally, she left her grief by the wayside. For now. "The biggest question I have is why Jean left. They both loved this place. The journal talks about gossip, but this was their home. They had renovated it together. Was she so sad that she had to pack up and leave?" "Your grandmother did not leave because she was sad. She moved because she was angry, so deep seated angry, I might add, that she threatened to – and I quote – 'Shove their judgment down the throats of those nit-headed idiots and laugh while they choke.' Your grandmother was a woman of great passion.

Maggie sat straight up. "What do you mean 'mad'? 'Mad' like crazy? Or 'mad' like pissed?"

Larry's face did a perfect impression of an irate principal. "There you go again with the language. I bet a fine lady like your grandma would not put up with that for a minute."

She set aside the journal and wine. When she looked up, Larry had disappeared. The rat! Her voice held a taunt. "You're supposed to be helping me! Play fair. Come out like a man – or the man you used to be. We have a deal!"

A voice floated above her. "Insults will get you nowhere. Miss Witkowski. When you're ready to behave yourself, let me know." Then nothing but silence.

She spoke to the air. "You win. I was overwrought. If you come back and talk with me, I'll be civil." The *civil* was a bit tinged with sarcasm, and she wanted to swallow the words, but she wanted more to find out what Larry knew.

She felt a brush of air on her hand. Larry materialized right beside her. She gasped as the hair on her arms tickled her, but she managed not to jump. Instead, she turned sideways to Larry as if he were a colleague ready to team plan, crossed her legs and arms on the sofa. "Why was my grandmother so angry?" Good starting point when reality is quivering.

Larry pushed his hands into his pants pockets, rocked on his heels once, and looked straight ahead as if for guidance. Maggie breathed in and almost forgot to exhale.

"You grandfather was a good man. A good, good man. The Judges made that perfectly clear."

No one had to tell Maggie about the goodness of Lou Witkowski. So why was there a *but* in this guy's voice?

"The townspeople thought that for many years."

Of course they did. All their trips into town while the child Maggie visited reinforced that knowledge. Everybody loved Lou. And Jean. The words of the phone call broke through, taunted her. *You should be ashamed of your grandpa after what he did.*

Larry walked to the sofa and sat down facing her. His face held the same expression her cousin Louella had when she was about to spill the beans on Maggie.

"I don't have all the information. Only what I heard from Jean when she thought she was talking to Lou. That and what I learned from the Judges."

Maggie leaned forward, head to head with Larry. If he didn't hurry up, she thought, she'd head butt right into his ectoplasmic brain and find out what he knew.

He shot her a look that said, *Don't even think about it.*

Her eyes shot back. *Enough with the run around. Spill it.*

"Alright. Some of folks in Hornsboro —not everyone mind you-- think your grandfather was a murderer."

Murderer and *Lou*. Larry's words entered Maggie's mind like dead wood, building up a pile of nothing. Then sensory bits fell onto that pile. Whispers. Condemning looks. Mocking smiles. The pillow flew from her hand across the room just as Maggie jumped up and turned toward Larry, arms outstretched and eyes flashing. "Are they nuts? He was the nicest guy in the whole world." People thought Lou Witkowski was a murderer. Dead was bad enough. But murderer? Fists clenched at her side, Maggie turned, stormed toward the fireplace and slapped the stones above the mantle. She stayed there, body leaning in, arms raised, hands splayed against stone, feeling the roughness while her chest heaved.

"Some bunch of sheep think my grandfather could harm anyone, must less kill? Who? And don't give me any crap about my language." She straightened and turned, locked eyes with her intruder. "Spill it."

Larry shook his head and shrugged. "Sorry, that's it."

"That's it? That's *it*?" Her voice was filled with tension, her neck tightened.

Larry stood up and gestured toward the couch. "Come on and sit down. We'll talk. I promise to tell you everything. At least everything I know."

Maggie was no longer tense. In fact, she was close to being a limp rag doll. Head dropped, she walked to the couch and sat down, then looked up at Larry. She listened to the words, sitting there on the couch, all the while trying to create a picture of motive. Who would have accused her grandfather? Why? She saw a man of humor teaching her how to cast for walleye, the man who promised the thrill of the first pull of a "big one." She saw the two of them digging for earthworms under a carpet of leaves, their fingers warm and moist in the rich dirt.

"How about a worm sandwich for lunch," he'd tease. "How about a worm down your back," she'd retort.

People like that did not commit murder.

Later, when she lay in her bed thinking about sleep, Larry's parting words from his visit pulled her from any hope of rest. Yes, someone had died. But not by the hand of Maggie's grandfather. Lou had been a good man doing good for another, a sad soul who needed him, he had told her, undone by an enemy with a friendly face. The Judges had been cryptic. Find the sad soul, find the deed, find the offender.

Thank you, Larry. That explains everything. Good deed? Lou did good for everyone. It was as natural for him as breathing. And sad? Of course, some of them were sad. That's why they needed him. Her grandmother's words came back to her. That woman who Grandpa took somewhere. What was her name? Anna? No. Something close, though. She'd look it up.

Then there was the last part of the directive. The one strangest of all. The real killer was an enemy with a friendly face. Why point out *friendly*? Who'd look for a grumpy face?

She needed to calm herself, get some sleep, figure this out when she was rested.

Maybe when she woke, she'd be sane again.

Good luck with that, a small voice mocked.

Luck, she answered back, had nothing to do with it. She'd find the killer and clear Lou's name. She had the whole summer to track down the bastard.

She bolted up. She *only* had a summer to solve this thing before she was back at school until the next summer rolled around. Who knew what could happen then? She sat in her bed, legs crossed, elbows on knees, hands cradling her face as the past and present played with her. Exhausted, she fell into the hope of rest.

As if.

Chapter 7

Nothing but a night of tossing, questions tumbling through her mind, no more than fragments merging and morphing. Here it was Saturday, two hours after a busy day at the store, and she felt nothing more than bone-weary fatigue, unresolved questions, and a strong desire born of fight or flight to hop into the car and head back to Chicago.

No rest for the weary. Might as well talk to the dead. Larry had left her alone for the night, gone . . . wherever with a promise to return by 3:30.

And so, Maggie sat at the long table just inside the cabin's front door, still as a nun in prayer – as some poet, equally dead, had once said -- to meet a ghost's eyes that leveled with hers, listen to his voice steadied with calm optimism. Maggie had her beer, Larry his self-assurance. She watched him, trying to see death in his face. *He was* a ghost for crying out loud. He should have pallor, at least the faint taint of former rigor mortis. Nope. All she saw was smugness, smugness on a rugged face that – what? Looked like a guy in a cologne commercial? He didn't have a morning stubble. Do dead guys need to shave?

Don't talk back. Listen.

She kept her spoon clenched in her hand, however. You just never knew.

He could have been selling her light bulbs. "I already told you. Last night. You're my mission." Obviously, he was working his own agenda and hadn't noticed her consternation. All business. "On the surface it's simple. I help you. You help me."

Maggie knew she should say something, but she couldn't utter a sound. Where Larry's eyes spoke of knowledge, her eyes were dull, the pacing of her breaths a slow rhythm. Headlines from the Hornsboro Herald began to shape inside her head. *Crazy Maggie Witkowski found in cabin, frothing at the mouth.*

What would her mother say if Maggie told her? *Told you to sell the place and run. What did you expect staying out in the middle of nowhere?*

Larry's voice brought her back. He had the stern voice Maggie used on those who chose to zone out, eyes locked on the victim, words bullets on a perfect trajectory. "Don't turn tail on me. You're my ticket out of here. If I'm going to go to wherever it is I'm supposed to go, I have to help someone. Want the white light, have to do the white deed. Seems I screwed up enough when I was alive to warrant a little payback."

She kept eye level with him. Stared a little, even. Rubbed her hands against her knees to check for signs of life. He scratched the back of his head while he shook it back and forth. "Sorry if I seem agitated. I have been here for a really long time. Believe-you-me, rural Northwestern Wisconsin does not teem with opportunities for humanitarian aid. I'm not allowed to leave the Witkowski property bounds. If I do, . . ." He drew his hand across his neck in the age-old sign. Strange movement for a guy who was already dead.

"And besides, you have no idea how much it's taking out of me to maintain my substance this long. I'll probably need to sleep for days after this."

Maggie nodded as if this made all the sense in the world – or in any number of worlds given the circumstances. At the moment, Larry's face had lost its agitation, even looked approving, the face of someone interviewing a prospective employee. Ah, it said, a woman who could be sensible after all. One who listens.

Nothing like a ghost who makes presumptions. All business, he gave his wrap-up. "I have been waiting here since 1963, October 12, 1963, to be exact for a project like yourself to come along. And here you are."

She had landed in a time warp.

"Let me get this straight. You've been here since 1963. That's a long time. How do you know *I'm* your mission?"

"Have you been listening? I had to wait for a mission. Only a decade ago it came. Finally. The Judges insisted I had to help Lou Witkowski clear his name. I am tied to this property. Jean left."

Maggie took in a deep breath and let her eyes slit.

"Sorry. That was insensitive. The point is, your grandmother could not clear his name before she passed. I thought she might be open to helping me, but . . ." He shook his head and gave Maggie a small, shy smile as apology. "That leaves you."

"Are you telling me I'm the only one who's seen you?"

Now he was grinning. "Yeah. Lucky girl." He raised his eyebrows in a leer."

Maggie snorted and looked downward. "Nice socks, stud."

Larry's face was paternal disapproval. "Don't forget your reward in this, young lady. All that guilt you harbor for not having *been there*?

"Goes away in one sweep of truth."

Maggie eyes slatted, a sheen barely perceptible. Jaws tight, she took in several deep breaths before her lips relaxed enough to speak, tone pure mean girl.

"So, what's it *like* to be dead?"

"Ah. So we play games, avoidance ones. Very well." He watched her, her complete lack of movement. One side of his mouth turned up and the space between his eyebrows furrowed. "Dead is weird. At first, sort of like ninth grade for the losers. They walk down long hallways full of strangers and nobody notices them. At least I never did." Larry's words were innocuous enough, but his face was guarded -- the kind of guarded that a chess player might be, or a psychiatrist about to interview a client that claimed extra-terrestrial abduction. "I never knew how those guys felt." He gave the slightest shake of his head. "Creepy."

"Doesn't sound like much of a final reward."

"That's just the initial phase. Just as you're about to beat the crap out of somebody to get a response, they whisk you to meet the Judges."

Larry looked at Maggie. "Thanks for asking." She turned sheepish and smiled back, her smile tight contrition.

Apology evidently accepted, Larry laid out his agenda. Maggie listened, nodding blindly to a ghost who assured her that she had to solve what she couldn't even contemplate. People thought her grandfather was a murderer. That sweet, funny man.

Her head ached. Her heart ached. All after-flavors of dealing with the impossible. Maggie spent the morning sitting on the couch, legs crossed, arms resting on her knees, listening to Larry plan their strategy. Or at least she played at listening. Her mind was hollow. Waves of panic, of anger, of coping with the surreal had left her sitting there, like a child listening to a parent, focused, yet tuning out.

Slowly, she responded to his logic. Coaxed on by the depth of his voice and the need to put insanity to rest, she began picturing what she had to do. If they had to find out who had killed her grandfather, they had to start with motive. Maggie had warranted little credence to the menacing phone call right before her encounter with her new-found ally. But she could not hide from reality. Someone had had it out for Lou, thought he was guilty of an unknown crime. An enemy with a friendly face, the Judges had said. The problem was who? And what had Grandpa done, good deed or no?

By the time Larry left her and she headed back off to bed to try to make up for lost sleep, even her bones ached, she was so played out. Later, she would take control. Right now she could sleep the sleep of the . . . oh good god, don't even go there.

The next morning, after the birds twittered her awake, Maggie managed one eye open and then the other. Nice morning. Not so nice stiffness in her body. She stretched out arms and legs to dekink and rolled her shoulders back.

"Rise and shine kiddo. Work to be done."

Stiffness forgotten, Maggie lurched up, banging against the iron bed head board. Larry was looking at her, kind of unconnected, like a television image gone bad, that is except for the naked grin that crossed her face when she shrieked.

"Don't have much time," he said. "Have to get back for some beauty sleep." He shook his head. This materializing is hard on the body." A yawn usurped his grin.

Eyes wide now, she grabbed a pillow to use as a shield. Her mouth gaped like a fish out of water begging for air.

"Don't get all in a huff, now. That isn't anything I couldn't see anytime if I wanted." He tilted his head. "Which, by the way, I'm too much of a gentleman to take notice."

"The town is full of people with answers," he insisted, "and daylight's burning. Up and at 'em. Where did you and your grandpa spend your time? Start there. Somebody has to know something." Then he disappeared.

"A faint laughter echoed in the room, near the ceiling. "Nice lace. You ought to dress up more often."

Maggie's eyes hardened. "Just what I need. A ghost pervert."

"Hey, I may be dead, but that doesn't mean I'm *dead*." The retort came complete with a raised eyebrow and a chuckle.

Maggie flung the pillow, pulled up the covers to her face. "Aaagh!" The she flung the bedding aside, stood up, and set to the task of getting ready for the day. While she dressed and brushed her hair, she peered aside and around the corner. Just to make sure.

So Maggie would chat with the locals. On her time off from Swoozie's, she would stop in at the bank, check out the hardware store for supplies. For sure, she would visit Winnie, the café owner who had snarled at her when she was with Will. Years ago, Winnie had teased Maggie but always called her "pretty" before she scooped out an extra dab of ice cream into Maggie's Green River soda. The other day, Winnie had snarled at her. One thing to have a bad day, another to get in a customer's face. Had to be more than a bout with lumbago with Winnie.

At least that's what Larry suggested before he dissolved.

Easy for him to say. He was a dead guy about to take a nap. She was off to work. Maggie walked into the kitchen to grab her purse. There was a ring of coffee on the butcher block counter next to it. She wet a sponge and wiped at it. Just a swipe and it was gone. Simple.

She looked out the kitchen window at the sweep of hill thatched with trees and brush. It swept toward the road that would take her to town. Simple. She said the word as a curse. Nothing would be simple again in this town. Simple had evaporated like the early morning dew.

The little girl had grown up and wanted answers. It would take more than a scoop of anything from Winnie – or anyone else-- to stop her.

Sunday started the reconnaissance. She baked two pies to take to the Catholic Church bake sale on Monday. True to her plan, while she was in town on Monday, she bought a piggy bank at Hornsboro State and Trust and gardening tools at the hardware store. Not exactly a reunion, but she established a few links. Betty Miller blessed her for the pies, said she hoped they were her grandmother's recipe. Arch Murphy helped her pick out a few perennials. Not a bad day at all.

Tuesday and Wednesday meant smiles around at Swoozie's. Could she help anyone? Make suggestions? Just let her know. And to those who seemed happy to see her, yes, it certainly was great to be back after all these years.

Then came Hornsboro's unofficial holiday. It was the second Thursday of the month. Even Swoozie knew better than to be open on the second Thursday. That was dump day. On the second Thursday of the month, the county landfill was open for perusal. Townsfolk liked to meet there to swap the best in treasures before lunch. Citizens were known to brag that they hadn't bought a magazine or a book since the Mud Ducks from the city had been coming to Hornsboro. The place was better than any store. Whole swaths of chairs and lamps, an occasional sofa all for the asking. Community members swapped stories and drank coffee from thermoses while they climbed through the piles. When she was ten, Grandma Jean had found two barrels she used as end tables and a great tin lamp. They still had their place in the cabin and in Maggie's heart.

When she arrived at the café, Maggie watched Winnie was pouring sugar into glass canisters to set on the counter, her back to the door. Maggie entered quietly and sat down, then stayed silent and watched. Impressive. Not a hair on the woman had changed since yesterday. The bun must be coated with superglue. She lowered her glance. The old girl's butt was a local monument – the two axe handles men in the North liked to use to measure derrières on their women.

An inner voice chided. She answered. *So I'm a bitch. Right. She dissed my family. And I could balance Hummel figures on her hips.*

The voice answered back. Enough with the butts and buns. Time for business.

"Excuse me."

Winnie jumped and knocked one of the sugar holders on its side.

"Look at what you went and made me do." The words were out before she had finished turning around, full of chiding laughter. She looked straight at Maggie. The laughter was gone. "Well. I guess I have a customer." She might as well have said 'cancer' given her tone. "What can I get you?"

A swift kick out the door, Maggie thought, judging by the woman's body language. Undaunted, she replied, "How about a cup of coffee and that piece of blueberry pie." A beat later she said, "Can I help you clean that up?"

Winnie didn't answer. She poured the coffee, slid the pie slice onto a plate, and brought them to Maggie. She set them down in front of her customer. Her mouth was a slash.

"Even Swoozie closes down during landfill time." Maggie smiled while she waited for a response. None came. "I'm sure you know that I'm working for her right across the street." Her words came out with the kind of enthusiasm that waited for a reply. Nothing. Winnie turned around and stepped back toward the counter.

"Winnie Listug, turn around and talk to me." The hands that had been scooping up spilled sugar dropped the spoon and gripped the counter, thumbs downward. Winnie kept her back turned. Maggie heard her snort.

"That's enough." The words came out in the teacher tone that corralled the most obstreperous children. "I spent ten of my favorite years coming here. You made me feel like I was the most special child ever. Now turn around and tell me what is the matter."

Winnie spun around and crossed to the counter. She kept the same handgrip there she had used just before. Her face was locked in anger. Not a molecule of friendliness in those eyes and mouth. When she crossed her arms, she pulled them toward her tightly and spat out, "What's the matter? I'll tell you what's the matter. Ida Ann Turnball was my best friend. Your grandfather – your happily married grandfather – had an affair with her.

"That's right, Missy. Your grandfather took my best friend, a woman with a heart of gold, to Bingo at the Casino every Tuesday and Thursday night. He puttered around her house whenever he had a chance and your grandmother wasn't looking, and Ida Ann fell in love with the old buzzard. And that old man fixed more than a dripping faucet."

Grandpa Lou a philanderer? Get out.

Winnie leaned in toward Maggie and spat the words. "Ida Ann Turnball died of a broken heart. That two-timing bastard wooed her, and then he killed her. While you were off at college, drinking beer and learning to be a smart-ass, Lou Witkowski was busy killing my best friend as sure as if he had driven a knife right into her heart. You'd 'a known about it if you'd been here. Everyone else did."

Yes, Winnie's face was even with hers, a face still stuck, now in smug self-righteousness. But the woman might just as well have said that a meteor was heading straight for Hornsboro complete with alien invaders riding on the tail. Shock wanted to course through her. It just couldn't move past the thickness.

"Can't believe it about your grandpa? Well, neither could we. At first. Sure, a few wondered where he got all that money to turn a cabin into a house. "Ain't no bowling alley worth that much, "they'd say, but most of us didn't think much about it.

Then we found the letter." Winnie looked down and wiped an imaginary spot. Her voice was choked with emotion. "Her suicide letter. Poor Ida Ann. Had plenty of beaus in her day, but couldn't choose one to marry. Then she swallows pills over the likes of a married man."

She raised her eyes but kept wiping. "Whatta' you think of that, little missy." Winnie's tears had been packed away somewhere in her heart. The words were no more than a low growl but clearly aimed at Maggie.

The intensity of Maggie's voice, Tasmanian in its intensity, blew clear to the kitchen. "You're nuts! That's what I think."

Adversaries, the two women looked at each other, jaws matched in their clenched anger, eyes unwilling to blink. Maggie lost the contest. Not only did she blink, she then closed her eyes against the sight of Winnie Listug, accuser in this inquisition. By the time she opened them a few seconds later, Winnie had turned her back, standing stiff in her dismissal. Lips pursed, Maggie studied the old woman's back while Maggie's inner warrior wanted to attack. *Crazy woman*, the warrior said. *C'mon, give her an earful. Let her know just how mean and crazy she is.*

A gentler Maggie, one that normally stayed hidden, shushed the warrior. Winnie sounded like she meant it. What if . . . nah. Righteousness stamped on her soul, Maggie listened to the warrior. She opened her eyes and slid off the stool.

The old bag probably sensed it, was smirking at a defeated Maggie even as she kept her back turned, a Maggie focused on hiding back her tears, one ready to run, tailed turned downward. Maggie grabbed a salt shaker, twisted the top open, and with one deft move turned the shaker upside down without spilling so much as a grain. With the best posture of a blessing from Sister Mary Alice, she escorted her anger out the door.

A heavy late spring fog had settled around the cabin. Fog transforms any landscape into somewhere sinister or mysterious. Perfect weather for a talk with a ghost.

Larry was unmoved. "What makes you think she was crazy?"

"P . . . lease." Maggi paced back and forth across the great room while she recounted the visit. Then she stopped and looked straight ahead. "Just because some small town gossip wants to turn my grandfather into a senior citizen Lothario doesn't mean . . . "

"Ida Ann loved your grandpa."

The words gripped the back of Maggie's neck. She turned to face the speaker. "And pray tell, how do you know that? What? Did you specter yourself during a compromising moment? See Lou and Ida in a clinch while Jean was away?" She blew her lips in a motion of incredulity. "Like that'd happen."

"I told you. I'm bound here now. But I didn't start hanging out in the house until after you grandfather died. No need to." His voice smacked of teacher tone and a bit of stuffiness. "Your grandparents had a wonderful relationship."

His comment stung. How dare he presume about them that way.

"How would you know?" Accusation leaked from every part of her.

"My mission started once Lou Witkowski died." He paused. "Before that, I hung around down by the lake, waiting." Head down and shaking, he gave a martyred sigh. "Day and night, years, nothing but water iris and bass boats." A bit of silence – no doubt for effect – and his head came up. Now he was all smiles. "Then I was invited inside the house."

"What? My grandmother asked you in? What are you, Larry, the private eye ghost?"

Larry chuckled. "There you go again, Miss Smarty Pants. No, I was swooshed in behind the sofa, without any choice on my part, one night while your grandmother was looking at a photograph album. Evidently higher powers had decided there was something I needed to see right then and there. A picture. Lou and said 'paramour' in the album.

"Those – they're not much for helping a guy out, so I knew head on, this was a moment." Larry shook his head, caught in the commentary.

"And?" The word was a snarl.

"Sorry. The album. The picture. Right. Your grandmother was laughing at it. Said only an old coot like Lou Witkowski could take a lonely old woman to Bingo on Thursday, clean out her clogged drain on Friday, and be accused of driving her to kill herself the very next week, even if she had fallen for him." He chuckled. "Good thing I was behind her and silent. I'd hate to scare anyone who can laugh for the first time after mourning for months." The comment seemed sweet. Maggie felt only sting. It was one thing to claim a mission, another to intrude on a woman so full of pain despite her trip into fantasy. "Well, aren't you the end all in compassion. Did you tuck her in and read her bedtime stories, too?" The thought of Larry hovering behind a grief-stricken woman was ludicrous beyond words. The thought that it was her grandmother made her hand itch, she so wanted to slap him.

Larry laughed. "You know that won't work. You've already tried it. You'd probably lose your balance and fall, and I'd only disappear." That's right. He could read her mind when she was agitated. Thanks a lot.

"So go ahead, Mr. Larry the Ghost. Fill me in on all your spectral wisdom. Let me know in lurid detail how much my grandmother cried and closed up inside over her loss. She walked around with a hole in her heart and you got to watch. Bet it was fun for you, watching all her sorrow. Better than a soap opera."

"Of course she grieved. You're missing the point, though. Think about what I told you. When I first saw her inside, your grandmother was laughing. A very nice guffaw, I might add." He paused.

Laughing. While she was all alone without her husband. And this buffoon thought that was so cute. Maybe it was the universe that had tilted. Maggie bit her upper lip to keep her mouth shut. What did he want? Validation for his keen insight? Forget it. Besides, Mr. I-Can-Read-Your-Mind-When-You-'re- Pissed knew full well how she was feeling right now. She allowed herself a small burst of self-pity and settled back to reality.

He was right. *Old coot.* That's what she called her husband all the time. It was a term of endearment. Grandma Jean's heart had broken when her husband died, but sometimes she had laughed while she thought about Grandpa. The couple had been married over fifty years. Memories consoled as well as tore.

Maggie wrapped herself in that consolation. At the same time, she felt a tinge of embarrassment. Truth was truth. She did not have to be a harridan just because someone other than she had been able to listen in on someone she loved.

She sat down on the edge of the hearth and focused on Larry. "All right. Potential clue number one. People thought Grandpa was having an affair with some woman named Ida Ann" She pressed her lips at the thought of that name. Ida Ann Turnball. Sounded like the name of a little bird-woman, certainly not someone who would match up with her burly grandfather.

She had to face it. The idea of any woman in Lou Witkowski's love life other than Grandma was pure tripe. Her jaw tightened at the mere touch of the suggestion. She had to get over it and find the truth.

But she didn't have to like it.

"So. They had some kind of arrangement. She was probably a spinster or a widow. Needed a little TLC. That would be just like him." Maggie's posture eased while she opened her mind. "Grandma probably made him go." She could just hear her. *Lou Witkowski, that woman's a storefront of hurting. Get down there and take her to the church to play. You love it. I hate it. She needs it. Move along.*

Better. If Jean could approve, so could she. She let out a huff of breath.

Larry's voice broke the reverie, as much an irritation as a signal to move on. "So. We're in agreement. Grandma knowing about the relationship – however that relationship was defined – suggests that your grandfather was not having an affair with Ida Ann."

"Damn straight he wasn't."

"Don't get touchy. We're simply analyzing the possibilities."

Spite driving her tone, Maggie slashed back. "The only possibility is that my grandfather was a nice guy who befriended some townie loser."

She put her hands on the edge of the hearth and cocked her head. One eyebrow was raised. "Oh wait. There's another possibility. You're a jerk sticking his nose into other people's business while you're dead!"

"That very well may be. The fact remains, however, that Lou Witkowski did a good deed for a sad woman. A sad soul. We have the first part of the puzzle." His voice held the same smirk that crossed his face. "We may be ready to move on to part two. The one that connects this Ida Ann to what happened to your grandfather. What was the deed?"

Now Maggie was down-right icy. "And that would be?"

The ghost tssked. "How would I know? I can't leave this place. You can. Thus, Maggie Witkowski, finding the deed -- or deeds-- is all yours."

Great.

Maggie snapped at her visitor. "Fine, let me think about it. Get along now. You need your beauty sleep."

Larry faded. Just as the last of him disappeared, the sound of his voice hung in the room. "I didn't know you cared."

Maggie curled her lip. "Don't press your luck, buster. Right before I got here, I swore off men. At the time I meant live ones."

— Chapter 8 —

Most of the next morning, Maggie moved around the store helping tourists who came in but bought nothing, the stress of last night a splinter in her mind, one of those thorns impossible to root out, a nemesis digging and demanding. Lou Witkowski wooing a senior citizen bingo Barbie. A ghost harping about clues. Every time she charged up her smile muscles to help a customer, she felt a corresponding pricking above her eyes, a jabbing with a name. Ida Ann.

Shortly before noon, she finally made a sale. Oh, happy day.

"Thank you so much. I'm sure that lamp will be just the thing. Can I help you carry anything to your car?"

Sweeping up her purchases, the lady from Duluth smiled appreciatively. "If you could get the door, I think I can manage."

"No problem." Maggie followed her, and like a dutiful aide, stepped in front to open the door. Swoozie's only customer of the morning left with three packages and an aura of contentment.

As she pulled away, Maggie gave her a "Y'all come back now" wave and leaned on the doorjamb. Not a single tourist in sight. Her eyes turned heaven word and she mouthed, "Thank you, Jesus" with enough attitude to make sure the Almighty knew how she felt about ladies from Duluth, the ones who spent thirty minutes trying to decide between teal and blue. She wanted to stomp her feet she was so tired of playing nice. Childish, yes. but perfectly understandable given the job of playing *Nice Maggie*. Instead of free falling into a tirade, she went back inside.

She hadn't meant to slam the door. What would people think? She gave a snort. Like she cared what anybody in this crazed out place thought.

A tiny voice, one sounding suspiciously like Larry, nagged at her. *You'd better care. You have the perfect cover.*

Yeah, yeah, she answered back. A summer career in selling junk to tourists so she could reclaim her possessions stashed in the back and held for ransom. A summer job with enough break time to make the schlepping worth her time. Since Swoozie -- bless the gypsy side of her heart -- preferred gathering stock over running her store, Maggie set the schedule. To a woman run by bells throughout the school year, this job was gravy even if she did have to smile.

That earlier pestering boiled up in her again one last time. Ida Ann and Lou Witkowski? Ridiculous. She swatted at the irritation, took a deep breath, and tamped down her ire before she peeked out to check for activity. Definitely ghost town today. Why not hang it up for an hour or so and get busy on other things.

She had just flipped the CLOSED sign and was outside locking the door when a tap on her shoulder made her jump. Lucky for her the key was in the lock far enough that it didn't fly from her fingers. Lucky for the tapper that she was sucking in air when she turned to face the miscreant.

Will Bentley.

The poor guy barely had enough time to lean back and miss the swing of her suitcase- sized bag much less the revenge of a hand that ached to punch someone. Grabbing at his polo shirt, she blurted out, "Oh my god, it's you!" Then she let go as if said hand were on a burning stove. He regained his balance, rubbed both palms down the side of his jeans. Fear induced sweat no doubt. Smiling sheepishly, she said, "A girl likes a guy falling for her, but not because he might get hit."

Still, he was laughing. "Put away that vinyl weapon, and remind me never to really stalk you."

Maggie put her hands on his shoulders and straightened out imaginary wrinkles in his cotton polo. "You might be the only friend I have in this town right now. Stalk away."

Wrinkles and ego back in place, she took her hands away, and clutched her purse with both hands.

Will cleared his throat. "I heard about a run-in with the indomitable Winnie. She's still muttering about crazy people who play tricks instead of listening to plain truth. What's with the salt shaker?"

Maggie's smile turned into a full course grin. "Guilty as charged, sir. The old bag deserved it."

"This has to be a good story." He pointed to the bench in front of Swoozie's store window. "Sit and indulge me in gossip worthy of the honorable citizens of Hornsboro."

Minutes later, after Maggie had narrated her encounter with Winnie, words at a fast clip, hands gyrating as her adrenaline level grew, Will was still laughing. He has dimples when he laughs, she noticed. Cute and hot at the same time.

When she finished her tale, she pulled herself into perfect posture, folded her hands into her lap, and smiled at him. "I am a horrible person. No sense of decorum whatsoever. My mother always said that what I couldn't defeat directly, I could wear down by mocking."

"Is that mother-speak for 'you're a smart ass'?"

"Guess so."

Will glanced at his watch. "I'd love to stay and hear more of your adventures, but I have a living to make, and you were on your way to . . . wherever." He stood up and folded his arms across his chest. "I must say, Ms. Witkowski, that it's been a treat."

Maggie smiled up at him. "I'll second the motion."

"Just one word of advice, my tall and lovely friend. Only play tricks when you want your fame spread far and wide. Hornsboro gossip is faster than the Internet." He unfolded his arms and stuck his hands into his jeans pocket. "Seriously, be careful around here. The natives get their panties in a bunch when an outsider – even one who spent a number of years in our fair town – takes on one of their own."

Maggie stayed on the bench watching him walk toward his office. "Her first thought was *Grandpa Lou was no outsider and they took him on.* Her second thought smoothed out the lines that had lined her mouth. *He called me lovely.*

Her inner sleuth rebuked her. No time for maidenly musing. Reconnaissance, not romance even if the guy could put a little tingle in a girl's heart. Lord knew she could use it.

She needed to find out more about what had happened to Grandpa. Not to mention the onus of Ida Ann Turnball, resident albatross around Maggie's neck. Winnie's was out as a source of information – at least until the old bag cleaned up her salt and her attitude, but that didn't mean Maggie couldn't ferret bits of the story from other members of the community. She'd start with Cal Dinsdale, realtor, mayor, and best of all, eternal gossip.

Cal's place of business was at the end of the street, what realtors called *cozy*, a small white clapboard house with pots of geraniums on the front porch. A white sign had been strategically placed under an oak tree, a bed of hostas circling each of the two posts. *Dinsdale Realty: The best place to find your place in Hornsboro.*

One can only hope, she thought as she opened the screen door and stepped in.

The business was in a front room that stretched clear across the front of the house, each end asymmetrically matched with bookshelves, desk, and accouterments of the job as well as two wicker chairs placed under side windows perpendicular to each desk.

On the wall above the end closest to the town's buildings, was a sign. *Hornsboro: where your heart lives*, surrounded by framed photos of the venerable Cal actively engaged in mayoral duties – standing on a dock with council members and their catch of the day, leading a parade, evidently on July 4th by the number of flags in hands of children and vets saluting. It was centered to match a picture of Jesus – or Jesus as Wisconsin saw Him, light-haired, blue-eyed, and serene.

A sign at the other end read *Where to place your heart in Hornsboro*, the latest in housing and business opportunities framing it. Instead of Jesus, this sign was matched by pictures of local wildlife opportunities. Different themes. Matching digs. In the center of the display was a framed map flanked by the announcement: *Future Site of Hornsboro Haven. Luxury Condos and Golf Course.* Ah. The source of in-fighting scuttlebutt according to Swoozie. "Let's have progress" versus "We ain't having no Las Vegas in our town."

And Cal in the middle as mayor.

Cute. Cal, old buddy, you're not in the pictures, but bet you would be if you could. Especially the one of Jesus.

"I thought I heard the door slam. What can I do for you, Maggie?" Cal walked in from the back of the house. Gone was his wild green and yellow attire of the other day. Instead, he wore a blue and gray sport coat, gray, pants, and blue tie. Same sense of matching, just notched down a peg. In his hand he held a coffee cup that read *Fritz's. The best in blue gills.* Raising it, he said, "How about if I get you a cup?" while he turned toward the kitchen. Maggie's sight followed him Still, nothing wrong with a little tingle in a girl's heart. Lord knew she could use it.

The kitchen was a study in white. White walls. White linoleum. A white stove and an equally white counter top that held a coffee maker and – surprise – white coffee cups. Th e coffee maker looked like an alien freshly landed on a planet of white.

The phone on the mayor's desk interrupted Cal's offer. Of course, it was an identical twin of the one on the other side that now set silent. Only this one had a china dish with wrapped peppermints next to it. Cal must have to sweeten his disposition, Maggie thought.

"Whoops. Better get Agnes. Some impending mayoral duty or even a potential buyer calling the wrong number." He moved toward the desk, sat his coffee down and picked up the phone.

He names his phones? Maggie stifled a laugh.

Cal put up his hand. "Just a minute, Maggie. Some sort of ruckus over a sagging dock," while he sat down in ergonomically perfect chair, an anomaly against the cabin chic. His chair tilted, and he leaned back laughing, waving one hand in circles while he held the phone with the other one.

When the last, "I'll be sure to take care of it" dismissed the caller and Cal had hung up, he turned toward Maggie. "Sorry about that." He pointed to a wicker chair facing his desk. "Come hang out on the mayor's side." With the beam of the righteous, he added, "Some men wear two hats at work. I hang out in two offices. Keeps the files straightened out better."

Maggie waited until she sat down and then matched his face, beam for beam. "How's it going, Mayor? Pretty impressive place of business. You have a great little two-for-one sale going on here."

Cal stood up and leaned in toward her, gave her a buddy wannabe look – the one that extended to a customer's pocket -- and extended his hand. "Let me give you another welcome to our fair town. The other day in Bif's wasn't enough." His eyes flicked doubt even as he welcomed her. He knew about Winnie's. Hell. Everybody knew about Winnie's. At this rate she'd be run out of town as a troublemaker before she had found out clue number two, much less solved the mystery of Ida Ann Turnball. She hesitated only long enough to reinforce her smile, stood up to meet his hand and shook it. The handshake felt oily.

"Cal, it's so nice of you to offer that greeting." Her smile wanted to turn sheepish, her conscience even more so, but she held her own. Every handshake was a road to information. A happy Cal is an almanac of the life and the loves of this town. Try not to choke him.

She imagined the friendliest smile and held it. *What's in your mind will soon be on your face.* Another one of her mother's maxims.

Might as well as get it over with it. She released her hand and sat down before she spoke straight ahead. "I suppose you heard about my faux pas at Winnie's."

While he sat back down, Cal laughed, a full chuckle that bounced off his chest. "Faux pas, huh. More like the heathen charging the City of God."

Maggie matched his laugh with a shake of her head. "I don't know what came over me." She bit her lower lip. Such concern. "Bad enough that Winnie treated me like a visit from the plague."

There was a flash of censure on Cal's face, only a flash before he took on his second-in-command-to-God look, the same one Maggie's mother wore when she was on a roll.

"Winnie, Winnie, Winnie. Such a girl." He folded his hands and leaned on his desk, the index fingers pointed up. Then he turned toward the display wall behind him. "She simply does not understand. She's caught up with the rest of those Luddites."

"Luddites?" Maggie scanned the wall, plying her face with a mien of interest. "So this is your big project. And I mean *big*. Looks pretty impressive, Cal."

The skin below Cal's cheeks flushed red. His index finger jabbed toward the map and project plans mounted on the wall.

"Read what it says, Maggie. 'Haven' Not 'Hell'. Not 'demise of everything in our town." He made it sound like a reprimand as her turned to face her. "Winnie and her crowd have decided that any project that might spell progress is against the interests of our community."

Evidently Cal didn't deal well with opposition.

What was it Swoozie had told her? Maggie searched her memory bank, came up with a fuzzy account of Dinsdale Realty wanting to build some kind of resort. "Could be money in my pocket," Swoozie had said. "For sure, Cal's pockets will be overflowing with the stuff if it goes through."

The stuff of juicy gossip not her concern today.

"Cal, I'm sorry to hear that your vision for Hornsboro isn't universal." Before Cal could do more than raise his hand, Maggie had hers in prayer position, her voice full. "Winnie has broken my heart."

Cal stationed himself, feet braced, on his face a mixture of attraction and concern. Don't be a martyr, Maggie cautioned silently. Just feed him the words.

"Winnie told me that my grandfather was a murderer. That he was responsible for Ida Ann killing herself." She paused. Her throat clutched in spite of intent, and she continued, more loudly than she had intended. "I mean, how tragic that the poor woman took her life, but my grandfather? Never."

Angry Cal had left. Public Cal was back. He turned to look at the picture of Jesus. Inspiration? When he turned back to face Maggie, his eyes were tender even while his lips pressed together. "Oh, Maggie. If only I could give you some comfort. Such a double loss to our town. We all loved Ida Ann." His face smacked of nostalgia. "She was almost a town mascot."

Mascot. Great. We have the town pet. What about Lou?

"And your grandfather. I could not, would not, believe that Lou Witkowski would knowingly harm anyone."

Then why are you and Winnie – probably the whole town -- blaming him, you moron?

"But the note. It was simply too damaging to be discounted."

"Note? What note?" *Note* played across her mind while the word left her mouth.

Cal was in full gossip mode. He leaned back in his chair. A beam of summer light from outside stretched across his desk, reaching across to his folded hands, fingers steepled heavenward. A ta-da from God? Maggie clenched her jaw.

"They found it right next to her body." His words tumbled over the exhale of his breath, holy stuff, indeed. The Jesus of his wall picture would be so pleased.

Maggie wanted to smack him. Pick the asshole up by his blue tie and send him hurling across the room, out the door, and onto the front porch. Her body tensed into fight mode, feet set to keep her balance even as she set her jaw to keep from blurting out words that would melt Cal's Jesus picture.

Evidently Cal was no judge of body language. He plowed on.

"There she was laying in her bed, dressed in her nightgown, just a sweet white angel in her bed. Her white hair fanned out against the lace of her pillow. She had been so down those days before this, her face just etched with sadness. We should have known." His voice turned stern. "The pill bottles were lined up on her bed stand." "The note was pinned to her pillow."

Oh please. Someone's been reading "A Rose for Emily." Steady, girl. Do not laugh.

"Cal, that's so sad. What did the note say?"

By now, Cal's eyes glowed. Figured. He must be in Cal heaven, Maggie thought, anticipating the sensation of the really good stuff about to roll across his tongue. Even his breathing had intensified. His body reached forward.

If he reaches for my hand, I'll pop him.

Evidently, Cal was a mind reader. He drew back, hands folded. "Maggie, I know this will be a shock. Do you think you can stand it?"

Cal, you're such a gossip. If I don't let you talk, you'll implode. "Cal, I want the truth. No matter how much it hurts." *Spill it, you fool.*

"I remember the words exactly. *Lou, I have to go. No matter how much it hurts. Never forget our time together. If only you could have left her.* "The last words came out slowly for emphasis.

"Oh Maggie, we all thought your grandparents were so devoted." He shook his head. His lips pursed so tight he could have been sucking lemons. After a full sigh, he said, "Jean never deserved such abandonment."

This time she didn't have to put on an act. Her hands covered her mouth and tears welled in her eyes. She swallowed – as if she could consume the words and let them pass through her. Only then could she understand something as tacky and humiliating.

She had come for information. Now she had to whittle down impossible supposition into fact.

No way in hell her grandfather could have even looked at another woman much less touched her. Much less driven her to suicide? Sad soul, my ass. More like crazy loon.

Cal, you're right. Grandma Jean never deserved such abandonment. From her friends that supposedly loved and respected her, that is.

She mumbled a goodbye and left, sure that Cal's eyes would follow her before he sat down to make the first phone call.

Chapter 9

The rest of the workday was a study in chaos control. Her body made nice with the customers while her mind whirled.

A note? A freaking note left on a pillow. Lou leaving the love of his life, his wife of forty-three years. And "I have to go?" What was she, the senior citizen version of Camille? Oh wait. Faulkner. Yup, the old bag was Miss Emily Grierson herself. Portly, bloated, and pallid. Hornsboro's answer to a southern town's fallen monument.

This was beyond absurd. Well past ridiculous. Brain, filter this. Figure out how I summered with two grandparents in a perfectly fine town only to come back to Nutsville. The people are loonier than the birds on the lake.

Maggie stepped over to the right of the cash register to a three-tiered display of bracelets, a collage of crystal, beads, and silver. Nothing better than jewelry for a little centering. Firmly entrenched in her need, she focused on fashion symmetry, aligning the rows first according to materials – crystal beads on top – then made sure that each bracelet was the exact same distance from each other. None of them dared break the pattern. Even inanimate objects could sense the mood of the struggling Miss Maggie.

Evidently, sorting jewelry wasn't enough. When a guy from Waseca came in, looking for a gift for his wife, he said, she wanted to stab out his eyeballs. Nice man, really. Too bad her hands itched to lash out.

Easy, big girl. He's a husband doing kind things for a woman he loves.

I bet no one thinks he's a destroyer of women.

Too close to the problem at hand – nice man acting out of kindness. No reason to project anger on a man helping out his wife. If a woman liked crafting from native materials, and her husband helped her out, that was a good thing. Maggie tried to feel the smile she forced.

Waseca man cleaned out a whole shelf of fishing lures, said his wife would use them for making picture frames. By the time she nodded a compliment, she'd relaxed her throat, sweeping away the dull anger that lodged there. Passion staid, she wished him well. How lucky, she said, he was to have such a talented spouse. She even meant it – sort of. His mission aided hers. Every commission brought her closer to reclaiming her stuff. Besides, none of the lures had belonged to Grandpa. Her horde was still safe.

Nothing better than resolved conflict. At 3:00, Maggie sneaked away to the back room. She had two quilts and this rocker in the back of the store, paid for with this week's check ready to return home where they belonged. Whenever she'd had a break for the past weeks, she'd sit in it, let the wicker scratch at her back just as she had when she sat in it as a child squirming next to Grandpa as he read her a "story" – usually a page out of *Fisherman's Quarterly*. The sensation rising from her memory storage relaxed her every time. And now it was hers once more.

What trinkets couldn't do, the chair did. She sifted through the bits she knew – the ' strange message, the scorn of townsfolk who had joked and teased with her not that many years ago. The rock that was Jean Witkowski loving her man, laughing at anything less than his devotion to good, however hapless. The world of rural Wisconsin was a mess, she thought while she sat and rocked. How the knots of its threads fit together was something she would have to figure out. Good thing she was on the job. What the heck, good thing she had an ally, even if he was unconventional.

Unconventional. The word applied to Larry made her laugh. What the hell. She'd have a couple of beers after work and sleuth away. Her mouth could taste the cold beer, her throat feel the trickle as it would make its way downward. Cold beer, conversation, answers. Good night on the horizon.

For now, Maggie was at uneasy peace.

Someone else rocked in a chair not so different from Maggie's. Northern Wisconsin loved its wicker. At the moment, however, the one doing the rocking didn't love much of anything. Quite the opposite. The walls of an empty house caught the venom.

They stare at you, Maggie Witkowski. Stare at your bumbling form, your outsider smile, your arrogance. Some chuckle. Some frown. All could care less about you.

The high keening of a rabbit in the throes of death broke the stillness. The form in the rocker smiled. Nature's way of weeding out the weak and the obnoxious.

Yes, Madam Maggie. No one would give a moment's thought if you disappeared. That's what happens to little girls who think they know everything. Ah yes, you know about the letter. Bummer for you. Knowledge is power. Trouble is, where will the knowledge take you? Keep on your silly quest, little girl. You never know where the journey will end.

The rocking figure smiled again, this time a smile of satisfaction. Time waits for all fools. A hand reached into the bowl of peppermints next to the rocker. A crackle of cellophane, the first jolt of sharp sweet as the candy hit the tongue.

End. What a pleasant thought. Such possibilities.

Chapter 10

Outside, clouds hung in the sky, but they were thin enough to promise a breaking by afternoon. Maggie had woken snarled in a sense of irritation, a tightness between her eyes. Bad day yesterday. Gertie Elerbe. The old hag. She'd been in the store hobnobbing with her friends, letting one comment rise above the din of hometown hens. "All I'm saying is that nobody I know ever made enough money to turn a cabin into a home by selling a bowling alley."

Almost Winnie Listug's words verbatim. What did these women do -- kennel up and practice choral reading? Too bad Maggie hadn't had one of Lou's bowling pins. Gertie would have worn one well.

If her fingers couldn't strangle the bat, Maggie would work out her spleen cleaning. By midmorning, the old claw bathtub in the bathroom sparkled. The butcher block counters in the kitchen smelled of lemon. Every nook and cranny dared not cling to dust. Lord help the spider that longed for a home.

By 1:00, the sun had won its fight with the clouds, and the June warmth reclaimed it place of honor. Good. Outside chores, usually her very own nature call to relax, would save her. Digging in the dirt. Hauling water and mulching. Guarantees.

Unfortunately, not today. Every time Maggie patted an annual or pulled at a weed, she thought about the looks, the suddenly hushing voices from yesterday. By the time she gave up on the planting and headed indoors, she was in a full-out Maggie snit. Just the thought of that smug old bat's face set Maggie's leg and foot pounding against the floor.

Night time should have been a respite. The sun had made way for an early June moon, leaving its comforting warmth, but the atmosphere inside the cabin was cold. Maggie and Larry sat in the great room, Maggie seated against the corner the sofa, leaning back, arms folded, Larry on a side chair, his body turned and leaning forward. Even though wet stains ringed under Maggie's armpits, and her forehead beaded with sweat, her expression was pure ice.

Larry laughed at her. She snapped back. "I *am* calm. If I were any more calm, I'd be a puddle."

"No doubt that's why your face is flushed and your heart sounds like a train headed for a wreck."

That Larry. He could so see inside her. Hard to pull off calm when she lit up for him like an X-ray. Maggie lifted her chin and looked him in the eye. Her voice was regal. "After lunch, I stayed outside planting the flower barrels and berm for three hours. I'm overworked, not agitated."

His sarcastic mouth curved into a half smile. "Nothing like a few marigolds to make a woman like yourself set her pulse racing. Perhaps if you went for the petunias, you could calm yourself into apoplexy."

"Well, maybe if you had showed up a little earlier, I wouldn't be in such a state. It's not easy being mad, especially if you're by yourself and need to yell at someone." She had her mean girl voice going. The one that third grade nasty girls used.

It felt good. Little buzzes of pissiness hopping along her neural pathways. "You yap about being stuck here, but if I'm your only out, you'd better be giving me a little assistance.

Larry stood over her, arms akimbo, his eyes and mouth warm with frustration. "Forget about me. This is about you. You'll never solve a mystery if you fly off the handle and get angry at every slight. Not all townspeople are out to get you. You're the one who told me that." Maggie's eyes narrowed. He ignored her. "I know. Obviously. Suspect behavior, a definite mystery . . . Never mind that look, young lady. I am on your side after all."

"Well, if you're so on my side, then why don't you do your ghosty thing?"

"Ghosty thing?"

"Yeah. Fly back to the Judges and get a few clues. They whisk you in and out and all over when they want you to know something. Seems like right now would be a good time for the big boys to come up with a little help."

Larry raised his eyes and opened his palms. A plea for divine intervention against her? Probably. She ignored him. "You gave me a mission. You didn't mention anything about torture."

He crossed his arms and shot Maggie a look. "This is not a game. This is my life. My eternal one. Get control of yourself. Grow up."

The burn of a retort nudged her. Go get him, Sic. Instead, she blew out her anger. He was right. She felt like she was lying in a dumpster, strangers throwing their garbage on her willy-nilly. No wonder she was knotted, all the strings of the week's events and her discoveries winding into a ball. They'd bury her with their bullshit if she didn't stop them.

"Ida Ann's a whack job," Maggie said. "Pure and simple. Most sensible explanation."

Larry shot her a look, the one she used to defuse the worst miscreants, the stare that cut stupidity at the knees. Her faced thawed and her shoulders relaxed. She'd even listen if he tried his lame charm.

"Hear any more through the village grapevine?" Serial killers in town? Errant Fuller Brush salesmen?"

"Not too many in said village want to share. Mostly they snipe. Good thing Swoozie loves to talk. I tried to find out some more about Ralphie Winnows. What was he doing out here when he found Grandpa?"

"Anything good?"

She frowned. "Not much. According to the boss lady, he's been getting into it with mayor Cal over this resort deal. The old Turnball place has fifty acres of land, mostly lake front property. Cal wants to play Donald Trump and develop it."

"And Ralph . . . ?"

"Ralph's family has some acres abutting it. The Winnows boys like to hunt and fish and drink beer until they pee sideways. 'Don't want no wine sipping boney-assed broads and jet-skiing punks from Minneapolis out there interrupting their way of life' according to the locals." She rolled her eyes. "Seems the whole Winnows clan is dead set on painting the project as entrance to Sodom and Gomorrah."

"Sound viable as a motive?"

"Not really. The only way any of the Winnows boys would hurt someone is if they sat on them. They're a hardy bunch."

"Is that a valid judgment or a fond memory?"

Maggie was out of her seat and pacing before Larry had time to listen for an answer. She stretched her head up, neck taut, and closed her eyes before she turned to him, remnants of snide comments like slivers of glass.

"One bozo had the nerve to suggest that my grandparents scalped money from Ida Ann. Bad enough that they blame grandpa for breaking her heart. ' Bet old Lou got paid a pretty penny for all those odd jobs of his. Wonder what tool he used.'"

"Somebody said that to you?"

"Nope. Not *to* me. Near me." Her face twisted. "Nobody talks directly *to* me. They'd rather sit around and gab at each other just loud enough so that I can hear." She looked down at her hands. Checked for a nonexistent chipped nail. She pictured her grandfather's smile, his meaty hands, his arms outstretched waiting for her to jump into them. Hugs were free. So were good deeds. No way would Lou Witkowski use someone on purpose for monetary ends. Even if he tried, Jean Witkowski would have skinned him within an inch of his life."

Larry scratched his head. "We need to consider the money issue. That seems to be what's in the town's craw." When Maggie shot him a look, he held up his hands. "Not because it's legitimate. Because accusation – however wrong – has to come from somewhere. Might be worth looking into." Even as he finished the words, Maggie's mouth tightened to a slit.

"It's the accuser I want to look at, not the accusation."

Just as Maggie was drawing in a deep breath – one of those to either still an outburst-- a June bug beat against the screen door. She started, shook off the sound.

Typical early summer sound, nothing to hardly notice, that is if you're not already halfway across walking barefoot on glass. Then it came. Rocks hit the side of the house. One, two, three. Big ones. Hurled. By the sound, they had missed the great room window by no more than six inches.

This time, Maggie jumped. Maggie screamed. Maggie felt the tears well in her eyes and then dissolve.

Larry held up his hand. "Wait here. I'll try to see who did it." Before she had time to react, he disappeared.

She stormed toward the door. "Not without me, you don't." Just as she was reaching for the door handle, Larry popped back in.

"What'd you see?"

"Nothing."

"What do you mean 'nothing'? You're a freakin' ghost for god's sake. You had to see something."

"That's right. I'm a ghost. I'm not Superman. I can't see any better than you can." By now, Larry was yelling.

Maggie held up her hand to slap him. And stopped. "I can't even hit you. You're not solid. You're just a dumb dead guy that can't see twenty feet past his face." She turned and stomped back to the end of the room, plunked herself down onto the sofa, and leaned forward, head and arms on her knees, right foot tapping. "Why are they doing this to me? What did I ever do?" She lifted her head. Larry remained across from her, "I can't get used to one ambush before the next one comes chucking at me." She dropped her head back onto her arms. Tears stung at her eyes. She swallowed hard and slowed her breath, then sat up straight.

No way would she succumb to crying. Didn't they know her blood? She was a Witkowski. Witkowski women are steel. They do not give in. They grind their feet to the ground and fight back.

Fists and jaw both clenched, she stomped her foot and craned her neck forty-five degrees toward where the last rock had thudded against the cabin. She snarled, right fist raised, cursing the empty night. "Hornsboro, Wisconsin, hear me out. I am pissed. Do you hear me? I am so pissed off that if I were any more pissed I'd go nuclear and they'd have to call Hornsboro, Chernobyl." Letting out a gust of breath, she lowered her shoulders, turned, and looked at Larry whose face was one large question. "It was a place in Russia that . . ." Her words were still steel. She shook her head and strode toward him, then stopped, immersed in teacher body language, looking down at the silent man before her, her eyes pure stone. "Never mind. Just get past it."

She sat back on the chair, pulled a pillow over her face, then thrust it over her head and leaned back, eyes fixed on the ceiling. Her words reached out to the silent Larry who had not moved a wisp and maintained a facial expression of pure stoicism.

"Look at me with that 'be a lady crap' and I'll kick you so hard your ectoplasm will squish." Maggie was on a tear, her words snapping, her finger pointed to the ceiling. Finally she faced her mentor. "My mother always said inner discipline is not one of my strengths." Her words dripped bitter. "Calmness is beyond the remotest of goals right now. It won't even fit on my list, I'm so out of room. So don't you dare think of spouting your calm crap at me right now. It won't work."

Ever the philosopher, Larry shook his head. "I may be dead, but I'm not dumb."

Clearing his throat, he tried a new approach. "I didn't see anything, but I assume those weren't raccoons." Perhaps he thought a little humor would lighten the moment.

Maggie snaked him a look before she stood up, paced past the furniture, and started for the door, her words more mutter than observation. "Not unless they were the 200-pound variety."

This time they both went outside. Maggie looked past the path into the thick of the woods while Larry stood by watching. The moon lit the end of the lane and the boat house. Nothing. Only a swath of trees under the moonlight and then darkness. No sound. Just the calmness of the lake on a summer night. Too late for mosquitoes, so the air was still. Off to the right, a few bullfrogs croaked a song. No rocks had flown out of the darkness at them.

She walked to the source of the attack. She almost tripped over one of the rocks, a round mini-boulder. The light from the cabin was dim, but she could see it was too big for her to lift, much less throw. No weanie terrorists out to get her. She found another, one that had ricocheted into a flower barrel. It had crushed two of the freshly planted marigolds. This one she could handle. Picking it up and holding it in her hand, she felt its heft. Someone meant business. Letting out an exhale of disgust, her mind assessed the situation. Morons in town. Morons out in the woods. Enough of morons. With a snort of disgust, she tossed the rock aside. Enough. Still shaking her head, she walked back toward Larry.

He looked like a beneficent parent. "Look at you Miss Maggie. You're a new woman. A fanatic just attacked your place and you've conquered your raging. You let it go."

Stow it, her mind answered back. I may have settled down, but that doesn't mean I'm calm. The night's still young, Larry, my man – or whatever you are –and we have our work cut out for us. Only when she had made the pledge to herself, did she notice that Larry was gone. Too bad. She opened the door and started to walk in -- in to her inheritance, her cabin, the place of her childhood, one that she would cede only when hell had turned as cold as a Wisconsin winter.

Someone was trying to drive her out of *sweet, friendly* Hornsboro, Wisconsin. Someone with an agenda and a whole lot to answer for.

She could picture the lot of them thinking. Her imagination ran with their pitiful clucking and staring eyes. *We'll holler and throw rocks and she'll go home. End of that nasty Witkowski clan.*

Do your best, you old fools, whoever you are. She might quiet her anger, but no way would she shy away from finding out answers.

She marched into the extra bedroom where she kept all the family photo albums, grabbed as many as she could carry, went back out to the great room and sat down. Legs resting on the old pine coffee table, her mind softened as she leaned back and filled herself with family images until she fell asleep, albums in hand.

A canoe slid through the water, the owner paddling in happy cadence. "Rock-a-bye baby, give it a hitch. When the rock hits, it falls on the bitch . . . " Let's hear it for the poetry of the night. Such rhythm. Gotta' love rhythm. The rhythm of screams. The rhythm of Miss Maggie seeking and finding nothing. "Rock-a-bye baby, soon you'll be gone. Your screams of pain, my favorite song." He chuckled at his expertise. "Slam that door again, Maggie. Tomorrow, look for tire tracks. What? Nothing to see? Too bad. So sad."

The figure mulling the night's adventure rocked away, sure that things were proceeding so smoothly. Think those rocks were unsettling? Maybe you can find a friend or two who'll console you. Not that many friends, you say? Just wait. Attack the castle, stir up the folk. Drop a hint here. *Well, I'm not sure why she's working at Swoozie's. Teachers often have summer jobs. She asked Harriet Mills what?* Who needed a newspaper when the citizens of the town spread news so well. And with such punch. The peppermint candy he sucked on tasted that much sweeter knowing that Maggie's days surely were numbered.

Oh such sweetness.

On Wednesday morning, Maggie headed toward Swoozie's with renewed energy. This job was more than a means to consignment ends. It could be a veritable path to all sorts of clues if she worked it right.

She climbed into the window space ostensibly to work on storefront displays. Those crocks and lanterns weren't perfectly perpendicular. They needed a tiny nudge for the best viewing. Cal had walked by, for the third time since 9:00, stopped and gave her a thumbs up. Maggie had craned to check his hands – pretending to reach for a tackle box. Were Cal's dirty from rock dirt? Callused? No? What about Ralph, the clerk at Biff's? Why wasn't he at work? And what was a guy his age doing standing behind the counter at a convenience store, anyway? The citizens of fair Hornsboro could hardly have a clue that the adult Maggie who had crashed their town was playing cop. Again.

"Hey beautiful, what's a pretty girl like you doing hanging out with antiques?" Will's voice. She hadn't even heard the front door's bell. Finally someone she wanted to see. Bent over to keep from hitting her head, she stepped across the land mines of goodies and jumped down to the floor. Not exactly the most graceful of moves, but no problem. It was Will, and he never judged. She had lunched with him every day this past week -- not at Winnie's, of course – and the lawyer never failed to make her laugh or put her at ease. Maybe she needed to introduce him to Larry.

As if.

She walked over to face him, fully smiling yet surprised. "Will. Is it lunch time already?" How had time so passed by that she had missed much of the morning?

She raised her wrist to check the time, and stopped halfway up. No watch. Good move, Witkowski.

Evidently he hadn't noticed. He only laughed and smiled back at her question. "Nope. Just thought I'd take a break and see my favorite town resident. How's it going?"

He could fill out a pair of Dockers like nobody's business. The guy was a hunk clear down to his attaché case. The first part of the thought surprised her. A pleasant surprise. When had Will gone from friend to hunk? She swatted it away. The last thing she needed was a romantic complication. But the thought refused to move. The swat had been too half-hearted to dislodge.

"Lunch can't come soon enough." Holding up her left hand – the right one had the dust rag -- she backed up two steps, "Don't get too close. Sweat doesn't mix well with candle scents and lavender." Yeah, right, her inside voice told her. You can't wait until he gets as close as you want. Lunch isn't all you want from this guy.

Maggie gave the voice an internal growl. *Down, girl.*

"How about a break? I've got the best of Hornsboro coffee and bakery doughnuts." He held the sack in front of him and headed for the sales counter. "Everybody has the right to sugar and caffeine. It's in the Constitution."

No wonder she liked him. He advocated for sugar rights. She craned her head toward the back of the store. "You're on." Behind the crinkle of her smile was as much a warning as an invitation. "Good time for a break. I need to tell you about some rocks and get your advice."

If she couldn't trust Will, whom could she trust?

Will insisted on lunch at Winnie's. The owner was gone for the day, so good food, good company. She and Will sat at a table next to the window. Maggie could see pots of red geraniums outside the diner with barely a turn of her head. The entire street, on both sides, was lined with large flower pots and flower boxes. Hornsboro had a thing for flower pots in their downtown. The town was quaint and well tended. She couldn't help think, *too bad about some of the people.*

"The cheeseburger probably tastes better than the flowers. You should really try it."

"What?" She brought her attention back to the man who sat across from her. The cute one who was smiling. "Sorry." She took a big bite of her sandwich to prove it.

Will turned serious. "Checking out the landscape is all well and good, but you need to tell me more about last night. Something about rocks?"

"Not much to tell. Pretty big suckers. One almost took out my dining area window." She tried to make a joke. "You can always come over and help me move them. They'd be a pretty good start for a rock garden."

"Funny girl. Tell you what, you stick to the subject and I won't tell you about the catsup right under your nose."

Maggie grabbed her napkin and dabbed at her face. She looked at the napkin. Nothing. "Funny yourself, big guy." She set the napkin down and grabbed a French Fry. "I really want to simply sit here and enjoy lunch with a friend. Plenty of time to worry about the unseen later." Unseen. Funny choice of words. If Will knew just how much unseen there was in her life, he'd bolt in a New York minute. She chomped her fry and gave Will her best smart-aleck smile.

"Okay," he said, "but I'm not letting this go. Promise me you'll meet me tonight after work. No way am I letting my favorite client be hurt, but you need a distraction. Besides, nobody throws rocks at *my* date."

A date. Tonight. With Will.

"It's time we had some fun. Tomorrow we'll worry about keeping you out of harm's way."

She made a lame joke about a lunatic local named Harm, but then smiled and agreed. On her way back to work, her mind played with the possibilities. He'd take her home to make sure that the bad guys were kept at bay. She wasn't about to let him sleep over – although the thought stirred a pleasure neuron here and there – even if Larry promised to hide. But Will could follow her home and scout out the place. Could become a nightly ritual. While she unlocked the door to Swoozie's and set up for afternoon customers, she played out several scenarios, all involving underwear and sweat.

A ghost that paced. I wonder how long he'll keep it up. Maggie wanted to laugh, but knew better. She simply watched through the screen door as Larry moved back and forth in front of the porch, arms flailing, kinetic energy sparking on occasion. When she went outside to stand on the porch, she let the screen door slam. Larry didn't notice, or he didn't care. Either way, he stood facing the road, his hands grabbing at his hair.

"Hey ghost boy, watch yourself. You may set the place on fire."

He turned slowly. The glare of a ghost in turmoil is an awesome thing to behold. The eyes become translucent, the skin fades to an icy white. A more intimidated Maggie may have feared the face that stared at her, but what the heck, she'd faced down nasty looks, phone calls, even rocks. Winnie and Cal. That in itself should earn her a break.

"What is it with you? You pop in and out of here like it's ghost camp and play snarky with me. *I'm* the one stuck here. *I'm* the one traipsing through Hornsboro trying to figure out a mystery I can't even define." "I get it. Solve the mystery. What do you think I've been trying to do since you showed up? I want a break. One night. I want to go out, have a drink, shake my booty in the face of all those self-righteous hicks that have tried to paint my grandfather as some kind of senior citizen Lothario."

Larry's form steadied. "One night?"

"Yes."

"Tomorrow you're back at it?"

"Promise." Maggie held up two fingers. "Scout's honor."

Larry shook his head. "I can believe a lot of things about you, Miss Witkowski, but you as a girl scout? Not hardly." Before she could answer, Larry disappeared.

Chapter 11

6:00. She had an hour. First up. What should she wear? She carted out clothes from the tiny bedroom until they lay strewn over most available pieces of furniture in the great room. City girl look? Not for drinks in Hornsboro. Naughty school teacher? That'd make those tongues wag. The thought made her smile.

Just as Maggie was checking out a jersey top, she heard a soft whistle behind her and turned. One of her thongs hovered in front of Larry, a deep purple piece of silk and lace he was studying as if he were an archeologist on a major dig. "You know, in my day we used to call these sling shots." His grin stretched clear across his face. "But they sure weren't made out of this stuff."

"Give me that, you moron." She marched across the room, snatched the thong with one hand and raised her index finger of the other smack dab in front of Larry's face. "I thought you had trouble with the material world." She held out the thong as proof. "Or does a big guy ghost like you get an ectoplasm surge from panties?"

Larry feigned pure innocence. "For you. Madam, my skills have no bounds. You fill me with force field."

"Well, *someone* is in a better mood. Not that I care. I am so not going to mess with you tonight. Leave me and my underwear alone. I'll be off checking out Hornsboro nightlife in less than an hour. The last thing I need to worry about is some smart-aleck ghost messing with my head." She put both hands on her hips, the thong hanging like a workman's belt. "Remember, you promised. One night. No hassle."

He pursed his lips and raised his eyebrows, then stared at the thong. "Better keep an eye out for hassle yourself, fair maiden." Then he dematerialized.

"Good riddance, lunkhead!" She scanned the area where Larry had stood. "And no fair peeking while I take my bath."

A chuckle wafted throughout the room. Maggie focused on her new Miss Me jeans. Later, when she stepped into the warmth of the claw foot tub, she checked out the mirror for any ghostly display, part of her warming at the thought of his smirking face materializing. She slid down into the bubbles. Good Lord in heaven, she *was* nuts. She picked up a handful of bubbles and threw them toward the faucet.

At 7:15, Will and Maggie walked into Wallie's, a local dive that boasted itself as "the oldest bar in Washekca County." From the looks of it, the place was the oldest bar in Wisconsin, one reminiscent of trader and trapper days. No flower boxes here like on Main Street. Just enough Carharts to qualify as hunter warren.

Like most small town taverns, the bar ran across the longest wall, a good thirty feet. A mixture of bar stools – a few wood ones sporting backs, more teetering and backless, most evidently garnered from the county dump exchange – housed the patrons, none of whom seemed to care about aesthetics. Yellowed newspaper stories of Hank Aaron shared the wall behind the bar with fishing tournament fliers taped to the mirrored tiles Most of the linoleum had been worn away. The sub flooring almost held back the dirt. A light bulb encased in a ball of barbed wire hung in the center of the ceiling. On each side, in an act of symmetry, hung a rusted mobile with bears and moose dangling from twisted wire.

Wallie's was a place for the Wisconsin version of good-old-boyism. Customers came to drink beer and tell lies.

The din of a few locals celebrating the end of a workday spread from the back. Every now and then, a burst of laughter echoed from one group or another, perhaps an invitation to a contest – the loudest man wins.

Maggie surveyed the bar from the doorway. *I dressed up for this?* Will put his hand on her back to guide her in.

Will's hand. Felt good, like it belonged. That touch sent . . . well . . . contentment, gave rise to a new thought. *I am absolutely the hottest thing in here.*

She used her naughty voice. "Nice place. Do they serve pickled animal parts?" Will laughed, pressed his thumb against her and made the slightest suggestion of a circle as his hand lingered. Warning or appreciation? Then he shot back, "Only in the winter when they've run out of popcorn."

A man at the far end of the bar turned his head toward her, picked up his beer and went to the back. Maggie gave him no more than a surreptitious glance. *Ah yes, we're in pitchforks and torches mode.* Will whispered, "Do you want to go someplace else?"

Maggie stiffened her spine, notched up her inner Xena, and walked in. "Not a chance. Besides, it's so dark in here that the guy probably thought I was his wife and figured he needed to hide." Just as Will shook his head and laughed at her, the customer turned his head and watched her, his head moving up and down her form. Something recoiled in Maggie's gut in spite of her goal to shrug him off.

Will and Maggie each took a seat at the front end of the bar, ensconced in shadows and privacy. Maggie's barstool had holes from cigarette burns in the seat. A cushion from another stool acted as a pad for her back. She swiveled the seat toward Will, leaned back, and crossed her legs. A diva never let her surroundings distract her. The bartender – a mountain of a guy at least 6'8"--reached over the bar and slapped his hands on each of Will's shoulders. "Hey lawyer boy, how's your torts?" He kept his huge paws there as the slap turned into a friendly clasp – at least Maggie hoped it was friendly – but he turned his head toward Maggie and winked. "And who's the pretty lady with you?" He let go of Will and, as Maggie turned to face him, leaned in closer, hand over his heart. "That Will gets all the hot ones. I'm lucky if my women have teeth."

The guy had dimples, deep gray eyes, and an obvious appreciation for play. And he hadn't run away. Maggie lifted the left side of her mouth in the start of a grin. Two men. Start of a good night.

Will slid his hands onto the arms of Maggie's bar stool and turned her back toward him, then broke in, both eyes and tone laughing. "Maggie, don't listen to him. Jeff is an out-and-out aficionado of beautiful women. All his wives have been down right smokin' hot." He gave a smug smile. "All three of them." The smile tightened into abject superiority. "Probably why all three left him." He nodded his head as if suddenly struck by a thought and then raised his eyebrows. "Oh, I forgot. Jeff here is dating wife number two right now." He turned back to face the bar and gripped the edge." How's that going, buddy?"

Big boy territory banter. Fun for them. Borderline annoying for a girl who spent this much time getting ready and was suddenly getting as much attention as the galleon jar of pickled eggs that waited forlornly on the counter. Besides, bartenders knew secrets. She adjusted her butt on the stool as an act of defiance and felt the tug of her thong pulling at her.

Sling shot, my ass.

Maggie waved a hand. "Excuse me. I'm the hot chick here. Let's pay attention."

She smiled and stuck out her hand. "Evidently Will has forgotten his manners. I'm Maggie Witkowski."

A "Yo" interrupted them. Jeff hollered down to the other end, "Be right with you Hank," then turned back to her, reached out and shook her hand. "Ah, the famous Ms. Witkowski. Lady, you are the buzz of the town. Let me get those guys their drinks, and I'll be right back. I want to *know* you.""

Once Hank and his buddies were appeased, Jeff was back. Will ordered a Hamm's beer, the nectar of choice in this state. That was no problem at Wallie's. The whole state drank Hamm's – straight from the bottle like real people. Maggie asked for a glass of wine. Jeff could handle the wine – they had a bottle somewhere – but when he returned with some Lambrusco, unscrewed the cap and poured, he had to use a plastic Pabst Blue Ribbon beer cup. "Sorry for the lack of amenities. The good folks who visit us usually don't ask for wine. We had two glasses, but Minnie Anderson broke both and we never ordered more." He leered at Maggie as he poured. "I, however, can appreciate the finer things in life. Dump prissy boy and hang out with me. I can swear in eight languages, and I *do* have crystal at my place."

Will broke in. "Too bad Crystal's the name of one of his wives."

Jeff ignored him, continued to focus on Maggie. "I left enough bottles down there in a couple of iced buckets to keep the boys happy so that we could chat. Word on the street is that you are looking for hornets' nests under every stoop."

Maggie raised one eyebrow. "That's one way of looking at it. Seems there's quite the to-do over my grandfather and the dearly departed Ida Ann Turnball."

"Folks around here won't let anything go. They make Ida Ann out to be some kind of wounded heroine." He looked straight at Maggie. "The woman was nuts. She fit in with the rest of the loons out on Lake Danbury. She was a boy crazy airhead as a teenager – not cool for the fifties – and dotty as a woman of a certain age."

Will coughed displeasure. "Ida Ann Turnball never had a chance."

Jeff looked at his friend as if Will were wishing for a star. "Have you been watching too many Disney movies?"

What was with these two? She wasn't here for guy spats. Maggie slapped the bar and stood up. Her feet held by the bar stool's metal rings. "Attention, please!" She slapped one hand on her rear. "My jeans here, designer, bejeweled jeans I might add, set me back two weeks worth of groceries. My top, if you haven't noticed is slinky. Sexy." She held out her leg. "These are killer shoes."

She took a deep breath and sat down. "Let me repeat. Ass. Rhinestones. Slink. Are you guys monks?"

Both men stared.

Jeff scratched his head and smiled. "Whew. You're a woman who knows what she wants." He cocked his finger at her. "And yes, what you're wearing is worth is every penny, smokin' hot lady."

Will held up his hands in defeat. "You have my vote. In all things."

Liars. Maggie knew resignation when she heard it. Even resignation laced with sucking up. *That's what you get for making this about you, lady rhinestone butt.* What? Had Larry sent a conscience fairy with her?

I know. I know. Stow the party and back to work.

She slid her hands down her things and groused, "What the hell. My party buzz is as dead as Ms. Turnball. Just be warned, if my party night is going to focus on a dead woman who may or may not have my stellar taste in clothes, I had better find something useful."

Jeff nodded. "I've heard the scuttlebutt. It's more fantasy than logic. Most folks around here live for bingo, polka feasts, and gossip -- mostly gossip. Finding the daughter of the local scion cold in her bed was an early Christmas present. Those a bit saner figured she'd had enough of life and offed herself."

Scion? Was Ida Ann rich? Was that part of the town's blame game? Lou was the senior citizen gold digger? Like that would happen.

Maggie turned to Will, her face asking the question. He stayed silent, his eyes straight on and neutral.

Right, she thought. Will had sympathy for the granddaughter of some kind of robber baron, thought the old gal was some kind of victim – victim of a man who was nothing but caring.

Idiot.

Will offered up. "Franklin Turnball was the son of the wealthiest man in the county. Franklin inherited his father's money, his brains, and his obsession to control."

Jeff tag-teamed the conversation. "Unfortunately, Miss Turnball was not at all what Daddy and Grandpappy ordered. "He cleared his throat. "Whatever genetic pool passed on brains was on vacation the night Ida Ann was conceived. She was a walking, talking caricature of every blonde joke told in this bar. And believe me, that's plenty."

"At the risk of being devil's advocate non gratis, I don't see it that way at all." Will's voice was matter-of-fact. He might as well have been in a courtroom. "Jeff, you've only lived here what – two years? The old girl was dead by the time you got here. You're only going on gossip."

"And what, you were her best friend? Come on, she was a batty recluse who rattled around in that big old house and probably talked to the wallpaper."

"She was a nice elderly lady who was doomed from the minute she was born female. No girl in town was good enough to be her friend. No man was good enough to court her. She only had one friend – Winnie – and they didn't even talk to each other until after her father died."

Will leaned forward toward Maggie. "I could be Mr. Nice, but if we're going to find the truth, we have to look at the possibilities. All of them."

Words from her grandmother's journal niggled at Maggie. *We lost a good friend. What she had to endure.* There were so many layers to this puzzle to yet be uncovered.

Only the slam of the front door sounded as Marv Federinc strolled in, and walked toward the bar, talking to the air as he lumbered forward to take a seat and to the mirrors behind the bar as he waited.

"Whoosh, what a day. The Peterson place on Route 14 had a backed up toilet. Jimmy Peterson decided to flush his sidewalk chalk down the stool along with a few toys. The stuff that came up – let's just say wasn't no artist ever colored with it, at least not in our area." He laughed. "Can't say that for Minnesota, ya' know. Elvira Holm called me out three times, all for nothing more than squeaky doors." Once he had plopped himself at mid-bar, his voice turned skeptical. "I think the old gal wants to get lucky." He laughed at himself. "If she has to flirt with an old geezer like me, she's gotta' be seven kinds of desperate."

He craned his neck toward the end of the bar, then his face broke out in obvious surprise. "Will. Miss Maggie. Good to see you." He grabbed his beer and moved closer. "Little lady, I hear you're tearing it up at Swoozie's." Chuckling, he looked straight at her – with one of his eyes. "Course, being's you're a city gal – a nice one, I might add – and Swoozie tends toward crankiness when she actually has to work, well I guess, it's no wonder the place is making it."

"Thanks for the compliment, Marv. But I'll bet that it has more to do with the summer people coming back than anything I've done."

"Nope. I have it on good account that you are one persuasive and friendly lady. Looks like Hornsboro's all the better for you coming back." His mouth twisted. "At least fer most folks."

Will took a swig of his beer and set the bottle down, one hand sliding down the neck before he spoke. "Not everyone seems to agree."

Marv leaned back, his friendliness hushed. Jeff watched the mirror. One of those uncomfortable silences ensued for a few seconds. Maggie watched her glass while she broke the lull. "Someone decided to toss a few rocks at my place Saturday night."

In truth, Marv did look surprised. "You're kidding me. Who'd do a dumb thing like that? Musta' been kids looking for trouble."

"If they were kids, they were big kids." Watching the handy man's face, she ventured, "I am not exactly Hornsboro's favorite daughter." She paused and widened her eyes. "Or granddaughter. I'd buy a chance encounter with ornery teenagers, Marv, if I hadn't had a run-in with Cal Dinsdale and Winnie Listug." She shook her head. "Cal tripped over his tongue about something between my grandfather and one of the local ladies, and Winnie all but called Lou a murderer.

"I remember our conversation the day you cleaned my fireplace. C'mon, Marv, level with me."

Marv took off his cap, set it on the bar, and scratched his head. It took several breaths before he answered. "It's like I told you, Miss Maggie. 'Bout the troubles. But I ain't got no right to butt in and make judgments. 'Bout you or anybody else."

If Marvin Federinc didn't make judgments, then he was in the minority of a good chunk of the citizenry. Before she could press him for more conversation, he chugged down his beer, plopped three one-dollar bills on the bar, grabbed his hat and made for the exit. Just as he was about to grab the handle of the door, he turned to the three and said, "If you want to know anything, Maggie Witkowski, ask Will. He was her lawyer and handled all her affairs Knew everything about all her business." He gave a snort. "At least the ones that were public. If anyone knows about the old gal, it's Will." He turned back to the door, opened it, and walked out.

Clearing his throat, Jeff announced that he'd better check on his customers. It'll probably take a few minutes, he assured them. Then he scooted off.

Will spread his hands his hands, palms up. "Yes, I was her lawyer. As far as I'm concerned, I still am." He lowered his hands to his knees and leaned forward. "If I knew anything that would help you – without compromising ethics – I'd tell you."

More new information. The focus she had demanded of herself moments ago left in the huff that she expelled. She bit her upper lip and made circles on the bar with her index finger.

Will's expression showed he was no dummy. He was a man who knew upset when it stared at him. "Maggie, I'm trying to be the good guy here. I'll go the extra mile for you, but I have to be true to my profession.

"I'd never for a moment believe that your grandfather was anything less than a sweet old guy trying to be nice. But what I said about Ida Ann is true. She was a harmless old lady, kind of pathetic, but just as sweet." He moved one hand forward toward her. "What kind of jerk would I be to jump to conclusions like the less enlightened of our townsfolk?"

"It's a good thing I believe you're on my side. Otherwise I'd have to waste my wine throwing it at you." She took a drink for emphasis. "That *is* why we came here in the first place. A couple of drinks. A little fun."

He grabbed her hand. "That's right. For tonight, relax. Enjoy the now."

Maggie popped off the bar stool and swayed to imaginary music, arms raised, drink in one hand. Why waste the evening? She was in a bar on the closest thing she'd had to a date in six months. The guy might be something worthy of a bubble bath and a snatch of lace even if Wallie's was hardly lace thong worthy.

Meanwhile, in spite of Marv's opinion, the town hated her, thought her grandfather a betrayer, even a murderer. The guy who, along with his wife, had befriended someone forced to endure. . . what? And the one who'd befriended her and listened unconditionally – that relationship had tilted. If Maggie couldn't untie this knot, how could she find all the answers? Was she strong enough, good enough to ever undo all the bad?

She watched Will watching her. He hadn't shaved. The stubble was sexy. Broad shoulders. Hard hands. The perfect complement to those dimples and good-old-boy smile. Of course he was on her side. Hadn't given any indication otherwise. He even brought her doughnuts.

Absolutely. So did another hottie you fell for.

I haven't fallen for anyone.

She took a sip of wine. The wine spoke to her. *Tomorrow, Maggie. Tomorrow the task is on again. Tonight, relax.*

Yeah, she answered, *that's what Scarlet O'Hara thought. Look where it got her.*

Later that night, after Will walked Maggie to her car and gave her a chaste kiss, after he squeezed her hand and made her promise to be careful, after those tender bits of friendship, even a little wooing, Will climbed into his own car and sat back in the driver's seat.

Not too bad. Maggie wanted fun. Maggie wanted answers. Of course, it was all about Maggie.

He reached over to the cubbyhole on the car's console and grabbed a piece of candy, unwrapped it and popped it into his mouth. Peppermint. His favorite.

Well Maggie, my dear, I'm going to give you plenty of answers. Wrong answers, but what the hell. Half the fun is watching you spin. *Bentley, you will be her best source of whatever she wants. After all, it's all about Maggie.* He crunched the candy for emphasis.

As for fun, little girl, you have no idea.

Chapter 12

After the tug of her date with Will last night, Maggie was in a snit the next morning in spite of her day off. Gone was the promise of back to detective. The ball was over and Cinderella Maggie felt like she had missed the prince altogether. A light goodnight kiss on the forehead – like she was fourteen, and an admonition. "I'm on your side, Maggie."

What a waste of her lucky purple thong.

She took her ire out on Mother Nature. In spite of the light rain, she took to reclaiming another perennial border, hacking at wild raspberry roots, scowling and huffing at the enemy that refused to budge – the enemy she could see. Mosquitoes swarmed near her ankles. She thought about spraying her legs with more repellent, but she kept at her task. *Let the little bastards come,* she thought. *I'll whack them too.*

Kill the roots. Kill the bugs. At least with them, she had some control.

She stared at the ground in front of her. The roots ran everywhere. *The damn things sending out shoots, and I keep hacking.* She walked around the closest clump, eyeing it, sneering.

You might have been here first, but you're mine, sucker. Think you can choke me out of here, think again.

For emphasis, she wielded her pointed shovel downward and stepped hard. When the root refused to break, she whacked at it once, twice, three times, and then stomped her foot down on the spade and pushed. Nothing. This was the root from hell.

Oh no you don't. This time I win. She set the spade aside and grabbed at the menace, wrapping the exposed root around her hand so that she could pull hard. The force felt gratifying, as if conquering the thing could pacify the restlessness that filled her. "Try to uproot my hostas after I spent three hours planting here? Don't even think."

"You know, they were here first."

Maggie jerked upward, root forgotten, then fell forward with a thud, hands splayed on the ground and knees plopped into freshly dug dirt. One hand lodged in a pile of raspberry prickles. Lucky for her she was wearing work gloves. Growling out a response more embarrassment than pain, she pushed herself up, dusted off her sweat pants, and turned toward the sound. Larry was chuckling. He swept down and plucked a wildflower growing in the pile of dirt, presented it to her with a flourish.

Her hand itched with the need to slap him. "Don't you ever knock? Or whistle? You scared the life out of me!"

"Poor choice of words." He was still smirking, flower in hand. "We have to keep you alive. Otherwise, I'll never get out of here."

"Funny." She faced him while she rubbed her hands across her pants. A smirk itched inside her. She bared her teeth, all coolness. "If you want me back on task, you have to play nice."

He tossed the flower aside with a shrug and sat down on an old tree stump. "Not playing nice was what sent me here in the first place."

Maggie eyed him while she swiped her gloved hands on her pants two. "Really."

"Let's say, shortcuts and a lack of indecision. That and too many martinis. Crimes not so much of commission as omission as the saying goes."

Maggie moved away from her work spot and leaned against a tree, looking down at him. "Anything you want to share?" Her voice was kind.

Hands folded, Larry met her gaze, his eyebrows lifted, his head moving slightly. "The Judges don't deal in particulars as much as they do in motivation. I, on the other hand, am interested in particulars. The particulars of what, why, and how that will solve this infernal mystery."

Maggie winced. He was right. Back to work. She filled him in on the facts of meeting Jeff and Ida Ann's status as heiress.

"Interesting," he said. "But what are you leaving out?"

Clouds had covered the sun for much of the morning. At this exact moment, they parted, letting the sun have its way with the day. A ray of light split through the trees and hit a boulder next to where Larry sat, illuminating him in what appeared to Maggie as a Catholic moment from her childhood. She felt like she needed a confessional booth.

She gave a weak, "Leaving out?" Not even the tree stump believed her.

Larry shook his head. "Don't forget. I can read your mind when you're in an emotional state." He paused slightly. "Like now."

Above them, a bird tweeted. Maggie thrust her arm up, middle finger of her hand extended.

"I take it, last night was not a success."

Face flushed, she exhaled, stood up, and began to pace. "Let's just say that when it comes Will Bentley, last night had all the success of a sack race in a swamp."

"What happened?" The words were firm and quick.

"I spent an hour getting ready. I am totally hot, and for that I get – wait for it – my *friend*. Will was Ida Ann's attorney. If I want to know about Ida Ann, the local handy man says, I should ask her legal counsel, the one resident of Hornsboro most likely to know about her. The whiz kid who took care of the poor little old lady no one seems to think had one extra brain cell above ditz. The one he thinks was some sweet misunderstood little old lady."

"That's it? That had you hacking away at weeds like General MacCarther stomping through Korea? Will Bentley was Ida Ann's lawyer? How many lawyers practice in Hornsboro?"

"One. The fink." Maggie's teeth gritted on the words.

Larry ignored her snit, looked at her like an adult telling a child to straighten up. "Right. He's the one full-time lawyer in a one-lawyer town. He looks like a lawyer, sounds like a lawyer. Guess what. He's a lawyer. He has to be on her side."

"She's his dead client, you moron."

"And what's the problem with sticking up for the old lady? Isn't that what your grandfather did? You don't seem to have any problems with his motivation."

"That's because I know it. Grandma knew what was really going on in his head. You said so yourself. I read about it in the journal." Maggie bit on upper lip while the lower one trembled before she spurted, "Will's the only one that's been upfront with me – at least that's what I thought."

The words were hardly out before she clenched her teeth and breathed in heavily. Then she turned and kicked the tree.

"You're jealous that a guy you're supposedly not emotionally involved with defended an old woman who happens to be dead." He sounded like an irritated father.

Maggie kicked another once more before she turned to face Larry. Planting her feet firmly, she placed her hands on her hips. "You don't get it! Will has been the one solid ever since I pulled up to this crazy place. He doesn't look at me as though I were some piece of litter on the sidewalk. He doesn't throw rocks. He doesn't make phone calls that accuse."

Larry watched her. "If you flap your arms, maybe you can fly away and all will be forgotten."

"He promised last night that he was there for me, like we were at least two of the Three Musketeers, and then he didn't even call this morning to see how I was doing."

Larry's voice was annoyingly even. "Again, let's take a look at this. A mature woman is upset because a man who is only her *friend* doesn't call her when he just saw her last night. That's what has you upset?"

Larry's voice settled to a coaxing. "I get it. This has hardly been a summer vacation for you." He paused. "And if my ill-spent humor offends you, I'm sorry."

"Apology accepted." Her words were clipped.

Larry's eyes softened to a lighter whiskey color, their normal brown even more flecked with green. He took a step toward her and folded his arms.

"Let's look at the bright side. As Ida's lawyer and town resident, Will knows as much, if not more than anyone, and he's been your staunchest ally since you first left his office. I'd call that a good sign.

"Besides, what's the worst he can be? Go into the cabin like a good little girl and call him. Ask him point-blank – if you need to – why he didn't call you. And after you take your foot out of your mouth, you can talk about his warped sense of professional obligation."

"We talked about that last night. He told me we needed to look at what we know objectively."

Larry beamed a little brighter. "Shame on him for that. Imagine, picking common sense over your ego. I bet you another plant, the problem is that he tried to explain, but he just didn't get down on his knees to do it."

Maggie sucked in a shallow hiss of breath and blew it out.

"Jeez, I hate it when you're right."

"I am. And watch your mouth. Now get going."

Scowling, she ground her foot on a clod of dirt. "You don't play fair."

"Fair is for sissies." He sounded serious, but his lips were twitching. He didn't mean it. Did he?

"Just making an observation." Maggie bent over to pick up her spade, grabbed it, and trudged toward the cabin. Tossing her gloves and the spade onto the porch, she opened the door and walked in just as the phone rang.

It was Swoozie.

"Maggie darlin', you best come on down here if you want your grandma's big pine case, that sweet one with the pewter handles."

Maggie could feel the southern charm oozing through the phone line. A customer lurked. One that could make off with something that belonged to *her*. Clenching the phone, she beat back a retort. Count, Maggie, count.

"Maggie? Are you there?" Charm had suddenly slipped into mandate, one swimming in the cream of Swoozie's Southern belle mien, followed by a little laugh. "Of course you are. Come on down to the store. And bring your checkbook."

The last sentence sounded like a tease. Maggie knew better.

In spite of the underhanded timing of the sale, Maggie's purchase was a link to the past. She perched on a porch chair, her rescue in front of her, her fingers touching memories while she stroked the smooth wood of the hinged top. Grandpa Lou had found the old wooden box at the dump, under an old mattress, dinged and smeared with paint splatters and circles. The last owner had stored paint cans on it, why she couldn't figure out. A much smarter eye had realized its possibilities and brought it home for restoration. It was too big, really, to be called a trunk by decorator standards, and besides, its top was flat. It had no drawers, so it wasn't a chest. It was just a big wooden box with a hinged top. One that her grandfather had seen for its own particular beauty. Her memory smelled the sanded pine, the hand-rubbed oil that had brought the piece back to its rightful beauty. She was silent while the past spoke to her.

"A piece like this is the same as a woman, Mags," her grandpa had said one afternoon on the very same porch while he worked his magic. It has plenty of beauty by itself, but with care, the beauty grows." Lou had clarified quickly. "Of course, your Grandma Jean never has to worry about that. She can't be any more beautiful than she is. I just treat her with care because I love her." He leaned over to his granddaughter, whispering, "Had to say that. Jean's in the kitchen baking cookies. I just want to make sure there's plenty for me."

"Don't think that I can't hear you, you old coot. I know that I'm the beauty of your life as much as I know how much you like cookies."

The words seemed rubbed into the longleaf pine, speaking softly to a woman who wrapped herself in the love they conveyed. Maggie was a firm believer that a girl made her own fate, but at moments like these, she could lean into the solace of knowing that there were those who loved her. Even if they were gone, the love lingered. She ached with the thought, a feeling both bitter and sweet.

Then she let the mad rise up.

Swoozie – the consummate bitch – had almost sold her heirloom out from under her. If she hadn't made it to the store in record time, a customer would have robbed her of her history.

From the time she slammed her car door shut to the last shovelful of mulch, Maggie had let her ire energize her. Nothing like a good mad to whirl a girl through her work. At the rate Swoozie was trying to screw her over, Maggie could double the size of the perennial beds by the end of the summer. Except by then, Maggie wouldn't have anything to put inside the cabin. Swoozie would have sold it all out from under her.

Leaning forward, her arms folded on her legs, Maggie looked out across the property. Thanks to forty-eight hours of rage-inspired gardening, the raspberry roots had been tamed, the hostas and clumps of Bleeding Hearts freshly watered and mulched. She had been a maniac. Now she was a woman content. From her viewpoint there on the porch, her additions looked like an infinity symbol weaving between the large oak trees. Infinity. Perfect. She sighed and hugged herself.

A voice crooned from behind her. "I see you have your purchase. It's a beauty."

"Larry." Maggie steadied herself, raised her body, and started to turn around.

"I used to make you jump. Must be getting used to me." Now he was directly in front of her, looking at her like a big brother who'd just read his sister's diary, his smile a smirk.

Maggie slitted her eyes. "Just because I don't lurch on cue doesn't mean you don't annoy me."

"I should be sorry that I broke through your mind nap? Don't think so."

"Why am I not surprised?"

"Probably because you know that we have work to do."

The words nagged at her. Who did he think he was, spoiling her down time, her moment that had so slid her into the past, she could hear the talk of family long gone.

He's the guy who's going to help you solve a mystery, that's who he is. Get back on track. You have bad guys to catch.

Fine. Whatever. Nothing like a conscience to spoil a party. Still, she fought it, begging for one last snippet of nostalgia. "Grandma had set this box right on the wall where the phone is. In the summer, it always had a pitcher filled with freshly cut flowers, bittersweet in the fall. In the winter, she'd put evergreen boughs around the pitcher and holly inside. Maggie tossed back her head and took in a deep breath. "I remember it all – the tang of the wildflowers, the scent of the boughs, the cookies on a plate waiting for me regardless of the season. I can feel the touch of the long pine needles, so soft when they were freshly cut."

When the tears stung the back of her eyes, she looked at Larry. "You're right. We have work to do. But first I want to keep reminding myself why I need to do it. This is so close to when I was innocent, before . . .." She let the words hang before she went to work in the present.

After lifting up the box lid, she ran her hands along the inside. "There used to be a spring that opened a secret compartment on the bottom. I used to write my grandparents outrageous stories about my summer adventures once a week and hide them, waiting until they'd magically *find* them." Maggie used her fingers to emphasize the game. "Grandpa said that certainly the bass that got away were as big as whales, otherwise why wouldn't I have caught them, but, truth be told, Wisconsin didn't have too many purple bears – at least as far as he had seen." While her fingers searched for the spring, she closed her eyes. "I don't know which was more fun, writing the stories or trying to convince Lou and Jean that they were true."

She started, as much in surprise as discovery. Larry watched as Maggie lifted the false bottom from the chest and set it aside. They both peeked in on the contents no longer hidden after so many years, pressed flowers, pictures partially wrapped in a folded sheet of note paper, and a yellowed envelope. Maggie gently lifted the flowers and set them aside, then pulled out the pictures. The ink on the note, faded against the aged paper, looked washed out. Maggie had to trace her fingers across the words to decipher them.

Jean. Thank you for keeping my secret and my treasures. You are a friend forever.

The signature stopped Maggie's finger, her mind following the circling of letters. *Ida Ann.*

Secret? What kind of secret? And Jean as friend and secret keeper? Ida Ann was a friend. The journal had said so. Friends kept secrets. Certainly nothing about Lou?

Maggie thought back to last night. Ida Ann's daddy was less than a doting father. Abuse? She turned her focus to the pictures, part of her shuddering at the thought of trespassing.

How silly, she thought. Everyone loves to look at old pictures. The Witkowski family was united in their passion for cameras. Every occasion, large and small, required a permanent image. Christmas trees. Summer jumping off the docks. Strings of fish. They were all dutifully preserved in stacks of albums, proudly displayed and eagerly cherished.

But these photos were from someone outside the Witkowski family unit. Someone locked in mystery and accusation. She slid the wrapping off the photos, pulled the pictures gently from their resting place and separated them. There were five of them, all in black and white, squares and rectangles with white edging. She picked up the first one. It showed a young woman, actually a teenager no more than fifteen, standing on a porch, her arm linked through a man's. She was pin-up girl pretty, porcelain complexioned, dimples clearly lining a smile that could only be called rosebud sweet. What could have been ash blonde hair fell in loose waves held back with a head band. The older man was dressed in a dark suit. He had a square jaw, steeled stare, hair slicked back. No smile.

No love for the girl on his arm. Pictures do not lie.

The porch spread across the front of a large white house, what looked like an upper class summer home. Huge pine tree boughs framed the edges of the photograph, requisite landscaping for Wisconsin. Wicker chairs peeked from behind the couple.

When Maggie turned the picture over, she froze. Neatly scripted on the back was *Ida Ann and Father, 1956.*

Larry broke her focus. "For you, snapshots like these are nostalgia; for me, they're yesterday." She could hear the sadness in his voice.

She turned to face him, her curiosity with their finds tinged with sympathy.

He coughed, returned to no nonsense Larry. "Back to business. The truth is there, somewhere in black and white."

Maggie nodded and went back to work. The next three pictures were of the same girl, one of them showing her standing on a dock, preening for the camera. The other two had been taken inside the house. The first showed her standing on a curved stairway dressed in a floor length gown, what looked like black velvet on the top – long sleeved and boat-necked, the skirt layers of white lace. Not exactly what might be expected in the small Wisconsin community of Ida Ann Turnball. In the second one, she stood on the same stairway, this time in a mid-calf dress, one just as elaborate. In neither one did she share the same smile as in the first picture.

The last picture showed Ida Ann in a fishing boat out on a lake, dressed in shorts and a halter top. Again, Maggie thought *pin-up*. This time, she was with a young man, a handsome young man several years older than she. Something was familiar about that face. It tugged at Maggie, but she couldn't place it. Ida Ann held her head back, and she was laughing. Her companion was looking at her, his eyes and smile all about the beautiful girl seated next to him.

The envelope. When Maggie opened the envelope, she gave a half snort in recognition of work she had seen in hundreds of notebooks scribbled by hundreds of dewy-eyed teenage girls. Hearts and roses, hand drawn and faded, lined the edges of a yellowed piece of paper. Directly inside the artwork, the author had penned *Mrs. Carlo Veraldi. Ida Ann Veraldi*, entwining the titles as they circled a poem in the middle, it too faded by age.

> *His eyes of brown gaze into mine*
> *My heart, oh dear one is truly thine*
> *He touches me and I feel such love*
> *My Carlo, you were sent to me by God above*
> *If you would ever say goodbye*
> *I know that I would surely die.*

The teacher in her reacted first while she reread the poem. Big on hormones, bad on content. As her critic self silenced, intrigue filled her. She put down the writing, picked up the picture. Hot guy. Not too hard to figure out this one. Ida Ann, you naughty little girl.

Larry stuck to the obvious. "Ida Ann had a beau named Carlo. Carlo Veraldi. Not much of a Wisconsin name. Where did he come from?"

"No kidding. Sounds like a kid I'd teach back in Chicago. Who cares, though. We have a name and a face. Couple of faces." She sifted back and forth through the pictures, excitement buzzing up and down through her nerve way. Where to start?

The more she studied the photographs, the more the thrill began to wane. The images of this young woman held her. Ida Ann had been sad as a woman. When had she moved from the laughing girl to the laughable woman? When had the cache of letters and souvenirs, the days of planning hairstyles and collecting stuffed animals soured into bitterness?

Larry's presence swept over her like a parent tucking in a child at night, complete with the sense of a goodnight kiss on her cheek. "You study these from a woman's point of view. We'll talk later." Then he was gone.

Who knew how long Maggie sat and looked at those finds, her mind wondering, stretching back to a time she had only heard about, a time of supposed innocence. Maggie slipped the contents back into the envelope and placed it back in its hiding place. Then she went inside to fix herself something to drink. Lemonade. The whole time she squeezed the lemons and stirred her drink, she was struck by the intensity of her find and the small nudging of guilt at the invasion of her discovery, that and Ida Ann calling Jean a friend. How had that turned to "If only you could have left her"?

Later, she would seek that answer, sure of it as a huge piece of the puzzle that she and Larry had to construct along with so many other questions. She would engage in what defined her as Maggie Witkowski, the drive to come up with an answer, as if the answer were a rose hip stuck in her finger, festering until she dug it out.

But as she stirred her drink, for that few moments, she let her imagination wander across the lake to a large house where a lonely girl smiled into a camera and dreamed of a handsome boy named Carlo.

— *Chapter 13* —

Bent over, picture in hand, Maggie reached for the far side of table in the middle of the store window and set it in the easel. She was alone in the store and on a mission. Good. The last of the photos. Five of them, the ones from Grandpa Lou's chest, each framed in antique pewter courtesy of Swoozie. She moved the easel a smidgen, then smoothed the quilt spread over the table.

Perfect. The edges of the quilt lay catty-whompas to the table. Maggie might say *juxtaposed* in Chicago, but the word sounded too pretentious for the tone of the display. She had picked the quilt in her mind last night when the idea began fermenting. Primitive flowers in deep yellow. Ivory background. Simple and gorgeous. People would take a look just for the quilt.

On top of the quilt, a stack of three over-sized alphabet blocks from children long grown set on one end, a crockery lamp on the other. Each acted as a backdrop for the photos, three by the blocks, two by the lamp.

Maggie had switched its lampshade to a black one to match the wrought iron of the easel and the script of the stenciled sign in the middle. *Hornsboro History. See if you remember. Or come in and take a guess.*

Witkowski, she bragged to herself, you are a genius. Way to use those years of bulletin board ideas for sleuthing.

Even the edges of her fingers were gleeful. Last night when she called her boss, she had told Swoozie the display would bring in the residents. She told herself that it would surely bring in some clues. Hornsboro blood ran thick with gossip. Maggie was about to cut a few nicks and let the flow begin.

Last check. She left the shop and stood in the street to test the overall effect. Two boys wheeling their bikes down Main Street slowed down enough to stare before they passed the window and shot off.

Perfect. If her ploy could get the attention of kids, who knew the response that might come. She had been open only ten minutes when the first of the townsfolk popped in "to get a closer look and take a stab at the challenge." Game on.

Deenie Clark was the first. She had been on her way to work at the hardware store and had stopped to take a look. She'd actually climbed onto the bench and, butt thrust toward Main Street, bent over to study the objects. Now she stood at the counter across from Maggie. "It's so darling. I told Clyde that I needed my break at 10:00 instead of 10:15 so I could look some more before the place was crowded with tourists."

Maggie's mind took a spin around the empty store. Crowded with tourists. Deenie, this is Hornsboro, not Palm Springs. She smiled and let Deenie ramble.

"Those frames are so great with the pictures. And the pictures . . . Why, it's like flipping back in time."

Back in time. Good going. Lady, you get the idea.

"I'm so glad you like it, Deenie. I found the pictures in an old trunk. They so capture the romance of Hornsboro in a simpler time."

Deenie fingered her way through a jewelry display, trying on rings and bracelets. She held up a large topaz cocktail ring to the light. "That house looks so familiar. Isn't that the Turnball place out by the lake road?"

Maggie's heart did a little flippy thing. You bet it is, Deenie. Tell me what you know. Her game face knew better than to show excitement.

"I have some great pearl and rhinestone pins in the back if you want me to get them. Just wait a second." Maggie turned around to go the stockroom behind the counter. Hand on door handle, she turned to Deenie. "You know, I think you're right about the picture. Of course, you'd know more about the place than I would."

When Deenie left, purchase in hand, she had been the first to jot down her thoughts in the journal Maggie had set on the counter.

By early afternoon, several journal pages were full. A lot of *Wonderful Idea* and *How Romantic* but a store of remembrances were registered as well. Maggie pictured herself weeks ahead, chatting away with customers, nudging conversation toward lakeside memories.

That boat belonged to your Uncle Alfred? How did he know the Turnballs?

Your mother cleaned for the Turnballs? Yes, that Ida Ann was a pretty thing. Did you ever get to play with her while your mother cleaned? Maggie adjusted merchandise on shelves, but her eye stayed fixed on the journal. Maybe, just maybe, a tiny detail scrawled on those pages would be a drop spilled from a tipped over ink well, one small entity coursing toward a full story.

Xanadu sank at 1:18. Swoozie's had a single customer. Winnie paid a visit. A very irate Winnie, from the sound of her outburst, standing in the doorway in full wrath mode. "What the hell do you think you're doing? Don't you have any respect at all?"

Maggie turned toward the explosion. The woman's form took up the entire doorway. She still had her apron on from the café, spotted and grease stained. It looked like a declaration of war. That and her face. It was red and furled, eyes mostly slits, mouth a slash of red. Her arms were akimbo, fingers digging into her considerable hips.

"Winnie. How nice of you to drop in." Winnie, how nice to let me have some fun. A two-for-one sale, watching you blow up and giving the town more to talk about. She felt the excitement rising in her, waiting for the woman to explode and make Maggie's day.

Winnie strode over to Maggie, grabbed her arm, and set her against the wall, away from any customers. Her voice was grit. "I may have been mad at your grandpa. I may think he was a two timing old fart who broke my friend's heart."

I know that, Winnie. C'mon, give me some good stuff.

"But, I'll tell you, right here and right now, that Lou Witkowski would be ashamed of you. Ashamed. No matter what he did – or didn't do – he would never have set out to hurt someone on purpose." *Purpose* came out like a curse.

This was no time for "Whatever do you mean?" Winnie knew fishing even if it meant fishing for gossip. Stay still and let it come.

"I know you're mad at me for bad-mouthing a man you think walked on water. But think about this, missy, while you run your little scam. Ida Ann Turnball was a victim. She was never good enough for that bastard of a father. She wasn't a son, and she wasn't smart. The only one who loved her was her mamma, and she died when Ida Ann was only a teenager."

Winnie pointed toward the front of the store but kept her face inches from Maggie's. "Go back and look at the picture of Ida Ann with her daddy. Look at that girl's eyes. You'll see it there. The poor girl was so lonely, trapped out there in that big house with an old man who either ignored her or told her she was nothing. No wonder she left town when she was fifteen." Winnie backed away but left her arms folded. Her mouth was pressed together in a knot of challenge.

Something in Maggie twisted, a remnant of last night. She moved beyond it. This was news. "She left town?"

"You bet she did. She went off to some private school in Ohio. Stayed there until she graduated. Came back and acted as Daddy's hostess for his fancy friends from Chicago until he died – from pure meanness. She was plain wore out, that and robbed of all her dreams. She should have been married and loved. Instead she stayed in that house and hid from the world until it was too late. She was an old maid. A *rich* old maid."

Rich? Will said Ida Ann didn't have any money. Maggie watched Winnie's face, let her words sift through her while her mind began to circle around Winnie's accusation. What had happened to Ida's money? She was so engrossed in speculation that she let Winnie strike a chord.

"Your grandpa knew that when he went sniffing around . . . "

"My grandpa could have cared less about her money." Watch it, Witkowski. Stay even. But that word *sniffing* made her grandpa sound like a dog.

"He couldn't help it that she fantasized about him. My god, Winnie, Grandma was the one who told him to be nice to her. They both wanted to make a lonely woman less lonely." Maggie said it as a reprimand, a little meaner than need be, but Winnie deserved it, she thought.

Winnie watched Maggie, fury in her eyes, but she said nothing, simply snorted a gust of derision from her nose. Then she turned around and walked out of the store. She didn't even bother to shut the door.

Maggie had expected this even while she was arranging the pictures in the window. Winnie would come in, throw a fit, be Winnie. Maggie would smile after she left, the winner of a snit contest.

She didn't feel like a winner. She had felt a nudge of victory, sure, but that was only for a few seconds. She stared at the door and waited for, if not elation, at least some satisfaction. That would make her feel vindicated.

Instead, she felt a sense of guilt edged with sorrow. Sorrow for a poor girl who had lost her mother, lost her money, lost . . . her life. She went to the front of the store, took one of the pictures down to look again, the one of Ida Ann and her father. Before she had scanned it, taking in the image of father and daughter. This time she looked at Ida Ann's face. Yes, she was smiling, that sweet rosebud smile. But her eyes, Maggie noticed. Her eyes were dead like the eyes of a whipped animal that didn't dare not obey.

Maybe this mystery thing wasn't so one-sided after all.

By 10:00, nightfall complete, fog had crept in from the lake, swirled onto the dock, tumbled up the path toward the cabin in a gray, damp hush. Inside, a fire burned in the fireplace, a pocket of warmth for a swirl of cold from Canada. Maggie sat on the floor, legs crossed in lotus position, a glass of Chardonnay on the floor inside her lotus position. She ran her index finger around the rim, watching it move, talking to a room empty except for her and a ghost.

"Girls today I get. At least the ones in high school. They swivel their hips and glitter their eyelids. Ready to go on the prowl. They think they're in love – fifteen minutes at a time."

"Doesn't sound like any girls I ever knew." Maggie looked up. Larry stood in front of her, his face as dark as his tone. "And it doesn't sound like that girl in the picture, the Ida Ann looking at a man she clearly worshipped. Whenever a girl looked at me like that . . . well, never mind."

"No. Tell me. I want to understand her. Tell me about love in the fifties."

"Back then, girls didn't prowl. And they loved for a lot longer than fifteen minutes. The kind of girls you were just talking about, we had a name for girls who played that game. Sluts." He reached into his pants pocket and pulled out a ring. A big thing, gold with a dull black stone, gold lettering edging the side. He rolled it in his hands and closed his eyes, then held it with his index finger and thumb while he set down on the hearth, his gaze centered on the ring.

"Girls used to dream about wearing this. A few got to." His smile held memory like a prayer. "Loretta would sit in study hall and wrap yarn around it so that it'd fit her finger. I liked the blue angora best."

He looked at Maggie, raised his eyebrows and smirked. "She loved wearing my ring. Loved me."

Maggie took a sip of wine before she spoke. "So you were a stud muffin, huh? Lucky girl, getting a hunk like you."

"Vi wore it on a chain as a necklace. Long chain. I'd think about my ring hanging inside her blouse right above her breasts." This time his smile mocked. "My ring got to second base before I did." He chuckled, then smiled. "Not by much."

All sorts of quips rose inside her, but Maggie shut them down. She let the belief that she was merely seeking clues guide her while she stayed quiet and sipped wine.

"The ring wasn't about any game. When a girl wore my ring – the whole time she wore it – she was mine. Not a possession. Not my challenge. No, she was a part of me. And the world knew it.'

By now he had fingers from both hands on his ring, turning it slowly as he studied it.

"You might think we were silly, those of us who lived back then, but we understood the concept of 'together.'" He stood up and put the ring back into his pocket. "I think that's why the Judges let me keep my ring. Watch? Gone. Tie clip? Zapped for all time. But when I want to know that I'm – or I was – human, I get to reach in and feel a piece of who I was."

They sat in silence, those two. Maggie had her senses on full alert. The night smelled of pine ashes. Outside, the fog hummed. If she kept alert for the outside world, Larry's words couldn't sift down and touch her in vulnerable places. The young Ida Ann's face, rapt with an adoring smile stayed with her, even when she closed her eyes. She thought of a summer when she was fourteen, how she hung around a senior life guard at the pool. He had the whitest smile and sun bleached hair. She'd spent all her babysitting money on a bathing suit and enough tanning lotion to brown the entire freshman class. He never spoke a word to her.

Larry's words played with the back of her mind. "She was a part of me. And the world knew it." Poor sweet Ida Ann Turnball. What happened to you? And how do I find out?

She knew there would be pain in the answer. And she knew she had something to do before she could allow herself to continue the hunt.

On Saturday, Maggie walked into the café minutes short of 7:00. Only a couple of customers checking out a menu. Good. She needed the space. That and some courage. A bit of luck wouldn't hurt either.

Winnie looked up when she heard the sound of the door opening. A smile of welcome that had started on her face turned rigid. She set her hand on the counter and squared her shoulders, thrust her neck forward.

This would not be easy. Maggie raised her arms in the universal gesture of surrender and shook her head, all the while keeping eye contact. Those few feet between Maggie and Winnie seemed like a gantlet. When she reached the end of the café counter, she spoke, her words hardly above a whisper.

"I came to apologize."

Winnie narrowed her eyes, but her head and shoulders drew down. At least that was some communication. Maggie walked closer while she talked.

"The whole time I've been here, I've felt like it's been me against the town."

Winnie's head moved to the side, a movement almost imperceptible. Maggie could see the intake of breath, but Winnie said nothing.

"The trouble with that, though, is that in a one-sided crusade, everybody else is the bad guy." Please, please, don't let my voice shake, she hoped. And please Winnie, don't reach over and slap me.

Maggie took a deep breath and continued. "You made me see something yesterday.

You're not the enemy and neither is your friend. I'm not sure what happened. Don't get me wrong. I'll never accept Lou Witkowski as a bad guy."

Winnie's eyes flared then settled. She folded her arms but kept her head positioned in the same still challenge. No words. Good.

"What I learned today is that a woman I saw as — I don't know how I saw Ida Ann to be perfectly honest — the woman who was your friend is not necessarily the enemy. She may even have been a victim."

Maggie paused. "Just like Lou Witkowski." Another pause. "That's all I have to say. That, and Ida Ann Turnball was lucky to have you as her friend."

Maggie nodded to a stone Winnie and turned around. She could feel the silence the whole time she walked to the door, opened it, and left.

Chapter 14

America was having a birthday party and Maggie had an invitation – actually a command visit.

Just when she was making headway as detective, she had to play float rider.

Hank Lockett had loaned Swoozie his hay wagon and his son-in-law to pull the float with his truck. No convertible for the Swoozie show.

Her employer had decided on a localized liberty theme. Maggie carried a fishing pole and wore her dress tucked into waders, but otherwise was the Lady Liberty herself. A string of letters, red, white, and blue, hanging from the end of the pole, spelled America. For the liberty element, Swoozie had set a crown on Maggie's head and painted her with watered teal eye shadow to mimic burnished copper. Why the woman had that much eyeshadow in a shade that smacked of Halloween was a moot point. Maggie was about to engage in the great Northern Wisconsin version of paradise, one foot firmly planted on the floor, another firmly planted on a large wooden box that spelled out *Muskie or Bust*. Swoozie, ever the belle, sat in a wicker chair dressed in the Glinda finery of that first meeting at Bif's, surrounded by merchandise from the store. Their sign said, *We Celebrate Freedom*. It should have said, *In the Name of Blatant Commercialism, We Celebrate Torture*.

She's paying me back for sneaking my stuff out of the shelves and back to my cache. If I live through this, I swear I'll let her have a couple of kerosene lamps, maybe even a few more salt and pepper shakers. At least the grizzly shakers.

Or else I'll shoot her.

At 10:30, Maggie climbed onto the *Swoozie World* float -- *climbed* not exactly the operative word – all the while praying that she would survive the half-mile journey.

Craning her neck, Maggie tried to take in the sights and sounds that surrounded her as the July 4th parade lined up to weave its way down Main Street. Soon, said street would be once again calm, only candy wrappers and a few discarded pencils from Dinsdale Reality strewn from curb to curb, but for now, it vibrated with anticipation. Kaylee Tock, this year's Freedom Princess, sat poised on the back edge of Hank 's convertible ready for first wave, followed by every fire truck in Washekca County. John Deere tractors would putt. Marching bands would play. Children would line the streets waiting for the tossing of candy.

Distracted by her self-pity and the distant sounds of the bands warming up, she paid little attention to the figure laughing at her from across the street. Only when he whistled, did she come back to reality and pay attention. Will. Hollering at her.

"Hey there, Lady Liberty, you're looking pretty hot. I always liked my women a shade of green. Very Spike Lee." He stepped from the curb and walked toward the float, stopping within a few paces. He just looked at her, one hand in his jeans pocket, the other carrying a paper bag. Some confetti had sprinkled onto his head. Great. He's the prince. I'm Shrek.

"The only hot thing about me right now is my reaction to the heat. And I may be green now – teal by the way – but I think I'll be blazing red by the time this parade is finished."

Will reached into the sack and pulled out a large water bottle. "You'd better get some of this down before the parade starts. Once you're on your way, it's all wave and smile."

"What I love about today. I get to stand here like a grinning rural Stepford wife and Swoozie gets to sit and throw candy." Maggie smiled at Will. "Guess there's something to be said for owning the business."

"Worse things have happened. Three years ago, the junior high band from Dunkerton Iowa came up. Somebody's uncle was on the parade committee. A Rathe, I think. Anyway, they put the kids behind the Danbury Riding Club."

Maggie made her worried face. "Horses? Nobody marches behind the horses. Parade rule #1."

"Unfortunately, no one from Dunkerton knew that rule. A trumpet player slipped on a horse apple and when he fell, he took out the whole brass section. Looked like red and black dominoes, one pushing down another. Hailey Garbes ran out to save the day. She slipped and fell onto the alto sax player. It was Rathe's nephew.

"That's awful!"

"Not entirely. Brett comes up every June to stay with the Rathes. That is, when he's not over at the Garbes house." Will shook his head. "But nobody from Iowa seems to want to visit us on the 4th anymore."

A voice interrupted them. The driver was standing by the truck, door open. "Time to let her rip." He looked at Maggie and grinned. "Make sure that you keep your center of gravity. Last year, Wayne Wilkin's wife leaned too far over and near fell off her float. She sat down and hyperventilated until the end of the parade. They gave her a sack to breathe in, but she was so shook, now she can barely ride out to the dump first of the month. Every bump reminds her of her near tragedy." He heaved himself up into the driver's seat, shut the door, and started the motor.

Killing Swoozie seemed more and more a mandate.

The parade wasn't unbearable. In fact, it was kind of fun. Yes, she swayed and heaved, but she also felt the spirit of a town that loved its country and its own personal culture. The bands played in tune. The local horse riding club pranced in perfect formation. Some folks laughed while they waved. A few yelled out greetings. Winnie, seated in a lawn chair in front of the café, nodded her head in the shared celebration and waved a small flag, a smile splitting her face as she watched "Lady Liberty" lurch by. Either the spirit of America was blessing its children to come together or Maggie's apology had done some good. Halfway through the route, the parade stopped and everyone stood and sang *God Bless America,* Yes, her Chicago friends might laugh at a woman, her artificial color half-melted and smeared, standing on a float singing her heart out, but for a moment, Maggie Witkowski put aside her anger and disdain and felt a sense of community.

Post parade cleanup was a chore. Normally, sweat was no problem. But green sweat, rivulets of it streaming down her face, patches embedded into her skin – that was another problem altogether. Dish detergent in the store's bathroom was far from spa treatment, but eventually Maggie left, freshly scrubbed and smiling, inside and out. She and Will spent the afternoon soaking up Hornsboro pride. At the fire department water hose fight, they lifted their heads and enjoyed the spray as Webb Lake battled Hornsboro for bragging rights. During the kiddie tractor race, both cheered for Ralphie Winnows' son, by far the fastest peddler, and truth-be-told, cuter than any six-year-old had a right to be, all red hair, freckles, and a grin that spread clear to his eyes when he waved his trophy.

Only one event totally threw her. Cow Chip Bingo. Quite the deal in the town. It was their answer to the gambling casino thirty miles away on the Indian reservation, and raised proceeds for the town's fireworks display. Marv Federinc had driven twenty miles to bring one of his cousin's heifers for the event. His honor, the mayor, had laid out the grid in the spare lot between the bank and Winnie's café – one hundred possible opportunities to win the $50.00 prize, not to mention bragging rights.

Maggie was stunned. "Let me get this right. The cow walks around until it poops on a square, and that declares the winner? "

"That's right." Will nudged her. "It's a hundred-to-one shot, but finally someone wins, and then everyone leaves to go eat real pie at the all-Hornsboro church pie fair."

Maggie looked at him, her face a prune. "That is so not right."

Will could only watch her and laugh until she recovered enough to ask, "So what happens if the cow's constipated. Does everyone get money back?"

Will grabbed her waist and turned her around, steering her away from the impending contest.

"City girl, guess you just don't know cows."

That night, when she and Will watched fireworks in the park, they rested against a huge tree away from the main crowd seated on blankets, picnic style. Will held her hand. When the finale came, he leaned in and whispered, "Ms. Witkowski, you set some off some of those very same fireworks in me." Then, under a sky streaked with reds and golds, silvers and blue, surrounded by the whiz of the rockets and the oohs of the crowd, he turned his body toward her, reached up his hands to hold her face, and kissed her.

It was a nice kiss. A first real kiss. His lips, warm and smooth, played with hers, awakened feelings set aside. When he nibbled at her lower lip, she let those feelings lay claim to herself as woman as she pressed closer and put her arms around him. Then she backed out of the kiss and lay her head against him listening to his heart beat a steady cadence. He gently kissed her neck and nuzzled at her ear. "Miss Maggie, if we were not in a public place, you would be in big trouble."

She kissed his chest through his tee, tasting man and a hint of sweat, before she answered him. "Not to worry. My mother always said I was ever on the lookout for trouble." She looked up at him, his face swathed in shadows. "So, if I found some, guess I'm just fulfilling my destiny."

— *Chapter 15* —

Another successful celebration in Hornsboro Wisconsin. The town settled back into normalcy, except for a few stray celebrants shooting off illegal fireworks and a covy of teenagers swilling beers they had swiped from their parents' refrigerators.

Oh yes, and one particular citizen who sat rocking, taking in the events of the day. Will Bentley was home in his cedar house on the lake, reflecting on the day. Heated words, no more than a low growling, spewed from a mouth tense with contempt.

"What a joke, waving to the townsfolk like she's the queen of the town. She looked like the fool she is. Tall and skinny and green, carrying a torch like she's royalty. Lady Liberty. Lady chump is more like it.

And she still had no clue about the truth. Pictures, a few facts. And yes, a new beau.

The tension in his jaw eased. Plans hovered as possibilities. His mind tumbled with possibilities. *Oh Maggie, you should listen to your mother.* "On the lookout for trouble," *she said.* You have no idea. Keep an eye on her, maybe indulge in a nice piece of ass. All the while watching her make a fool of herself over clearing the name of fool rotting in the ground.

Don't worry about fulfilling your own destiny. I'll help you along.

Candy wrappers lay strewn on the floor, cellophane pressed by fingers tense with anger then flicked into the night air. Peppermints, crushed by angry feet, ground into the floor, bits of sweetness normally soothing, now white powder on a wooden floor.

The room silenced, only the creak of the rocker's legs accompaniment to the swirl of thought.

You may think that you're a part of our town, now that you've been here for a few weeks. Bake a couple of pies for the church, climb up on a float. Hornsboro's newest Mother Teresa. News flash. No one likes you. Some hate you. Maybe even somebody wants to kill you.

Keep waving Maggie Witkowski. Keep talking. Have your fun in Hornsboro.

While you can. While I let you. This is my town. I own it. Bitches don't snoop unless I let them.

In the late afternoon of July 5th, Maggie and Will were on the deck of his house, Will grilling steaks while Maggie sat facing him in an Adirondack chair. This morning, someone had left a note for Maggie at the store, taped it to the bottom of the door. Maggie was holding the note between firmly between her thumb and finger, as if it might disappear , whipped by a gust of wind that wasn't there. *Maggie Witkowski*, it had said on the envelope. Perfectly innocent. Perhaps a fan letter after her performance on the float? Hardly, she thought with a laugh as she snatched it up and opened it.

The message smacked of some of the town's critics of the resort project Maggie had first seen in Cal's office. *Why don't you check out our mayor? He's had more than one meeting with Chicago big wigs over this resort deal. How much profit does a relator/mayor make on a multimillion dollar deal that he arranges? Maybe they should call the place Cal's World. Time to find Ida Ann's heir is just about out.*

Maggie's voice was firm. "What's the deal with time running out and this heir?"

"Legal stuff," Will explained, "Ida Ann's will left the property to the town, its future use to be decided by the mayor. She might have been broke, but she had acres of lakefront prime land ready for whatever project the mayor thought best. Except, the town had to wait ten years after she died in case there was a claim."

"And so far no one's come forth?"

"Nope. Cal's been rubbing his palms over it for the past six months." He grabbed at one steak and turned it, then the other.

"Development I can understand, but I can't believe Cal would be dumb enough to tie himself to a bunch of Chicago thugs bent on building a jaded utopia." She dropped the note next to her. Pointing a finger to her head, she looked up. "Wait a minute. We're talking about Cal."

"You only have a note from some stranger. Don't jump to conclusions." Will leaned against a dock post. "Then again, I have to wonder where a guy like Cal would get his financing. Sure, Ida Ann left the property to the city, but it takes more than owning land to build a resort." He looked out over the lake. "We're pretty pristine here. Folk like it that way. Can't see anyone lining up to let in city people. And the only big city person I've seen lately is you."

"I found something in an old chest my grandparents left me." There. It was out.

Maggie laid out the news about her discovery. As she gave Will the information, she punctuated it with vows to reclaim Lou's reputation. "This town turns on the best of who lived here and keeps a Blagojevich clone as its mayor."

A white cloud edged with darkness swallowed the sun and the air turned instantly cool. Maggie looked up, eying the nuisance. How dare darkness spoil the moment.

While she chastised the interruption, Will's face turned cold as well. Veraldi. Yes, a name he knew.

The cloud finished scudding past and Maggie turned back to Will. "Enough business. Obviously the weather wants us to lighten up."

"Got it. These steaks are about down. Can you go in and fix the salad?" As Maggie shoved the note into her pocket and went inside, Will watched her move, a glint in his eyes that did not speak of fireworks and a first significant kiss – rather something more, much more, and vile.

Chapter 16

Days went by, toiling toward a week. Yes, Will was there at night. Steady, dependable Will. She touched her lips. Hot, sweet guy Will. But the rest of those days, nothing more than haggling with Swoozie, and fruitlessly searching for clues. She would sit on the porch of her cabin, feeling pinned against a wall of frustration. Even the frogs and crickets around her seemed to mock the lack of progress. The summer was growing shorter. Life back in Chicago loomed more heavy, taking her away from her focus. Three days in a row at work. *Eye on the prize*, Maggie kept telling herself, but her feet and back had a few things to say to those eyes with a work ethic. The only prize her aching parts wanted was a day off. Wasn't summer living supposed to be easy?

Maggie stretched her sore shoulders and walked over to rummage through the old kitchen pie pantry looking for a can of whatever for supper. Tin clinked against tin as she shoved one, then another container aside. Nothing seemed to catch her attention. With a shrug, she stopped, jar of pickles in hand, and stared at the back of the pantry. Why bother? She was tired and stuck out in the middle of nowhere without so much as a ghost to keep her company. Will she could understand. He was out of town on business. But where was her mentor and guide, the guy who was in such an all-fire hurry? Larry had been gone for three days now. Nobody – not even a ghost – needed that much rest.

She snorted in self pity. Even the pickles could care less.

A sound broke through her thoughts. Three raps on the porch door. Maybe fate had taken pity on her. She had a visitor.

Maggie didn't mean to jolt. Really. After all, she'd already faced down a ghost in her home. But she stepped back anyway. The sole of her shoe slipped on the wooden floor as she went to open the door. There, on Maggie's porch, stood Marv and Winnie. Marv was smiling, his good eye twinkling at Maggie, his wandering eye -- still twinkling though not directed much of anywhere. Winnie was . . . smiling? Winnie? And they both were arm in arm. Behind then, the sun shone under a bank of clouds in a weird kind of blessing.

"While you're inviting us in, why don't you put your tongue back in your mouth?" Winnie's voice was a tease, but her faced invited friendship. The woman, only weeks ago, had been a snarl with a black topknot. Now she was Aunt Winnie again. Her hair looked a little less stark, her hips less a joke -- actually more part of a lap waiting to invite a child for a moment of tenderness.

Maggie looked directly at her, absorbing the change in perspective. Stepping back, she laughed and gestured a welcome. "Winnie. Of course you may come in." She kept on walking backwards, one, two, then three steps, unable to take her eyes away from the new Winnie Listug.

Marv interrupted. "Glad you two are having a moment, but what about me? We're kind of a matched set, you know."

Winnie turned her head to Marv, unlocked her arm, and patted him on the back. "Sweetie, looks like we have an invitation." She shot a look at Maggie. Watch where you're going. Wouldn't want you falling on account of us."

While Winnie held the screen door open for both she and Marv to step through, Maggie stopped dead on. Winnie called him *Sweetie?*

Marv closed the door and the three of them stood inside. His laugh broke the silence, a laugh that swayed his belly and moved down his squat legs. "Winnie, I haven't seen this kind of reaction since Dave Weeston ran off those Willson twins trying to get into his truck." He scratched his head and looked straight at Maggie while his lips stretched into a smile, one side of his mouth jutting higher than the other in amusement. "That Dave. He ran out to their trailer buck naked, nothing on 'cept the pellet gun in his hand. Them two boys charged out of there like the devil hisself was after them." He leaned in. "Went right back in took advantage of his – ah – special excitement, if you catch my drift." He winked. "His wife looked up and there he was, looking like a spaniel making point on a pheasant."

Scowling, Winnie hit him on the arm. "This child doesn't need to hear those kinds of things. She'll kick us out before we have time to visit."

"Nah." Marv was chortling by now. "Maggie has a Wisconsin girl's sense of humor. Besides, Alice said it was the best sex they'd had in twenty years. Told me she was gonna' mount that gun right above the bed as a reminder of what old Dave could do if he put his mind to it."

While they sat in the living room, a trio of – if not friends, at least allies, Winnie started. "We've decided to give you a chance."

Maggie first felt a stab of resentment. The day had not exactly been fraught with kindness. But then she calmed herself. Listen to her, Witkowski, and keep your mouth shut. Either Winnie hadn't noticed or she had expected the reaction. She didn't even take a pause. "At first we thought you were an upstart, just an outsider wanting to nose your way into things that were better left unsaid." Her lips and jaw trembled slightly. She swallowed and her lips turned tight. "You have to understand, I still don't trust Lou." Maggie balked and Winnie kept on. "Don't get your back up. It's a fact. But that's not why we're here."

Maggie had faced too many teacher union negotiation talks to let her pique ruin the moment. She listened, eyes and mouth in taut control equal to Winnie. "The older woman's body relaxed in what? Appreciation? Then she sat up straight and raised her head. "Marv and I talked. You haven't been in Hornsboro, in and out like a wanna-be townie. You got a job. At least that's what did it for me. Lord knows dealing with all that southern butter all day has to mean something. Anybody who can stay in the same room with Swoozie all day has to have some grit."

Maggie smiled, laughter now in her shoulders instead of soreness. Winnie had Swoozie nailed. Good going, Winnie. Even her feet forgot to protest. Winnie sat back, crossed her arms, and broke out in a chortle. "My lord, that day – you on the float trying to look like Lady Liberty and all you did was look like a green fish wishing for water." Winnie leaned forward, put her hands on her thighs. She wiped away a tear, her shoulders gleeful with the laughter. "That had to be the funniest thing I've seen around here since the mayor slipped in the mud at the Cow Chip Booth three years ago." Winnie turned to historian mode. Maggie's mind rode the image and waited for more.

"That year it rained for a week straight. Wherever in town wasn't cement, all we had was brown slop. But Hornsboro can't have an Independence Day without tradition." Her voice was a smirk. "At least that's what the good mayor said. Personally, I never thought cow pie and mud made a good combination. Too much alike to let you know where the danger is."

Maggie's imagination filled the picture. Cal in red, white, and blue, the cow, no doubt in a really bad mood. By now, Winnie was on a roll. "There was that fool Cal Dinsdale standing in the lot next to City Hall reading The Declaration of Independence with Ryan Rausch's cow in the background." Her voice took on a smirk. "God only knows what that document has to do with Cow Chip Bingo, but then, that's Cal. 'Mr. Drama.' When he finished reading, he turned to motion to the cow – like she was gonna' listen to him – and he went down on his ass, legs up, holding onto his copy of the declaration like it was God's word." Winnie stopped and turned serious. "Not that it isn't, mind you, but in Cal's hands – well, even one and one is two seems screwy."

The minutes went by like that, an evening of sharing, stories and recollections tumbling one upon another, each teller thrusting into the conversation. Sometimes, while Maggie listened, Marv and Winnie bent over in laughter, other times they smiled in sweet remembrance. Always, they opened and shared, what they told punctuated by a "Oh, I remember him!" or a "You've got to be kidding" from the teacher who had come to live again in her summer home.

Finally, Maggie leaned back against the back of her chair. "I love this place." She joined in as an active participant, letting spill her memories of life as a child in Hornsboro. She talked about pine-scented days and cool nights, about splashing in the lake and wolfing down treats, about shooting the bad guys with make-believe oars turned to guns, about hide and seek and watching for deer from her bedroom window.

The memories had to come first, a glue that cemented the three, the past carefully unfolded. Winnie and Marv let her ramble, often smiling, occasionally laughing outright.

Then Maggie prepared to face the present. What did Winnie and Marv already know And how would they react to anything she might share about the now?

She wanted to test the waters. Her hesitation hung there, snuffing out the joy of their camaraderie. Where could she begin?

Winnie solved her dilemma. Leaning forward, elbows on her knees, jaw jutting forward, she issued the challenge. "So why did you stop coming if you were so dog-faced in love with the place. You know, young lady, you hurt your grandparents. Broke their hearts. Whatever I thought about them, they didn't deserve to have you up and stop coming here for the summer." She sat up straight, her mouth and eyes stern. "Well, at least your grandma didn't deserve it."

Marv was the echo, his voice gruff and deep. "Yep. Wondered that myself." He paused. "Wanted to believe that there was some natural reason you'd up and leave us." The question hung in the room.

Maggie looked at her fingernails. They had nothing to say. "I have to agree with you. I should wonder about it. All I can say is that by the time I turned thirteen, my priorities changed." She looked up at her guests and rolled her eyes. "Charlie Magee, big and burly hunk that he was seemed much more a priority than fishing off the dock." She let out a disgusted sigh, more at herself than anything else. "I was the typical teenager, sweaty-palmed over boys and stuck to the telephone with my girlfriends over them. Summer was for hanging out at the pool and watching high school boys play baseball."

She shook her head. "I see girls like that every day in my school room and my throat knots.' Marv and Winnie let her ramble. "They called me Maypole Maggie. I was six-feet tall by tenth grade, all legs, big hands and feet. How could I expect to ever catch a guy? I'd trip over my size ten's before I'd even come near him."

Winnie slapped her thigh and chuckled darkly. "I was Bomber-Butt Listug'. The kids in my class never suffered from any sense of grace. It took me until I was thirty to even think about forgiving them."

Marv's face was pure cream. "Winnie, your ass . . . 'er . . . " He dropped his head in embarrassment and muttered, "You know what I mean, your posterior . . . " then, head raised up, continued. "Your body is just fine, always has been. In high school, I always enjoyed the way you handled the hallway, kind of like a boat tied up to the dock and swaying." Then he cleared his throat and sat up a bit straighter.

A blush crept up Winnie's neck. The blotches of red on her cheeks matched it. Then she chuckled. "Why Marv, I always thought it was my pie you wanted. Who would have thought."

Who would have thought, indeed.

"Enough." Winnie's voice snagged their attention. "Maggie Witkowski, Marv and me have come to offer our assistance. We know all about the shenanigans out here, and we want to help. At first, with the phone call, we thought it was just dumb kids." Winnie glanced over at Marv who nodded his head in agreement, mouth set tight. "But when we heard about somebody throwing rocks, well, that just too mean spirited to be the worst kind of kids causing trouble."

Winnie reached out and patted Marv's knee. "I know we can help you. Nobody knows more about what goes on here than the two of us."

That Maggie couldn't argue.

"And we may find out that Lou wasn't the buzzard that we – or I – think he was."

The change to singular was said with two knee pats. Evidently Winnie and Marv differed on their opinion of the love life of Ida Ann Turnball -- or the lack thereof.

"But girl, you're one of us – even if you did drop out of sight for all those years."

Winnie cleared her throat. "And the folks of Hornsboro take care of one another."

Winnie's face clouded momentarily and then she set her jaw and nodded. "At least those of us that aren't nut heads."

So, how about we three put our heads together and get this whole mess figured out."

Maggie didn't see him at first, She was too focused on her alliance. When she lifted her head and looked past Marv and Winnie, there was Larry, beaming, his arm raised, thumb tucked into his palm.

That's right, he gestured. There's help all around. All four of us.

Maggie leaned forward. "You can't know how much I appreciate hearing this, not just for the help you can give, but for the promise of friendship." She stood up and turned to them, arms extended, palms up. "Don't you dare move. I was just about to cut up some cheese and sausage for supper. Let me get that, and a couple of beers to go with it."

She lowered her arms and took a couple of steps, paused, and said back to her guests. "No hanky-panky now, you two, while I'm gone." Then she lopped forward, glad that supper would be more than pickles. On her way, she muttered to the air, "Larry, get in here!"

This was it! Allies. Human allies who could help out. Larry leaned against the counter while she sliced away at the snacks. "You bet this is something big. Allies. Real human allies. Ones who knew Ida Ann."

"I bet those Judges are warming up their welcome speech as we speak," she whispered. Right before she shot him a look. "No monkey business!"

Larry looked the picture of innocence while he tipped over the Ritz cracker box and spun it around on its side.

While she lay in bed that night smelling the light rain that drizzled outside her bedroom window, she measured Winnie's words. She had walked away from her childhood here. She pictured her grandparents sitting on the porch, her grandfather sitting alone on the dock, wondering what their granddaughter was doing, trying to accept that children grow and move on but mourning the passing of a piece of their lives.

They had cherished her, given her stability. She had run off into adolescence without so much as a thank you.

Maggie hugged her pillow as if she were hugging them.

She did love them.

She should have shown it.

Her voice was a hoarse whisper. "Grandma. Grandpa. If only I could go back. What times we would have. I'd make it up to you. I swear I would."

A gust of wind sprayed raindrops through the screen, misting her face.

Isn't that what this is all about?

Had she said that?

What did it matter? Tomorrow she would barrel forward, let nothing rob her of her focus. Tonight she would dream and remember. In that blessed state of relaxation, she reached out to turn off the bedside light. As if by magic, the room went dark. She startled and sat up, Rolling her eyes, she called out. "Larry! Knock it off."

Nothing.

"Larry, we have a deal." Her voice raised as the irritation clambered through her.

A blue cloud, vaporous and iridescent, wavered at the foot of her bed. "Maggie. Shhh. It's not me. The dark. It's not me."

With a consciousness born from panic, she grabbed at the bedside lamp, pressing the light switch again and again. Nothing, just darkness and the clicks of fingers against a switch.

"Then who?" She had meant the question to stay in her head, but it was too terrible to keep from tumbling out.

When Maggie finally fell asleep, she slept only because a blue cloud rested next to her, warming her cold body. Outside, footsteps waited to be found in the morning, those and severed power lines clipped during the night.

Chapter 17

Thank God for Will. He not only called the sheriff, he insisted that this time, vandalism for Maggie Witkowski was not the matter of a few kids looking for trouble. Lyle Stout professed agreement, but looked through them, his voice sounding like Maggie's when a student tried to talk away late homework.

When the sound of the sheriff's car grinding on gravel faded, Maggie and Will sat on the porch steps, bodies parallel, Maggie staring straight ahead, Will head down, hands running along the sides of his head. Maggie ached with a squeezed numbness.

"I hate cops," she said. Inside, the words ground at her.

Will sat up and pulled her toward her in the universal sign of safety. "Lyle's not so bad. He'll come around."

There was something so comforting and safe about that arm, something that softened a bitter wall in Maggie, the one that she had built that past spring. She had worn that pain like stigmata after David's betrayal. Even now, the memory drew a numbness, a chronic shell of deadened hopes, icy and hard.

Too soon to let your guard down. And yet that arm, its warmth, its promise wrapped around her. Could she trust again? Maggie nestled against Will, felt her forehead and neck relax. Yes. "I think it's time to talk about David."

Will's body stiffened but he kept holding her, his hand massaging her upper arm, one press, then two. "David. Is this some former boyfriend? Is he the one hassling you?" By now, Will had let go of Maggie; he grasped her shoulders and searched her face.

Maggie breathed in deeply and rose from his hold, stepped down from the porch and faced the lake, arms crossed. She scanned it, just a quick glance to focus herself before she turned to face Will who still sitting on the top step of the porch. Her mouth was smiling but her eyes were not. "I guess it's time for *the talk*."

"You were vandalized last night, Maggie. What could be more important than that?"

Maggie looked toward the top of the porch. She rubbed her hands. A bird had built a nest there this spring. Funny that she hadn't noticed.

"Maggie, talk to me."

Now her hands were clenched. "I had a messy breakup this spring. Very messy. David was exactly what I wanted. Strong. Funny. Honest. He's a cop, a detective in Chicago. All my friends told me I was nuts, a no-rules girl like me falling for Mr. Authority."

"Okay. Nice guy. Good cop."

"That's the problem. He wasn't."

"Wasn't what?"

"A good cop. In fact, he was down right dirty. Kept drug money, it turned out. Even used kids as drug runners." She rubbed her forehead with the palm of her hand. "Imagine. I'm a teacher. Sworn to teach kids. They're my mission. Drugs screw them up. Turn them into vegetables. Kill them."

Her arms wrapped around her, held her secure even as her jaw trembled. "David's betrayal smashed me, destroyed what I believe in, or at least the love I thought I believed in." She cocked her lips on one side, bit against the inside of her mouth.

"I like you Will. I like you a lot. I *like* liking you."

Will stood up and crossed to her. She felt like she could break. The terror of last night. The outing of her betrayal. He took her hands between his, caressed them. "That is the best news of the morning." With one hand, he led her up to the porch door. "Time for some rest. Do you want me to stay?"

She looked up at him, eyes glaring. Her whole body stiffened.

"No," he said. "Not stay *that* way. I could run back to my place for my laptop and get some work done while you rest."

"No." She managed a smile. "I'm much better." She opened the door and leaned on it. "Thanks for the help with the sheriff . . . and thanks for listening . . . and thanks for being such a friend."

After Will gave her a quick kiss, she watched him head down the stairs and walk toward his car. When she looked away, she saw Larry standing at the edge of the trees watching the car leave. He turned toward her, his face solemn, and he shook his head, firmly back and forth. What was wrong with Larry? She called out, but he strode into the woods, body language hidden by the foliage, his form merging with the shadows.

Nothing like a good nap to turn the day right. That and warm sun on a lake ripping under its rays. The thousand pound albatross that had pulled at Maggie for weeks was gone – slain and gutted by a confession and self-forgiveness. How light Maggie felt this afternoon. She and Will sat on the dock facing each other, tossing red licorice at each other like a couple of ten-year-olds. A fish flipped near the end of the long structure, a glint of silver and then a splash breaking up the candy fight.

"Maybe he wants some candy too." She grabbed a stick from her lap and gnawed. "Can't blame him." She turned toward the lake. "Too bad, buster. I have one licorice maniac to contend with. That's enough."

Will laughed, but then pushed himself onto his knees and bent toward Maggie. While she watched his movement, she let the strand hang from her mouth in invitation. He yanked it away, and right before he kissed her, he said, "That's not the candy that interests me right now." His kiss hardened. He pulled her head toward him, clutched her hair in his hands, his tongue opening her mouth even more. Her nipples hardened under her tee, an ache stretching in her breasts. It had been so long, too long, her body protested since . . .

David. Too soon, her mind protested. She backed away from the kiss. "I can't do this. I can't. Still panting, she took his face in his hands, the face that now registered shock. Her voice turned raw, a growl. "I am so sorry."

She dropped her hands and closed her eyes. Will stood up. She could feel his rise of his body, the disappointment, the tension of his anger. She opened her eyes and watched him walk away toward the end of the dock, his hands stuck into the pockets of his shorts. Were his hands clenching and unclenching like hers did now? Did he want to hit her?

She waited seconds, hours, minutes for him to turn around, who knew how long?

He walked toward her and crouched down, fists kneeding his thighs. He didn't look at her; instead, he scanned the lake, perhaps for some answer or even question that Maggie could not begin to imagine.

"That David. Hope what they say about cops in jail is true."

Maggie had walked in that tunnel of gray for so many weeks now after David that she could hardly bear the sensation of relief that bled upward now. Her throat caught as she whispered, "So do I."

Will turned to her and sat, legs crossed. He reached out and took one of Maggie's black curls, wound it gently around a finger and smiled. "Then I'll have to be a better man."

Maggie picked up a strand of licorice and held it out. "You already are."

Maggie sat there in the sun, on the edge of a summer afternoon, an adult silently eating candy and enjoying the silence and the belief that here was someone she could trust.Finally Will spoke. "I'd like to think that I'm kind of growing on you – in a nonmossy sort of way of course."

Ah yes. Banter. The salve for wounds of heavy conversation and heavier lulls. She studied his face and smiled. "I was thinking that there's a sort of green tint to you. I thought it was because you recycle."

"Funny. Back to the point.

"Which one?"

"David. Why you broke off what was obviously a hot moment."

She let the breeze calm her, even while her fingers played with a splinter of wood sticking up on the dock's floor. "I couldn't agree more – that is about the moment and its heat. God, I want to hear that you understand what I'm trying to say. Limits. I have to set them, and I suck at them. Whole foreign territory given my manic bent"

Will leaned in toward her even as she backed away. "I'm listening to what you're saying, and I respect your words. I'm just having a hard time tying your words right now to what happened between us just now." He reached next to him and picked up his bottle of beer, chugged a swallow and set it down, spent a few seconds turning the bottle so that the label faced him. Not a good sign, Maggie thought.

When he turned his attention back to her, Maggie could picture him in court. She hadn't seen much of his attorney face. She watched him while he continued. "A week ago, you joked about reveling in trouble. Now, you're setting up boundaries. It's like you gave me this great surprise, and now you want to take it back."

Maggie was not one to tip-toe. Normally, she plodded as if subtly were an insult. She tried a light touch. "That's not it at all. I'm all about trouble. That and having a good time. You are talking to the woman who gives nuns new kinds of sin to fret about." Maggie hands and arms reached behind her, supported her as she held her face skyward, took in the warmth of the sun. "And when it comes to feelings, I usually wear them, not only on my sleeve but tattooed all over my body. I am a walking, talking burst of emotion." She relaxed her shoulders, brought her arms back around her and bent forward.

Will opened his mouth to speak. Maggie touched his lips, shook her head. "Just now, please understand, Will. Just now, I'm still tumbling from David. That's part of why I came up here, not that I wouldn't have otherwise. I wanted to find peace."

She laughed, more snort than laughter. "Look how that's turning out."

Will covered her hand with his. "I get it. I really do. Let's enjoy the time we have. If you want to talk about David, I'm here. If not . . . I'm here. What you see is what you get."

Maggie slipped her hand out and pressed it on top of Will's, patted it once, twice before she spoke. "I'm not leading you on. You are my died-in-the-wool summer time camp hottie. Let's have fun. Play in the sun. Play in the moonlight." She squeezed his hand for emphasis and leaned in. "Don't get me wrong. I am all about kissing up a storm. My response to your very talented kissing should have attested to that." She gave him a soft kiss as punctuation and gratitude, then backed away. "But I have to have boundaries. I'm just not ready for anything more.

And as naughty as I seem to be – and I am – boundaries means no commitments. And contrary to this age of hooking up, no commitments means no sex."

Will didn't make a sound. Not so much as a breath or an exhale. What was he thinking? She made a fist and poked at his shoulder. "Lucky you to have found the only woman on the planet younger than fifty who doesn't hook up." She said the words, but her face asked a question.

He did take the time to reach over and grab another strand of candy. The bag made a crackling noise and Maggie was sure that she could hear the candy slide from the sack. He stuck the end of the candy in his mouth, leaned back, and folded his arms. The he laughed – just a snicker, leaning forward as he took the candy and waved it at Maggie. "First of all, I personally know two or three women under forty who don't hook up with guys." He paused, brought the candy to his mouth and took a bite. "Of course, they're gay." He made that pronouncement sound almost tragic.

When Maggie glowered, he turned serious. "Do you really think I'm nothing more than some schmuck looking to hook up?"

"What I think about you, Will Bentley, remains to be seen," she said as she looked out as the water and pictured dragonflies flitting near the docks. How easily someone could come along and pluck one from the air, pin it to a corkboard in the name of love.

She stood up abruptly and rubbed her hands on her shorts. "Listen to us. A couple of make-out sessions and we're analyzing." Holding a hand out to him, Maggie said, "Summer's all about having fun. Let's go have some."

Will grabbed her hand and rose. He kissed her forehead. "How can I say no to Lady Liberty in wading boots?"

She made a fist and smacked his arm. "Just make sure that I don't have to say no, and we'll get along fine."

Will leered back. "I'm just going to trust in the fact that I'm irresistible."

Maggie shot him her teacher look.

"Hey," he retorted. "A guy can hope." He wrapped her in his arms and let his mouth do some talking, firm talking, the kind of kissing that says there's more fun to follow if you dare. He finished with a soft touch of his lips, more a caress before he backed away, arms out, hands open, the barest of smirks enjoying itself.

Maggie's smile was pure cream. "You are going to be a problem."

"Who me? I'm just the guy waiting for you to know that I'm the guy."

"Just watch where you're going."

Will shot her a quizzical look. "Is that a challenge?"

"Nope." She laughed. "There's a loose board right behind you. I'd hate to see you trip over yourself while you're so immersed in hope, and all."

He turned away from her, walking away with just enough swagger to make his exit interesting. "Have a nice day and don't eat all the candy, little girl."

After Will left, Maggie trounced into the cabin. Larry was waiting for her. Larry was not amused.

"Nice lips. Certainly they're not swollen from the sun." He had that disappointed Catholic dad look about him, the one that pours water on a daughter's after glow.

"Need any help getting the splinters out of your butt? Hope that dock holds after all it's been through. What happened to 'We're on the verge of discovery?' You're supposed to be solving a mystery, not lip-locking with your lawyer. Didn't last night send a message?"

Good lord. She had enough men issues to house her own retreat. "What? Jealous? Want a little specter nookie? Maybe I can search around and find some hot chick who'd *die* for you." She widened her eyes and shrugged. "Oh wait. She'd already have to be dead."

Maggie waited for a retort. She got empty space.

The air in the cabin chilled a touch, and a rustle of air swept across her face. His voice barked. "When you have your hormones back in place, I'll be back. We can have an adult conversation."

Maggie called out to the empty room. "Okay, I give." Even as she said the words, she felt the sinking. Still, she finished. "Will can wait."

Nothing.

Her throat tightened and she rasped, "Get back here ghost-boy. Since you're so all-fired in a hurry to let my love life sink and drown before it's even had a chance to swim, help me with a plan." Even as she said the words, she pictured Will with her on the dock – under that full moon. The image faded, curling into nothing as Larry's voice came at her from the kitchen. "Ah, the Miss Witkowski I know and love."

She turned and looked at him, six feet of irritation standing in the doorway.

"So now what?"

"It's pretty obvious. You find out more about Ida Ann's mystery child. And why her records were in your grandfather's possession." When he disappeared, he left with a chill.

Lunkhead. The least he could have done is apologize for ruining her love life. She kicked at the doorway in front of her, a little kid trying to send an empty can careening down the road. Then she took a deep breath and headed to the kitchen for the cold beer with her name on it.

Later that night, Will stood at his kitchen window, fiddling with a delicate chain wrapped around a bottle on the counter, his index fingers sending the touch of metal through his hands in the darkness. His eyes peered out. He and Maggie should right now be sharing the beauty of a lover's moon, a lover's star-lit night.

Ludicrous.

"Poor poor Maggie. You had a trauma, a betrayal." He grasped the chain and pulled, nearly breaking it. "You want peace? How's that – peace for a piece."

The lake was so lovely tonight, smooth, rippled only by rays from the moon.

"Okay, sweetheart. I'll be a good boy. I'll be your lap dog, your guard dog, why the best pet ever. After all, play time with a pet means less time on the job. And little girl, we don't want you nosing out too many answers.

He dropped the chain, letting it rest again on the bottle's neck.

She thinks she's been betrayed. She doesn't know the meaning of the word.

Just remember, Ms. Witkowski, the best of dogs can turn on their masters and bite.

— *Chapter 18* —

Sleuth Maggie was back. The hunt was on, with a vengeance. Maggie had spent her dream time last night tossing while images announced her guilt. She and Will on the dock twirling licorice while bodies floated nearby, faces frozen in pain and disappointment. It didn't take a shrink to figure out that bit of remorse.

Lucky for her, the city library had a strong sense of history. Once, the building had housed a local newspaper -- saved money for the taxpayers—but now, newspaper long folded, the lone institution was the only place for digging into Hornboro's past.

The building, a thick square of bricks, had once been an icehouse. Maggie remembered hearing stories about huge blocks of ice cut from the lake to be carted and stored in the cellar, packed in sawdust from the lumber camps. Sounded romantic, but she nonetheless preferred her ice fresh from the refrigerator door. Kind of hard to fix an evening cocktail if you had to run into town every time you needed a cube or two.

When refrigerators became a household necessity, the town solved two problems at once. What to do with the building, and where to put a library some of the more enlightened citizens thought as necessary as chilled milk and butter. The building as ice house was well insulated but dark. Natural light did not go well with maintaining freezing temperatures. Once the townsfolk carted out the old equipment, local builders, professional and recreational both, installed windows in the front and an exit passage in the back. A few fluorescent lights suspended from a lowered ceiling, and the Hornsboro Public Library building was ready for filling. The guts of the library still had a North Woods feel – a mixture of smooth cedar walls and wide planked floors.

While she waited at the desk, she told herself that she was meeting Ellen Campbell, town librarian and county historian, as research, but as she glanced around the inside, attention on the endless rows of shelves and books, her mind turned to the past, days of sitting on the floor next to the book stacks, books at least five-deep in a stack next to her.

She could hear his voice still edged inside her. "Granddaughter, you are a reading machine. Let's get these checked out before you read them all." She'd gather up her pile – mostly biographies – and together they'd head to the check out, a behemoth of a counter, thick pine, some of Hornsboro's history carved into its top. The librarian at that time enjoyed keeping a record of her clients right in front of her. "If you sign your name, that means you're one of the regulars. Anyone smart enough to spend a life reading is smart enough to be president. When you're famous, I'll have your autograph."

"May I help you?"

Maggie gave a little start at the intrusion, then turned toward a woman in her thirties dressed in cargo shorts and a black tee that said *Librarians are stacked*. She was short, slightly chubby, her hair dark brown with blonde highlights. Librarian Campbell? Just in case, Maggie extended her hand.

"Ellen? I'm Maggie Witkowski. We talked on the phone yesterday afternoon."

The woman clasped Maggie's hand warmly. "Glad to meet you. I understand you want to do some research on our town? Lucky for you the history of Hornsboro Wisconsin, in fact most of Wascheka county, is right here." Gesturing for her to follow, Ellen walked past Maggie along the beaten brick lined interior wall of the building. Shelves of books lined one side, pictures the other. Each picture was black and white, a few of them sepia tinged, all framed with black metal, all enlarged to 18X12.

She stopped just short of the first photograph, turned and folded her arms, facing Maggie who had trailed slightly behind. "I noticed that Swoozie had a few pictures of the Turnballs in her front window last week. Have to admit, I was pleasantly surprised. The family was the closest thing we have to royalty or founding fathers, but we don't have much left of a legacy. I always thought our library's collection was pretty much it." She stepped back and gestured toward the first one. "Let me add a few images to what you already know. This is Harlan Turnball, Hornsboro's founder on the right and a hunting partner we've never been able to identify."

The image seemed cold and ancient, two men, rifles in hand, standing on each side of a felled deer. While Maggie studied it, a tinge of unease crawled across her shoulders. Leg stationed on the carcass of the deer, Harlan's hunting mate preened, all smiles and testosterone. No problem there. Next to the stranger, though, was the same stark figure, tall and lean and totally without facial expression Maggie had seen in her smaller photo. Harlan could have been a wax statue brought in as an extra. *Ida Ann was the offspring of money and power all right. This guy could kick widows and orphans out into the street without flinching.* The guy must have one expression, she thought. Hunting, hanging out with daughter. It was all the same.

Working her innocence tone, Maggie said, "I don't remember hearing the Turnball name mentioned when I was a kid visiting here. I suppose that was because my grandparents were relative newcomers. Still, people as important as the Turnballs – I'm really surprised their names didn't turn up."

Ellen shook her head. "There's not much written about the founder, but from what I understand, Harlan was well connected to some of the forerunners of the mob." Her lips curled into the smile of a well-laced storyteller, and she tilted her head. "Town history has it that Hornsboro was a getaway for the worst of Chicago's bad guys – at least those who liked to hunt and fish – and occasionally a hideout for some of their cronies. Harlan Turnball even had a railroad line built to cart his cronies to their getaway Wisconsin playground."

Very interesting, Maggie thought. Some families have metaphorical skeletons in their closets. The Turnballs may have had a few real ones. A name tugged at her. The one in Ida's poem. Veraldi. What did they say in *Jersey Boys*? All Italian names end in a vowel?

Italian name. Chicago Italian name?

Maggie studied Harlan's hunting partner more closely. It wasn't the same mystery man with Ida in the picture Maggie had found but they shared characteristics. The coloring was the same. The sense of cockiness, too.

The tour continued, more lore about building the railroad, fishing lodges in their glory days before tourists rented cabins, a sense of sadness that a founder's family had died out. Harlan had been an only child, his wife as well. They had carried on the tradition with their son, Franklin, who in turn, married and had one child, a daughter. Ida Ann. When she died, a single woman with no children, the line had died as well. Evidently,

Ida Ann had left her estate in trust to the town to be administered by the mayor. Too bad for the town that there was little more than the Turnball house and the acres of land surrounding it. Cal talked about developing it, had the bragging rights platted in his office. Maggie thought back to the anonymous note and Will's conjecture nodding her head through all this. But her brain was on high alert from the news about Harlan's mob connections, ones no doubt inherited by his son.

Ida Ann Turnball, you little tart. I bet you were a mobster's babe.

She had to wait until the next morning to tell him. She'd showered, cleaned the bathroom and kitchen, even cleaned the baseboards with Uncle Jones' Bees Wax. Finally, after five cups of coffee and two peanut buttered pieces of toast, Maggie had her wish. There he was, the freshly materialized Mr. Know-It-All Larry. *Wait until you hear this*, she thought, as she stood in the kitchen doorway, feet planted, her hands at a gallop, each finger flipping in opposition to the other, the universal sign for gunslinger r' us.

While she reported her findings, he watched her with a stony gaze, hands folded in front of him, his face full of that "don't get ahead of yourself" that always drove her crazy.

"Excuse me, Mr. Ghost. Are you listening? Don't you know anything about Chicago and the mob? Gun molls. Bad guys. Guns and bombs. Duh. Don't you think it's a little odd that 15-year-old Ida had the hots for a guy with an Italian name? Here in Hornsboro, Wisconsin? An Italian name in a place full of Gundersons and Listugs? An Italian name in a place where mobsters gathered to unwind after shooting each other?"

He stared at her before he responded. Like he was making up his mind but couldn't believe that what he was hearing was worth the effort to listen, much less respond. "Don't forget. Nowhere does it say Carlo Veraldi, Capone's best friend.

Maggie was unswayed. She walked past him toward the dining area window. Late morning light shafted into the room, motes swirling in the rays. She watched them in their dance. She didn't bother turning before she spoke.

"Plenty of mystery here, Larry, my man."

She stayed at the window watching the lake. She could see the outline of his reflection in the window. The hands that had folded in front of him now were at his side, in fists. The image was too weak to show his face, but Maggie could feel him, the ice wrapped in resentment.

"If there's so much mystery, madam, so much intrigue, then why did you waste so much time playing with the locals? We could have known this days sooner."

Maggie turned to face him, hands on hips. "Playing? C'mon Larry, lighten up. For crying out loud, I just made a huge discovery. Ida Ann had been mixed up with some nasty guys. Maybe some that carried a grudge." She crossed her arms as if to underscore the point. "Don't you find it at least little suspicious that this 'pure misunderstood spinster' had a sordid past?"

He didn't answer right away. He just looked at her wearing neutrality like armor. "Not really. If there's anything to universal principles, seniors no more resemble themselves in adolescence than Mickey Mantle resembles his sandlot self."

"I'm sure there's a point there." Maggie had always preferred to be the one with the attitude. Her voice let him know that.

"What I'm saying is that all that information and five pennies will get you a nickel. Our mission has always been to clear your grandfather's name."

That hurt. Of course, that had been their mission. What else had she been thinking about these weeks?

"What else, indeed, Maggie."

Maggie felt just like she had when she had been six and eaten a cricket on a dare. Sick to her stomach and immediately rueful, not exactly sure what was roiling around in her, but sickened nonetheless.

"If you come up with anything significant, let me know. I need some rest." He yawned for emphasis and disappeared.

She closed her eyes and gave herself a second or two of snit. Here she'd been itching to tell him all her discoveries. And what does he do? He carps at her. Then leaves to catch some sleep. What had been doing the whole time she waited for him to show up? So much for putting her head on the line spying on a town that was only now beginning to stand her.

So what if she had spent time with Will? She deserved a little happiness, especially after the disaster of last year. And besides, Will helped her see things objectively. She walked into the kitchen for another cup of coffee, spilled half of it – damn that coffee maker never poured right – and took a sip. It tasted like dregs, lukewarm dregs. She'd turned the pot off and forgotten about it. She slammed the cup down right in the middle of the spilled coffee. It pooled in reaction.

Just like her life.

She pulled out one of the wooden chairs and sat down, leaned back and sat there. Had she an audience, she might have yelled obscenities, but she was alone. With her left hand index finger, she played with the coffee spill, running a small circle in its middle. No impact at all. Exactly how she felt.

Slowly, the bits of her conversation with Larry sifted through her, her mind examining each one, rearranging, looking for perspective. Was she looking for a killer or for scapegoats? Was she using Will as an ally or a means to run away from all sorts of things she hadn't wanted to deal with? She had told him flat out that the last thing she needed was any kind of relationship. "The closest thing to hooking up I can handle right now would be selling a vintage corset," she had told him. He had laughed at her words, but agreed when he acknowledged the hurt in her eyes that had not yet vanished.

Our mission has always been to clear your grandfather's name. Larry's words inserted themselves in every segment of her reflection.

Down at the lake, bullfrogs croaked in the late morning hung heavy with summer moisture. Even frogs were telling her off.

Was she was playing summer camp romance with the original Mr. Nice Guy while Larry waited for a trip to eternity? Was she was rejoicing in sleeze that may or may not be true?

Her gut said no. Especially about Ida Ann. There were too many possibilities swirling in the Turnball history. Maggie just had to find out which ones were true.

She stood up and headed toward the bedroom. The pine chest was there, at the foot of the bed. Maybe looking at those pictures would shake something loose.

— *Chapter 19* —

Happiness is a strange thing. It perks us up, makes us think that all is golden, then disappears, nothing left but a remnant of a smile and life ready to bite us in the butt any time soon.

Today, a Tuesday, had definitely been a butt biting day.

When Maggie had driven down the lane to the cabin, she had been in a snit about a day of absolute chaos. Every time twigs and pine cones crunched under the onslaught of her tires, her shoulders tightened. Some alien force had sent every tourist in Wisconsin to Swoozie's place on the day her boss was gone. No help there. Life was no better when she closed the doors at 5:00. Will was still over in Eau Clair. No help at the end of a long day to take the edge off the tightness banding her head,

And Larry, demander of action? No where. Still.

Could be a three-wine night she thought as she edged the car to meet the railroad ties separating the end of the lane from the span of grass in front of the cabin.

Yep. The wine was clearly calling.

She had slid out of the car and heaved the door shut – one of those mad slams that doesn't solve anything but feels good – made her way halfway around the front of the car before she noticed the mess. Lumps of stuff on her porch.

What the hell?

Intrigue turned to fury halfway to the first step. Someone had dumped garbage, enough for at least two bins in front of her door. The late afternoon light hit crevices, sending streaks of light off of old cans. Nasty globs and streams lay in the murky darkness not so readily lit. Craning her neck, she looked for empty sacks – as if that would somehow make the mess disappear or give her answers. Nothing. Just a six-foot- wide pile of refuse left as a calling card. Cans, cartons, coffee grinds, bones and meat waiting for critters to forage through the mess. Globs of grease, waded up paper, all ilk of unidentifiable effluvia glopping the pieces into a wet, sloppy pile of rot at least a foot deep.

And at the top, centered like a tiara on a princess sat the final insult. A skunk. A dead skunk, a piece of road kill, head and body smashed flat, only its tail three- dimensional. Not enough that someone had left a clear message for her with garbage. No. Whatever miscreant had used her porch as a dump had left an insult. A dead one.

She stormed forward and kicked the first step leading to the porch, all the while swearing. Maggie Witkowski was a virtuoso of cussing, but this brought out variations on words long forgotten, a stream that matched the reek of what lay before her.

This was pure evil.

Moving forward, she grabbed the handle of the door, all the while trying to protect herself from sinking into the muck. She shuddered at a meat bone laced with maggots, then pulled the screen door toward her, using it as a shovel to clear a path, ignoring the rock that had formed in her gut the whole time she pulled. Then, one hand braced on the door, she stepped over the pile and opened the main door.

Lucky for her, she had been late for work and hadn't locked it. That thought brought a snort. Good news – no one had broken in. Bad news – well universe, take a look around.

As soon as she was inside, she heaved off her shoes, marched into the kitchen, and tossed them into the garbage can. They were polluted, toxic. After rinsing off her feet in the sink and swiping them with a towel, she walked barefoot to the phone and called the police.

Darlene Weber answered. "Hornsboro Police Department. How may I help you?"

"This is Maggie Witkowski. I'm out at my place on Route 151."

"Why Maggie, good to hear from you girl. Saw you rushing around in the store today. Good thing that Swoozie's got someone to handle business for her."

Maggie's head started to throb, and she felt her lower jaw begin its trembling. She breathed in deeply and steadied her voice. "Thanks,

Darlene." Still, the words had come out as a snipe. She breathed in deeply and let the air out slowly. "Darlene I've got some trouble out here and need some help."

"Again? Goodness, dear. What happened?" Maggie could hear the hope of good gossip in the woman's voice. She bit off a retort and kept calm – considering.

"Someone decided to use my front porch as a garbage dump. There's a month worth of nasty out there right now, topped off with a dead animal."

"Oh my gracious, that must be awful. Not bad enough they had to cut your wires, now this. You poor girl." Darlene's voice grew conspiratorial. Maggie could picture tightened lips and knowing eyes as Darlene went on. "Somebody's just hell-bent on causing you grief, for sure. It's those kids, I tell you. Must've listened to those old hens talking when you first came to town." While the *tsk* in Darlene's voice crackled over the phone, Maggie gritted her teeth.

Darlene kept on. "Why just last week Lyle caught Hiram Bosch's kids right in the act. They'd been riding their bikes out on Danbury Road, flinging baseball bats at mailboxes. That Jeremy had a bat right in his hand and a you-know-what-eating grin on his face."

"I'm sure the sheriff gave them what-for, Darlene, but what's all over my porch couldn't have been biked in. I'd really like to have Lyle come out and take a look."

The words were an understatement. She wanted Sheriff Lyle Stout to bring in the CSI team and get the bastard. Enough was enough.

Darlene sighed. "Maggie, Lyle's awful busy trying to clear out that beaver damage near the north shore. I'll make a note for him and have him call you. Don't worry, sweetie, I bet it's just kids needing a good thrashing. Can't imagine what this world's coming to."

Right. You look a dead skunk in the eye and tell me it's just kids. Getting help from the local police department was about as likely as getting Swoozie to turn over Maggie's horde for free. Might happen. Not likely.

"Thanks, Darlene, I'll be waiting to hear from him." After hanging up with a scowl, she stilled, bent her head against the wall. Getting through to the people of Hornsboro was like putting out a wildfire. Just when she felt safe in one patch, another would start smoking, ready to ignite. Who was friend and who was . . . foe didn't begin to cover it.

Later, armed with cleaning supplies and flip-flops, she shoveled her way from the cabin threshold outward, dumped them in front of the porch steps and took pictures of the chaos with her cell phone. Then she went to work, loading plastic bags with the essence of this calling card before she them aside at the back of the cabin for whenever the sheriff finished with his own wildlife. She scrubbed. She hosed down once she had cleared the refuse until puddles formed in front of the porch. Then she sat inside, alone at the dining room table, the memory of the insult wafting in her nostrils. She could still smell it – the garbage strewn onto her porch like a swath of loathing. It was cleaned up, but the odor lingered. She turned her chair away from the table. Facing the porch was too hurtful.

A sheen of tears glossed her eyes, that and the retching in her stomach.

You're a Witkowski, a trooper, never indulging in weakness, she told herself. Buck up. Be a trooper.

Shut up, her eyes retorted as they strung with the threat of defeat. The sting of those tears sent her over the edge. Jumping up, she yelled at the raftered ceiling.

"Who are you, you son-of-a-bitch?"

No one answered. The silence was insult.

"I haven't done anything except come back to a place that's mine. I haven't done anything except remember the people who loved me, tried to find the truth about my blood."

Even after a marathon cleaning, anger trumped neatness . She turned toward the table, grabbed the wildflowers out of the pitcher in its center, and beat them on the table. "It's not fair! It's not fair!"

A familiar voice spoke. "What's not fair?"

Maggie turned toward the familiar sound, her face white except for two red splotches along her cheeks, flayed wildflowers clutched at her side.

"Where the hell have you been? Four days you've been gone!" Her voice was feral.

Larry crossed his arms and shook his head. "Gone, obviously, at an inopportune time." He stepped forward.

Maggie started to lunge for him, caught herself before she fell through him. The wildflowers flew from her hands and scattered onto the pine planks of the floor. She threw her hands up in disgust. "Take a peek outside, buster." She tilted her head to the side. "Oh wait. You won't be able to see anything. It's cleaned up." She fell silent.

You won't see the heap, smell the reek, feel the sludge on the bottom of your feet while you try to wash away the hatred. Why weren't you here?

"I know. I was here earlier." He spoke the words evenly, his tone neutral.

Maggie turned her back on him and strode toward the front door. She leaned against the door jam, her body steel as she fixed her sight on the porch. "Some guardian you are." She turned around to face him, her voice seething. "I'm not upset." She wiped her arm across her eyes and kicked at the wilting mess on the floor. "And I'm not crying. Witkowski women do not cry."

Fists clenched at her side, she tightened her mouth into a knot, her eyes slits before she said, "What I am is pissed. I'm so pissed that I could blow up this whole freakin' place, walk away, and never look back."

"I would say that definitely qualifies as angry." He crossed his arms and glanced back and forth. "From the sound of things, you'd better get some answers while you still have a home to clean."

Maggie drew her breath in sharply and held it. She might not – just maybe might not – lose it, even though the slightest tic could send her into permanent rage. Her home had been violated and this bag of ectoplasm wanted to talk strategy.

Fury surged within her – both at her circumstance and the dismissal of someone who should be an ally. She pounded her left hand on the door frame, fingers splayed, her fingers pressing so that she could drive some of her storm into an inanimate object.

"I can't get out from under this." She walked to the window and looked out at the lake, scanning the familiar scene, the banks slipping down to the water, the dock worn gray, the old boat house the color of the dock. She arched her back, jutted her chin forward, stood arms crossed, feet spread hip-width apart.

She felt the warmth of him behind her as he spoke. "Come. Sit. Breathe."

Maggie managed to reach up and rub her face, pull her fingers over her eyes, down the sides of her nose, over her lips. Breathe? She couldn't very well *breathe* when what she wanted to do was spit.

He tried teasing. "Can't let a dead skunk send you packing."

"The skunk's not the problem. Someone wants me gone. Hates me. Watches me. I see glimmers in the stands of trees, hear the creaks of twigs in the night."

The stranglehold on her throat stayed while she turned around. Larry fixed his eyes on her face, his scrutiny void of interpretation. Teasing had turned hard in just a second. "You have to stay, have to finish this. Don't forget who has the most to lose in this project of ours." His words spit out into the room. His body smoldered with a whiteness that made Maggie's mouth gape.

"Besides, you can't play tonsil hockey with Mr. Wonderful if you run back to Chicago." He disappeared. Larry had cut and run. Only the words lingered in the air.

That night, while she soaked away grime and misery, she lay back in the tub and relived their encounter.

When the last of water had long been drained and she'd headed off to bed cleansed – at least on the outside – and exhausted, she closed her eyes and slept while the wind rustled through the pine trees like a grim omen, dreaming of a raccoon dying while angry hands pummeled it with rocks. She would wake in the morning chased by dream tears, tears that could fall in that special part of a Witkowski woman who faced the world with the grit of her lineage yet allowed herself the privilege of being human, tears that would not wet the pillow but still shame the woman.

— *Chapter 20* —

8:30 Wednesday morning at Winnie's. The breakfast crowd regulars by and large were gone; the few that had stayed, sipped coffee as they meandered from table to table, hoping for a final tidbit or two of gossip. Plates were stacked in the sink. Crumbs lay on the floor. The cafe had a pile of clean-up detail before the lunch crowd came in.

Maggie hunched in a booth seat while she picked at a dime-sized hole in the fabric of her chair. Winnie sat across from her.

"Look, why don't you get it out before I have to rip out the upholstery." Winnie's eyes were motherly, her voice laced with a laugh even as her face strained with concern.

When Maggie reached out to run her finger around her the coffee cup rim, Winnie clamped her hand on top of Maggie's and held tight. Maggie only lowered her head even more.

"Don't coffee cup wrestle me, young lady. I've taken down better than you. You can't work out a good mad when you don't face the fact that you're mad in the first place."

Maggie bit on her lower lip, but at least she raised her head. Someone's car backfired outside. A plate crashed in the kitchen followed by a "Sorry" from the hapless Mollie Sygman who scurried trying to do the work of two women.

Maggie's face showed a swath of emotion. Loss. Questioning. Suspicion. Her eyes and lips showed the tumbling as she set her teeth tight in a futile effort to deal with the previous night's chaos.

Winnie watched it all, silent as Maggie's rode her emotions. The diner would take care of itself even if Mollie broke every dish in the place.

Finally, Maggie' breath steadied and her mouth and chest relaxed. She lifted the coffee cup and took a drink, set it down on the booth's table. "I keep thinking about the smell. On any given day, my place is fresh air and cedar and the richness of the earth. The worst that happens is that I get of whiff of fish every now and then." She brought her hands up to her mouth and tapped twice, made a fist beneath her chin. Her focus was not on Winnie. It had turned inward once again. "Whoever thought that hate could smell so vile. The alleys in Chicago on a hot day can't match that smell. It swarmed over me the whole time I tried to clean."

She lowered her hands to grip the edge of the booth and focused on Winnie. Her voice tapered off. "That poor damn thing. He was nothing but a pancake with a tail."

In the kitchen, business played on, pans rattling while water sluiced inside the dishwasher, elegy for a skunk mocked in death by a bandit garbage man. The refrigerator hummed a second beat.

"You should have seen that thing. He was propped up on the side of a mayonnaise jar head side down, what was left of his feet stuck in a glob of old grease."

Winnie's lip trembled. She bit down on it. And laughed.

Maggie's immediate reaction was to suck in her breath. Her lips quivered at the lack of respect for her troubles. Then Winnie's laughter broke through distraught Maggie to amuse the old Maggie, and felt it rising within her, a percolating that unclogged the mess inside her. And she laughed. Not a snicker. Not a titter. No, Maggie Witkowski gave into a full-out chortle. She wrapped her arms around her sides and rocked, her voice rising, sounding boyishly pubescent. "The poor thing would have drowned in that stuff if he weren't already dead." When enough emotion had been spilled, when her ribs ached and her stomach clenched from tightening while she worked out her dread, she blew out an exhale. "I thought my green body on that float was the sorriest sight I'd see all summer, but I've got to say, that skunk was the winner hands – nope --paws down."

That sent her into another gale of raucous glee.

Eyes rimmed with tears of humor, Winnie reached across and took her hands. "Young lady, I think we sent mad back where she belongs." Then she laughed again and squeezed. "But I've got to say, that thing must have been pretty ugly to be worse than you all green and sweaty riding next to Swoozie."

A squashed piece of road kill meant to intimidate. A six-foot green living mannequin bumping along a small town street. The images lent a sense of grace to the morning. There had been a shift in this small town and in Maggie's life. She had been alone, and then picked up one friend. He had found another, a bartender who practiced law better than he practiced marriage. They had come to her, and she appreciated them. Now Maggie had new allies. But these were different. At least one of them had seen her as enemy.

That had changed.

After work on Friday, Winnie, Marv, and Maggie sat at Wallie's sharing a pitcher of beer and conjectures. Maggie was in charge of keeping notes, but so far had only doodled boxes on the legal pad in front of her. A sign on the wall opposite her advertised Yuengling beer. *How appropriate*, she thought. Sounds like what we're accomplishing here. They had met to brainstorm, but so far hadn't had so much as a brain drizzle much less a full out storm.

All four of them had passed around the pictures and Ida Ann's love poem enough times to have it memorized. They touched the pictures as if gleaning for a psychic connection. Will had scrunched up his face at the poem twice now. A man of good taste. Marv seemed noncommittal.

Winnie set down her picture and spoke up. "I know I didn't meet her until she came back from out East, but I spent hours with that woman. Not once did she ever mention anyone named Carlo, much less a Carlo that had been the stuff of romance." She stared, first at Marv, then at Maggie, then back again to Marv as if they might provide some inspiration. Then she pursed her lips and shook her head. "Makes sense that she'd go ape over someone like that now that I think about it. I loved her to death, but she was the kind of girl who'd move into the castles she'd built in the air. She was the princess alright. Dress up and be ready for the ball. Always hoping for that prince that would glide out of nowhere and take her off to happy land.

"Ida'd go one for hours about the in's and out's of shoulder pads – as if I could give a toot about what a woman did with her shoulders – or she'd sigh about how some perfume had undertones of vanilla." She gave Maggie a smirk – albeit a friendly one. "Undertones. Imagine that in this town. And she'd talk on and on about shopping up at Wall Lake or playing games, 'specially bingo, like that was the be-all of life. No wonder she liked Lou so much. He'd laugh and tell her he was the lucky one to be driving her to the games, she made his car smell so fresh."

Winnie lowered her eyes and sighed. Then she looked up at Maggie and shook her head, eyebrows slanted in thought. "I guess it was just too easy to jump to conclusions."

Her voice sounded matter-of-fact although Maggie doubted that. A woman like Winnie did not let go of a mind set easily, and Lou as spurning lover had been settled in the woman's mind for years.

Winnie went on. "Rhonda Everling used to call me about every Thursday morning, all full of attitude. "You should have seen those two again, him all doting on her like she's the Queen of Persia and her giggling every other minute. 'It's disgusting,' she'd say, 'pure disgusting the way those two carried on with poor Jean sitting at home waiting for that no good to drop off his floozie and make an appearance.'" Winnie's voice had been high and airy, no doubt in homage to a woman priding herself on her ability to discern newsworthy trash.

Marv broke in, his voice deep and sympathetic. "Never mind, Winnie. Rhonda Everling's been spreading gossip since she learned to talk. Come to think about it, I bet she hasn't shut up since the first time she opened her mouth."

"That's probably why we believed her. She brainwashed us. Tell a lie often enough, it becomes truth. It's even worse if you believe the lie in the first place." Winnie patted the paper in front of Maggie. "Time for truth, people. Where do we start?"

Scrunching her face and beating a rhythm with her pen, Maggie let the tasks click into place in her mind.

"I think we'd better find out about that school she went to in Ohio. Maybe they have a yearbook with names. It's a long shot, but right now that's my best guess. Will gets back tonight. I'll ask him to start using his legal voice to sound official."

Winnie nodded. "Yep. Nothing like a lawyer to make snooping sound like important business. And that Will can talk a hen out of her eggs without a peck to be had."

When the bar door slammed, and a voice called out, "ladies and gentlemen of Hornsboro, may I have your attention," everyone looked up.

Cal stood at the front of the bar, his beaming face only slightly brighter than his Kelly green tie. He looked at Jeff. "Barkeep, a draw please." Then he faced his citizens in full mayoral splendor. "I would like to announce some news, some very exciting news."

Random buzzing surrounded Maggie and her tablemates. At the table next to them, Dennis Stempke muttered, "What's got Cal in a bundle? Fresh cow chips for next year?" His wife, Liz, shushed him. "Hush, now, I want to hear."

Cal waited for full attention, his arms held in a presidential pose as he took in the room. "As most of you know, McClean Development out of Chicago has expressed an interest the lake front property deeded to our fair town from the estate of the late Ida Ann Turnball. I would like to report that representatives from the company – important representatives – will be arriving on Monday to explore the property firsthand and meet with me. My friends, think what that will mean to Hornsboro."

Marv raised his hand. "Cal, I thought the estate was tied up. They had to find Ida's relatives."

"That's the point, Marv. The time for the search is three months from legally being over. McClean's wants to do preliminary work now in anticipation of a very big deal."

Now the room sounded like a classroom five minutes before the school day ended. Lots of animated chatter, low enough not to be chaos, but lively just the same. Development meant tourists. Tourists meant money or trouble depending on the perspective. Everyone had something to say.

Maggie grabbed her purse and stood up. "I'll be right back. Gotta' call Will."

Winnie scowled. "Hold your panties, girl. He'll be back later tonight."

Maggie looked at Winnie. A laugh barreled forward at the suggestion she wait. "Nope. This is too juicy for later." She looked at the two friends over her shoulder as she started off. "Besides, we'll have better things to do than talk about property."

While Cal made the rounds toward the back of the room, the Hornsboro think tank group had one more pitcher of beer before they adjourned. Marv and Winnie needed to take off for some evening fishing – much more exciting than the business talk in the bar. Maggie had a date.

Will would be over at 10:00. Business was over, he had said when she had phoned him, lawyer business out of town and Cal business in town. Time for some definite pleasure.

His nonchalance surprised Maggie. She had expected at least questions, but hey, a girl would take pleasure over business any time. Pleasure. What an alien concept after the past two days. Not a bad idea at all. Ten minutes after Marv had polished off the last gulp of beer, Maggie let herself back in at Swoozie's. She tramped through the store like a scout on reconnaissance loading up on merchandise she probably couldn't afford. Let Swoozie grumble, she thought. She'd leave an IOU and sell more stuff to customers who didn't need anything but would help her buy back her own property.

— *Chapter 21* —

Less than ninety minutes after she had locked up at Swoozie's and hauled her goodies to the car, Maggie looked over the changes she had made to the cabin – changes that put more of her own stamp on her home, and, she had to admit, lent cheery colors to help lighten the scar of vandalism. Wine glasses and snacks were ready on the pine table, bunches of freshly picked Black-Eyed Susans sat in a butter yellow vintage pitcher courtesy of Swoozie's. A large antique copper plate rested on an easel next to the pitcher. Filling half the window next to the table, a stained-glass prairie scene hung from iron chains. Tonight, the dark greens and gold would be muted, but today – and every day after -- light would send the colors spilling onto the table where Maggie took her meals. The symbolism of the changes made her smile while she fussed with the finishing touches. She wasn't ready to grab a wine and chill out on the porch yet, but the area immediately inside the house helped damper the remnants of yesterday's foulness.

Will would be here.

She needed him.

Maggie fussed with the flowers, then sat in the rocking chair on the opposite side of the window, grabbed a magazine from the tin barrel that served as a table, and read while she waited for Will.

The wine might be chilling in the ice bucket by the sofa, but she was warm. He'd be here in another hour. They'd sip wine and make plans. She could count on his arms, his words, his help.

She read through another speculation on the latest in Hollywood breakups and laughed to herself. Hollywood. Hornsboro. Not much difference between the two. Everyone had an agenda. Everyone had a spin.

The air split with Will's reaction.

"Are you out of your mind? That wasn't garbage someone left. That was a message. Loud and clear." There on the couch, where he was supposed to hold her, Will had Maggie by the arms as if she were a child who needed to be shaken into understanding.

Maggie had worked through her dread, let it slip away like a nightmare lessened by morning light she told herself. She had called the sheriff. Three times. No return. That had her madder than the original crime. But the news was fresh for Will. She reached up and drew his arms down, intent on soothing his concern so that he would set aside his reaction to see her side.

"I don't blame you for reacting. In fact, it's sweet that you're so worried." She reached up and touched his face, pulling her thumb along side his lips.

Will grabbed her hand and held it firmly with both of his. "Either I stay here or you find somewhere else to live until we find out who's doing this."

Maggie pictured herself moving in with Swoozie, padlocking her possessions to keep them from becoming store fodder. Not a pretty sight. Besides, she couldn't very well plot with Larry since he couldn't leave the property grounds. And Will moving in? Wouldn't that set the town talking.

"Last night I might have taken you up on your offer. I was that angry and scared." She looked down at his hands, then leaned forward and lightly kissed him. As she leaned back, she watched his face. It was neutral. Good. He was open to suggestion. She pulled her hands from under his to reverse the handhold, then held them gently while she talked.

"Can you imagine the gossip that your moving in would cause? Maggie Witkowski – granddaughter of a cad shows the family blood by playing slut."

Will tightened his lips but otherwise stayed steady.

Tread easy, girl.

"Winnie and Marv are on our side now. They'll start a 'Maggie is one of us' campaign, and by the time I have to leave at the end of August, people will be asking if I want to move here permanently and teach their kids." She moved closer and gave him her naughty-girl smile.

"Besides, you'll be with me most of the nights anyway."

No reaction, or at least not a visible one. Still paranoid Will?

Maggie kept on smoozing. "Admit it. You'd be here on my doorstep even if Mr. Garbage hadn't made an appearance. You like me. You think I'm cute." The words were a whisper in the air, each phrase murmured as Maggie closed in on Will, until her face was inches from his. "You know you do."

"Cute isn't the problem." Will said it lightly enough, but his eyes were hard and his mouth a slit.

Maggie felt the frustration flowing from him, the tautness of his throat. *He's worried about you. Hell, he's scared stiff.* She kept her gaze level and took his hand.

"I know." Then she leaned forward and gave him a kiss, just the brush of her lips against his as a gift. She backed away from the kiss and smiled, still holding his hand. "You are the absolute best, Will, and I'm so sorry to have dragged you into this mess."

"Sorry?" The word was filled with wonder and anger and a sense of derision. "Sorry is for someone who doesn't care."

Will stared at her, his eyes searching, before he grabbed her face with both hands and kissed her. It was a dominant kiss, the kiss of a man on a mission, a kiss that shook her with its intensity as he lowered her onto the couch. This was a kiss from the man who had always been gentle, the one who joked and teased, the one who knew the boundaries even as he played at seduction. But now, this Will was kissing her neck, moving down her chest, easing his way to her breasts where his lips teased her nipple, drawing it hard through her tee shirt and bra. His right hand edged upward on her leg, the lightest pressure of his fingertips touching her thigh, moving higher, his thumb making a circle on bare skin in rhythm to the beat of his kisses.

This Will stopped only long enough to raise his head and rasp, "There is no 'sorry' between us. And no one drags me anywhere." His voice was throaty, an animal growl as he lowered himself onto her body. His hands worked closer to the stretch above her thighs.

Maggie felt panic even as she sank into desire. Her hands had been busy, one gripping the edge of the sofa, the other the back of his head. Instinct had welcomed him, but now she brought both arms forward and pushed at Will's chest. Or at least tried to. Primal Will took hold of her hands and pressed them down even as he attacked her neck, again stirring the play of both desire and fear. His lips were hot, his body hard.

Fear won. This was too sudden, too alien. What had happened to the man who knew her boundaries?

"Will, stop."

Once again, he raised his head to look at her, this stranger, eyes hooded and clouded with intent.

'Stop? I've hardly started. His voice was feral." Gripping her hands, he raised her arms above her head and attacked her mouth. His hands went back to the business of foreplay so fierce, her heart pounded with fear as much as desire. His hand was under her shirt, under her bra, grasping at her nipple, his thumb and index finger rubbing, pulling, making her want to scream.

Wine doused Will's head, a full glass. The empty glass thumped to the floor onto the rag rug. Will jerked up, shaking his head. "What the . . .?" He breathed in heavily. His jaw shuddered.

Maggie's mind took in the stunned Will as her ears heard a voice. "Naughty, naughty."

Larry?

She didn't have time to speculate. Will sat up and hunched over, drawing in deep breaths, hands on his knees pressing hard, his only movement the rise of his chest as he breathed. Even as she scooted away from him to seek refuge in the corner of the sofa, she could see his jaw clench and listen as he took in gulps of air. Fury etched his face. Perhaps regret? The back of his hair lay matted where the wine had wet it. A few red drops had left marks on his pants.

When he spoke, his voice was rock. "There has to be a drier way to let a guy know you're not interested."

Maggie waited, listened for the rush of blood to subside in both of them. Part of her wanted to touch his face, a small part. The child part of her wanted to crawl into the fetal position and hide. A deeper part wanted to slap him silly. Will had morphed into primate Will, a throwback to some mottled ancestor that roamed the savannah. The emotions settled like leaves on a windless fall day, replaced by questions. What had she done? Had she led him on? He knew about David, had promised to respect her need for ease.

The answer was quick. Hell no, she hadn't led him on. Her teacher voice spoke sharply. "No means no. That's true for everyone. You, too." She let that side of her settle the rest.

Will sat up and stared straight ahead. His hands grabbed at the sides of his head and moved upward until he grasped his fingers. His breath had calmed, his jaw relaxed. He would not look at Maggie.

"That was not me. Not me." He still would not look at her. "I behaved like an horny frat guy. I . . ." He lowered his hands, paused, and turned. His eyes were clear, his face chagrined. The old Will. Or the old Will that Maggie thought she had known. He sat still, his eyes searching her for a reaction. Maggie supposed she should say something, but her mind was only capable of questions. Was the man who had what – attacked her? Was that man still wedged inside the friend she had thought would give her comfort? She let her fear sift through her, like gray ash sifting downward, remnants of exploding pops of a campfire. "I can't even find the strength to slap you. I can picture it in my mind. A hard slap. Maybe one that ends with clawing your face. You'd better go before I find it."

Will stood up. Without a word, he turned and walked around the sofa, across the length of the cabin. Maggie heard his feet move against the floor, heard the screen door open, heard his words as he stood in the doorway. "Tonight was a mistake. I hope that tomorrow will be something better."

"Just remember one thing." Maggie could feel the pause. "My name's not David." The words had come out a stern disappointment. His eyes, however, glittered, his lips tightened coldly, his head slid a deadbolt on the need to turn around , march back to the bitch, grab her by throat and end this charade.

The door closed. Maggie listened for the sound of footsteps down the front steps, for a car door to open, for tires to crunch gravel as Will's car left her property.

Only then could she relax. What in the hell had just happened? And even more pressing, now what?

Maggie sat still, knees drawn up, in the corner of the sofa. She clenched at a pillow. "You didn't have to soak him." She sounded like a child freshly slapped for raiding the cookie jar.

"Oh really. It seemed to me that he needed cooling down." His retort echoed in the room, the rawness of his voice hanging in the room. A door slammed. Larry? What was he doing – venting?

"Come on back here, Larry." Even as she said the words, she listened for a break in the silence, the flutter of a ghost, a friend.

Nothing. She let out a small "Please?" No more than night sounds answered.

"I hate it when you whisk yourself out of here. Get back here. Coward!" Maggie laid her head down on the sofa arm. The question of cowardice niggled at her. Who was the coward. Will for turning boor and running away? Her? Time passed. Hours. Minutes. She wasn't sure.

Eventually she uncurled, stretched her legs and managed to set them on the floor. She picked up the wine glass. As she ran her index finger around its rim, she thought of her friend.

"Thank you Larry."

She reached over for the other wine glass and carried them both across the room and into the kitchen. Maggie Witkowski had a strange taste in her mouth, like she had eaten sad.

She never sensed the silent visitor that paid her shoreline a visit. She never heard the boat's motor humming as the craft slid across the lake passing over the shallows, past McGraw's Island, the best site for walleye, and neared her dock. The lights of the cabin had been out. The visitor had smiled, knowing this, watching in the darkness.

A voice had replaced the hum of the engine as the boat sat still in the water. "So you've lost that lovin' feeling, eh Maggie? Think that means you can hose me down with wine? I felt you want me, you stupid cow. You think tonight was a mistake. Perhaps. Little Miss Maggie isn't ready."

She'll just have to wait, then for the moment to be right. Give her some time.

"Tonight was nothing compared to what's coming," Will said before a sneer followed the promise.

Beautiful night. Like so many of the summer. Enjoy them, Maggie. Pretty soon you'll learn to fear the dark.

Whistling a little Righteous Brothers, Will turned the boat around and turned back home, the trails of *Now it's gone, gone, gone wooooooh* sounding like a moan.

— *Chapter 22* —

S unday night had been long, a few hours of scattered sleep, many more
spent looking at the ceiling. Maggie had slept with the bed stand light
on. Outside, moths beat against the screen, their bang startling at first but
then settling into a timely rhythm. A mosquito inside her bedroom had
joined in, buzzing a warning. She had waited for it to light, itched to slap
the intruder into pulp. Sometime around 3:00 she got her wish. Then she
went back to counting the slats in wooden ceiling above her. Eleven on
each side of the center rafter. If she squinted just right, the knots looked
like constellations.

Monday morning wasn't much better. Good thing she had negotiated
Mondays off. After a hopeful blast of cold water from the shower, she
dripped her way to the bedroom, threw on sweats, and headed for the
kitchen. The refrigerator was a sorry sight. Some bologna. Half a bag of
wilted spinach and two carrots. She needed to go to town for groceries.

Fat chance. If she went to town, Will might be there. Then what?
She pictured running into him. Hesitation. A couple of awkward looks.
One of them would make the first move. So what? She wasn't ready. Will
represented balance – or at least he had before last night. Before his hands
and crotch had made themselves clear on their intent. His breath hot with
thirst for a drink she wasn't ready to serve. His voice. His walking away.

Leaving the refrigerator door open, she checked out the cupboard.
Bologna and spinach sandwich with a little ranch? She sneered but thought,
what the hell, it fit into the scheme of things.

The phone rang.

Sometimes intuition is right. Maggie could feel him on the other end
even as she said "Hello."

"Don't hang up. Please." Will.

"Why would I do that?" Easy question. She could hear his two breaths on the other end, more than an intake but not quite a snort. Good. A little squirming never hurt anyone. Especially a guy who needed a slapping, as her cousin Cheryl always said.

"Can we talk?"

"That's usually what people do over the phone."

"I deserve that. I probably deserve a lot more."

"Can't argue that."

"You're not going to help me out here, are you?"

His laugh was a sigh of rue. Good.

"Maggie, I swear that wasn't me last night. The horny boor on the sofa."

"Sure felt like you." The retort surged through her. Body memory could be such a nasty thing, a trigger for all sorts of feelings. "We talked about this, buster. We had boundaries, remember? Summer fling. No commitment. No complications."

Now the anger spilled out full-throttle. "Grabbing at my crotch, slamming at me with a hard-on, is full time over the edge. I don't know what they call it up here in Hornsboro, but in Chicago, we call it date rape."

Nothing but silence. Maggie stiffened, waiting for a reply. What would he say now?

"I called to wave a white flag. I was wrong. You told me about David. Told me you're not ready. I forgot to listen." He paused. "No. I chose not to listen."

It was Maggie's turn to only breathe into the phone.

"I can't justify what I did. When you're ready to talk to me again, I hope that we can try to salvage the good between us before last night.

"I guess that's all."

She looked at the phone. Once. Then she strode to the desk in the great room and grabbed her grandmother's journal from desk drawer, took out the envelop with the pictures and poem. She settled onto the floor, legs crossed, and spread out her evidence in front of her. If she wrote out all the evidence, something had to click. She flipped through the journal until she found a clean page for her notes. If she was on her own, by god, she'd be on her own and organized.

Her fingers tore away at the paper. Ida Ann had died ten years ago. Maggie jotted down her age and figured the approximate date for the boat pictures. What did she know about mob activity then? Lots of raids for prostitution. B-girls the newspapers called the women. Drugs. Dirty money.

Nothing much had changed. What about the dirty money? Would a resort be a perfect place for money laundering? Cal was over the moon about this project. Was it more of an opportunity for wealth than just a relator's fee?

The afternoon was perfection. Sun. Warmth with enough breeze to deny a sweat. Maggie never even noticed. She was too busy. Arrows crossed and crisscrossed. Evidence columns crossed into hunches, hunches into a to-do list.

Two days of work at the store. Biff's for groceries. Then back to the puzzle. She and Larry would go over her notes looking for answers but the whole thing was a giant puzzle box invented by a demented wizard. No key. Hell, she and Larry hardly had a door. They needed outside help.

The silver lining – the tiny silver lining of her time with David was that Maggie had friends on the Chicago police force. She could have them check up on the Veraldi name and any scuttlebutt involving a Turnball. One question from her journal notes, the one she had underlined three times grabbed at her again. Why had Ida Ann left to live with her aunt in Ohio for those years? That had to play in this mess.

Maggie scowled. She needed to clear her head, get some fresh air. Only when she was headed for the porch chair, sipping coffee, journal in hand, a present stole her concentration. A bundle of flowers – daisies at first glance – stuck in a glass jar. She eyed the bunch more closely. Inside the daisies, wrapped in white ribbon was another kind of flower, green leafy foliage and golden buds.

Tansy. It grew wild in patches throughout the area. Drove gardeners crazy, the way it spread. Daisies she could understand. They were her favorite flowers. But why would anyone want to give her tansy?

She set her coffee mug and journal onto the porch floor and walked over to the gift. A note stuck out from under the jar.

Yes, daisies are your favorite, that I know.
But consider poor tansy -- nothing but a weed.
Weeds are just flowers that have to try harder.
With enough forgiveness
Even a weed can be pretty cute.
I'm sorry.

Maggie bent over and grabbed one of the yellow buds, crushed it between her fingers. She understood tansy. Pretty flower, nasty smell. She recognized only a broken promise. Will's assault moved through her; she felt it like a phantom limb. She stood up and flicked the piece of tansy over the porch rail. Dumb man. Way to ruin a good break.

She turned and walked down the porch steps, headed for the path opposite the one leading to the dock, the one that led straight across the property deeper into the woods. Rows of birch and aspen and oak rose tall on each side of the path amid clumps of green growth. She decided to see them as soldiers, standing straight at attention ready to serve and protect.

Sunlight dappled through the trees. Shadow and light made a hopscotch pattern on the dirt path. Maggie walked for a few minutes along the way, occasionally playing a child's game of avoidance. "Step on a crack, you'll break your mother's back," she had called as a child on her way to school. This time, on this walk, she designated gnarled roots as the cracks. This time, instead of avoiding the omens, she stomped on the roots. She just wasn't sure who's back she wanted broken.

When she returned to the porch, she picked up her coffee cup and bagel and went inside. The coffee was cold. She dumped it and a couple of stale bagels into the sink and ran the garbage disposal. As the machine churned away, Maggie looked out the kitchen window, the clunking sound of the empty disposal chewing nothing strangely comforting. After a few seconds, she turned off the disposal and started cleaning a kitchen that wasn't dirty.

Might as well clean. Nothing else seemed to work.

As the last of the red, then pink, then bands of purple fell behind the shoreline on the opposite side of the lake, she disjoined herself from the chair and went to the bedroom, turned the fan on and plunked down on her bed. She laid there, covers off, the sweep of air from a fan directed toward her. As she yawned and took the blessing of the fan's coolness, the day's tension lost its edge.

"Are you sleeping?"

Maggie shot out of bed. Larry was standing at the foot of his bed, his form tingued with that strange light, like the aura around a darkened moon. She flipped on the light.

"What?" It was more curse than question. She knew better than to complain. Her bones told her Larry

"We have all this information and a thousand ways it can tie together."

She rubbed her eyes. "Tell me something I don't know."

"We found most of what we know from things hidden in this house. The journal. The pictures. The notes and poem. Lou liked to play hide and seek."

"I know. I've poked through every crevice and hidey-hole in this place."

Larry's form grew brighter even in the light. "But you haven't searched the things that aren't here."

Swoozie's. Maggie started to jump up, wanted so to hug him. Oops. Instead she punched the air. "I know just the place." She said it like a battle cry.

— *Chapter 23* —

On this Thursday night, Maggie had intended to stay neutral. But she couldn't help the rush that sluiced through her as she unlocked the back door and skulked into the store. The sky had turned dark thirty minutes ago. So the only light in the room was a beam of her flashlight focused on the merchandise in the back room. Swoozie would never know she had been here. Shadows reached out like claws, but Maggie refused to be distracted. She knew this room, and she knew the furniture in it. She climbed over a maze of furniture to get to the night stand. Boxes. Trunks. Old metal milk jugs from the dairy, faded remnants of scrolled letters mere chips to remember days long gone. Her foothold had stayed steady as she navigated the maze, looking like an ostrich climbing over boulders. She slipped once, threatening to dislodge the pile but regained control. Up and over. The Hardy boys could not have done better.

The bed stand. Finally. It stood on top of a weathered bureau, two iron lamps flanking it on the right. All day today, while she had been at work, she had sneaked breaks to peek at it, her hands itching to finish reclamation. It wasn't much of anything, mostly walnut boards cut and jigged. Two drawers. Nicked legs. Missing one pull. But she had to have it.

The iron bed was the more valuable. Probably the item that needed rescuing more. An antique dealer from Menominee had been in yesterday yammering with Swoozie about its form and price, how the chips on the headboard's balls would lower its value – like Swoozie would care what the munchkin thought. Maggie knew full well about those chips. She had put them there herself in a perfectly legitimate snit over not being able to roller skate off the dock.. Yes, the bed was precious, but the piece had no siren's song. Not like the bed stand. Something about the bed stand demanded that Maggie grab hold and return it to the bedroom.

She lodged the flashlight under her chin and reached, right foot held steady on two dining room chairs wedged together on their side. Neither one of the wooden pieces probably would support Winnie's bottom on a good day without wiggling, yet here Maggie was, planning on using them like a rock wall pinion. With a firm oomph, she grabbed onto the night stand and lifted. Thank you, Pilates class. And thank you, gods of wobbly chairs. Flashlight still under her chin, bed stand ready for up and over, she edged her way down, her chin tucked, holding the flashlight, her hands holding onto merchandise, her will dedicated to keeping her balance. As a guide, the flashlight was worthless, its beam bobbing to the left instead of focused on her footfall. Plus, the damn thing threatened to choke her. Maggie lost her momentum only once, fell forward, the nightstand slipping from her hands. She grabbed and steadied, made her way down. Finally. Terra firma.

She grasped the flashlight and stood up, rolled her shoulders. The cracking in her neck was a victory dance. She switched the flashlight to her left hand and started examining the bed stand, pulled out the top drawer, ran her hand along the sides and back of where the drawer had set. Nothing. She checked the drawer for a false bottom and struck out, slid the drawer back into place. Down on one knee, she started in on the lower drawer. Bingo! A thank you went skyward, this time for hard fingernails. She pried open the drawer's false bottom and held it with her left hand, shined her flashlight on the discovery with her right. There it was, waiting for her after how many years. A manila envelope. A sense of grace filled her. This was big. She could feel the telling inside the envelope, waiting for her to air its secrets. She wedged the flashlight against the slat of wood that had so long closeted her find and reached in. Holding it between thumb and index finger, the aged paper stiff against her fingers, she pulled the envelope back, out from the weight of the flashlight and up toward her. There. She had it. She started to stand, was halfway up, when the lights went on and a voice called out.

"Hornsboro Police. Step back down and turn around slowly."

The sheriff. Her stomach flipped, then pulled down, contracting. Flight mode went into full throttle. She lurched. The envelope slipped from her fingers. Before she could react, it fell and stuck between the iron bed stand and a pile of wooden boxes. She felt her face tighten. What the hell. She grabbed her flashlight out of the drawer and let the false bottom fall back into place, upside down but tight enough to stick. She gave it a shove for good measure. Nice timing. The envelope was beyond her reach, but hey, nobody would know about the bed stand's secret compartment. Perfect Witkowski luck.

"Ma'am, I said step back. Now."

Flashlight in hand, grimace in place, she stood up and faced the sheriff. Mr. Authority. Where had he been when she needed him back when some madman was decorating her porch with filth? The jab of anger squashed any fear she felt at being caught. "It's just me, Sheriff. Maggie Witkowski. I work here.

— *Chapter 24* —

Legs spread wide in official stance, one hand on his gun hip, Sheriff Lyle Stout watched Maggie with a wary eye, the picture of police detection. Great. He knew who she was, sure. He had spent a whole five minutes at the cabin dismissing the garbage fiasco as a prank. The entire Hornsboro police system loved to think that all distress lay on the backs of prankster kids. So why did he decide to become official and go after the bad guy – in this case, Maggie? So she was in the store scrounging around in the dark? So she had the bed stand torn apart? Couldn't be worse than dumping road kill on a lady's porch.

Maggie watched him looking at her sharply. Saw his hand near his gun. Lyle Stout was in no mood to think prank. That was obvious. Was his hand sweating? Did he have an itch to use that gun? Chances were, the only time he had ever pulled it was at target practice. Criminals, if they ever stepped foot onto the streets of Hornsboro were only passing through, gassing up for a trip elsewhere.

Or out at her cabin scaring her. But that was no criminal. That was a psycho bastard. Sheriff Stout didn't include psychos in his view of Hornsboro criminology. Only kids bent on mischief.

Come on, woman, think. You're the one who talked a Chicago cop into letting you dance on the bar because the Cubs had broken a losing streak.

Maggie put on her contrite smile – the one that said, *yeah, I know I screwed up but I had a really good reason* – and made sure that she kept her hands in the air and her eyes focused. "Officer Stout – Lyle -- this looks really dumb, I know, but you're going to laugh when you hear the story."

Officer Stout displayed no visible signs of humor. Nor did he move his hand away from his hip. If fact, it looked like it was inching closer to his weapon.

"Miss Witkowski, ma'am, I'm going to call Darlene down at the station. We had a report of strange lights. She's going to call Swoozie and have her come on down." His face took on a smile, one that was tight-lipped and void of anything remotely friendly. "Meanwhile, you and I are going to stay here and wait. I'll let you lower your hands and have a seat, but don't think about doing anything foolish."

Foolish? Like anything could begin to seem more foolish than she felt now? Oh wait. What if he searched the area? What if he found the envelope stuck between the bed and the boxes? She didn't even know what was in it.

For a few seconds she imagined Larry popping in and rescuing her. He might be tied to her property, but wouldn't the Judges relent a little? Let Officer Stout deal with a ghost. That would change the chemistry in the room. She silently cursed authority figures who mandated that ghosts stick to boundaries. She didn't stick to any. Why should Larry have to?

She decided to stay standing. All she needed now was to have the sheriff come toward her and notice the envelope boldly asking to be retrieved. Two legs cramps and a headache later, Maggie heard the front door shut and footsteps headed toward them. Swoozie glided in, all magnolia charm. She stood in the doorway to the back room and pulled her reading glasses up to face. "My, my. Whatever do we have going on? Why Officer Stout, I believe you have caught my assistant in . . . tell me, Maggie darlin', just what is it that the good officer has found?

Maggie rubbed the top of the bed stand, touching it like it was a favorite pet. "I feel so foolish now, but this whole thing is basically innocent." She managed a catch in her throat. A little Camille might go well with Southern belle. "You know how precious my grandparents things are to me, how much I've wanted to rescue them." She let "rescue" slip out with a sigh. Lyle Stout raised an eyebrow but let her go on. Swoozie looked noncommittal. Like that could happen. "I've had my heart set on the iron bed – that has to be the next purchase. I knew that there's no way I could find the money for both the bed and the night stand, so I thought I'd spend some time alone with both of them – try to get a feel for what I should choose. I'd been thinking about it all evening, telling myself that

I was seven kinds of silly for thinking the furniture might kindle a vibe, but finally, I hopped into my car and came to town." She took a breath and tried a half smile. No takers. "So, I was sitting here in the dark trying to figure out what to do when I remembered how I used to hide things when I was a kid. I got all hepped up about maybe there were trinkets or notes or whatever stuck somewhere, so I started . . . "She pointed to the space in the bed stand where a drawer should be. "Well, you get the idea."

Swoozie fingered her glasses chain. "And this couldn't wait until tomorrow because . . . ?"

"Oh, you know how hyper I am. Now that I think about it, I should have listened to that voice that told me to stay home, but obsessive me, I fret until I have to act." She faced the sheriff. "I didn't want to turn the lights on," she said with the most self-deprecation she could muster, "because I figured you'd come running and I'd have to explain and sound like a muddle head." She let a sigh work as punctuation. "Now look what I've done. Everything I wanted to avoid has come tumbling down."

She looked from the sheriff to Swoozie and back again. "I am so embarrassed and so very sorry."

During this speech, the sheriff had gone from Hornsboro professional to skeptic to cynic. He shook his head and made half an effort to keep a smirk hidden while he turned to Swoozie. "It's your call, ma'am. What should we do here?"

Swoozie waved her hand like she was dismissing an annoying child. "You just run along now, Lyle. I think we have everything settled here."

Maggie's mind hammered. Swoozie did not settle. She swooped. Break into her store and try to pull something over on her? Might as well tell native Texans they should ship the Alamo to Cancun as a tourist attraction.

Swoozie's voice floated after the sound of heavy footsteps heading toward the front door, all sweetness. "You take care now, Sheriff Stout. Don't get caught speeding on your way home." To Maggie, she said, much more quietly and much less sweetly. "I'll see you tomorrow. We shall certainly have a chat about this."

Why couldn't things be simple? Pop into the store, search, pop out again. But no, Sheriff Lyle had to be on duty. So did the busybodies of the town, their noses fine tuned to sniff out the unusual. She was so close. Close to uncovering a clue. Close, she told herself, to probably to getting fired.

By 10:00 most of the crowd at Wallie's had cleared out. A bit of good news, considering. The last thing Maggie wanted was friendly banter. There would be plenty of that tomorrow once news of her escapade swept through the rumor mill. Right now, best thing was to hide in some place conspicuous. Make her look innocent. Scatterbrain beats thief any day. After a couple of drinks with her bartender friend, Jeff, she could sneak back into the store and retrieve the envelope.

So hide she did. She sat at the bar, her purse in protective custody in her lap, elbows on the bar, chin resting on her palms. The sheriff had never asked for the key. Neither had Swoozie. Lyle Stout would forget and just go home. Swoozie? Maggie's inner detective warned her that her boss never let anything slide, but like Tara for Scarlet O'Hara, that could wait until tomorrow. She itched to get back to the store, but what the hey, a diversion with Jeff couldn't be all that bad.

Jeff served her the draft. She took a long draw and set the glass down, ran her finger along the rim as she watched the narrow rim of foam now half way down the glass.

"From the looks of things, this hasn't been your best night." That Jeff. What a master of subtlety.

"From the looks of things, I'm probably getting fired, and if things are really in the toilet, I may be going to jail."

"Sounds like maybe you could use a lawyer. I know a guy who'd be glad to take on your case – that is, if you have one." He paused and his voice grew hopeful. "Or even if you don't. Be glad to give him a call."

Will. Not just Will the lawyer. Will the guy, Will the friend, the confidante. Will the out-of-control tool. Maggie's face stayed neutral while her mind spun a wheel, each version of Will spinning one atop the other like clothes in a dryer, each piece equal and unique, all of them bumping along together. She stuck a mental stick in the wheel. Enough on her mind to think about him right now. Still, the wheel continued to spin. Great. Double duty in the what-to-do department.

"If the guy were any more repentant, he'd be sprawled out on Main Street in sack cloth and ashes." Jeff hesitated, leaned forward. "But then, you know that, don't you, Maggie."

Maggie met Jeff's look, eye to eye. "This is not night to start in on me about Will."

He smiled. "Well then, pretty lady, when would a good night be?"

Maggie studied Jeff's face, held up one finger and let out a long breath. "After our little run in at my cabin, 'night' is most likely off the table."

Jeff backed away, arms extended upward in submission, toward the bottles lined up to call out to Wallie's customers. "Why, oh why, gods of wheat, barley, and malt? What will it take to melt the ice in her heart?" Maggie watched him without response, but then she laughed. Couldn't help herself.

"Put your hands down. You don't do supplication. Any more than I do submission. Give him a call. Tell him he has fifteen minutes to get here before I leave. I need to hear a little groveling to raise my spirits. That and a promise I won't be locked up in the town slammer."

Will was there in twelve. He tried nonchalant, as if he had just meandered into Wallie's for a late nightcap. He looked at Jeff, nodded. Then he switched his focus to Maggie, watched her from half eyes, cocked a smile and shrugged.

She rolled her eyes and patted the seat next to her. "Good thing we're hanging out with Jeff. He has your best interests at heart, and besides, he makes anybody's sins wane in comparison."

"I acknowledge his omnipotence as screw-up. Even as I acknowledge my own." Will's smile was beatific. "Later tonight, I will stand in my yard to face the stars and pay homage to both." He raised his hand and spoke to Jeff. "Until that time, barkeep, how about a beer?"

Maggie said, "Jeff's got you beat in the supplication department." His face had a look of such mixture – a stab at humor but even more curiosity, even atonement. The revelation surprised her. She took herself back to their fiasco at the cabin. Felt nothing. She felt a little yelp of surprise even as she considered her response. What the heck. How many guys had gone too far, messed up a relationship? Bet most of them hadn't wound up drenched in wine. The relationship she shared with Will had been clubbed by an act foolish but certainly not lethal. She shuddered. It wasn't like . . ."

He caught her attention and spoke, "What's up?" Her grip tightened on her beer glass. She startled. Will reached out. "Easy, girl. It can't be that bad. Jeff says you got yourself into a scrape. Vintage Maggie or real criminal?"

Before she could answer, she set her hands on the purse in her lap, smoothed her fingers and palms along the leather as if she were pressing out a wrinkle, then kept her hands on the edges. She worked a smile. "No biggie. Just a little breaking and entering. I needed to check out a few things in the last of my stash at Swoozie's." she raised her eyebrows. "Secret stuff. Unfortunately, Sheriff Lyle and Swoozie did not share my nonchalance about what I consider my own property."

"Ah, the venerable Lyle Stout. Always there when you don't want him. Off somewhere when you do."

"The good sheriff is not my problem. Sweet Swoozie, that's another issue altogether. She is not amused when people visit her store after hours. Even the people who work for her."

"And the visit was for . . . "Will said it like a skeptical parent. Maggie had heard that tone many a time. She leaned toward Will, held her hands on each side of her mouth in secret mode, and whispered, "Don't tell anyone, but I rifled through a couple of secret places and found what might be a . . . very valuable clue." She drew out the last three words, punctuating them with precision. For just a second, Will looked like something had twisted inside him. Maggie suppressed a laugh, a need to slap him on the shoulder and ask, "What's up?" Was he mad that she had scrounged around the inside of Swoozie's? He was such a stickler for rules, that Will. No wonder she had flipped when he'd made a move on her.

Before she could even finish her speculation, much less pull it in, his face relaxed into simple interest. "So, I give. What's the big clue? More pictures?"

She shook her head and wagged a finger. "Oh no you don't. I've got dibs on this. If it was hidden, it must be really good." She smirked her Cheshire Cat smile and hopped off the bar stool. No need to let him know that a second breaking and entering was on tonight's to-do list. Leaning in, she taunted. "For me to know and you maybe to find out. Talk to you tomorrow" Then she gave a quick kiss – a really quick one --this was only the beginning of a reconciling after all – and headed for the door. She had only gone a few feet when she turned and said, "Don't get your knees too dirty out there praying to the gods of contrition."

She laughed as she walked out to the street. She might not have a job tomorrow, but she'd have a good time tonight with whatever was in that envelope. She whistled all the way to her car, kept it up while she hid it behind the store, but was all stealth when she went back into the store.

Maggie sat across from Larry at the trestle table, the manila envelope in front of her unopened. Larry was frowning. "Get on with it girl."

"Shut up. I'm sensing its importance." She closed her eyes and ran her fingertips back and forth over the envelope. "Be a mystery breaker. Be a mystery breaker," she pleaded in her best swami voice.

"The only breaking will be me breaking your fingers if you don't start opening."

Maggie opened her eyes and laughed. "I thought I was the impetuous one. Haven't you been riding me about jumping into situations without thinking?" When Larry snarled at her, she lifted her head up a notch and did her best snooty voice. "Guess I just have to give in to a big old meanie like you."

Larry kept his snarl and kept his silence. But his face said much.

Maggie turned the envelope over and unlatched the clasp, pulled out a document on its flip side. A lock of hair -- no more than a few wisps and a pink bow, just a sliver of satin ribbon had been stapled to the paper. From it dangled a tiny silver necklace, half of a heart on a silver chain, fashioned for a baby. Underneath were the words, "You'll never wear whole, sweet baby."

Baby? Maggie flipped over the paper. It was a birth certificate for a baby girl. Mother – Ida May Turnball. Father – Carlo Veraldi.

Ida Ann and the guy from the pictures. They had a baby. Maggie checked the date and did the math. 1953. When had Ida Ann been born? She scrounged in her mind, pictured the grave stone at the cemetery. Something about Margaret Mitchell. 1936. That was it. Ida Ann had been born in 1936, the same year *Gone with the Wind* made the bestseller list. That made her fifteen when the child was born. Maggie set her jaw and bit her lip "Holy crap," she said. "Ida Ann didn't go to Ohio because her mother died. She went because she was pregnant. In 1953, girls who *got into trouble* went away to have their babies, and then gave them up for adoption."

The shock of their discovery took time to settle in. Larry sat back in his chair, arms folded, lips pursed and eyes narrowed. On her side of the table, Maggie bent forward, forehead braced in her left hand, elbow planted on the table. It should have felt good, a major find like that. It didn't. At least right now. It felt like ache.

With her right index finger, Maggie traced the edges of the birth certificate, as if by elfin magic, secret writing would appear and explain the tale. She turned the paper over to look more closely at the silver heart half, all the while fighting against the tragedy of the pink ribbon. This was a clue, not an exercise in emotion. The heart was so tiny, and yet an artist had engraved something on it. Maggie lifted it closer to the light to examine it. One half of a butterfly, beautifully scrolled, clear to cleft edge. A heart broken. A butterfly in need of its other half.

"In my day, we didn't even talk about such things." Larry said the words with the censure of a critic straight out of a long ago decade. "Girls disappeared, went off to live with an aunt for a year. Nobody said a word, even though everyone knew that girls did not suddenly rush off to live with aunts real or imaginary."

"*The Scarlet Letter* alive and well in suburbia – or rural America." Maggie shook her head, not sure whether she felt sympathy for the girls or scorn for the times, or, good Catholic girl that she was, something entirely different, the blow of guilt and foolishness rent from trust in the wrong man.

The image of Ida Ann's adolescent letter came back to her. Scrawls of romantic daydreams, large letters proclaiming a wish. Mrs. Carlo Veraldi. She let the sense of sadness tip the end of her fingers and edge her jaw. She saw Ida Ann in her mind. Moon struck face, smile of innocence as her pen led her through a fantasy. Had she been in her bedroom on a bed, stuffed animals surrounding her, blonde hair curled and young cheeks blushed with anticipation of a boyfriend's next kiss?

And the boyfriend. Ida Ann had gone off to a place that housed girls marked with sin. What about young Carlo? Son of a mobster if Diane's information was true. Hornsboro Wisconsin, vacation land for the scourge of Chicago. Had Carlo cared? Had he even known?

Where was he now? An old man living in Skokie, eating pasta and listening to jazz at Billie's while escorts hung next to him? Woman from the city, Maggie had seen mobster recreation – at least from the outside --could visualize an ancient Carlo, diamond rings, girl friends, and entitlement.

Mobsters. Hornsboro as recreation spot. The thoughts tugged at Maggie, that kind of niggling message from the unconscious begging to come to the surface but too deep to be identified. At the library, Maggie and Diane had laughed about Harlan Turnball's shady past. But where else had she seen this?

"What are you thinking?" Larry's voice interrupted. Damn. The thoughts dissolved like fog hit by sun.

"Reading my mind again, ghost boy?" Her tone was less than friendly.

"Not at all. Your mouth was so twisted up, I was worried it'd pop off." His face was flushed. Pretty weird for a ghost. Guilt?

"So, you're the *expert* on life in the fifties. You know, when bad girls were somehow impregnated by their own sin, and not some horny boyfriend. Was our Ida Ann whisked off to Ohio to bear a daughter, not because she was grieving for her mother as the townsfolk believe?"

"Got me. Bet a modern woman like you could find out. And when you do, we'll tackle the next question. How is this related to your grandfather's reputation?

Maggie's mind was already playing with Google. When she looked up, Larry was gone. She went to the kitchen for a pad of paper and a pen. Maybe if she wrote about what she had found, the pieces of this mess would start to click into place.

Ten minutes later, a sound from outside broke through her thoughts. Something had been knocked over, or someone had fallen. She pressed down the panic that grabbed her, stood up, and went to the door to check. The porch light sent a blanket of yellow ten feet out beyond the porch. Nothing there. The shadows looked safe. No movement.

Maybe a bear had been stumbling around or a deer. Something big had made that sound. She shut the door and locked it, left the light on. When she went to sit down again to research, she thought to herself, *I might have heard a bear, and I'm relieved.* She shook her head while she let out an exhale, and went back to her task.

Chapter 25

By the end of the next day, the afternoon light had scared away any fear of bears – or whatever wildlife had scuttled near the house last night. But critters were the least of her problems. Maggie had to talk to Winnie about the latest findings. Friday was busy at the café, so no worries about Winnie dropping in. Maggie had closeted herself in the store all day – thank god Swoozie was off on a collecting trip –and dashed to her car as soon as she locked up. But now Maggie leaned against the door frame, phone in hand, for a response. Winifred Listug was silent, an unusual state for the woman, but then, the news about poor departed Ida Ann would silence anyone. An eternity of seconds went by. Maggie could tell. She had been thumbing her free fingers against the doorjamb long enough for dents to form on her fingertips. She intervened.

"Say something, Winnie."

Maggie heard a long exhale. At least it was a beginning. Then Winnie began her rant, first a heavy exhale and then the litany. "No way. No way, no way, no way. She would have told me. Ida couldn't keep a secret if it was super-glued to her backside. A baby? Are you sure? Uffta nada."

Maggie thought about assuring her, but before she could even begin, Winnie was off again. "That Ida. Oh that poor, poor Ida. All alone, her mama dead – I thought that was why she left. Her iceberg of a father in that big house on the lake. No one even gave it two thoughts when she took off for Ohio. Who'd want to be stranded out there in the boondocks with Franklin Turnball?" Winnie took a breath before her voice rose and she asked, "Are you sure, Maggie?"

Maggie's glee at finding the birth certificate waned. Even after all these years, Ida Ann could reach out and inflict pain on those she had left behind. A tug of guilt teased.

She swatted it away.

"I really need your help, Winnie."

"That's for sure. I'll probably have to hire you after Swoozie kicks your boney behind to the curb." Winnie's voice was censure, payback for the news about Ida no doubt, but by the sound of the sarcasm, at least Winnie had one foot back into her old self.

Maggie matched the tone. "Funny, Hornsboro lady. I'll deal with Swoozie later this morning. Soon as I have one of your cinnamon rolls and enough coffee to wire some courage. Right now I need you to remember the name of the town where Ida Ann went to finish high school."

Nothing from Winnie. Was she trying to think of a name or getting ready to come back at Maggie with more denial?

"Findlay." Winnie said the word as an insult.

"What?"

"Findlay, Ohio. That's where she went. I teased her. 'Find the friendly in Findlay,' I said right before she left." Winnie's voice started to choke. "Poor, poor Ida Ann, all alone and pregnant, and I'm making jokes about a name."

Maggie pictured Winnie, saw in her mind the stern face twisted with guilt. Her own throat tightened. "Winnie, when she came back, you were a friend to her, the only one she could count on."

"Some friend."

"Exactly. Friend."

"Then let me tell you, missy, be sure that you're Ida Ann's friend too. She deserved a friend back then, and she deserves one now. This isn't just about justice for Lou. This is about justice for Ida Ann." The words had snapped through the phone lines. Now they softened. "And for a woman out there, who knows where, who never knew that she had a momma who cried because she couldn't give her baby a silver necklace."

The baby. A little girl. With her mother's blonde hair. A little girl born in Findlay Ohio. Finding whatever institution that had housed Ida Ann would be easy, finding the child another matter altogether. Sealed adoption records were iron clad. But there were birth registries now that connected adult children to their birth mothers.

"Are you listening?" Winnie's voice snapped her out of her reverie.

"Sorry, Winnie. My mind's already on the road to figuring this all out. I'll get back to you as soon as I have something. Promise." She put the phone back in its cradle and stood still in the doorway, her mind in that state right between figuring out a plan and making those precious first steps, that stage when possibilities are promises.

A couple of diet sodas later, when she had set her laptop on the big trestle table and was typing in Findlay, Ohio, the crunch of gravel announced a visitor. She closed the laptop and went to the door.

Swoozie. Could timing be any worse?

Maggie's boss had a big old Chevy truck that begged for hounds in the back and a beer in the driver's hand. It had belonged to a trapper over in Wall Lake who wanted to trade up. Swoozie spent the first six months she owned it cleaning the smell of dead animals out of the cab, but she said that her heart belonged to the vehicle because it reminded her of home. Right now it was parked in Maggie's drive, door open, while Swoozie slid down to plant her feet on the running board and then jump down. She shut the truck door and swatted at her hands while she hollered out at Maggie – or hollered as much as southern lass Swoozie would do. "I just finished hauling junk back from an auction down over by Danbury." She kept up the conversation as she marched toward the porch. "Between now and then, I have to turn them into homespun rustic treasures. Thought I'd stop out here and see if you wanted to help, seeing how you're so slick at climbing up piles of furniture." By the time she had finished, she was looking up at Maggie, one foot on the front step, her hands on her hips, a grin plastered across her face.

Perfect. The acerbic tongue of an employer who dangled Maggie's possessions in front of her like a carrot. Maggie's jaw ached, her fingers itched. She was on a roll, ready to finally come up with lines to connect the dots and Swoozie showed up. *Steady. Don't blow it. Stay quiet.*

"What," Swoozie mocked. You think I'd fire you? That'd mean I'd have to work all the time. We're coming in to the busiest time of summer. And besides, I know every square inch of my inventory, especially the things you want. Now let's go inside and you can explain what you were doing crawling all over my store in the middle of the night.

"And by the way," Swoozie smirked, "Don't make any plans for this Monday."

Chapter 26

She hadn't eaten since breakfast. Her back hurt from leaning over the laptop. And she had skewed the world of a good woman. Shortly after 10:00, Maggie gave in to her sleeplessness. No answers inside the cabin. Once again, like so many times in her life, the dock called. The night tingled with the promise of cooling and a full moon held court over the lake. Too much beauty to ignore with the act of sleeping, even for the untroubled. Double reason for Maggie to be outside. She could sit there and watch the streaks of moonlight play across the water while she weighed decisions – or ignored them if she chose. Fat chance of ignoring her troubles, she thought. They were strung through her mind. There simply wasn't room for anything else.

As she headed down the incline between the edge of the cabin's clearing and the dock, Maggie stumbled over a root and lurched forward. Before she could even react to steady herself, a hand grabbed at her hair and yanked her upright. Sharp pain filled her head. Even her eyes hurt. She screamed, as much from the shock as the pain. The scream was muffled by a coarse burlap bag thrust over her head, the opening twisted by a strength of a hand that held tight. She could feel her attacker's knuckles pressing at the back of her head as he pulled her head back. She knew it was a man. No woman could be that strong. His other hand grabbed around her waist and he lowered her to the ground, then twisted himself to kneel above her, cementing his knees and thighs to keep her pinned. In the midst of what she so often had seen as beauty, she could feel the dried branches underneath her, the piles of leaves, the clumps of grass. She tried to squirm. Only scraped her back against the edge of a rock half buried.

My god, I'm going to be raped. She was struck by a fierce desire to deny the possibility, but every cell in her body knew better. Her right heel dug into the growth, seeking leverage as her hand reached out to grab a stick. His hand clamped her wrist before she could reach anything remotely resembling a weapon. Now his body was directly over her, the one hand on her wrist, the other holding her down by her throat. He had moved one knee between her legs. She could feel the bone of his knee as he pushed upward against the crotch of her pajama shorts. The hand against her throat tightened as the pressure increased.

She couldn't breath. Dirt and must from the sack filled her nostrils. *He's going to kill me. I'm going to die.* She gave into the terror and lay still.

His hand released some of the pressure against her throat even as he kept the rest of his attack steady. She felt the loosening of the sack, just a slight gift, but one that might keep her from dying in the immediate future. One day she might feel guilt over the relief, but a gift this was. Instinctively, she breathed in, trying not to choke on the dirt embedded in the burlap.

"I'll be still. I promise." Her words were muffled by the sack, but to her, they thundered inside. With one musty breath after another, her mind coaxed her muscles into relaxing in spite of her terror, first her legs, then her middle, then her arms and hands. She was no more than a rag doll, limp and waiting.

Hands that had held her down began their work. The attacker lifted up her top with one hand while he lowered her shorts with the other and cast them aside so that he could begin his work. His hands were big, fingers long, unweathered but strong. They groped her breasts. Pinched her thighs. Thrust between her legs with neither remorse nor caring.

Maggie pulled down walls between her body and her mind. He could touch her body parts but never reach the real Maggie. If she lay there, refusing to let him inside, then this wouldn't be rape. It would be sex with a shell.

His breath increased. Through the dirt and the burlap, she could smell something sweet. What was it? Dear God, his breathing smelled of peppermint. To her, it was a stench. She wanted to retch.

By now, he was kneading her breast with one hand. The other had stopped its attack. He rose up slightly. The sound of a belt unbuckling, a zipper being lowered made a ripple outside the walls she had erected. She waited for the inevitable. Would she feel pain? She was as dry as a virgin. She reinforced the walls of her protection.

He bent forward. His left hand stroked his erection while his right hand kept at her breast, his harsh grunting beating in time to the strokes. His knuckles grazed her pubic hair while he worked. Finally, Maggie felt the wetness. While she lay there, waiting, she felt his hand spread the sticky mess upward, over her stomach and between her breasts. Her walls crumbled. He had won. He had broken through, raped every part of her. She could no more have fought him then and there than she could have grown wings and flown away.

While she lay there in a bed of forest floor as broken and twisted as she was, he stood up and dressed. Moments passed. How many? Who knew? She could feel him watching her, know the smirk that crossed his face. Still she did not move. She heard him pick something up, then felt a branch across her throat, a quick press of warning.

She could hear the scrunch of leaves and twigs as he walked away, the sound growing dimmer until finally all was silent. Even then, she laid still, barely breathing in a nether land of shame and disbelief until she found the strength to reach up and grab at the branch lying there on her neck and fling it away. Only when its faint thud broke the silence could Maggie move. She pulled at the sack until it was above her nose, but refused to lift any higher. She did not want to see, could not see a beautiful night in Wisconsin. Her head partly covered by burlap, pajama top still pulled up, shorts around one ankle, she turned on her side and waited for nothing.

Who was she, this beast, this clod of refuse? She thought of her porch, defiled by garbage. Was she garbage? Was she no more than road kill heaped on a mass of stench rotting where no one could see or smell? The sheriff had ignored her when she had called about the garbage. Why should now be any different. Garbage was garbage.

She sat up, pulled off her clothes and sat hunched over underneath the moon. Finally, she reached over for the stick that had imprisoned her throat and used it to pull herself up – or upright as much as her battered body would allow.

Then, while out on the water a loon called, its sound mocking her, before she could struggle up the hill that now met her like the mountain of Sisyphus, Maggie Witkowski cried.

Chapter 27

It was her kind of morning, full of sun and possibilities. It was her bed. The one she had slept in every night since her first night in the cabin. So why did the light hurt? Why did the bed feel so lumpy? She felt like she had slept on rocks. Why? Not much future in possibilities if her head felt like it was caved in.

Poor Maggie. Those first few seconds of innocence after awakening in hell are so blessed. That is, until they fall victim to reality, in her case, a wall of pain that slammed both body and mind.

She breathed shallowly, petty little breaths that could slip by unnoticed. She had to. The very act of breathing let the pain win even more.

"Shhh."

The sibilance of the sound brought panic. When warm water and cloth touched her arm, she screamed. Inside. She couldn't make any noise worth hearing. More warmth touched her, this time a touch that had no physical sense but filled her nonetheless. It entered her mouth, rose through her sinuses, behind her eyes, into the part of her head that had turned to cement. It moved through her throat, through her lungs, into her gut, down her legs, her arms. Such a lightness. Like love and peace had come to visit. No more smell of dirt. No more heaviness impaling her. Her body gave into the warmth, let her eyelids close. As she drifted away from the pain, she heard the softest of voices, one itself touched with ache. "Sleep, Maggie girl. Sleep and heal."

All she could think was, *Grandpa, you came. Help me, grandpa. Take it away. It hurts.*

She fell back to sleep, lulled by that warmth, but the edge of a nightmare lived behind her eyes. Her. Walking – no stumbling back to the cabin. The wracking sobs that had ruled her. The image blurred in mist as she slipped away into a sleep void of sensation and memory.

When she woke, the moon had replaced the sun, its rays casting a blue sheen in the bedroom. She was dressed in a dull ache except for her knees and throat. They full out hurt. Every sensation morphed and merged together, one on top of another, moving and blurring like an Impressionist painting gone rogue.

She needed water. Lifting her head was too much work. She settled on opening her eyes a little wider as if seeing better could stave off her pain. She'd die of thirst here in this bed but at least she could see it happening. No. Too much. She shut her eyes and tried not to feel.

Water touched her lips. Just a sip. She let it run over her them, move across her tongue toward her throat. She found the strength to swallow.

She opened her mouth and let the words rasp out. "More." Her jaw sagged in anticipation.

There. A trickle now. Her throat ached but the cool wetness was too much of a gift to not swallow. She strained to take in the blessed water, lifted her hands to grab at the cup offered while she opened her eyes.

Hands. A man's hands. Pain faded in the wake of panic. She yanked back her hands, balled them into fists. Her throat tightened.

"It's okay. No one can hurt you." The voice was tender, familiar. Grandpa? No. someone else. Someone she trusted. Maggie knew the voice promised safety. She turned and looked up.

Larry. It was Larry sitting next to her, feeding her that blessed water. His hands were strong, callused palms and huge fingers wrapped around the cup. How could that be? He was a ghost. He had no substance. Yet here he was, cup in hand, a savior.

Don't think. Lay your head back. Drink. Rest.

Were the words a prayer from her mind or an order from this nurse who should not be able to tend to the wounded? Maggie didn't care. She let Larry give her more water and she fell back to sleep.

A cold front had worked its way from the northwest by the time Maggie woke. The night air had a nip to it and the wind had picked up. Maggie sat up in bed, shivering, a good shivering, a normal reaction to a normal stimulus, the cold air that thrust through the cracks in the bedroom window frame welcome. Her body still ached but she would live.

She sat up slowly. A day in bed, not to mention what had put her there, had taken its toll. The bedroom had not changed. Same pine paneling, same rustic shutters on the window Jean had rescued from the dump. Only Maggie was the single altered entity in the room. Wrapping herself in the quilt she had grabbed from the end of the bed, she turned her body and scooted, set her feet squarely on the floor, and stood up. Her head felt light, but she didn't sway — much. She breathed in deeply, tightened the quilt around her and walked to the main room. Larry was sitting on the sofa, head lowered onto clasped hands. While Maggie watched, he raised his head slightly, unclasped his hands from on top of his knees, and made two fists, then drove them across his legs, just the slightest movement, one wrought by anger and helplessness.

"You can hold things. You held that cup. You held the wine when you dumped on Will. I always wondered about that. You're supposed to go through stuff, not hold it."

He set his hands on his knees and looked up. "You're awake. How do you feel?" His voice was even, the words spoken tentatively.

"Sore." Pin points of pain made her body a quilt of aching. She retreated from them. "Don't change the subject. Explain the ghost rules." Hysteria edged her voice. She beat back against it. "Gotta know the rules if I have to live with you."

Rules? Who was she kidding.? There were no rules. Rules had been stomped on. All there was . . . no. She wouldn't . . . couldn't go there.

He stood up and took a step toward her. Her gut told her to run. The rest of her knew better. She waited for a reply. If they could talk physics, she wouldn't have to talk about . . .

"I'll make you a deal. I'll explain all about ghost rules if you tell me your story."

Cocooned in that quilt, still Maggie shrank. Her voice shook. "I'll make *you* a deal. I'll talk to you all right, talk to you about the cup thing, the weather, the state of American education. I don't care." She waited for her jaw to stop trembling before she finished. "The only thing I won't talk about — yet — is 'my story' as you so glibly put it."

"Deal."

She settled into the wicker rocking chair that she had rescued from Swoozie's, the one that had reminded her of her goal the whole time it had waited for her in the store. Larry pulled a dining room chair over and sat straight across from her. She managed to unwrap the quilt from around her shoulders. Now it lay across her lap.

He spoke. "I heard you first. There was this god-awful sound, like the keening of a dying rabbit, coming from the cabin. I usually can't hear you when I'm away, but the pain in that sound reached me."

"Did you not hear the deal? We talk about the cup." Her voice was a rasped scream.

Maggie watched his face. His lips were drawn together. His eyes had darkened, gone from whiskey brown to almost black. He wore a stoic look, but his substance, his Larryness—whatever that was—quivered, faded out then came alive with blue intensity around his edges. Larry of the "we're all about the mission" was in turmoil. He nodded at her, acknowledging. Part of her felt a bond of satisfaction. Selfish? Who cared. The bond felt warm.

"What do you mean, you were 'away'? Where do you go when you're not here?" She sounded like a suspicious wife.

"Sometimes I rest. You know how I need a lot of rest after materializing. Sometimes, I just *am*, mostly when I need to think." He raised an eyebrow. "I've been doing that a lot lately. Thinking."

Maggie passed on the temptation to talk about that subject. Too close to bringing up the source of all her pain.

"You still haven't explained how you could feed me water."

"I told you. I heard this awful sound and came here. You were curled up in a ball on your bed, rocking and crying and making that noise. Then you just stopped." His mouth showed a squeeze of fear."

"Never mind me. That's part of . . ." Her body stiffened.

"I tried to talk to you, but when you heard my voice, you started shaking. He was breaking the rules, damn him. She was too tired to care.

He kept on. She might as well have not been there. "It was dark in the room, but I could see you in the moonlight. You were on all fours, looking like a cornered animal, backing away toward the edge of the bed. I couldn't do anything, couldn't turn on the light, couldn't call for help. Nothing." Larry ran his hands down the sides of his face and over his mouth. He blew out two breaths and lowered his hands, breathed in and out once more. "I had to get stronger, had to be able to focus. I mean, if a guy can send a glass of wine hurling, he should be able to handle a light switch."

He looked at his hands, then up at her. "It's all about energy, harnessing it. Just takes practice. That's another reason I'm gone a lot. I'm practicing."

Normally, Maggie would have spit out some smart-assed retort. She stayed silent.

He leaned back in the chair and rocked, no longer eye-to-eye with Maggie. His mind was trapped in last night. "At first, it was like grabbing at shadows. I needed that light on. I just kept at it, spitting out spurts of energy until – it was the damnedest thing – the switch flipped up and the lights went on."

Larry leaned forward and shook his head. From slitted lips, he blurted the words. "Maggie Witkowski, you scared the whatever out of me. You were cut and bruised, naked, hunched over like an old woman fighting the wind, you had dirt all over you . . . "

Maggie backed against the chair. Her voice was a whisper, soft and harsh at the same time. "We're not going there, not yet."

"Then let's sit here and I'll talk." He waited. "I can do this."

"Good. You talk. I'll try to remember how to breathe."

So Larry obeyed. He talked about his first crush, his best friend's hot older sister. He talked about drag racing at sixteen, about his brother who had died in Korea. While he talked, Maggie started arranging the parts of her back together. She felt the edge of her hurt fade, burn away like the edges of a letter set on fire first curling. She might recover. Her hope stayed long enough to be touched before she crushed it and went inside herself again.

Her chair rocked. Her own unconscious need to find a rhythm and move. More of Larry's help? His words moved with the rhythm of the chair. She felt it, the gentleness of tone and movement as it sifted onto to her while she let herself feel the movement, emerge and breathe out her spite. The dank sweat of remembrance would its way into every hollow, but she could rock and breathe and come back to herself.

"That's right, Maggie girl. Witkowski women may cry, but they do not fold."

Something snaked from deep within, coiled and writhing as it worked its way up. She growled, "He threw me on the ground. He put a sack over my head and threw me onto the ground. I couldn't move. I couldn't breathe."

By now Maggie was crouched over, hands over her head, rocking as if the movement itself could bring on the words. If words had taste and texture, hers would have burned her. "He came all over me, rubbed it across my body like I was a fucking paper towel." Maggie sat up, heaved the quilt aside and jumped out of her rocker. She leaned forward, her index finger pointed at Larry. "I want to find that bastard. I want to kill him. I want to throw him on the ground, stand on his chest, and ram a stake down his throat.

With that outburst, something cracked inside her. She remembered a fourth grade teacher doing an owl pellet lab. Kids broke the shell of hardened owl droppings – disgusting yes, but intriguing as well. Inside were the bones of the owl's prey, the tiniest of bones waiting for someone to reconstruct them and give them a last sense of meaning. Yes, she thought, quite an analogy. What her attacker had done was no better than animal shit. And the bones? They were her bones of anger, isolated inside some capsule in her self and now laid bare. Only she could reconstruct them into a being, give them form.

When he's helpless, staked there like the snake he is, then I'll laugh." She sat back down in the rocker and folded her arms. "That is, of course, only if he apologizes first."

She watched Larry to gauge his reaction. "C'mon. Laugh. Other people drink themselves to death or slice on their wrists when they're angry. I indulge in sarcasm.

Besides, if you laugh, then maybe I can. Some day."

— *Chapter 28* —

Monday morning brought a sense of normalcy to the cabin. Or as much of a sense of normal that was possible. "Eight messages. I think it's some kind of record." Maggie sat on the kitchen floor, legs crossed, observing the landline phone and message machine in her lap.

She had dressed herself, if shorts, sports bra, and flip flops could be considered dressed. A red 8 blinked at her like a watch tower signal warding off planes.

"You might think about answering the phone," Larry said. "Just a thought."

"Why? I know who called. Swoozie wants me to come in to work today." She shook her head. "That Swoozie. She's trying to blackmail me into working Mondays." She traced her finger around the blinking number. "Five of them are from Will. He's worried about me. Wants to know if I'm all right. Vows to do anything to make things right after Friday night. "Please, just call,' he says." She looked up. "Think I should call? I'd hate for him to think I hold a grudge against the men in my life." Her voice was a razor.

Maggie set the phone aside, stood up, and walked over to the sink. With one hand, she grabbed a sponge, with the other dishwashing soap. "People say, 'Get over it. Life goes on.'" She doused the sink with a shot of the soap and ran the water. "Think that's possible?" Her hand ran the sponge over a perfectly clean sink like an old crone trying to wash away sin. "Get over what? The smell? The touch? "

She set the sponge down and ran the spray on the stainless steel, then dried her hands. Turning, she was all business, posture erect, face centered. "Yep, life goes on. No point in bending over like an old woman walking against the wind." She stepped over the phone like it was a toy left by an indulged child and headed toward the front door.

"Where are you going?"

"I have to get evidence."

"What?"

"Evidence. My clothes are out there from last night. The police will, no doubt, insist that this was the work of churlish kids. I need the DNA to prove them wrong."

Larry had seen enough crime shows courtesy of the cabin residents to know about DNA. Right now, he was more concerned about sanity. He watched as Maggie took the porch steps two-at-a-time and rushed off. He watched as she bent over and beat the brush next to the path heading toward the water. When he heard the scream and saw her fall to her knees and beat the ground, he moved, as only a ghost could. Instantly.

"He took my clothes. That bastard. He took them." Her fists banged the brush in front of her body. Acorns. Twigs. Leaves. She never felt them. She kept hammering like an enraged drummer. Slowly, Maggie became aware of Larry, the feel of hands that did not exist, of warmth that should have been an illusion.

"Shh. We'll find them. Maybe an animal ran off with them. He's – whoever *he* is – is gone. Let me look. I'll find your clothes."

Maggie did not respond. She just kept kneeling there, her hands making outward circles in the debris, while Larry scanned the area.

"Maggie. There's nothing here." The words slipped into her consciousness. "Nothing."

Water iris, their green fronds twined, bobbled as a boat stirred the water. A bunch of flotsam stirred by a force beyond its control. How fitting.

Then it hit her. Forget DNA. That was probably a fantasy anyway. An awareness crawled through her, a perception of truth as it lay in wait to molest her standing there, woman of no power next to man of no flesh.

He had come back.

A cold rock of emotion hit her. She drove it inward, let it become the magnet of her every thought, every emotion. There was no pain. Just the beauty of the anger drawing her molecules toward it. Her neck relaxed, her shoulders, her legs, her core. She smiled as she breathed in the elixir of her emotion. This was her emotion, her rock, what held her solid to the ground. She embraced it, letting its crags and splinters give her joy, let it settle within where its pain was only known to Maggie.

When she spoke, she might as well have been asking the time. "What does it feel like when you die? Does it hurt?"

Good thing Larry could read her mind. His jaw hardened. He looked at her with those darkened eyes "Not the dying. By the time you're there, your pain nerves are shut down. Right before the dying isn't pleasant. I remember the pain of the impact and the sting of gravel as it cut my face, but not much else. Right before I died, it was peaceful."

"Too bad. I want the son-of-a-bitch to hurt the whole time I kill him." The rock within smiled.

The first week was surreal. The outside Maggie practiced life in Hornsboro. She smiled at customers, shared a couple of jokes with Ralph at Bif's. Dealing with Will was tough. She met him once for lunch, but drew the line at drinks. And Will at the cabin? Out of the question – for now at least. He probably thought her limits were about him, but Maggie wasn't ready to care. He understood a break. "But make it a short one," he had said. "Time's slipping away, and I miss you." She smiled and agreed. "Just a few days – time for me to regroup." That was the key. Regroup. Get strong enough to fight back.

The dance was to relish the good moments, minutes – second even -- and hide the pain from others on the bad. She had looked her pain in the face, smelled its copper fear. It couldn't hurt her anymore, so locked within had she secured it. She could smell the forest without panic. She could feel the wind and not cringe. How bad could life with Swoozie and Will be? Then she thought about Will, or any man for that matter, touching her, and her skin crawled.

She moved a rocker out to the porch, the chair that she had reclaimed from Swoozie. The porch was her safe play, the one where she had made a deal with herself to use as a healing base. When her body would clutch tight, when she felt his suffocating presence, she would head to the porch. The porch was home base. Even Larry wasn't allowed there.

One week after the attack, Larry stood outside the cabin and watched Maggie. She was parallel to the porch, holding an old fishing reel. A worn bucket set some fifty feet away from her, dab smack in the perennial border.

"What are you doing."

"Casting."

"Casting. Why?"

"Grandpa said before I could catch a big fish, I had to learn how to cast. He wasn't about to let me snag him while we were on the boat." She set her eye on the bucket, pulled her arm back sidearm and flung.

"If you cast, Maggie, don't you need a rod attached to the reel?"

"Nope. Not for practice. I had to use one when I was little, but this is like a golf swing. All body memory." She set the line brake, put her thumb on the reel, pulled her arm back again. "I was always better at sidearm. Grandma could do sidearm and overhead. Used to be jealous, but what the heck, sidearm will catch what you're after as well as any.

"See? It's all in the wrist. Gotta focus." She let go again. "Bingo."

Maggie turned to Larry and held out the reel. "Grandpa had this when you were alive. Quite the antique."

"Quite the funny girl. Let's try this again. "Why are you casting?"

"He made me cry. The bastard stole from me. He stole my assurance that I was strong. He won't steal anymore."

Maggie put the reel in her left hand and ran her right index finger against her thumb. "Had a lot of blisters from keeping that string tight. Couldn't let anything knot up my string.

"That's how it is, Larry my man. Taut string. Perfect form.

"Let's go catch us a fish."

Larry cracked, "Just don't yell at the fish and let them know you're coming."

Maggie let go of one more cast. "Not to worry, my friend. I've swallowed enough pain in the last days to turn me into a shadow. Someone's worried that I'll dig up some real nasty dirt, or find out some real nasty secret." She smiled. "I'll be the shadow that can kick ass and take prisoners."

They had done a lot of walking, Maggie and Larry. He might not have been able to leave the property, but there were paths aplenty. They were in a cluster of wild plum trees overhung with oak and maple just feet away from the jumping tree, a knobby behemoth whose upper branches hung over the water. She walked forward and raised her arm, felt the bark of a childhood friend. "My cousins and I used to scrabble up its trunk and walk the plank," she said. We'd balance on the arms of these branches and then plunge into the cold lake and roar like pirates."

Tracing her way down the trunk with an index finger, she kept on. "When I was twelve, I decided I liked Richie Nesbit. He had a bright green Sting-Ray bike. Right out of the 60's. I could watch him skid out all day long." She stopped at a carving, almost invisible in the gnarls of the bark. "He did a somersault into the lake off one of the upper branches. I came back here later and carved this. Larry peered in. *MW/RN. Forever.* He was the gutsiest kid I ever knew. Wonder what happened to him."

Maggie bent over and picked up a stone. She hurled it into the lake, then slapped her hands against each other in a signal of finality. "Guess its time to get ready and dive in." She grabbed at a tree branch and began climbing, walked foot-over-foot along one of the diving branches and leaped into the lake with a scream. "Geronimo!"

This time when she ran, the red spandex shorts had a little less wiggle room. Amazing how, in a few short weeks, a few short beers with friends could put more span in the spandex.

Maggie stood on the porch, stretching, readying herself for a run, the first one since her arrival day in June, the one that had left her panting. Just like then, little crunches, knots of tension, snapped in her shoulders as she stretched them. And again, her hamstrings wondered what she was thinking.

But this time she was ready to run. This time she knew the pain that would lie ahead. She whisked it aside. What was a little sweat compared to what she had endured. What she had left to do. Morning wetness hovered above the grass. Everywhere, the sound of birds chattering broke through. Maggie looked past the lawn, up the lane where a sun-drenched road waited for her. She finished stretching, padded down the steps and started jogging. Slowly. No sense slipping before she made it off her property. Acorns and twigs crunched under her feet in spite of the morning wetness. As she headed up the lane, the dirt road widened and the trees on both sides thinned. Sun light cut through shadows, its promise of warmth soothing.

She reached the paved road. To the north, where she would head, just shy of the curve, Black-Eyed Susans filled the ditches. Queen Anne's Lace split through the grass on the roadside, tall wisps of green with ivory heads. Maggie breathed in, acknowledging them all, then hit the pavement. The run was strenuous. No doubt of that. But as she ran, she fell into that inner strength that she had found, a gentle strength, not so much worn as armor as it was carried in her core. The attack was behind her now. She was not free of it, no. But its power had loosened its control. Feet against pavement. That was her power now.

Mile one, she started easy, took on her battle with Swoozie. Still, they played the game. Maggie worked to refurbish her home. Swoozie worked to refurbish Swoozie. Time was speeding by and Maggie still needed the old iron bed, dishes, canisters – the list went on. She might even have to work a Monday. Bring it on, boss lady.

Mile two, the spider web of the past. The need to clear her grandfather stretched through her, up her shins, her thighs, the core where her emotion lived. She had not come this far, endured this much, to turn around and crawl back to Chicago. Ida Ann, the beautiful heiress. Ida Ann, the loony old maid. Father. Mob. The biggest question of all – how were these linked to her grandfather? Snatches of possibilities rose up in her mind as she ran, only to twist and tumble and fade before they took form. Midway through the second mile, she had felt her face flush, beads of sweat collect between her breasts. How much was exertion, how much frustration?

Mile three. By now she was full out panting. Her arms and back itched from the sweat. Her legs and chest begged her to stop. Mile three had no agenda other than survival. Thanks the good lord the last of the mile was the downhill trot on her lane.

She reached the porch steps and sat down, pulled off her headband and shook out her hair. Not much moved. It was mostly sweaty strands. She pulled off her shirt, wiped her face, and toweled her hair. Better. The hang of wetness on the ground had gone, replaced by a gentle breeze that cooled her and made her tingle. She jumped up, went inside and grabbed a bottle of iced tea, then came back out and sat on the steps. After chugging half of it, she held the bottle against her forehead, let the cold bring her back to normal, or as normal as a post-running Maggie could be.

Only then did she think about the third problem, the one she had avoided during that last god-awful mile. What to do about Will? Did she even want to do anything about him? The phone calls had stopped. He was true to his word to give her space. But Hornsboro Wisconsin was not big on space. She saw him somewhere every time she went to town. He'd look at her, give a half smile and then look away. She had no anger, no resentment. In fact, she felt sorry for the guy. What they had was broken, but next to what she had endured, Will was no more than a nice guy turned alpha male for a few minutes. Could they put things back together? She let herself feel the sun warming her neck. Yeah, Will would be part of her life again. He filled in too many spaces not to.

She shook her head. Swoozie was an annoyance, no more than minnows nibbling. Will, a piece of tomorrow not yet defined. With Will, the pieces would fall together in whatever pattern they should. No need for direction. Just as her feet had found their cadence, she and Will would find their rhythm in the weeks ahead.

Maggie squared her shoulders. The strength of her feet hitting the pavement had connected her to priorities. Ida Ann and Lou were a commitment. Those two and the bastard who had attacked her. If she were going to cast for the big fish, she would spend her energy on that prize. She grabbed the bottle and clothing, stood up and went inside to shower. Clean body. Clean hair. Good immediate goal.

Then time for the heavy stuff.

Larry sat at the trestle table, leaning back in the chair, Maggie's empty tea bottle twisting back and forth in his hands. His eyes followed Maggie as she paced.

"Are you sure you're ready for this?" Oddly enough, the same thought nagged at her. All the commitment in the world did not a hero make. Motivation, yes. Going out and picking up the mystery trail, another story altogether. Yet within this misgiving was an excitement, an itch to move, to take control, a roiling of desire to set life right again.

Larry spoke. "My bet's on Cal. He's a realtor. Realtors make money off of what they sell. What's seven percent of a few million dollars?"

"Enough to kill for."

"My point exactly."

Maggie nodded. "Let me remind you of the bad news. We're a few days short of four weeks until I go back to Chicago. Time to boogie. I'll pay a visit to the good mayor tomorrow. Tonight I have some other ends to tie up."

"Do I want to know?"

"Probably not."

— *Chapter 30* —

Gooseberry Days. That time in August when townsfolk smiled and tourists poured in. Booths started going up on Thursday night. Arts and crafts booths. Fishing paraphernalia booths. Even one devoted to saving the wolves – which never quite set well with the farmers, but then this was the time of the year to all get along for the sake of the town. The Larrsen family set up first – a matter of respect. In 1978, on a Monday morning, Gert Larrsen, a spry eighty-four and founding member of the Washekca County chapter of Daughters of Norway, had picked up a few groceries at Bif's and headed home in her canary yellow Oldsmobile. By 5:00, when her daughter had stopped in, Gert was nowhere to be found. No car. No groceries. No Gert.

The town scoured the countryside for a solid month. A few postulated a senior citizen getaway. Most shook their heads and looked toward the lake. Gert's eyesight just wasn't what it used to be.

So every year the Larrsen family set up their booth selling gooseberry jam, gooseberry chocolate pound cake, and lefsa next to a basket of flyers asking, *Have you seen this woman?* By now Gert would be well past a century, but no one wanted to discourage a family so rooted in gooseberry tradition.

So life in Hornsboro focused only on preparing for the festivities. Maggie ached to get out and put her plans in order. Unfortunately, for Maggie, Swoozie had big plans for a slow day herself. "Don't you worry about a thing, darlin'. I know it seems like a lull right now, but two days from now the town will be popping, and we'd best be ready." Cinderella's stepmom had surely held that same tone when she talked about cleaning the manor. *Ready* was the definitive word here, as in *tasks that could break your back in the name of a weekend named after orange berries.*

Maggie was up on a stepladder hoisting a bicycle onto a sideboard. She had spent the morning painting it Dunsmore Crème, then wove twinkle lights through the spokes and around the seat and handlebars after the paint had dried. Cute, but what a waste of valuable time. She had to figure out how to haul it up onto the sideboard for display. She had one foot on the sideboard, the other on the ladder, her arms lugging the bicycle into place when the front bell dinged. A customer. She looked up and her brows furrowed. While she shouted out, "Be with you in a second," she gave one final tug. The bike cooperated and stayed level. She leaned it against the wall and climbed down the ladder, glad for the respite. "Can I help you sir?" She had the words out before she even got around to the front of the counter.

The man was the last kind of customer she would have expected, a bald guy, middle-aged, a good thirty pounds overweight, mostly in the belly that strained against his shirt. The folds of his neck hung over each other. On a dog, that might have been cute.

What the heck. A sale was a sale. And since her escapade the other night, she'd better make some sales or Swoozie might regret her decision to keep her on. Painted bicycles only went so far.

The man eyed her she walked toward him. Not the *I need help* kind of eyeing. *More* the *I'm looking into you, not at you. You'd better not be hiding anything* kind of looking.

Smiling broadly, she ratcheted up her perky level. "We have a sales section in the back of the store. All kinds of bargains." She sidled toward a display. "Or can I interest you in some pottery – fresh in from Alberta Williams. She's one of our best sellers."

The man didn't reply, didn't even move his facial muscles one bit. His hands were stuck in his jacket pockets. That was strange enough – a tourist wearing a sports coat on a hot August day. Maybe he was a couple of days early for the Gooseberry Festival, as if an impending Hornsboro holiday might explain dressing up.

He started toward her. Maggie startled – why she would never be able to say – but the back of her neck issued one of those flight warnings that sprang unannounced from deep within.

"You know where I can find Cal Dinsdale?" His voice was deep, abrupt. The guy was from Chicago. Maggie didn't have to even ask. His voice gave him away. Hard core city guy. Fought the consonants coming out of his mouth instead of pronouncing them.

"Cal? His office is just down the street past the bank. Can't miss it. It's a white house with Dinsdale Realty in bold letters on a yard sign. Looking to buy in our fair town?"

"We'll see. Oh. He turned toward the pottery exhibition and pointed. "Nice stuff you have here. Like the fishing design. Never know what you're going to catch in the water."

He started to turn around to leave, stopped and reached into his pocket, pulled out a small white card. "Here's my card. Just to say hello." Held it out more as an order than request. Maggie took it, but before she had time to check it out, he had walked out, the door slamming behind him.

That was not a tourist. Maggie laughed as she held up the card to read the name.

Veraldi Investments the card said. *Real Estate and Finance. Eddie Balconi Sales Representative.*

She walked toward the front of the store and looked out into the street. No strange vehicles. A couple of bikes, three cars, one Winnie's, two belonging people who worked in the bank. Walking back toward the counter, Maggie kept her eyes fixed on the business card she held with her index finger and thumb. Her Chicago friends were searching the Veraldi end. And now a guy from Chicago, a consonant pounding guy, a guy with *Veraldi* on his business card was in town looking for Cal. Why had he stopped here to ask for directions. Her radar dinged and she shuddered. Winnie always said her money was on Cal being the connection to the truth about Lou, but Maggie had figured that was all sour grapes. Now this guy.

Holding the card between her thumb and index finger, she went to the side room to post it on the bulletin board that kept track of messages and notes to self. She had just tacked it up when two hands settled firmly on her shoulders from the back. Maggie was not one to jump, any more than she was one to jog. But jump she did. All the while screaming and flailing her arms. She flung herself around and slapped the intruder.

Will. His head jerked back and his glasses sailed off. A mouse in the corner would have a hard time determining who was more startled. Both of them spoke at once, Maggie a "Oh my god, I can't believe I just did that," Will, a "What the hell!" While Maggie watched, Will bent over and picked up his glasses, took some measured time to straighten up and face the woman he had scared half to death.

Once he was upright, Maggie reached out and touched his arms, smoothed her hands up and down his shirt. Then, biting her lip, she looked directly at his face and straightened glasses that were perfectly set. She finally managed a ragged smile, drew in a deep breath. Will's face was passive but his eyes looked hard. Nice going, she thought, you just let him back into your life and now you tried to beat the crap out of him.

She turned back to the bulletin board and straightened two of the messages. Her hands were trembling. Running her finger along the perimeter, she searched for something equally errant to buy time, pressing into the cork to steady to steady potential spasms.

"Kind of hard to organize things when your can't keep your fingers focused. Here, let me help." Will bent forward and pressed in one of the tacks more firmly. Maggie could smell his aftershave, a sensation smooth and soothing, but the presence of his arm so near her face made her throat tighten. She could feel an unnerving tension in her gut. She tried to shoo it away; she had, after all, just had a run-in with a potential mobster, but her insides refused to relax. At least her fingers had stopped trembling.

Stop it, she told herself. She felt silly, superstitious. You're a grown woman, not some middle-schooler on a first camping trip startled by a squirrel in the middle of the night. Will's hand was still pressed against the tack in the bulletin board, his arm still near her. She swung her hip to the side to bump his, then took his arm and raised it. "You win. I flinched first."

They both laughed at the same time. Will bent over and gave her a kiss on the forehead, just a quick peck. "That means I get to kiss the princess."

"Only if you want to turn back into a frog." Her voiced was a shade too harsh to be purely teasing, but Will gave no reaction. "Just thought I'd drop in and see how you're doing. Swoozie gets a little nuts around this time of the year. Gooseberry Days is Swoozie's answer to Black Friday in Minneapolis, make it or break it time. I noticed the bicycle out there. Last year she wired together branches with gooseberries and hung them clear across the ceiling. Looks like you got off easy."

"Don't even say the words. She's not done with her decorating list yet. She'll probably wire me to the ceiling before this whole thing is over."

"I'll stop in tonight before I head for home, make sure that you're not part of the ambience. Maybe we can stop at Wallie's for a drink."

Maggie had her hands on her hips, her head slightly tilted, her thoughts moving to tonight. Her mind said, *You bet we'll have a drink tonight. I'm gonna rock your world, big guy, with all the news I have. That is if I can I get you to leave so I can get the dish on Mr. Chicago.* Her words were much simpler. "You hold that thought while you're slaving away figuring out how to beat back the bad guys. As soon as my stint as decorator is finished, I'm going to have a chat with the mayor." She put her hands on Will's shoulders and turned him around, then gave him a push. "Now, leave me to my tasks." As Will walked away, Maggie caught herself watching his butt. Nice sensation. At least some things were back to normal.

Will kept an iron control all the way out the door and toward his car. No one had been there to notice the tic in his jaw, hear the slamming of his car door. What the hell was she doing with a business card with the name *Veraldi* and a Chicago address? He gripped the steering wheel and leaned his forehead against it. No. No way could she connect the dots.

Then what the hell was she doing with that card?

Chapter 31

Dinsdale Realty had not changed all that much since Maggie had dropped in on Cal in June. Sure, outside the geraniums were bigger, and the hostas had sent up their purple spikes, but inside, Jesus still smiled from one wall, His beatific image directly across from the sign that promised Hornsboro Haven: Luxury Condos and Golf Course. Evidently Cal promoted that the good Lord wanted progress in their fair community. And there were a few more pictures and blueprints for Hornsboro's stake in resort living.

Cal was standing behind his desk talking on the phone. From the looks of it, all was not well. His face was flushed, and he kept grabbing the bridge of his nose, rubbing it with his thumb and index finger. He didn't even notice her standing inside the doorway, arms folded, mind musing about what was causing the good mayor such consternation.

When he hung up the phone, he rubbed his hands through his hair and let out a long exhale.

Maggie couldn't resist. "Bad news on the housing front or did someone cancel the Gooseberry Days parade?"

"What?" In a fumbling kind of lurch, he looked up at the source of the noise, his face twisted. Maggie expected Cal's politically correct mien, the one that spread across his lower face and worked toward his eyes. Instead, she saw mouth and eyes narrowed with suspicion. This was about to become fun.

Chameleon Cal took over. "Maggie Witkowski! You are such a trickster. Come right on in. I've had one problem after another and would love the attention of a pretty girl to set the day right." This was the old Cal, the one with the serpent smile and sure-fire path to happiness for anyone willing to pay.

Maggie walked over, grabbed a chair, and sat herself down across from him. She plopped her purse onto the desk and started rummaging. "Swoozie asked me to bring over some flyers for the upcoming weekend. She's sure that you'll be besieged with visitors who'll pick one up and dash over to the store." Shaking her head, she pulled out the flyers, leaned forward, and held them out to Cal. "That woman thinks what's coming is Christmas, Fourth of July, and St. Patty's Day all rolled into one."

Cal put his hands onto his knees and bent forward to meet her enthusiasm. "That pretty much sums it up. The whole idea of the celebration started years ago. The town council thought we needed something to bring people in as a last hurrah of the summer. Mabel Wente had baked a couple of gooseberry pies to serve at the council meeting, one thing led to another, and what do you know, we had ourselves an official holiday." Cal lit up his naughty smile. "Good thing Mabel hadn't brought over pickled pig's feet or Rocky Mountain oysters."

While she set the advertisements down, Maggie gave a perfunctory laugh and then straightened up. She smoothed her hands over her purse and looked up at Cal. "I bet this year's festival will be especially exciting, with all that's going on with your project." She turned her head toward the wall holding the resort plans. "But I can't believe the old codgers who are worried about the Haven. It's too beautiful to be anything but a selling point for our town." Even with her head turned, Maggie could feel the mayor's pride – or was it the aura of impending wealth from managing such a project?

"Those are the same Luddites whose grandparents worried about building a bank and letting cars come into town. Hornsboro would be an ice house and a bar if they had their way." Cal's voice was downright professorial. He was starting to roll.

"I bet Ida Ann's somewhere looking at this and smiling." Maggie still had her head turned. The words were spoken simply, made to sound like an afterthought. The best way to sneak in a bomb.

"For sure. She was very generous." He sounded like he meant it.

Turning her head back to meet Cal's eyes, she shook her head, just the slightest movement. "This is certainly a key year for you. Will said . . . "The mention of the lawyer's name caught his attention before Maggie could get out her third word." Something glittered in his eye, and his lids became hooded. Maggie caught the change and plowed on.

" . . . the legal time limit for searching for an heir is ten years. Isn't that time period up now?"

"As a matter of fact, it is. August 18. Ten years exactly since we found poor Ida." Cal said "poor Ida" like it was the title of a bad country Western song, then, as he sat in his chair, he lifted his posture and struck an evangelist pose. "We have that lovely lady to thank for what could be the best investment in this entire area of Wisconsin."

Lovely lady. Hard concept to grasp. Maggie gave a short prayer to Ida Ann, the young girl of the pictures, the one who had saved a lock of her baby's hair. It was as much a prayer asking for forgiveness as asking for grace.

"Every time I see what Hornsboro might become, the sweep of potential progress, I think about how she died. So sad. What was on her mind the night she swallowed those pills?

"Little is known about Ida's state of mind on the last day of her life." The words bit the air.

"Ah yes, the unknown truth. The state of mind of a spinster missing a few billion neurons." Maggie shook her head. "That's the image of poor Ida Ann burned into everyone's collective mind, isn't it Cal?" Maggie reached toward her purse, unzipping it slowly. She couldn't see Cal's face, but she could picture him, dressed in pure sanctimony, wondering what crazy Maggie Witkowski wanted. This was so fun.

With her left hand, she pulled the business card out of the purse and held it at eye level. "I guess what has me going about this, why I'm so glad to talk to you this afternoon – other than the pure pleasure of your conversation, of course – is this business card. A man stopped into the store this morning. He didn't buy anything. He was just looking for you, Cal. Had to find the mayor, he said right before he handed me his card."

She studied the card. "Eddie. That's it. Eddie Balconi, a sales rep from Chicago." She lifted her eyes skyward.

"That's right, Mr. Balconi and I are working together on the Haven deal." His tone was a studied neutral. Maggie could hear the subtext. *What does this woman want?*

"That makes perfect sense. The whole point of Hornsboro, in the first place, was to provide a place for Chicago businessmen to relax. How fitting that the granddaughter of its most illustrious citizen reclaim its purpose."

"I really don't think Harlan Turnball's initial intentions have anything to do with our modern resort."

"Really? I think they have everything to do with it. See, I keep thinking about a name, a Chicago name, one very important for the Turnballs, one evidently still important to you, Mr. Mayor. Let me see." She raised the card as if trying to discover a name she knew so well. Then it was ready to come out, that magic word that had tripped over Maggie's tongue waiting to fill the office air. "Here it is. Veraldi."

Maggie gave her favorite smile, the sweet one that said, *Gotcha*, while she waited for Cal's reply. He looked at her, his face a mask of stoicism, except for the slightest tic at the edge of his right eye. "Veraldi? That's the name of one of the backers of the project."

"It's also the name on a birth certificate. One that I have in my possession as a matter of fact." Cal's eyebrows furrowed and he drew back. Maggie went for the kill. "Veraldi is the name of the father of Ida Ann's illegitimate child, the one she gave birth to in Ohio when she was supposedly too distraught over her mother's death to stay in Hornsboro."

Maggie waited for the impact, glee lodged in the back of her throat. Her face was ice.

Cal's face matched her stare down, that is, except for the eye tic, the one in his right eye, that started to tap dance. Some kid outside was yelling a taunt against another. The high pitched sound floated through the screen in the window, words unclear, but intent right on.

Cal sat back in his chair, his brow once again furrowed, his lips pulled together, his hands folded in front of the lower part of his face. He tapped his index fingers against his mouth, once, twice before he let out a breath.

"Let's see. You're saying that Ida Ann Turnball had a child, fathered by someone named Veraldi." The statement hung in the air. This was too much fun to warrant a comment. Cal rose, his body bent forward, hands clenching the edge of his desk. His face morphed into rage. That mouth, so thoughtfully pursed just moments ago, morphed with Hulk like action. His jaw jutted out, lips tightened. His eyes darkened and narrowed.

"Who the hell do you think you are? And to whom do you think you are speaking?"

Maggie met his stare coolly.

"I think I'm the granddaughter of a man who's been royally screwed by this town, that's who I think I am." Fiery words delivered in utter calmness. "And I think I'm talking to someone involved in said screwing."

Cal sat there stunned, perhaps by the insult, perhaps by the insight of this intruder.

Maggie reveled in a Cal subdued into silence. She had only begun.

"My grandfather, the finest man I have ever known, the kind of *Christian* a pompous wannabe like you could never hope to be – has been slung onto a cross by this town. So if you're walking around thinking you're the hand of the Almighty because you've brought in some rock-solid project to this burg, I'd suggest you look under those rocks. Lots of creepy crawlies there, my friend."

The good mayor leaped out of his chair, fists clenched. While his eyes locked locked onto her, two words spewed from him like bullets aimed at a mortal enemy. "Ms. Witkowski!" But Maggie had turned and was walking to the door, outwardly a study in calm.

"Don't you think you can sashay in here and accuse me of whatever, then leave!" Maggie could picture his face. Purple. Matched his tie. When she left, she made sure not to slam the door. That would be rude.

Chapter 32

Hot, humid morning, sitting on the porch floor, jawing with a ghost. Rural life in Hornsboro at its best. Maggie took a swig of beer, let the coolness slip down her throat. She drew her lips inward and closed her eyes, the images of yesterday's meeting with Cal sliding by her in a row.

"Cal's probably rounding up his hatchet men as we speak. I'll be wearing cement blocks by tonight." She took another drink and set the bottle down on the step below her seat. "Might as well enjoy the morning while I'm still breathing." She leaned forward, rubbed her hands against the sides of the bottles. "Food for the fishes. That'll be me. Maggie Witkowski, bass bait."

Larry shook his head. "Buck up. This is no time for weak knees."

Laughing, Maggie kicked her legs out straight. "Just funnin' with you, buddy. No weak knees here, my man. I'm on a roll." She straightened back into a boat pose balancing on her sit bones , arms and legs out, and closed her eyes, her voice a sigh. "I am one with the mission."

With a whoosh, Larry was in back of her, leaning over, his hands on her shoulders lightly pressing. "Just make sure that the mission doesn't eat you for lunch."

Maggie jolted at the feeling of his hands on her, a warm sensation just short of electric, then fell flat onto her back, legs still straight up but balance mere memory. Larry had wisped to the path in front of the porch steps and watched, mouth smug in spite of a darkening of his eyes.

While she righted herself and crossed her legs, she grabbed the beer bottle and held it in front of her. "If you were solid, I'd smack you with this." She slammed it down onto the porch floor, taking the brunt of the impact in her fingers, then waggled a finger at him.

"You have been on me for weeks now to solve this thing so that you can skip out of here. Now you're warning me?"

"The idea was that you find out why this town turned on your grandfather. You're not supposed to make the entire town turn on you."

"Too late. In for a penny, in for a pound. Not that many days ago, I was jogging, my mind focusing on what's important. Solid commitment. Since then, I've been caught breaking and entering and I've given the town's mayor reason to off me." She cocked her head and studied the beer bottle. After another swig of beer she said, "Maybe I can get the city council to come after me too."

Beer bottle in hand, she pushed to her feet, turned toward the cabin's door and stomped forward, then turned to address her partner, wrapped in smugness. Some things were simply too funny to evoke fear. "I'm going to take a shower and give myself a pedicure. If they're going to find my body, it'll be clean, and I'll have good toes." She headed into the cabin.

Larry stood watching her, his face drawn, tension firm at his jawline. He took his ring out of his right pocket and stood there twisting it, concentration on thoughts known only to him. Had Maggie been watching, she would have teased him about anxiety or a guilty conscience. But she was off readying herself for a little quality girl time, not one inkling or question about a ghost standing outside her home, twisting a ring, deep in whatever thoughts had webbed him.

Between the time she stepped out of the shower and slipped into a well worn t-shirt and shorts, Maggie was well on her way to girl time fever. Yesterday had been such a rush watching Cal swim up to the bait on her hook while she yanked him in. Sure, this morning, she'd worried about being the victim for a nanosecond, wanted to run back to Chicago even if that was where the bad guys lived, but a surge of gloating had swatted that fear away like it was a pesky gnat.

Revel time. That's what she wanted. What she deserved.

Right now, sunshine was shafting through the windows, her hair and body was clean, and no pushy ghost hovered near to heap guilt in buckets or give orders like she was his private PI. Her biggest task was to choose between *I Wanna Be Red* and *Plum Dilly Delicious* for her toes. She spread a towel on the floor in front of her chair, grabbed the heel scraper, and sat down ready to work her feet toward nirvana.

Twenty minutes later, her feet were not only happy, they were downright gleeful. Smooth, creamed, toes polished. She sat back in the chair, legs jutted out in front of her to admire her handy work.

"Are we done now?"

Maggie jumped, then lurched forward. While her eyes widened and her arms flailed, she let out a shriek and her heels smacked the wood floor. *One. Two. Eight hundred and thirty.* She scanned the room, "Where are you? And why do you have to ruin my every relaxed moment?"

"Because you *are* relaxed." Larry materialized in front of her, hands in his pockets, feet shoulder width apart and solidly planted. "That means there's a slight chance that you'll listen to what I have to say."

Oh for the love of God, he was going to be at it again.

"Larry. Lighten up. Have a seat. We're the good guys. We're winning." She wiggled her toes for effect. "And my feet are a thing of beauty."

He stared at her face, stared at the floor, brought his head up again. But not a word. This was not a guy who appreciated the significance of good toesmanship.

"There's more to it than just clearing his name." His words spilled out like a small boy's confession.

Maggie lowered her feet to the floor and leaned over, hands folded, forearms on her knees. "What in the hell are you talking about?

"I haven't told you everything."

The edges of her shoulders stiffened, tension sluicing toward her neck. Her eyes locked onto his.

"I want you to understand," he said. "I really thought you didn't need to hear this. The more I listened to you, the more I believed clearing Lou's name would be enough.

"That was before this thing started getting dangerous."

Dangerous? No. She was done with that. Done with checking out her closets when she came home. Done with letting the gnawing in her gut and throat keep her awake at night. She had climbed more than that pile of furniture at Swoozie's to let Larry get to her now.

An intuitive snatch of dread clawed inside of her. She packed it down.

"If you take more than five more seconds to tell me what I don't know, I'll pack up and leave you here to float in limbo. I swear I will."

"Your grandfather was murdered."

While a warm pine-scented breeze blew through the window, the words hung there in front of Larry. Maggie would not draw them to her. Her face blanched, her limbs tightened. When she spoke, the words barely moved from her mouth as if they were mere wisps too fragile to mix with the air . "No way. Lou Witkowski? Murdered?" Maggie Witkowski stood up slowly. Her jaw were clenched, teeth pressed against each other, feet and fisted hands grounded. But her posture was perfect as she moved toward the cabin door and opened it, held onto it like an old hag borne onto a cane.

Still, she mumbled, "You're not just dead, you're nuts."

She stayed perfectly erect as she walked across the threshold and let the door slip shut, faced the lake, her eyes taking in the spot where evil had been done to her. What did it matter now? She stayed standing on the front porch while the beauty of a world too naïve or too uncaring continued to play. Sunlight hit the water, rays shooting across the blue. Dragonflies romped near the dock. A hawk swept across the lake, its flight a poem in and of itself.

While the beauty gathered outside, Maggie only knew a sense of numbness standing there at the window waiting for Larry's news to settle into a reaction.

Chapter 33

On any given day, all sots of news could have jolted her. The fundamentalist minister out on Goose Grove Lake could have been caught playing spank-the-walleye. The Swinton boys could have stopped spitting Doritos at Maude Elway's mailbox. Ralphie Winnows could have decided to ask out that sweet Ellie Carsten. Sixteen years of flirting was long enough.

But nothing had prepared Maggie for this.

Murdered.

Her grandfather had been murdered.

Tsunamis must feel like this. The sucking of water toward a fissure somewhere deep. The force of energy unleashed as a wave hurled, gathering energy. The inevitable geyser flaying the skin of whatever surrounded the explosion. Maggie felt it all. Not water. No. Emotion. A rumble of emotion at first, sucked down to places where other anger bided its time.

Weeks ago, she thought she had felt the worst pain of her life. It had smothered her, driven her to go within, wrap herself in a blanket and rock until she could face its trauma and own it. So compartmentalized she was, so sure that could carry on and be just fine. Now this. This pain hurled, tore at her insides. This pain was shock, the shock of reality fragmenting around her. The shock that she had played at solving a mystery like she was Nancy Drew, after the bad guys and full of hubris, bad guys who called her grandpa names while a heinous truth lay buried.

Murdered. Someone had murdered Lou Witkowski. Someone in this town had watched her, a silly twit making vows she had kept half-heartedly while she sold trinkets and made out with the local golden boy.

The phone call. The rocks. The garbage. The attack. They all took on a new light of viciousness. Each one its own circle of hell. Even the attack she could handle. It was against her. But her grandfather? She shook with the morphing of this new reality.

While Larry watched her, standing near the window, a nimbus of sunlight outlining his form, Maggie sat on the floor. She was surrounded by all that she had loved from her childhood, and those bits of girlish beauty she played with as a woman. Who cared? All that Maggie saw, all that she felt was fury at a world bathed in beauty and violated by the caprice of some mad man. She sat on the floor, pounding at the boards with her fists while she wailed for a world gone wrong.

The onslaught of the guilt came in a wash -- the wasted time, the wallowing and sarcasm and the self-deception of her summer. She reached up to grab a pillow from the chair, sank her head into its form whether to buffer her sobs or capture the wetness of her tears. Tears for her lost childhood, her grandparents, her own pain, a pain webbed into ugliness begun on an afternoon of blood years ago. Lou had not lost consciousness and fallen, hit his head on those rocks. Someone had killed him.

She had been joking about Cal coming after her, tossing her into a lake – joking about it while she wore her confrontation with Cal like a badge of honor. Her shoulders sank and the jaw that had been so tight moments ago trembled.

"You've got some explaining to do." For all she knew, she was talking to an empty room. Oh wait. She was here even if Larry was gone. But how could she explain herself, her hubris. That was explanation every bit as incriminating as Larry's.

The words floated from the back. They reached out and covered her like a pall.

"I knew I'd have to get to this point. Deep down I knew. I just never knew how to get the words out." He stopped. "I still don't."

"I'll bite my tongue while you figure it out. Take your time. The pain will feel good." Maggie looked around the cabin. There was a large ding on the trestle table leg. Funny, she had never noticed that before.

She hadn't noticed a lot of things.

The rug in front of the fireplace was dingy. When Grandma Jean had woven it, the colors had been so bright. Now they lay there, aged and tired.

Funny. That's how she felt right now. The pine floor had a few scratches. Maggie had thought about refinishing it, but each mar was a piece of history, a contact from someone who had been part of her world. Erase the scratch, erase the imprint of someone who had loved her.

She pushed herself up from the floor and turned to face her ally. Motioning toward the table, she said, "Have a seat. We have some work to do." She kept her eyes locked on Larry. Funny how he didn't have to pull out a chair. He just was there. Kind of like her now. No movement. Just there. She churned over possibilities, the same way she had been churning questions since she found out the truth about Lou.

"Ralph Winnows found him," she said, as if she were realizing this for the first time. "Said he had fallen, hit his head. Bad heart. No one questioned. No suspicion, no autopsy. No clues."

"Would this Ralph guy have any reason to hurt your grandfather?"

"Ralph? No. He and Grandpa were friends. Besides, Ralph was not like the rest of the Winnows brood. He had issues hunting squirrels. Hated blood." Maggie thought about the Ralph she knew. She also wondered if there were a Ralph she didn't know.

"Just a minute," she said while she stood up and walked into the kitchen to grab pen and paper. When she sat down, she started the list. *Ralph Winnows.* She looked at Larry. "Let's go back to what the Judges told you. They're the ones with all the answers." Unsaid was the addition, *them and the killer.*

"Lou was killed for doing a good deed for another, a sad soul who needed him."

"'Sad soul' is Ida Ann. We've known that all along."

"Find the deed, find the offender."

Maggie drew boxes and circles, joined them with arrows, her hand unconsciously seeking possibilities. "Ralphie's family owns the property next to the Turnballs. It'd be part of the buy out if there's any development." She tapped the pen against the table. "What if *deed* has a different meaning? What if it's land? She wrote down *property connection to Ida Ann?* under Ralph's name. Good thing she and Will were back in good grace with each other. He could do the research.

Would he wonder why? Clearing Lou's name had been a project they shared. But his murder?

Maggie's hand moved the pencil around her notation, more graffiti on the paper as if the answer needed to flow from her mind through the pencil and onto the paper. When she was done, all she had was a mess. That and determination. She would talk to Will. As soon as he got back to town.

Chapter 34

The news of Maggie taking on Cal took a good twenty-four hours to spread. After all, a visit from the Witkowski girl and a snit from Cal were not earth shattering, especially given that the festival was right upon them. Still, Irene Cmelick's kitchen window had a great view of Dinsdale Realty, and since it had been open on a fine August day when Maggie slipped over to Cal's after work, Irene had been intrigued enough to stay stationed – just in case. Mercy, the comings and goings of that man. A body never knew who was going to show up.

When the noise began, Irene not only saw Cal stomp out of his office, she heard the slam of the door and the tone of his muttering. She watched him connect on his phone and heard what sounded suspiciously like cussing. From Cal!

She would have loved to understand his words, but she would have had to go outside outside, and that would have been prying. Instead, she watched and let her mind dance with possibilities. Then she headed toward the phone to call her best friend, Janiece Spratt.

"I'm telling you, sister, our mayor used the you-know-what word more than once! And him always complaining to the school board to control hoodlum cussing. And take the Lord's name in vain? I couldn't hear the words clearly, but I can read lips enough to know that kind of language when it's spewing. I'm surprised his hostas didn't curl."

Janiece called Elvira Holm who called Annie Poremba. By then it was past 9:00, so the calling waited until the next morning to start up again. By mid-morning – just about the time Maggie was polishing her toes in happy oblivion – Winnie heard the news from Marv.

He had slid into the kitchen at the café while she rolled out pie dough, the canary that he had proverbially swallowed supplying a most naughty grin.

"Guess Maggie put a burr up Cal's butt yesterday. Came right out and accused him of being tied to a bunch of crooks. folks say she even accused him of fathering Ida Ann's child."

"Crook I can see. Always thought that of the old fart. But fathering a child? That'd be kind of tough seeing as he wasn't even born yet."

Marv scratched his head and frowned. "Hadn't thought about that. Arithmetic was never my strong point. Okay, guess Cal can't be the dad." He smiled. "But he can be the bad guy. And Maggie sure gave it to him."

Ah yes, so many of Hornsboro citizens were joined in the thrill of a tiff. Nothing like juicy tidbits to liven up a slow late summer couple of days.

In another part of the town, however, someone else was pondering the gossip, someone not nearly as amused as the neighbors, someone who ignored the idiocy of speculation and concentrated, rather, on truth and its implication. Will's breath ran hot and harsh, his hands pounded, his teeth gritted like grindstones against fresh wheat.

"That bitch! She's a Pandora, stupid woman, sitting on her box of woes, fingers aching, ears wet with the need to listen inside.

Maggie was not a myth. Before long, she might open the box. Only there will be no hope.

"I should have killed her. I should have beat her fat mouth shut, pounded her head against the rocks while I had her on the ground, broken her wind pipe and cut out her tongue.

She'll ruin everything."

The words, coarse with rage, continued, spread like plague. The creak of the floor echoed the wrath as footsteps followed the sound, matching the tone. Finally, the speaker sat down, crossed one leg and held on at the knee, hands folded, a slow smile stretching lips.

"I'll be coming for you Maggie Witkowski. Soon. So soon.

Hear me in the crunch of leaves under my feet. Smell the want I have for touching your throat before my hand chokes the arrogance from you. Taste your own fear that rises within you as you watch me kill you."

— *Chapter 35* —

⊰≈⊱

Today, the official start of three days of celebration, the weather more than cooperated; it opened its arms in blessing. Blue sky, a drop in humidity, just enough warmth to appreciate the stately pines and ash lining a lake streaked with sunlight and shadow into a work of art all its own.

At 8:45, Maggie stood behind the long wooden counter, ostensibly ready to meet and greet. Swoozie swept through the store, nudging and tucking at the products already perfectly displayed. She was decked out in her silver Glinda outfit, wrists, neck, and ankles wrapped in strings of garnet – not quite the color of gooseberries, but close enough. "We're going to have all sorts of folks here today. Be ready to do your magic."

Maggie wanted magic alright. Just not the kind her boss had in mind. It was August. Full blown dogs days. That time when summer began to say goodbye. The morning light waited longer to visit. The evening approached sooner. And all light lost the edge of June, diffused as a reminder to make the most of now.

She felt a hunger for action. So many pieces coming together, but still there was just this mental exercise.

"I'd give a penny for your thoughts, but from the look on your face, they'd probably cost me a dollar."

Will. On her mind. At her door. Maggie hadn't even heard the bell ring, much less sensed him.

"Hey you. My first customer."

"Thought I'd check in and see how things are going."

"Going?" She flung out her arm. "They're going great. We're armed and ready to take advantage of another Hornsboro celebration."

"That's not what I meant. I came back from Stansbury last night and heard that, once again, you're the talk of the town."

Waving a spray of gooseberries like a fan, Maggie teased, "Little old me? Why you naughty boy, Will Bentley. Watch yourself or I'll have to swat you with my berries." She tapped his shoulder with her spray.

Will shook his head. "Just try not to get arrested. For you, that's a good day." On his way out, he said to the ceiling, "Patience Lord. Give me patience." Good thing he was laughing.

Maggie called after him. "Don't get too busy. I need a lawyer."

Will stopped in his tracks and turned around, gave her his 'not again' look.

Maggie laughed. "No worries. Just a little research on a property issue." She watched his face cloud. "Go. No big deal. Talk to you later."

The day sped by. Tourists. Townies with friends and relatives. By mid afternoon, Maggie's feet were begging for mercy, and her back threatened revenge. The bustle of people meandered toward the park where the entertainment pavilion stood. The Sons of Norway had organized a show, just as they did every year. Hannah Jacobsen and her cousins had traveled all the way from Eau Claire to open the show. They were the Scandinavian answer to the VonTrapp Family singers, and sure to be a hit.

Just as Maggie turned away from the counter and headed for the back room for a cup of coffee, the customer bell rang. She closed her eyes and let out a sigh, careful to hide her thoughts from the potential customer, then turned around.

There, on the threshold stood Eddie Balconi. Evidently he had no interest in Norwegian folk music. But he had an interest in something, judging from the look on his face. Maggie thought of *Vampire Diaries*, bad guys who had to be invited in. Only this wasn't a television show.

"Mr Balconi, right? Here to look at our fishing motifs again?"

A trace of a smile flicked across Balconi's face. He might as well have bared his teeth. "Good memory young lady. Ms. Witkowski, isn't it?"

Somehow Maggie knew that was no guess. Balconi edged his way forward, his hands touching merchandise he had no intention of buying. Maggie watched his hands lightly touching the objects, his index and middle fingers playing with edges, his thumb following in kind. Her throat pulsed. She looked past him at the street. Empty. Silent. No sound there, not even the waft of music.

"Can I help you?" Her voice suggested pleasantry. Her stomach felt sourness.

Balconi picked up a mug. Lime green and orange. Yellow flowers on it. "Thing about pretty things like this. They break." He held it out in front of him and dropped it.

"Oops." His grin reminded Maggie of a picture in a children's book she had once seen of a cobra ready to pounce. She'd wondered why someone would scare kids that way. Right now she wasn't scared, though. She was pissed.

"Oops? Perhaps you didn't take a look at the sign on the door. 'You break it, it's yours.' Usually we mean it for children."

"You're a funny lady. Maybe even a brave one." He stepped on one of the shards from the cup and ground it under his feet. "Just don't be stupid. Big lips sink ships and all that." As he walked to the door, he waved. "Cal sends his regards."

Maggie went to the back room to get a broom and dustpan. Her hands were shaking. Should she tell Will about this guy?

Duh. He'll go all ballistic and want to take charge.

Maybe that's not such a bad idea. You can't solve a mystery when you're dead.

Chapter 36

Will Bentley was moving quickly now, this dark mass in a canoe stalking the lake. The oar dipped into the water quietly, hardly a splash breaking the hush of the night. Quarter moon covered with wisps of clouds. No stars. Good thing he knew his way. Boulders jutted out from the shoreline like humps of a black sea monster ready to slink into the depths of the lake. He was five minutes past Harp Wallace's place.

He had brought the bowling pin, set it next to him on the floor of the canoe, its rounded top touching against his leg. Perhaps he'd use it to bash in her head. He chuckled at the thought. Keep it in the family. She had told him she wanted it the first time he met her, that day back in June at Swoozie's. She might just get it now.

He sat in his boat and smiled at the thought. Maggie had some legal issues she had said. Couple of concerns. Oh sweetheart, if only property deeds were your biggest trouble.

He tied the canoe up to the dock. No need to worry about a quick getaway. Soon there would be one live figure on the place instead of two. While he climbed up the ladder, each hand-over-hand movement spurred a surge of excitement, until he stood strong at the top, feeling the cool of August in Wisconsin. The pier stretched toward the cabin like a bridal path. No more Will the patient lover. Will the friend. Will, the dolt without a scrotum. He tipped his face upward to honor the truth of the real Will Bentley.

He left the bowling pin in the canoe. More fun to just use his hands. Pretty soon Lou and Jean wouldn't be the only Witkowskis in the graveyard. Or what the heck. Maybe he could dump her in the lake.

On the way up to the cabin, he crouched down at his favorite spot, filling his hands with the leaves and twigs and dirt. His mind could smell her terror from that night, taste the agony of her helplessness. He let himself chuckle, just a soft laugh, one that he felt in his groin, his hands. So much to do. He stood up and headed for her and his pleasure.

Maggie startled when she saw him standing inside the doorway. "Will. I didn't hear your car." She had just come out of the kitchen carrying a basket of laundry. When she jumped, the clothes on the top jumped as well. Amusing. If things went according to plan, he could use those towels on top to wipe up the blood.

"Sometimes I like to be a man of surprise." His voice was harsh, monotone. Her face changed all at once, scrunched itself up, eyes wary. That was the thing about Maggie. Her body language. A guy knew where he stood even before she did. And knowing her would be especially important tonight. A man must know his lover's mood, especially when he plans to choke the life out of her.

Maggie's hands clutched the handles of the laundry basket. Will was here, in front of her. The feral Will. Will, but not Will. Back to the Will from that awful wine dousing night. Normal Will would be smiling at her clear to her eyes, some cute guy quip ready. Nothing about this Will smiled. In a small part of her brain, she reinforced this Will to the one who had so shocked her that one night not so long ago, detected it in his bland eyes and the way he tilted his head. She felt the press of that thought, like a headache looking for a channel. The floor boards beneath her feet felt rotten. She could fall through any time now.

Knock it off Witkowski. You've got fight or flight going full throttle here just because you didn't expect him. Friends can drop in unannounced.

She wondered where Larry was.

Will took three steps forward, slow steps, like something on the prowl, an implied sense of the feral in his movement. His hands were in the pockets of his chinos. Any second now, she told herself, he would break into that silly smile and say, "Gotcha!" She edged toward the pine table and set her basket down. It slid across the wood easily. She held onto the handle with her right hand.

He didn't say anything. Just moved toward the table, pulled out a chair and sat down. Through the window, the porch light surrounded him in an eerie yellow. His shoulders were well lit, but his face was cast in shadows. Even shadowed, now his eyes bored into hers. His smile was a thin line. He leaned back, his feet planted solidly on the floor under the table.

Maggie eyed him while she spoke. "So. What's up?" Her tone was friendly even as her hand clutched at the plastic of the basket's handle. She tightened her grip. The edge pressed her thumb, a good feeling. The pain of the rough plastic countered the stoning of her stomach.

Will shrugged, the one side of his mouth scrunching up, typical old Will. Maggie allowed herself to breathe while he bantered back, "Not much. Thought I'd bring a little late night Gooseberry Days celebration out to your place. We didn't have much time to talk today."

Maggie felt a touch of comfort. Her relationship with Will was undefined right now, but she knew she could count on his friendship.

Couldn't she?

She looked through the screen door onto the porch. The porch light was coated inside with dead bugs. How did they get in there? Why hadn't she noticed that before? She'd have to clean the light. As soon as Will left.

His voice brought back her focus. "The thing is, Maggie, in one short summer you've managed to turn this town upside down. You rode in here, an outsider, and took over the place. Hornsboro folk don't like their banal little lives askew."

Banal? Askew? A squeeze of indecision gripped her. No way did Will use fancy words. He was the original Opie goes to law school. Her face registered surprise even as she stayed silent.

Will sat back in his chair, hands folded across his middle, thumbs tapping. "This whole time I have been so impressed with you. You grab onto a project and hang on until the end," He shook his head. "Such loyalty you have. I never sensed that at first. Thought you'd be in and out and back to the big bad city."

"That was pretty much the plan. At least until figured out that I had to work to buy back my own inheritance."

On *inheritance*, Will's lips tightened just slightly, then pulled back. Something was bugging him, something beyond anything Maggie knew. What did Will care about a bunch of furniture at Swoozie's?

"Yeah," she continued. "The minute I figured out that my mother had turned over my cabin stuff into consignment, I . . . "

"That's the thing about mothers." Will said the work like he might have been saying *serial killer*. "They act like it's all their's, like the pixie dust settled on their heads and everyone else is inconsequential to their life story."

Will had never as much as mentioned his family. Now this. Maggie inhaled deeply, then nodded. "And here I thought all we had in common is a love of red licorice."

"Oh Maggie, my dear, we have so much more in common, so much that you still need to discover." Maggie had planned on sitting down. Bad idea. She forced herself not to look at the door.

He still had his thumbs tapping, a slow cadence. Maggie tried to reimagine him as Opie, maybe even Atticus Finch then slapped herself inwardly. Most definitely neither the innocent Opie nor the good Atticus. More and more this night screamed *weird*, like she had been transported to the black hole Hornsboro where everyone was an opposite. She looked at Will's hands. They were broad and strong, two scrapes on the right hand knuckles.

"What did you do to your hand?"

He held out his hand and looked at it. "This? Just practicing."

"OK, Will. Enough with the mystery." Calm, Witkowski. Key concept here. She did her best wry smile. "By now you should be feeding me cheesy jokes and laughing about some dumb cluck down in Eau Claire. Instead you're musing about scrapes and practice. What? A gang fight with a bunch of fascist law boys? Duke it out instead of settle?"

Still watching that hand, he tssked like an old biddy scolding a child while he shook his head. "I worry about you and that mouth of yours. That smart mouth could get you hurt." He laughed, rural boy lawyer relaxed and mulling over a friend's mishap while he flexed his fingers. "Oh yeah, that's right. You're going to get hurt."

Outside, a rabbit screamed in the night air. A hawk was happy. That or a feral cat. Will looked up. Maggie hurled the clothes basket at Will running while she slammed open the screen door and pounded down the porch steps into the night. "Bitch!" cut through the air from within the house. She ran blindly, caught in the thatch of leaves and brush that crusted the woods' floor. Not a good night to be wearing flip-flops. She grabbed at her shoes and threw them off. Cut feet beat slowed feet. The boat house. It was no more than a shot away. She could hide there and think. She sped toward the lake hoping that speed outweighed stealth as an escape mechanism.

Where the hell was Larry?

"Maggie. Sweet Maggie. Come out, come out, come out and play." The words floated in the darkness.

What the hell. Who was this man who called himself her friend? Maggie waded into the water. Her feet, legs, clothes, took on the lake. The wet promised hiding. She swam until she reached the water's far end of the boat house and grabbed onto the wood skirting the building, went hand over hand, then sank underneath the old behemoth, her memory guiding her in the darkness. Her feet and hands found the metal first, and she grabbed, pulling herself forward, then she crouched in the old lift brace on the underside of the boat house, her body in the water, her arms wrapped around the wood poles, only her head out of the water. Even as water lapped at the edge of the shore, she listened for Will's voice.

When it came, it was from the rim of the trees near the shore. "If you come out, I'll solve all those mysteries that have been driving you. Let's start with Ida Ann. You always like to call her the old tart." His laugh had an edge to it. "I actually prefer the term grandmother, even though I couldn't use it."

Ida Ann was his grandmother? Maggie almost lost her balance on that piece of information.

"That's right. Surprise. Surprise. She was my granny. She was also a gullible old bag, stupid and needy." The voice came nearer. He was on his way to the boat house. Maggie heard the crunch of his footsteps as he neared the pier. "So easy. 'Oh Miss Turnball, come on in and have a seat. Can I fix you some of that chamomile tea you so like.' Wasn't I the good grandson. Too bad she only knew me as a young lawyer fresh out of law school and wanting the small town life. 'Wholesome' she called me." He paused. Maggie could imagine his expression, those eyes of his searching.

"So I kept that tea coming. Too bad I couldn't fix her hemlock. But then, I couldn't have talked her into all those investments that made so much money -- for me. Except for that one night when I brought her tea to her bedroom and she spilled her heart to me. Oh how she loved that Lou Witkowski." He laughed. "That's not all she spilled. So sad when she conked out. Tea all over that lovely bedding."

Ida Ann in her bedroom. Spilled tea. Could such a thing be possible? Did Will feed drugs to Ida Ann. Did he kill her?

Then the chilling nudge. If he killed his grandmother, whom else did he kill?

"Shocked my dear? How could I kill my own grandmother? Aren't I just consumed with guilt?" His taunts stopped. Collecting his thoughts? His voice broke through once again. "Guilt comes in all degrees, sweet Maggie, and I can't rustle up enough for a woman who gave away my birthright. And any asshole who threatened to expose me."

Silence hung in the air between them. Somewhere in the dark, bull frogs croaked their songs, but Will was done -- at least for the moment. Was he waiting for a reply? He'd killed his grandmother. A germ of memory coursed through her more as emotion than facts, tied itself to her question -- who else? Lou had been murdered. The bastard had murdered her grandfather. She gritted her teeth as rage filled her and gripped the edge of the posts, scraped her hands against the wood crusted with nature's refuse. *You bastard. If you hurt Lou, I'll.* . . . She couldn't finish the thought. But she sure as hell felt it, burrowing into her like the rot and the ancient gnarl of wet wood.

"I could tell you about how I had a difficult childhood -- bastard son of a bastard mother. I could tell you about the bullies at school and the bully step fathers at home, step-dads defined as guys who stayed more than one night. He laughed. "I could even bitch about not getting laid in a real long time. Of course, you know about that. Poor little Maggie. Nasty boyfriend didn't turn out to be the hero. I gave you a clue. And how did you repay me? Doused me with wine." The mocking voice turned nasty. "Dumb cunt. What has that got to do with fucking?" Will went back to mocking. "But I don't cry over spilled milk. After all, I spilled my milk all over you and you never heard me cry."

Maggie hugged the old metal even tighter and bent her face into her arms to muffle a sob. Her attacker. It had been Will. She rocked against its hardness and wore her grief.

The wood on the opposite side of the dock creaked. Will was near the boat house. Another creak, then quiet before Will started up his taunt again. "Enough about our love life or lack thereof. The bottom line, sweet Maggie, is that the old bitch who happened to be my blood had a lot of money, and I wanted it." The boat door opened, its ancient hinges squeaking, the bottom of the sagging door dragging in disapproval. More steps.

"Now you know so much. What a waste. All that confession and no one else will know. See, you're going to die."

The ancient light bulb in the structure's ceiling came on, its glow wedged in the cracks of the old eroded slabs of wood and spilling out through the open door. Maggie watched shadows play on the walkway. Maggie felt the heft of Will's weight as he stepped out and called into the night.

Chapter 37

Larry woke with a start. That was the weird thing about being dead. No dreams. No reacquaintance with morning reality, the blurry realization that another day awaited. Nope. One second nothing, the next, depending on his choice of resting place, cabin or trees, maybe a rabbit scampering to make it a Disney kind of day. Mortality was so much more interesting. Unless, of course, it came with a hangover.

Larry took in his bearings. Night. What was he doing waking up at night? He was in his "Denison Hotel" as he liked to call it, the cabin's bunkhouse, lying on a bed frame, no more than a bunch of springs, quilts rolled up at his feet.

A scream interrupted his musings. Not a damsel in distress kind of thing. It was a roar of rage, vaguely familiar, definitely male. And it was coming from the near the lake. He leaped up and tore out the door of the bunk house at full run. He checked out the cabin, then focused on the boat house just as Maggie crashed through the brush and leaped onto the dock. She scurried down the side of the old building and slid into the water. Up to his left, he heard that voice again, this time hollering, taunting. Will's voice.

"Come out and play," the voice called, but the tone suggested anything but playing. It was something out of a B movie that promised, "Come out and I'll slash your throat."

"Okay," he said. Running girl. Bad mood guy. He headed toward the voice, all the while fuzzy with the serious weirdness. Will liked Maggie. He was a wuss, a pussy boy, but the last one to be a threat. Except for that one night when Will turned into horny guy and Larry had to douse him with wine. Was that the real Will? Larry scowled even as he searched the landscape. Nah. Will was a puss.

Then he heard him again. "Mysteries." "Ida Ann." "Grandmother." The words hit Larry's mind like cosmic stones. He was hearing something infinitely more essential than man chases girl.

His response was simple. Get to Maggie. Save Maggie.

Will was on the dock, facing the boat house, not more than ten or twelve yards from a well-soaked Maggie hiding in the dark of the water. He could feel her pain, the coldness of fear and water that seeped deep and held. Larry bent over to pick up a sizable branch. If he knocked Will unconscious, Maggie could climb out and dash to the cabin to call the cops. His fingers grasped the branch and pulled. Nothing. He forced his resolve, moving all his energy toward his fingers and pulled again. Then his fingers moved through the branch, not so much as disturbing a molecule. He dashed toward Will, took a flying leap -- and wound up in the lake. He could see Maggie under the structure, hanging onto the lift posts, her body wrapped around the old wood.

Panic seized him. He'd lost all control. All those years of focus and practice, and when he finally needed to be able to manipulate matter, he was as inept as a gnat swatting at a mastodon. He climbed out of the water onto the dock, took a last ditch turn at Will, and sailed right through him.

No time to panic, buddy. His mouth twisted into a bitter smile. "So, you can't do this yourself," he said to the night air. "Maybe you can get some help. What the hey. The Lone Ranger rides again." His mind begged, "Just let there be a Tonto somewhere."

Just then, the wind picked up and the temperature dropped. He looked up. No stars. Great. A storm. "What else you got for us up there?" The wind rattled the old boat house just as Larry took off.

Minutes later, he squatted on the ground, weight on his heels – at least in his mind he thought of it as weight. Not much chance to imprint the ground when he had no substance. He leaned into the quiet for a last second of predictability. Once he crossed the property line, all hell could break loose. For him, permanently.

Great image for a dead guy looking consequence in the face.

Strange how fear had tastes and smells and ways of wrapping itself inside the body when he was alive. Copper pressing on the tongue. Lead weighing down arms and legs. The kind of belly numbing fear that pressed on him when he was a kid sure of monsters in the closet. That was what he felt now. Wouldn't you know it. Here he was, dead, the only link he had to life the same stupid dread that had made him want to piss his pajamas when he was eight. He forced down the panic. No point chewing on the past. It certainly wouldn't save Maggie. Around him, the wind howled and the rain pounded the tops of the trees. Nothing much reached the forest floor, too much of a canopy here.

His instincts screamed at him one last time before he set his feet and steadied himself for the leap. "Go big or go home," Maggie had said to him once. He got it now.

Then he leaped like the track star he had never been and landed . . . right on the other side of the property line maybe three feet from where he had jumped. What the . . .? The trees still bowed to a sky boiling with storm. A blanket of leaves and tree branches still lay underneath him, his feet still making no mark. He brushed himself off out of habit from a lifetime long ago. Then he started to move. Fast. Fast turned to bounding. Miles swept by. He was guided by an instinct bearing no resemblance to his own survival mode.

Hornsboro's outskirts. Hornsboro's main street. *Wallie's* the sign said. Help was inside. He didn't know that, not in a logic sense of the word. He just *knew* it. He entered, scanning the place. Just the kind of bar he used to love. Sticky floors, warm people, cold beer. Probably had nickel draws on Wednesday night.

Larry surveyed the room. Three people in a dim and grimy hole-in-the-wall. A bartender named Jeff – how did he know that? He was leaning back against the booze counter, arms crossed, shaking his head side to side. The two customers he knew from that day at the cabin. That guy with the funny eye and his girlfriend. They were both gripping the bar and talking fast. He heard the names *Cal* and *Maggie*.

Now what? Materialize and scare the crap out of them? Not like there's a lot of time to explain metaphysics. The room started to take on a weird sense of coloration. No. Not the room. Just the bar and those three people. They were outlined in red, then blue, then back to blue again, kind of like watching *Thirteen Ghosts* without the 3-D glasses. He spat out an extra heave of energy and leaped toward the bartender out of pure instinct, washed completely through him, crown to toes. God, he was in another guy's body. This must be what Frankenstein's monster felt like. All kinds of molecules and energy inhabiting a space that only wanted to recognize some of them.

He willed Jeff to move and – nothing. All that merging and fusing and Jeff didn't move so much as a hair. That is until he blinked and put his hands up against the sides of his head and opened his mouth. The voice was Jeff's when the words came out, but the order was all Larry. "Get to Maggie's place. She needs you." Larry felt the twitch and jerk of Jeff's body as his host reacted. Larry watched Jeff watching the reaction of the other two as they looked at him in stunned belief.

Too many kinds of weird. Let's get going Larry's energy said. Jeff's body obliged, lurching forward at Marv and Winnie. "Will's the mystery guy. He's trying to kill Maggie. Knock it off and move!"

The couple each inched back in sync.

"You were all about helping Maggie the day you showed up at the cabin and shocked the holy bejesus out of her. Get a move on!"

While the man they knew as Jeff headed for the door, they looked at each other and ran after him, climbed into his car, Winnie riding shot gun. The driver threw the car into reverse while they managed to shut the doors. Before either one could get out the first of who knew how many questions, Larry spoke and Jeff glared. "There's two possibilities here. One, I'm nuts and we're going for a ride that'll end with Maggie laughing her ass off. Two, I know what I'm talking about because I'm psychic, just like I know that you, Winnie Listug, used to skulk around and take pictures of the cabin when Jean was still alive, muttering how you'd 'find something to pin on that bastard or die trying.' Jean caught you once and made you come inside and have a beer."

Marv laughed from the back. "Boy was she pissed about that. Woman hates to get caught."

Winnie looked straight ahead, her lips pressed tight, right foot tapping on the floor of the car. "I don't know how you know that, and I believe in psychics like I believe in Bigfoot." She turned her head left. "If you're wrong, you owe me free drinks until Christmas."

Larry's words came out low, shoved out into the dark car. "But if I'm right . . . "

No one answered as they sped toward Maggie's.

Chapter 38

Submersed, hugging cold, alga slicked braces under the dock's lip, Maggie felt the temperature drop and the wind pick up. The water sloshed at her in anger, attacked her head even as she set her forehead against the wood, raised gooseflesh on any skin not already well bumped by fear and water temperature. When the rain came, it came in torrents, slashes that rattled the old boat house and slicked the decking. She listened for thunder. With her luck, a lightening bolt would slice under the frame and fry her before Will had a chance to slit her neck. She clung tighter, her face roughened by the coarse wood, the splinters a strange comfort. If she could feel them, she was still alive.

Even with the roar of the storm, Will's voice reached her, an eerie swirl of sound competing with the rain. "Maggie, my love. Why keep fighting me? It's inevitable." She could no longer hear his steps, but she followed his voice as he moved. Right now he was immediately above her. Crashes thumped as Will threw objects -- oars, barrels, old rusty bars of metal Lou had saved for some project he never had a chance to begin. "Where the hell are you?"

Maggie knew he had no idea she was only a matter of feet under him. She knew darkness and weather worked to keep her hidden, that Will could rage until the contents of the boat house were splinters. She also knew the shivers that gripped her were an omen. Her fingertips burned with cold and her toes throbbed. The heels of her palms cramped and stung at the same time. Cold lake water was not a friend. She ran a mental inventory of her surroundings. If Will kept up his fit, she could edge over under the dock and swim to his boat. There had to be something in it to use as a weapon. Her eyes fixed on the darkness in front of her, she measured in her mind, the distance under the dock, where the water irises lay in wait to pull down an unwary swimmer -- and she pushed off. Luck held. Will stayed in the boat house and Maggie missed the irises, except for one clump of tendrils that grabbed at her legs and made her want to scream. Just what she needed. Undone by water weeds. She pulled herself up the dock ladder and bent over to peer into Will's boat. Strips of light and shadow from the boat house gave her a sense of form; she could make out a life jacket, a boxy object, probably an old cooler. Maybe the cooler would work, if she could heave it. Lightening streaked. She pulled her hands in defensively. Why worry about a killer stalking her when Mother Nature could take her out with a little electricity.

Even as the threat shook her, something set near the front of the boat caught her sight in that instant of illumination. In the dark once again, against the echo of the last of the thunder -- at least for a moment --she climbed in and grabbed at it, let her hand search for identity. The object was anciently familiar, wooden, yet round and smooth, heavy on the bottom, a curved neck, knob on top. A bowling pin. What was Will doing with a bowling pin in his boat? No time for wondering. She clambered out of the boat and slipped her way down the pier. Should she run? No, that would alert him. She took a stance, then while torrents of rain and Will's anger filled the air, sidled to the wood skirting around the boat house, careful not to slip on the decking until she could take her stance. Bowling pin over her head like Thor's hammer, she waited for Will in front of the one unopened door.

Could he sense her? Fear had attacked her entire body. Now it solidified into a single mass that wedged behind her breastbone. She breathed in slowly, stretching her breath to reach her lungs in spite of the barrier, ears primed for Will's movement. There. The creak of a footstep, then another. A growl of frustration and a slap against something hard.

Will's stepped out of the boathouse, one creaking step then another. Maggie reared back with all the might born of months of gym workouts and swung. Contact. Will staggered forward, dropped to his knees and crashed down onto the deck face down. She bashed him again just for good measure, a club across his shoulders, then backed away to stand under the eave of the boathouse, cradling the bowling pin to her chest, feeling the blessing of its heft next to her pounding lungs and heart. Will was nothing more than a dark lump, face down, arms extended.

There in the dark, arms and shoulders aching, chest heaving from the cold and the danger, she indulged herself for a moment, pictured water pooling around his body washing away the danger of the man she had called friend. She burned with the need to pummel him, strike back at all the betrayal and hurt that balled up within her. Her lungs heaved. She gulped in air and still they demanded more. Then the shaking began. Legs. Arms. Torso. Jaw and teeth. Her fingers begged to let go of her weapon, that silly bowling pin that had saved her life. Not in this lifetime, she told them. Xena had her sword. Maggie had her weapon of choice.

What next? What did a girl do after she took out the bad guy? Do a victory dance? Sure, if she could convince her body to move. Call the police? Much more likely. That is if she could make it to the cabin without passing out. She knelt down and shook him; her fingers ached to dig themselves into his throat, the rest of her recoiled at the thought of touching him. She lifted his head and let it plunk down on the wood. Such a gratifying sound.

She stumbled into the boathouse for rope. Safety was a hogtied Will. While she manipulated the rope, that's when the satisfaction began to rise, like a howling within her, the knowledge that she had broken his power over her. She checked her knots and yanked. Lou had taught her well. When he was conscious maybe she could press a branch against his throat and press.

When he was conscious. The thought sickened her. Before she rose, she spit in his face for good measure, then on her feet, kicked him once, twice, three times in the crotch. Then she left Will lying there, left the man, the lies, the viciousness and headed for the cabin. Lord, she was tired.

The last thing on her mind was that loose board. She knew about it, had told herself for weeks to get it fixed before someone tripped. Just now, she had a few other things on her mind. Like staying alive. Her foot came down on the wood, hard, and it gave way, pitching her forward. Had she been watching this, she would have laughed at the irony, her sprawling forward six feet away from the end of the dock, spiraling downward to land in three inches of water, ending up a twin image of her attacker. Only, he was able to breathe -- if he ever came to -- and she was face down in the water. Off toward the cabin, car doors were slamming and people were shouting. She heard them just as she lost consciousness.

— *Chapter 39* —

The three of them -- four counting Larry -- headed toward the lake, Jeff leading the way. The guy could run. Larry gave him that. Good thing. He needed the fastest body possible. There, at the end of the path, the boat house stood out against the night. The rain had stopped, but the only light came from the building. Wisconsin did not give up its storms gently. The sky was still a stretch of blackness, the boat house looking like a luminary floating on the water.

Marv and Winnie had stopped to check out the cabin. Larry knew better. Maggie was out there on the dock. He knew it.

He almost missed her, she was so silent, so still there in the water. Steps from the shore. Steps from dryness. She lay there, face down, the lake lapping against her body.

Once tonight, he had tried to save her and failed miserably, no more than a wisp of air battling a giant. Now he had a man's body. That and a couple of years experience as a lifeguard back in the early 50's. Long time since basic lifesaving, but he would not fail. He couldn't.

He sank down and turned her over. Pulled her to him and listened to her mouth for breath, checked her neck for a pulse. Nothing. He tilted her head back, moved Jeff's fingers into her mouth to clear a passage for air, bent over to send air to her lungs. Her lips were so cold. One breath. Two. Three. He checked for her pulse again. Nothing. He blew air again. And again. At some point, Winnie and Marv found him. Flashlight in hand, Marv knelt next to him. "Keep going Jeff. Keep going buddy." Jeff? That's right. He was in another man's body, using another man's air, another man's lips, hands. It felt like a betrayal. The ritual became automatic, a meditation, his mind numbed in the sameness. Breathe in. Check for a pulse.

The ritual drove on until Maggie's chest heaved and her neck wrenched backward. She turned onto her side and spewed water. He rubbed her back in circles, offering silent apology for not protecting her, then pulled her inward, cradling her like a child he never would have. She was still so damn cold. He kissed her forehead, tenderly, reverently.

"What the hell do you think you're doing?" Maggie was awake. And storming.

He kissed her. "I thought you were dead." His voice was a growl.

"Jeff?" Maggie was on her knees on the rock-strewn shore, peering at his face.

He leaned in. "Not hardly."

She smiled in the knowledge as it wrapped her in its warmth.

Realization came in slow strands, like a pack of cards shuffling themselves into reverse order -- into some kind of final sense out of total mixture, but the gestalt of the order was a new mystery all of itself.

Of course it was Larry. Sure, the guy had Jeff's face, Jeff's body, Jeff's hands. But at the core of what had saved her, who had kissed her, that was Larry. Her mind never even suggested the insanity of her perception. Her body -- not so much. She pushed against this man who had held her as a child, as a lover. She touched his face.

He closed his eyes, a smile borne on his face, no more than a wisp of happiness, but a smile nonetheless, and shook his head. It was the slightest of nods, almost imperceptible. It opened the world to Maggie. Her ghost. Her friend. He was here.

"You two done over there?" Marv's words brought them both back to the crisis. Will. An unconscious Will. A Will that had tried to kill Maggie just as he had eliminated Ida Ann, and the thought crawled through Maggie's body in its horrible truth, maybe someone else so dear to her. A murderer was lying unconscious on her dock, and she was the only one who knew the truth. She should be able to summon up enough adrenaline to let them know the truth -- that the man they had all called friend was a sociopath who had tried to kill her, just like he had killed . . . she couldn't even get the rest of the thought to rise past semi-awareness as she slipped into a blackness that felt so good, so safe.

She sucked on ice chips while the sheriff questioned her. Her throat hurt. She must have swallowed rocks while she was out. Good lord, she had almost drowned. At least the ice melted in her mouth instead of disarming her limbs and she had managed to sit up in her hospital bed. Dr. Phillips stood by as chaperone, her eyes on the machine registering Maggie's vital signs. The sheriff had asked her to stay.

"Do you have any idea why Mr. Bentley would have wished you harm?" Perfectly legitimate question. Maggie wondered what would go through the doctor's mind during all of this as insect Will would unfold. Did she know Will? Dumb question. Everyone around here knew everybody.

"Well, yes. Like I said before, he saw me as a threat to his plan to get rich off of his grandmother." The blip of the machine plodded on in perfect timing. Machines did not care.

"Ida Ann Turnball." The sheriff's voice was firm

"Look officer. I know you're doing your job, but that man tried to kill me, probably killed two other people. So instead of questioning me, how about questioning Mr. Bentley."

"Don't worry Ms. Witkowski. We will have someone doing exactly that as soon as Mr. Bentley regains consciousness."

Will was still unconscious? What if he stayed that way? Her throat tightened, this time not from lake water. Maggie shot a glance at the doctor. Ann Phillips was a study of objectivity except for her eyes. Curiosity cannot hide in the eyes.

"Again, let's talk about your threat from Mr. Bentley."

Maggie lay back against the upright top of the bed and pressed her head to the pillow.

"The man came to my place in the dark. In a canoe. He has a car. He has a boat with a motor that makes noise. Instead, he slipped to my place without so much as a hum. He brought a bowling pin with him, one that belonged to my grandfather, whom I remind you died from trauma to the head. Who carries a bowling pin in his canoe?" She closed her eyes and let a deep breath work through her. "That is not your typical social call."

"I would have to agree with you, Ms. Witkowski. Unfortunately, Mr. Bentley is in pretty bad shape as well. Much as I feel for what you've been through, I need to get this all sorted out."

The sheriff's pager interrupted. He stood up, eyes on the message. "Looks like we're about to hear from Mr. Bentley. He's awake. The sheriff stopped at the threshold and faced Maggie. "No one can say it hasn't been an interesting night. You try to get some rest, Ms. Witkowski. I'll be getting back to you . . . soon."

The doctor nodded to Sheriff Stout. "Be sure you focus more on letting my patient rest than getting back to her," then turned to her patient. "Goodnight, Maggie. I'll check on you in the morning."

When Maggie was alone, she let herself smile. Ann Phillips had heard her story. Ann Phillips would check on her in the morning. Maggie could rest.

Rest. Funny word.

Beats the hell out of dead.

Chapter 40

Maggie and Will had both been released from the hospital two days ago. Plenty of time to recover. That is, if recovery didn't include nightmares of gasping for breath underwater while strings of slime-coated roots wrapped around her ankle, cutting her while they pulled her down. If she didn't hear Will's laugh snake around the corner of a room while she least expected it. If she didn't have to fight the urge to retch every time she looked out toward the boat house. If she didn't have to think about that kiss, play it over again in her mind, feel it again, the warmth against her lips.

Do not go there.

Deal with Larry. He hovered. She hated hovering. And a ghost that looked like a basset hound in need of depression medicine, that was beyond the pale.

"Damn that sheriff. He said he'd get back soon. Two days is not soon." Maggie's impatience had her tapping her heels against the floor while she vented.

"Time moves slowly out here. Have a little patience. Can I get you anything? A beer?"

"If I don't hear from our illustrious constable in the next twenty minutes, you can get me a gun."

As if on cue, the phone rang.

Maggie listened after the initial greeting, but then burst into a "He actually took the bait?" After a pause, "His suggestion?" She managed a few more mumbled responses before she ended with "See you at 10:00."

Larry waited for some control to assert itself and simply said, "And . . . ?"

"And Sheriff Stout will be picking me up at 10:00. We'll be meeting Will at his house to try to, let's see how Will put it, 'hash out our differences.'

Poor Will feels too weak to come into town, and feels that a conference around his table will put things to right." Maggie lowered her voice and looked official. "I'm sorry, Miss Witkowski, but given the nature of this brouhaha, that seems the best to me."

"The sheriff's official down to his belt buckle."

"He certainly is. Let's just hope this 'brouhaha' winds up in our favor. I want to see that bastard laid naked for the world to see."

Larry glowered. "Naked?"

Maggie crossed her eyes at him. "Exposed, ghost boy. As in 'I am a sociopath cretin cockroach.'"

"Gotcha. Let's get busy."

Minutes turned to hours as Maggie and Larry laid every clue, every picture, every scrap of paper, every object remotely related to Ida Ann, Lou, and the possibility -- not the actuality -- of Will the grandson. Maggie fingered the objects, hoping for a shaman's wisdom. Larry questioned, murmured agreement while he leaned in. At times, Maggie felt his breath -- an impossibility for sure --often his anger and frustration, warmth and heat directed inward as much as toward her.

At one a.m. Maggie pressed her palm down over one of the objects. "That's it!"

Maggie had been to Will's house a number of times. In the morning light, nothing had changed. Same cedar shingles and slate roof. Same French doors leading from the eating area to the wrap-around deck. Same Old World distressed beams and floor inside. The place was gorgeous, a hobby his designer cousin had dived into, he assured her when she had first visited. Back then, and several times later, they had grilled to their hearts' delight.

Wasn't that eons ago?

Today, a whole new kind of grilling would take place. Pulling up to the end of Will's lane, Maggie felt the excitement grab her. Today yes, the house was the same, but so much was different -- the air, the tilt of tree limbs, the breath of forest creatures well hidden, all the intangibles that had changed. She could feel the excitement of the change in her stomach. A portent, perhaps a blessing. Yeah, right. How about an invitation to hell.

When the sheriff and Maggie stepped inside Will's house, Will was standing to their left at head of the table, chairs pulled out on adjacent sides. Maggie shot a glance to her right, to the kitchen counter where they had sat on rainy mornings sipping coffee and munching cinnamon rolls.

"Good morning, Maggie. Why don't you have a seat here." He pointed to the chair at his right, then quickly gestured to the right. "And you, Lyle, have a seat here across from Maggie."

How sweet, she thought. The good lawyer was seating the crowd. How nice to have a killer tell you where to sit. Where was the cinnamon now? She felt her leg want to tremble, her foot desperate to tap. No way. She'd stay steady. she was ready.

"Maggie, I'm so glad to see you're feeling better." Will kept his voice friendly, no doubt how the wolf had talked to Red Riding Hood as he was sizing her up in the forest. Oh if only the good Lyle would turn out to be a huntsman. She pictured Will with sharp fangs and a whole lot more body hair. Alas, she had to slay the wolf herself.

"Maggie?"

She jerked her head up. "What?"

"Have a seat. We're ready." Will was in his lawyer mode again. While Maggie pulled herself closer to the table and sat down, he said, "Make yourselves comfortable now. I'll get us some coffee."

While he scooted his chair in, Sheriff Stout piped in, "Thank you Mr. Bentley. I take mine black."

"C'mon Lyle, call me Will." He nodded toward Maggie. "And for you, one spoonful of sugar as always?" Without waiting for an answer, he started toward the peninsula, hesitated a couple of seconds as he rested his hand on Maggie's shoulder, let it graze before he eased his way toward the coffee maker and began his hosting duties.

Maggie did her best not to flinch. She wouldn't give the bastard the power. She leaned into Sheriff Stout. "You know there's a reason he's doing all this, right? He wants me gone at the very least, not sipping morning joe with him."

Stout's eyes stayed steady while he pursed his lips. He shot one glance toward the welcoming Will. "This whole set up is hinkey, but hinkey isn't proof."

Proof. Nasty word. Please lord, let this work out.

"Coffee's a little bit hot so be careful." Maggie started at sound of his voice behind her. Calm yourself, girlfriend. Work to be done. When he set her coffee down in front of her, she managed a terse thank you.

Will took his seat, and took a sip from his mug. Shaped like a fish. Muskie Mug she called it. Maggie had sold it to him only last week. Hopefully, it was laced with mercury. She shut down her sarcasm, steeled herself. For Will to win at this game, he'd need her skewed. Someday she would look at this moment and remember the crackling of her resolve.

His words slipped out like honey as he picked up his pen and jotted a few words on the legal pad in front of him. "Lyle, I'm sure that you'll be taking notes. Be careful now. Don't let any of that coffee blot out any details."

While the sheriff pulled out his notebook and clicked his pen, Maggie watched Will, his upper body forward, hands folded, mouth and eyes neutral, sensed the smile that wanted to curl upward even as he bathed himself in neutrality. She hadn't meant anything to him, wasn't so much as a piece of lint to be plucked from one of his lawyer suits. She steeled her resolve.

C'mon, lawyer boy. Bring it.

The sheriff cleared his throat and spoke. "Let's get started here, begin with what we can agree on." He looked at each of his interviewees, one at a time. "You've known each other most of the summer, have in fact, been seeing each other."

Both Maggie and Will nodded in agreement. Will smiled and looked at Maggie. Maggie tightened her lips and looked straight ahead.

Stout focused on Maggie. "We know that Will often visited you at your home, and that occasionally you and he spent time together here."

"Yes." Maggie said the word with perfect neutrality even while the thought of *visit* twisted in her throat. Will stayed quiet, reached over to his mug and took a sip of coffee.

"We know that Will visited you, Ms. Witkowski, two evenings by boat. Is that a normal occurrence?"

Visit. Normal. Not on this planet. "Yes. Will often visits -- but always by car, never by boat."

Will interjected. "Like I told you, Lyle, I wanted to surprise Maggie." He sat back and did his innocent routine. "Needless to say, 'surprise' was an understatement that evening."

He wears his smugness like a prize. God, I hate that man. "Surprise? Not hardly. You sneaked up on me. In the dark. After I had been riddled with phone calls and rocks and garbage by God knows whom. What kind of an addled brained . . ."

"Just a minute, folks. Let's get back to facts." At the sheriff's words, Maggie shut off the valve to her outrage. Keep quiet, girl. Will's the sociopath, not you. Rile him up and he becomes ice.

"Sorry. I'm as interested in the facts as you are. I'm sure we all are." She kept all emotion out of her tone even as her legs tried to shake and her toes begged to tap. Steady.

"Let's continue." Stout turned to Will. "So, you came by boat, after dark, to surprise a woman, your friend, someone you obviously care for, who has been, like she said, threatened a number of times."

"I guess I have to plead guilty to stupidity." His eyes locked on Maggie's face. His hands, in fists, rested on the table, thumbs up. "You see, Maggie, I had brought a present for you. Had it all planned out. I'd walk you down to the boathouse, flip on the light, and give it to you where your grandfather stored so many of his possessions."

Maggie imagined the word. The sheriff said it. "Present?"

"The bowling pin. The one from Lou's place in Blue Mound." Maggie's stomach lurched. He had brought the bowling pin alright. He brought it to bash in her head. How ironic that it had saved her. She felt the heft of the pin in her hands even as she imagined Will lifting it as a murder weapon.

"Let me get this right," the sheriff said. "You wanted to give your girlfriend a bowling pin that had belonged to her grandfather?"

"Yes." Will looked at Maggie, tenderness plastered on his face. "Maggie's determined -- obsessed if you will -- with reclaiming her grandparents' belongings.

That's why she's working at Swoozie's."

"He's well aware of that relationship." Maggie tried to make the comment sound light. The sheriff simply cleared his throat and smiled -- tightly.

Will scratched his head and let out a grin. "Right. The break-in last week. Quite the night. Actually, that's what gave me the idea about the bowling pin in the first place. We had joked about the pins the first time we met. I had bought the entire set from Swoozie, and I figured, why not share one of the pins and make the lady happy."

"So you walked up to the cabin, without this present." Stout's voice was neutral.

"Yes. Maggie was busy with laundry and certainly had a lot on her mind, what with work and the end of summer." He shook his head. "I have to tell you, though, I never expected her reaction." Will stopped. Was he pausing for effect or waiting for a reaction?

Lyle picked up on the conversation. "Maggie, do you agree with what Will has given?"

"On the surface, yes." What could she say? That she'd sensed danger? She had looked at a friend who had the face of an enemy? That'd go far in this interview. She watched Will, questioning. "But when I ran, and you called out 'Bitch,' a present from you was the last thing on my mind. Slurs make me uneasy, I guess."

"I called out 'Wait!'" Will widened his eyes and looked insulted, the little boy with his hand in the cookie jar pleading innocence. "I would never resort to such a pejorative."

Bide your time, Maggie. Any deviation from calm only works against you. She rubbed her legs along her thighs, then stood up. "Excuse me for a minute. Third cup of coffee this morning," she said before she headed toward the bathroom. Bladder not withstanding, she needed a break from the tension. That and time to collect her thoughts.

"You know where everything is, Maggie," followed her. She gritted her teeth. You think I'm a bitch, buster, just wait. Pay back is coming.

Lord, she hoped so.

She had to pass by Will's bedroom on the way to the bathroom. She shot a look as she started to pass by the doorway, then stopped abruptly. There, placed ever so neatly on the bed was a pair of shorts and a tee. Hers. The very shorts and top she had worn the night Will had attacked her in the woods. Clean. Folded with military precision. A peppermint candy lay atop, right in the center.

Her breath shook as she heaved it in. Anger lodged inside her chest, her throat. Her stomach ached, her chest, her heart -- everything. She stuck her hand into the pocket of her shorts and fingered the item she had placed there. A talisman. Her hope. She rubbed it between her thumb and index finger, letting its touch still her breath. That bastard would not break her power.

She strode into the room, picked up the clothing, careful to balance the candy and returned to the men. "Why Will, how kind of you to launder for me." Her tone outbuttered even Swoozie's. She set the clothing down on the table, picked up the peppermint, and leaned forward toward the sheriff. "Remember, Lyle when I described my clothing the night I was assaulted?" Candy still in hand, she held up the tee. *Paranoia burns calories.* "Golly Will, it's not every attacker that cleans up after himself." Then she unwrapped the candy, stuck it into her mouth and crunched, followed the crunch with a sigh of pleasure.

"Whatever are you talking about? Assault?" He was the veritable choir boy. "Maggie, my love, you never called it an assault when we were . . . together. You called it marvelous." The choir boy's voice held a tinge of naughtiness.

Maggie slipped toward the kitchen peninsula, coffee cup in hand. After she poured herself a cup, she ran her hand along the granite, sipping slowly, her index finger slipping along the glass jars, the wood of the knife rack, until she picked up a bottle of olive oil, one decorated with a silver chain holding one half of a heart. Moving back toward Will and the sheriff, she said, "While we're talking about clothing, let's nudge over a little to accessories." Then she set down her coffee and the oil onto the table, slipped one hand into her shorts' pocket and used the other to pull the chain from the bottle. "I've always been fascinated by this little trinket. Will, where did you get it?"

"I don't know. At some little trade swap place." His words were short. He had just bragged about prowess, and Maggie was dismissing him. He frowned. This wasn't the way it was supposed to go. He needed Maggie furious, hurling insults and snarls. He needed her wrath. It fed him, that beautiful, hopeless, fog of outrage that turned her into a bumbling fool. It kept him balanced when he wanted to bash in her face. And why did she care about some trinket?

"Lyle," he asked, "Aren't we supposed to be staying on track here? I don't think a bottle decoration has much bearing on our agenda."

Ignoring Will, the sheriff leaned toward Maggie, arm extended. "Can I see that please?" Maggie placed it in his hand. It sat there, a tiny circle of silver in the big man's paw.

Dammit. The sheriff was ignoring him. Will felt a crack in his control, not more than a nudge, but one that eroded his supremacy. Nonsense. This whole sidestep was ridiculous. Back to the script, people. He rubbed his head where a knot of pain had started.

"Do you mind?" Both Maggie and Lyle stared at him. Easy now. His voice was too forceful. Keep the show going. You're the director of this play.

"Sorry." He made his voice sound contrite while he rubbed his forehead with his fingertips. "My head's still thudding a little. Nothing like a good dent to give a guy a headache." The sarcasm dripped before Will regained his lawyer voice. Let's review what we have, shall we."

Lyle fingered the chain with his left forefinger. "I want to see what you have here." He joked at Will, "Never figured you for much of a bottle jewelry guy" before he set the piece on the table. "Look here, it's a little kid's necklace." He picked it up by the heart. "What's this on it?" He peered at it, his brows furrowing. "Looks like half of a butterfly."

Here it was. The moment. Maggie let its excitement slip through her, replace the roiling and the stoning, the sum of her fear with a childlike glee. She slipped her hand into her pocket and drew out a tiny piece of jewelry. A silver chain with a heart.

"Why look here," she said. "I have one almost identical." She placed the heart onto the table and matched it against the one that the sheriff had set down.

"Perfect fit. Whatta' you know."

Something slipped. In his head. Sort of like gears before the engine came crashing apart, all the symmetry shattering into a pile of useless metal. Then the wall of sociopathic perfection crumbled. Will was on his feet, jaw turned to steel, his fists clenching, unclenching, aching to reach out and strangle. He grabbed Maggie by the hair and yanked her toward the kitchen counter, grabbed a knife from the cutting rack before Maggie had a chance to scream. By the time Stout had a chance to stand, Will had one arm around Maggie's neck, the other pressing a knife at her throat.

"Just sharpened this last night. Kind of a freaky thing about me. I like sharp knives."

He nudged the knife upward, the tip against Maggie's underjaw. The skin broke and a drop of blood shed red against the aluminum of the knife tip. He made sure that his arm swept hard against Maggie's breast.

"Maggie, where's the fury? You're bleeding, babe. And you've lost." He felt the weight of her head against his chest, laughed inside at how she had to bend her knees to keep her feet on the floor. She was a beanpole, alright, poor little Maypole Maggie, subject of scorn at the very end.

Stout's voice broke his revelry. "Just let her go, Will. This is all going to end badly if you don't."

"End badly? What. You think I don't know the drill. 'Let her go and we'll talk'?" He shot scorn at the sheriff. "What kind of dumb fuck do you think I am?

"I didn't just kill Granny; I killed her grandfather. Bludgeoned him. The crack was so beautiful." He spit the next words while he stared down the sheriff. "Lyle, you fool. You can't even tell the difference between a fall and a murder." He didn't notice Maggie's right leg edging toward his foot.

The crunch of gravel sounded from outside. For a mere instant, Will lost his concentration, loosened the pressure of the knife. Maggie stomped on his foot, her boots hard on his sandals at the same time she lurched her head back against his and flung her forearms up against his. She had a second to slide down.

A shot broke the air. Lyle had drawn his gun, placed the shot right in the center of Will's forehead. The knife slid from Will's hand and clanked to the floor. Both Will and Maggie fell in a jumble, Maggie on the bottom. She shoved Will's body off hers and rolled out, away from the man, away from the blood that poured from his wound.

The sheriff rushed forward, grabbed her hand and tried to yank her up, but she fell forward, away from Will's body, kneeling, bracing herself with her arms against the floor, heaving in gulps of air.

"You'll be alright, Maggie. It's over." The words hovered behind her. The sheriff opened the door and called out, "C'mon in, boys." Then he holstered his gun and went to the kneeling Maggie while two uniformed men clomped up the deck stairs.

"I am so sorry you had to go through this, Ms. Witkowski," he said, "But like I told you, 'hinky isn't proof'. Even in a country burg like ours."

"Sheriff, if there's one thing I've learned, it's that 'country burg' is a compliment." She said it, arms still on the wood, to the floor, but she meant it to the whole town.

While the sheriff held the door for her to leave, she relished in the moment, even as tired as she was, knowing that grace had come to her life, but in the back reaches of her mind, she centered on Larry.

What would happen to Larry?

Chapter 41

Two mornings later, Maggie barreled through the screen door and leaned against the wall. She raised her fist in victory. "Three miles, and I don't want to melt," she crowed as she padded into the kitchen for a glass of water.

"Not bad," Larry called out from the great room. "I'm more impressed that you didn't cuss out the birds, however."

"What?" She brought out the water and sat down across from him at the main table, gulping a huge swig.

"Birds. The first morning you ran. You acted like they were the barbarians banging at the gate, said a cuss word or several as I remember."

"You never told me you were there."

"I've been here," Larry said as he swept his arm, "for a long time, or have you forgotten?" He leaned back and crossed one leg over the other. "Looks like I may be here for a while longer."

Guilt tinged Maggie's tone. "You still haven't heard from the Judges?"

"Nope. Evidently, court is still in session. Without me."

"But we solved the mystery. We caught the bad guy. Justice. That's got to count for something." She looked skyward. "C'mon, he only broke one little rule. And that was to save me. Extenuating circumstances."

"That doesn't cut it."

"Must be Republicans."

Larry scoffed. "The afterlife is totally nonpartisan."

"Must be why they get things done."

Larry was quiet, his face edged with the stress of the past five days. "The point is, I broke their rule."

Maggie took another long drink. "You didn't even know that you could leave. You were stuck here for over fifty years."

"That's the thing. I did know that my body -- and I use the term loosely -- could cross the property lines. I never said, 'I can't leave.' I said I couldn't."

Maggie frowned. "I'm the language expert here. They mean the same."

"Nope. Can't means glued in place. Couldn't implies choice. I made the choice. Here I am. Forever is a long time. Might as well make the most of it." He looked at her water glass, now nearly empty. "How about a beer? My treat."

"That just means you go to the refrigerator. Don't get too cocky."

A beer. Easy. Puts off the inevitable -- Maggie leaving. Only one more week before she had to return to Chicago for inservice.

That night, Maggie and Larry sat on sofa, both of them still. The August air was cool enough for a fire. Maggie had taken a shower and was wrapped in a terry robe over her tee and shorts. Warm inward, warm outside, she watched the flames and the lamp light cast a golden glow throughout the room. It was her room, a complete room. After the Will fiasco, Swoozie had caved and given her the rest of the Witkowski cache. "Good lord in heaven, sweetie, if anyone deserves a present, you do." Of course, Swoozie made her promise that she'd work the next summer at least, and Maggie had said yes, providing, of course, that Mondays were free.

Danger was past, treaties promised. Only the obvious remained. The two of them. They had battled a monster, battled each other. Larry had saved her life. More than once. Shadows of him after the attack, both of the attacks hovered but held no power. Here, next to her, was the best friend, the clown, the nurse, the savior.

Her eyes glistened, and she swallowed hard. Surely she was not about to cry. She had cried only once, after the attack, a deluge of shame, and reaffirmed her vow to stay strong like all Witkowski women. But now, glisten those eyes did. Looking straight ahead, she reached her hand across and held it on top of Larry's, thumb against his palm underneath, four fingers caressing the top side. His fingers squeezed her thumb, his index finger rubbing against the lower part of her palm. Maggie felt the tension of that finger, a coursing of sensation that heightened her awareness of the colors, the sounds, the smells of the night. A tension that awakened a response in her body that she had not felt in a long time.

She never even considered fighting it.

While the two of them sat there watching that fire, Larry so seemingly calm, she so . . . what was she feeling? . . . she started to muse. "I was thinking about kissing."

Larry didn't change, not a movement of his head, not a cessation of that finger on the underside of her hand. "Really?"

"It's a lost art, you know. Couples hook up, jump each other, nobody enjoys the flavor of a good kissing session anymore.

"When I was twelve, kissing was a big deal. Not for real. Just in the abstract. At night, I 'd hide out near Johnny Delorean's boat house and watch him kiss Amy Butler. The way their bodies moved into each other. I obsessed over kissing that summer. Pressing my lips to the pillow didn't cut it."

He leaned into her, watched her as she leaned her head back before he moved his head toward hers. One arm reached for her shoulder. His hand, so large, so hard, touched her shoulder, the warmth of it spilling through her, its substance seeping into her arms, downward through her own hand. Skin and yet not skin. So much more. The other hand tipped her head closer to his. "Pillows don't know how to kiss back." I do."

His lips were warm and full. Nice. He rubbed his tongue against her lower lip urging her mouth to open. He moved in closer, his arms enclosing her. Those hands, those warm, strong hands stroked her waist, her back. She opened her mouth, let his tongue enter her, discover her. When he withdrew, his lips made love to her mouth, pressuring, then receding, nipping, then moving in on her lips again. Maggie had been kissed in her life, but never possessed by the energy that pulsed from this man. Lips and yet not lips. Skin and yet not skin. So much more.

Then he stopped. Drew away from her, laid back stiffly against the back of the sofa.

He wasn't looking at her -- she knew that in her gauzy state -- but she could feel his eyes as if they were still on her, small pulses of intensity that ran along her face, then downward along her neck until they stopped below the base of her neck.

Imagine. The ghosts of desire left after a kiss.

Okay, buster, you can read my mind when it's in an emotional state. If this isn't an emotional state, I couldn't possibly know what defines one.

Maggie felt the movement, the subtle beat as watching grew in intensity, as his eyes grazed across the tops of her breasts. Little circles of sensation made them tingle and her nipples tighten. Maggie shuddered, inhaling breath and pleasure. Her head arched backward as she took in the air. She could feel her neck muscles tighten even as want stirred in places ignored for so long.

If you're going to do something, you'd better do it now. Her thoughts were screaming at him.

"Close your eyes." His voice was low and no more than a whisper. The sound, itself made love to her. She felt his mouth, the tip of his tongue run down her jaw line, his teeth starting to nip at her along the way. Nothing spirit about that sensation.

He stood up, reached for her and swept her into his arms, carried her toward the bedroom. Moonlight covered the bed, fell onto the floor, surely an invitation. He pulled the covers aside with one hand, laid her on the bed. He was looking at her, those whiskey colored eyes of his glazed with want, his mouth feral and grand. Ghost and yet man.

He knelt between her legs, kissed her again, this time his hands kneading at her as he brushed them through her hair. She was dizzy with the wanting. Her mind, her body wanted more, so much more.

His mouth was a litany sung to her body. He worshipped her neck, her breasts. Nothing was complete substance; he was a symbiosis of raw man and god. A wetness touched each nipple and the breeze of a hot tongue played against one and then the other. She could feel her breasts move forward with the arch of her back.

When he entered her, she was filled. She had heard *melted* as a term for response. This was a different kind of melting. He melted into her even as his hardness drove her to madness; his essence spread through her like warmth curing a winter body of its coldness. When she came, it was not merely an orgasm. That was for mortals. This was the moment of creation, the touching of supremacy to the receiver of creation.

They made love until the first graying of the sky and the chatter of the birds. Sometimes they made love by talking. Sometimes by giving of each other in other ways. Softness. Hardness. Teasing. Passion.

Larry stroked her. "Time for sleep."

"Will you stay here? Sleep with me?"

"I'm here."

"And so you are. So you are." She closed her eyes, still cradled in the power of the man beside her.

When she woke, morning was a gray promise of a sun that had yet to fully rise. She was alone.

"Larry?" At first her voice was a more purr than call. When no answer came, she sat up and called again. Nothing but quiet. She rose, threw on a robe, and padded out to the great room. Nothing but the silence of morning awakening.

He was gone. She knew it. She sat on the sofa and pulled her knees inward, hugged them and bent her head down. Gone.

The mission was over. She had her answers; he had his great reward. The weight of the truth hung over her as she replayed the night in her mind. Had she meant anything to him, other than a job well done.

Don't be a fool, her heart said. If you can't recognize love when you find it, you'll never be the woman he deserved as friend.

David. Will. Their names were ash. Larry. She laughed. What a name for a ghost.

There it was. Lying on the hearth. A ring. Larry's ring. The one he carried, the one he had showed her when he talked about giving his heart. Maggie reached out, let her fingers move across its hardness before she picked it up. *Lincoln High School* it read on the gold, above and below a black onyx stone. She let the ring settle into her hand, sketched its rim with her finger and smiled. When she put it into the pocket of her robe, she felt its weight settle, and gave it a final pulse with her thumb.

Once she settled herself on the porch steps, she pulled the ring out and slipped it on her finger. It slipped sideways. She thought of Larry's hands, those large hands that had stroked her.

She gave the ring a kiss, just a soft grazing while she thought of him, and leaned forward, crossing her arms onto her knees before she sighed. "I would go steady with you anytime."

A breeze mussed her hair. With a sweet laugh that warmed her, she sat and watched the day begin.